D0535893

"*RED DECEPTION* is a Thriller with a capital "T"! Not for the faint of heart. The doomsday scenarios depicted in this fast-paced, **can't-put-down nail-biter** are real-world accurate and truly scary. Dan Reilly is a terrific new hero for today's troubled times!"

RAYMOND BENSON

AUTHOR, *BLUES IN THE DARK* AND *THE BLACK STILETTO* SERIAL
AND *JAMES BOND* NOVELS

"*RED DECEPTION* provides **an in-depth and realistic ground-level view of the type of asymmetric Nation-state–sponsored threats faced by the Agencies tasked with protecting the United States both domestically and abroad.** Thoroughly researched with thrilling pacing, it follows a worst-case scenario with the resulting fallout and a complex investigation that unfolds all over the Globe."

EDWARD BRADSTREET

SPECIAL AGENT—DEPARTMENT OF HOMELAND SECURITY
HOMELAND SECURITY INVESTIGATIONS (HSI)

"As the former Director of Intelligence (J2) for the U.S. Pacific Command in Hawaii and Joint Chiefs of Staff in the Pentagon, I know these dangerous scenarios are plausible, which makes *RED DECEPTION* all the more thrilling. Infrastructure attacks, Russian aggression, bumbling national leaders, North Korea malign activity, Venezuelan dangers—**Fuller and Grossman's exciting story mirrors reality.** Oh, and the U.S. needs more heroes like their daring CIA Officer Dan Reilly!"

REAR ADMIRAL PAUL BECKER, USN (RET.)

FORMER DIRECTOR OF INTELLIGENCE, U.S. PACIFIC COMMAND

"*RED DECEPTION* is **an adrenalin-laden thriller and as true to life as it gets.** As a former intelligence operative (linguist/analyst—Soviet/Warsaw Pact) with assignments to Field Station Augsburg, Germany and the Defense Intelligence Agency at the Pentagon, I know that all of the explosive events, all of the alliances, and all of the deceit detailed in this book are realistic. Grossman and Fuller possess a keen insight as to the interaction(s) amongst governmental, military, intelligence, and business leaders and operatives. Compelling insight into the world of high-stakes drama, deception and intrigue; full of intricate relationships, and the complexity of independent, yet interconnected scenarios. *RED DECEPTION* just can't be put down. I want more. Outstanding!"

G. MICHAEL MARA, JR
FORMER MEMBER OF THE U.S. ARMY INTELLIGENCE
& SECURITY COMMAND (INSCOM)

"**Heart-pumping excitement—another page-turner from Fuller and Grossman.** RED DECEPTON paints a picture of reality in our world today. Politics, economics, terrorism, travel, intrigue, deceit at home and overseas. An above-the-fold thriller by any measure!"

FRANK HELMICK
LIEUTENANT GENERAL, U.S. ARMY, (RET.)

"With their novel, *RED HOTEL,* acclaimed journalist and thriller writer Gary Grossman and international hotel executive and Army combat veteran Ed Fuller showed how the world we live in has changed. *RED DECEPTION* takes the genre to another level, demonstrating how a true-to-life thriller can deliver vital information over even what the news media provides. Besides keeping us on the edge of our seats, *RED DECEPTION* is so prescient, filled with deep insights into the real worlds of espionage and politics, while giving us **a window that sheds light onto the darkest aspects of political intrigue and human nature**."

BARRY KIBRICK
HOST OF NATIONAL PBS SERIES "BETWEEN THE LINES"

"Gary Grossman and Ed Fuller have done it again in *RED DECEPTION*. Plot, characters, and details are gripping and captivating. **A page-turner by authors who might as well sit on the National Security Council.** A fantastic read!"

PAUL DEBOLE

FORMER AIDE TO SENATOR JOHN MCCAIN
AND SENATOR LAMAR ALEXANDER,
ASSOCIATE PROFESSOR, HISTORY, LASELL UNIVERSITY,
AUTHOR, *CONSPIRACY 101: AN AUTHORITATIVE EXAMINATION
OF THE GREATEST CONSPIRACIES IN AMERICAN POLITICS*

"Another thrilling masterpiece from Grossman and Fuller! A real inside view into the shocking behind-the-scenes world of international politics and intrigue. *RED DECEPTION* is **a fact-rich page-turner, expertly fit together like a giant jigsaw puzzle** that will keep you completely fascinated right up to the surprise finish. Wow!"

WG GRIFFITHS
"RENEGADE WRITER" HOST, BEST-SELLING
THRILLER AUTHOR, "MALCUS"

"*RED DECEPTION* starts with a shocking series of terrorist attacks against America, then races along at break-neck pace until the mind-blowing ending. There are inept political leaders; new threats to world peace from Russia and North Korea; deadly assassins; and secrets and betrayal everywhere. Gary Grossman and Ed Fuller have given us **a must-read thriller that truly feels like it's ripped from today's headlines,** or even scarier, tomorrow's."

R.G. BELSKY
AWARD-WINNING AUTHOR OF THE CLARE CARLSON SERIES

"Wow! Here we go again! I thought *RED HOTEL* was an adrenaline pumper, but *RED DECEPTION* takes it all the way up! Each chapter is incredibly realistic, making me hungry for more. **No one knows more about operating hotels in hostile environments than Ed Fuller! Grossman and Fuller hit the 10 ring with their latest thriller!**"

ALAN ORLOB

TRAVEL SECURITY EXPERT, CEO THE ORLOB GROUP,

FORMER VP OF GLOBAL SAFETY & SECURITY,

MARRIOTT INTERNATIONAL CORPORATION,

U.S. ARMY SPECIAL FORCES, (RET.)

"*RED DECEPTION* delivers **another loud wake-up call that rang so true in *RED HOTEL*.** This time, Fuller and Grossman take us even further into the new Cold War that shows every sign of turning RED hot. Reading *RED DECEPTION* shows us how fast the map of the world could change yet again!"

ROGER DOW

PRESIDENT AND CEO, US TRAVEL ASSOCIATION

"**It doesn't get better than *RED DECEPTION* for weaving true insider business and anti-terrorism experience into a heart-pumping international thriller!** Ed Fuller has been there. Done it. Lived it. I've read all his books, and now his latest collaboration with Gary Grossman exposes more of his world and the dangers that lurk just below the surface. A political reality thriller of the highest caliber."

DOUG MULDOON

CHIEF OF POLICE (RET.), PALM BAY, FLORIDA,

2013 PRESIDENT FBI NATIONAL ACADEMY ASSOCIATES

PRAISE FOR *RED HOTEL* BY FULLER AND GROSSMAN

"*RED HOTEL*, a terrific, fast-paced, stylish, eye-opening spy thriller, with a knowing, insider's look at the intersects of terrorism, the CIA, and world politics. Ripped right from the headlines, *RED HOTEL* will forever change the way you look at hotels, and use the phrase Road Warrior."

BRUCE FEIRSTEIN

JAMES BOND SCREENWRITER, *VANITY FAIR* CONTRIBUTING EDITOR

BEST-SELLING AUTHOR

"Welcome to my world. *RED HOTEL* is a thriller that dramatically covers a very real global threat that could redraw nation boundaries and lead the superpowers to the brink of war. Fuller and Grossman echo the warning, 'If you see something, say something.' They're saying it loud and clear in *RED HOTEL*."

STEVE TIDWELL

FORMER FBI EXECUTIVE ASSISTANT DIRECTOR, CRIMINAL, CYBER, RESPONSE AND SERVICES BRANCH

"Dire exploits. A beguiling read. A battle of wits that heads up every page."

STEVE BERRY

NEW YORK TIMES BEST-SELLING AUTHOR

"Feverishly paced with surprising twists and turns, *RED HOTEL* starts with a bang and the action gets faster and tenser from there. Get ready for one late night when you dive into this gem of a read!"

"Laced with drama culled from recent events, *RED HOTEL* places the reader directly into the role of intelligence analyst and operative as well as business and political strategist. Read *RED HOTEL* and it's doubtful you'll ever travel again without conjuring up possible intrigue from observations that used to seem like normal occurrences."

"Grossman and Fuller deliver gritty insider detail in their thriller *RED HOTEL*, bringing fact and fiction together in an explosive mix. *RED HOTEL* is a must read for international travelers and anyone seeking to understand the new Russia."

"I got to know Ed Fuller in Iraq when I was Deputy Commanding General US Forces Iraq. *RED HOTEL* takes me right back to our in-depth discussions and it spells out tomorrow's threats that we better pay attention to today. Take a deep breath, jump into this novel scenario from authors Fuller and Grossman. I dare you to try to go to sleep tonight once you begin."

"There is nothing more deceptive than an obvious fact."

SIR ARTHUR CONAN DOYLE

RED DECEPTION

GARY GROSSMAN

ED FULLER

BEAUFORT
BOOKS

9780825309465 Hardcover
9780825308505 ebook

For inquiries about volume orders, please contact:
Beaufort Books, 27 West 20th Street, Suite 1102, New York, NY 10011
sales@beaufortbooks.com
Published in the United States by Beaufort Books
www.beaufortbooks.com

Distributed by Midpoint Trade Books
a division of Independent Publisher Group
https://www.ipgbook.com/

Book designed by Mark Karis

Printed in the United States of America

To my beautiful Italian wife Michela for your support, patience, friendship and never-ending love. And to our beautiful growing family, Scott, Elizabeth, Alex, Cameron and Nolan.

ED

To Stan and Debbie Deutsch. Through all the years and all the miles, true friends.

GARY

REAL WORLD NEWS

NORTH KOREAN SPIES IN THE U.S. DEFECTORS REVEAL STARTLING NUMBERS

CNN conducted interviews with two former North Korean agents revealing that hundreds of North Korean spies are working in the United States at any given time. One man talked about their lives as spies saying he was first recruited in high school and received years of special training from martial arts to rigging explosives.

CALIFORNIA ON HIGH ALERT

State and federal law enforcement agencies have boosted security patrols on and around the Golden Gate Bridge and the Oakland Bay Bridge after officials learned of a potential terrorist threat. "The best preparation," said the California governor, "is to let terrorists know we know what you're up to. We're ready. It's not going to succeed."

NORTH KOREA, VENEZUELA AGREE TO STRENGTHEN DIPLOMATIC, COMMERCIAL TIES

North Korea and Venezuela held a series of high-level meetings and inked multiple agreements. According to the North Korean ambassador to Venzuela, the Democratic People's Republic of Korea will continue to "strengthen solidarity and cooperation with socialist countries in accordance with the ideology of self-reliance, peace and good will." The relationship immediately binds diplomatic, economic, and commercial ties between the two nations. US State Department officials voiced concern.

RUSSIA'S WORST KEPT SECRET: IT WANTS ITS FORMER SATELLITE NATIONS BACK

From Sofia to Prague, Warsaw to Budapest, people all across the former Soviet East bloc are looking uneasily at Russia to see how far President Vladimir Putin will push his more adventurous foreign policy and his new pique with the West.

PRINCIPAL CHARACTERS

WASHINGTON, D.C.
Dan Reilly
President, International
Kensington Royal Hotel
Corporation

Alexander Crowe
U.S. President

Ryan Battaglio
U.S. Vice President

Pierce Kimball
National Security Advisor

Elizabeth Matthews
Secretary of State

Carl Erwin
Former CIA Director

BD Coons
US Army General

Tom Reardon
Former FBI Agent

Donald Klugo
Private Security Consultant

Bob Heath
CIA Case Officer

Vincent Moore
FBI Agent

Reese McCafferty
FBI Director

Gerald Watts
CIA Director

CHICAGO, IL
Edward Jefferson Shaw
President/Founder
Kensington Royal Hotel
Corporation

South Atlantic
Chad Barquist
U.S. Air Force Cpt.

Lou Tiano
Kensington Royal COO

Alan Cannon
VP, Global Safety and
Security

Chris Collins
Senior Vice President, Legal
Kensington Royal Hotel
Corporation

Brenda Sheldon
Executive Assistant to Dan
Reilly

Pat Brodowski
Kensington Royal CFO

Lois Duvall
Kensington Royal VP
Public Relations

Spike Boyce
Kensington Royal IT
Executive

RUSSIA
Nicolai Gorshkov
President, Russian
Federation

Martina Kushkin/Maria
Pudovkin
FSB Agent

Pak Yoon-Hoi
SVR Agent

LONDON, ENGLAND
Marnie Babbitt
Barclays Bank Executive

NEVADA
Richard Harper
An Engineer

NEW YORK
Savannah Flanders
New York Times
Investigative Reporter

BRUSSELS, BELGIUM
Nato Secretary General
Carlos Phillipe

KIEV, UKRAINE
Ilya Volosin
Former Ukrainian Special
Forces Officer

PROLOGUE

CANADA/US BORDER
NEW BRUNSWICK/MAINE
MARCH

The rented Cessna 207 dropped to fifty feet above the tree line. One hundred fifty feet below Boston Air Route Traffic Control Center and NAV Canada's radar sweeps. The flight originated from a private airport outside of Edmundston, Canada; a week-long rental by sport fishermen who boasted about catching bass at Témiscouata-sur-le-Lac, to the northwest.

For three days the tourists flew the route to the fishing destination, landed, even fished. Just before dawn on the fourth day, today, the fishermen were overheard saying they wanted to explore other regions. They flew east, then south, skirting a stretch of the 611-mile border between the Canadian province and the state of Maine. Fifty-two minutes into the flight, the plane suddenly dropped down off its current course. Boston lost them. So did Bangor, Maine's radar, which swept Area D low altitude sectors. Calls went out. Urgent calls. The pilot reported that he had a fuel line issue, but control of the aircraft.

"Do you require assistance, Cessna 4251?" asked Bangor control.

"Negative BGR. Negative. Checking all systems. Stand by."

The standby bought the pilot time to hug the border between the

US and Canada below the MVA—the minimum vectoring altitude. In other words, below approved altitude. And soon below radar.

The pilot, experienced and trained elsewhere, shot across the border, then suddenly climbed higher. High enough for his passengers, who weren't good at playing fishermen, to prepare to parachute.

The heading, practiced abroad, took them over flat farmland, clear of trees, roughly two miles from the small Maine town of Limestone in Aroostook County, population 2,300. For a few hours it was about to be 2,300 plus four.

Approaching the drop zone and reporting he had gained control, the pilot leveled at 7,300 feet and announced "Ready" to his passengers in their native language. One by one, twenty seconds apart, they stepped out onto the fixed landing gear and bailed out.

The moon provided enough light for the men to touch down within one hundred yards of one another without incident. They silently gathered up their chutes, removed backpacks reverse-strapped to their chests, stuffed in the silk and laid low for ten minutes.

The lead skydiver searched the sky for the plane. But it was already out of earshot, heading back on its intended course, and, according to plan, radioing that he would set down back in Edmundston after dropping off his passengers for another day at the lake.

Convinced the route was clear, the leader gave the signal for his team to rise and begin walking across the field. If all had gone well on the ground, there'd be an SUV waiting for them in a 4H—whatever that was—parking lot. It was chosen because unlike a shopping center or convenience store lot, there were no cameras. The order was to stay out of sight.

Decades ago, they would have been easily spotted on radar, intercepted, caught and questioned. Not today. From 1947 to 1994, Limestone was home to Loring Air Force Base, one of the nation's largest Strategic Air Command bases. Until its closure at the end of the Cold War, it provided immediate eyes and ears against incoming threats. Now the land was part of the Loring Commerce Centre, and nobody saw who or what was coming. Not here or across America, as the first of the rogue strike teams moved into position to prepare for their attack.

There were more on the way.

LOS ANGELES INTERNATIONAL AIRPORT

APRIL

Three men deplaned at Philippines Airlines, Terminal TB. They had sat separately on the nonstop flight from Manila, pleasant to the flight attendants all the way. They talked politely to seat companions, but gave no biographical information to anyone onboard. They looked like many others on the plane—friendly when required, but most of the time connected to headphones or sleeping.

At US customs they each took different security stations, providing the rehearsed responses: "Thank you. Yes, I'm a graduate student beginning at"—here they filled in different school names—UCLA, USC, and Loyola Marymount University.

"What department?" one agent inquired.

"Engineering, sir."

The Customs and Border Protection agent smiled. "Engineering…."

She looked up, compared the international student against his passport and continued, "Well, good luck."

With that, the hardest conversation of the day, the agent stamped the passport and returned it with the student's visa.

Engineering, the agent thought. That's what her son was going into. *Perhaps they could…* But the Korean student was gone, already hooking up with two other fellow travelers.

Odd, she considered. Friends, but separate lines. By the time the next passenger stepped up to her, the notion was gone.

Strike team two was on ground.

FIFTEEN NAUTICAL MILES EAST OF FORT LAUDERDALE, FLORIDA

EARLY MAY

The skipper of the 65-foot Viking Sportfish cut through gentle waves at a comfortable eighteen knots. His luxury three-stateroom vessel normally booked at $4,500 for a full day, but he had no outgoing passengers today. Only five incoming, whom he met twenty-one miles out. The captain, like those he took onboard from a boat sailing out of the Bahamas, was deeply committed to the cause.

The pickup was surprisingly trouble-free. United States Customs cast a blind eye to pleasure vessels leaving a homeport for international waters if they didn't make a call at a foreign port. Under that circumstance, it didn't satisfy the requirements of a foreign departure. It had not, in a legal sense, "departed the United States."

And so, a third set of foreign insurgents slipped into the country. And still, there would be more.

PART ONE

THE LONG FUSE

NEVADA

JUNE

Summerlin, Nevada. Fifty miles from the key water distribution center in Henderson. Miles from the thirstiest city in America, Las Vegas, but integral to its survival.

Springs fed the area for 15,000 years, quenching desert Native American tribes and the white settlers who drove them out. In time, with ever-growing need, the healthy flow reduced to a trickle. Now every minute of every day, residents and visitors of the sun-scorched valley relied on water from the Colorado River, piped through a complicated system and accessible at the turn of a tap.

The journey begins at the southwestern shore of Lake Mead where the Southern Nevada Water Authority's Intake Station No. 2 draws water through a 20-foot-wide straw from the bottom of the reservoir three miles away.

The water is propelled through twenty-two powerful vertical pumps—powerful because one gallon of water weighs eight pounds. The water authority's pumps have to lift nine hundred million gallons every day. No other pumping station in the world can match that capacity and the volume.

The pumps send the water another thousand feet higher to the River Mountains Water Treatment Plant, eleven miles away in Henderson.

There, the untreated water flows into a tunnel carved through mountains. It's first put through an ozone chamber where electrically zapped bubbles break up microscopic organisms. The water then passes through sodium hypochlorite (or bleach) and then is hit with disinfectant before being sent to a multi-stage filtration process where it pours through anthracite coal and sand. For a single gallon of water, the trip takes four hours from Lake Mead through the plant. It's stored in three basins, then travels through nine-foot-wide underground pipes at three to five miles per hour. This takes the flow under Interstate 15—the main route southwest to Los Angeles—to a reservoir and pumping station in Las Vegas.

The entire system makes the water available and safe to drink. But there are any number of stages along the way where this most valuable resource can become vulnerable to a terrorist attack. For the past eighteen months, Richard Harper, a mid-level engineer at the plant, had been tasked with reviewing threat analyses. He felt he knew more than almost anybody, and early on he surmised that a crippling terrorist strike would require much more than opportunity. It would take a deep-rooted supply chain and a backup network, engineering experience, ample funds, and a great deal of patience.

On this 98-degree day, Richard Harper scanned the data on his computer screens and had a single word on his mind: *Summer.* One hundred fifteen degree scorching heat was only a month away. And then, the thirstiest city in America was going to get even thirstier.

WASHINGTON, D.C.

JUNE 5 7:42 AM

Morning rush hour traffic was basically normal, just typical commuters into Washington with the squeeze occurring at the 14th Street Bridges across the Potomac between Arlington and the district. Three options: one northbound, one southbound, and the busiest route, the bi-directional Rochambeau, named for a French Revolutionary War general who accompanied George Washington in the 1781 Battle of Yorktown.

More than seventy-five thousand vehicles cross the Interstate 395 bridge every day. Right now, 392 vehicles were bumper-to-bumper for all 2,483.1 feet of the Rochambeau's span. Two sixteen-foot U-Haul delivery trucks (which had seen better days) were in the slow traffic approaching the bridge. They were roughly twelve car lengths apart, in separate lanes. The drivers crept along, stopping and starting every few feet. It was one of those mornings. Soon it would be another kind of morning.

NEW YORK CITY

THE SAME TIME

Inbound Manhattan traffic was moving surprisingly well in the center tube of the Lincoln Tunnel under the Hudson River. Two self-driving cars entered from Weehawken, New Jersey. Usually it's hard for autonomous vehicles to recognize lanes in darkened tunnels, but the cars' Chinese software (developed by Baidu, the nation's version of Google) worked exceptionally well. For now, the cars sensed the traffic flow and maintained constant speed. For now.

ST. LOUIS
THE SAME TIME

Nathan McGowen had piloted his 10,000 horsepower pusher for more than thirty-three years, most of it along the same stretch of the Mississippi. He knew the river in good weather and bad, day and night. He had an innate sense for how much time it would take to bring his haul to a stop in any conditions. He knew how the wash of another passing barge would affect his steering, or how close he could pass an approaching shipment in the channel.

There were few Mississippi pilots, if any, better than Nathan McGowen on the mighty river. But none of his experience would serve him today.

WASHINGTON, D.C.

The pair of U-Haul trucks headed toward the nation's capital and onto the Rochambeau, the center vehicular span of the 14th Street Bridges. A morning storm had cleared out, but the roads were still slick. Accidents would happen—most unintentionally, but one now on purpose.

In the right lane, the lead U-Haul lurched forward and hit the back of a black Nissan with out-of-state plates. The impact caused the Nissan to slam into the car in front of it, a Chevy Impala. Traffic stopped. Some fifty feet back, the second U-Haul did the same in the left inbound lane. Predictably, commuters began yelling at one another and pointed to the trucks as the cause. But when they approached, the Hauls were both empty.

The drivers, wearing identical jeans, black mock turtlenecks and baseball caps, were moving fast, weaving around the stopped traffic. They tipped their hats low to evade the bridge surveillance cameras, hopped the railing to the pedestrian sidewalk, and ran toward the Virginia side of the bridge, where two motorcycles awaited them. The first man covered the .22 miles in one minute and five seconds. The second arrived ten seconds later.

Precisely two minutes after leaving their vehicles, both trucks, each loaded with 30 pounds of C4 in the undercarriage, exploded. The blasts tore a 35-foot hole in the cement. The trucks plummeted into the Potomac along with 16 other cars. The blast zone took out another 37 vehicles, killing nearly 100 commuters in seconds. The shock wave blew windshields and windows out of cars in both directions, seriously injuring scores more. Many on the bridge were instantly blinded.

NEW YORK CITY

At the pre-programmed location, the two self-driving cars slowed to a stop. That was at the 4,108-foot mark in the tunnel: the halfway point.

There were no drivers to get out, only nearby commuters to die. Twenty-three immediately, 44 more injured when they understand-ably panicked and ran. The tunnel's ceiling held after the twin blasts; 97 feet of earth protected the tube from the river. But smoke bellowed out from both ends and the twin explosions immediately closed the route. The city's three other tunnels were shut down within minutes, as were the subway tunnels between Manhattan and New Jersey and Manhattan and Brooklyn.

ST. LOUIS

McGowen whistled an old Irish tune, "Whisky in the Jar." He looked forward to seeing lots of friends at his upcoming retirement party. *One more month*, the 63-year-old pilot thought; he was still pondering the milestone when a 9mm bullet tore through his head and exited the win-dowpane of his towboat as it navigated three barges up the Mississippi toward St. Louis. He was the last of his crew of seven to die.

The assassin, with seafaring skills to match his ability to kill, set the port azimuth stern drive (ASD) to seven knots and a degree course that would bring it directly into the base of the west tower of the four-lane Stan Musial Veterans Memorial Bridge. Finished onboard, the assassin, a man of medium build with dark hair, was met by an accomplice on a Jet Ski a quarter-mile from the target. They sped away, as had three other accomplices. The collision alone would not do enough damage to the bridge, named for the great St. Louis baseball player, but the explosives strategically placed on the barges ten minutes ago would.

Two minutes later, the ASD brought the lead oil barge to a collision course with the bridge support, whereupon the first explosion sent a fireball upwards that instantly incinerated 62 morning commuters. The second and third explosions succeeded in dumping more than 3,600 tons of oil in the channel, which caught fire and in turn consumed all other craft within 500 yards.

Billowing black smoke could be seen for miles.

WASHINGTON, D.C.

Commuters fled the bridge in both directions. Many were on their phones, calling loved ones or their offices in the District or Virginia. Others just ran for their lives. Some stopped to help victims—one of them was Dan Reilly.

Reilly was on his way into D.C. in the backseat of a taxi. He'd flown into Reagan National from his Chicago corporate headquarters at Kensington Royal Hotels. He had a meeting scheduled on the Hill that clearly wasn't going to happen now. Not today—probably not for many days. The fact that he was in the backseat of the taxi and behind an armored car probably saved his life and his driver's.

Reilly opened the car door, got out, and quickly assessed the situation. *Disastrous,* he reasoned. *Definitely an attack.* He'd experienced it before. Others hadn't, so he helped those he could. First, a woman struggling to get her infant out of a back-facing car seat. Next, a disoriented older couple, a pregnant woman, two executives carpooling who clung onto each other, and a group of students on their way to D.C. on a school tour.

He found a middle-aged woman unresponsive in a car. Her doors were locked. Reilly grabbed a small slab of cement that had been blown forward in the explosion. He smashed the driver's side window, reached in, unhooked the seatbelt, and pulled her out. Her breathing was labored. She needed immediate medical help. Reilly looked around. There were dozens of others slumped over their wheels, on the ground in pain, or scrambling to get to safety.

Some automatically shot cell phone video over their shoulders as they escaped. Reilly ignored them. And because Washington was Washington, there were uniformed military personnel commuting to and from the Pentagon. They quickly volunteered, and one came to the aid of the woman Reilly had just extracted.

"She needs attention. Might be a heart attack," Reilly said.

"I'll check, I'm a medic. See who else needs help."

Reilly went from car to car in his immediate area. He helped those he could get to. They included people in shock who were otherwise unharmed, but so disoriented they walked toward the blast zone. Reilly turned them around, pointed the way off the bridge, and had them hold hands to make their fleeing a purposeful group activity. Reilly tried to get closer to the twisted and smoldering vehicles in the blast zone, but the intense heat and toxic smoke that came in rolling waves prevented him from making real ground. Besides, he couldn't tell if the bridge section would hold.

He stood and took stock of what to do next. The answer came to him. *Run!*

A truck, just feet from the spreading fire, was leaking gas. It was flowing in his direction. In a matter of seconds another fifty feet of the bridge would be engulfed in flames. Reilly caught up with the group he had walking hand-in-hand. He took the lead and shouted, "Move, fast! Now!"

Dan Reilly was in complete crisis mode now. There was no time for calm. He used all the authority in his voice and body language to get people through the chaos. The sounds, the smells, and the sight took him back to other locales, other attacks—all too recently, a terrorist attack in Tokyo, and years before that, Afghanistan.

Now, as President of Kensington Royal Hotels' international division and the force behind the creation of the company's global threat assessment program, known as Red Hotel, Reilly relied on instinct. He was, after all, Army-trained and State Department-tempered. Experience drove the dark-haired, six foot, 180-pound corporate executive in this new moment of crisis.

"Faster!" he yelled.

They only had seconds before the gasoline explosion that would undoubtedly trigger others. He guided people past ringing cell phones that would never be answered, past body parts, past debris. Past death.

"Keep going. Don't look back! Faster!"

The group had swelled. Now everyone was running for their lives.

And then it came. The boom and the heat flash at the same time.

Reilly and the servicemen and women carried those who couldn't walk. *Fifty feet more. Forty,* he said to himself. *A few more steps.*

Once on solid ground, Reilly, like the others, collapsed and took in the scene: Billowing gaseous smoke, one car after another engulfed in flames, loud popping and louder explosions. And approaching overhead, Coast Guard rescue helicopters, while fireboats headed midstream from the southern shore.

Dan Reilly had done enough. Others would do better.

He rose and began walking away, but spotted the corporal who had administered to the woman. The young enlisted man shook his head in sorrow.

"She didn't make it," he said. "But a lot of other people did."

Reilly simply nodded and patted the soldier on the back. He walked toward the line of oncoming emergency vehicles, military and civilian, their sirens screaming. He wasn't sure how he'd get anywhere, or for that matter where he should go. But he had a friend to call in cases like this, a friend who would surely be into what the hell just happened.

He was surprised when he got a clear cell line out. He figured they'd either be clogged, or Homeland Security would have had the towers silenced. Crisis protocol usually dictated that cellular communication be cut to prevent potential wireless signals from triggering explosive devices. But for now, they were on.

How much time had actually gone by? Reilly wondered. It felt like an hour since the blasts. Reilly looked at his watch, and for the first time saw that his arm was bloody—and that it had been just seven minutes since he last checked his watch in the cab.

"Hello."

"Bob, it's Reilly."

"Can't talk now, buddy. Busy," came the reply. "Suppose you heard."

"Heard?" Reilly helped a woman who had fallen. "I'm there!" Bob Heath gasped.

"There? 14th Street Bridge, there?"

"Yes. Awful." For the next minute Reilly described the scene, minimizing his own efforts.

"Jesus Christ, are you okay?" his friend asked.

"Yeah." He looked at his hands. The blood was not his. He felt his head, touched his chest: no injuries. His grey-green suit was a mess, his shoes were covered in soot, but he was fine.

"This was well-executed," Reilly noted.

"Timed with the others," Heath replied.

"What others?"

"You don't know? Minutes apart, attacks in New York and St. Louis. Each at major transportation choke points." Bob explained more.

Reilly took a deep breath. He thought long and hard. The 14th Street Bridge across the Potomac, the Lincoln Tunnel, the I-70 interstate span across the Mississippi at St. Louis. Targets all too familiar to him.

"But there's more." Reilly snapped back into the conversation.

"Where?"

"Not here. Latvia. The Russians are at the border. Looks real this time."

The man had reason to know. Bob Heath worked for the Central Intelligence Agency.

3

THE ROCHAMBEAU BRIDGE

VIRGINIA SIDE

Panicked commuters fled the 14th Street Bridge in both directions. Sirens blared. Thick smoke blew Reilly's way. He tore the inside lining of his jacket out to cover his mouth and nose and cupped his hand over the phone to block out ambient noise. Even with everything going on within eye and earshot, Reilly's thoughts went to Europe.

"NATO?" he asked.

"Some chatter," the CIA Officer replied. "Can't really say."

He couldn't and wouldn't; they were on unsecure cells. However, Heath added one consideration:

"Awfully coincidental." Reilly turned away from the growing cacophony of sirens and talked louder.

"You know what Malcolm Nance says?" Reilly asked. He was referring to the counter-intelligence expert, a former US Navy officer specializing in Russian affairs, as well as a bestselling author and go-to cable news source.

"Coincidences take a lot of planning."

"Right. Any discussion on invoking Article 5?" Article 5 is the catchall collective agreement that declares an attack on one NATO nation an attack on all.

"Nada. But you tell me. What's going to matter more—infrastructure attacks here or a Russian threat to a country most people couldn't find on a map?"

Reilly didn't need to respond; the answer was obvious. Heath went silent for a moment.

"Still there?" Reilly asked.

"Yup. Incoming text. Double whatever I just told you: I just got word that Russia's doing the same thing to the south. Ukraine."

OSTROV, RUSSIA
THE SAME TIME

A thousand paratroopers, the third unit of equal size, from the Russian 76th Air Assault Division waited for go orders at the 444th Center for Combat Employment in Ostrov, Russia. Nearby, they were supported by another four thousand ground troops from Russia's 6th and 20th Guard Armies, along with their tanks and missile brigades, and Russia's 1st Air Defense Forces Command from Severomorsk. MiG-29 and Su-25/Su-25SM fighters and Tu-22M3/MR bombers were fueled and battle-ready. The objective was to take Riga, Latvia in under 36 hours.

THE BLACK SEA OFF THE CRIMEAN COAST
THE SAME TIME

Captain Yegor Gleba of the Ukrainian frigate *Hetman Sahaydachni* radioed for orders. Ukraine's naval command had been through this before.

"Surrender."

The alternative was too great to consider, and if the scenario played out as it had before, the *Hetman Sahaydachni* and its crew of some 200 would be released within a few days. At least that was the initial thinking when the captain weighed anchor as the Russian crew came aboard in the Kerch Strait, the narrow strip of water separating the Black and Azov Seas. But this time, the Russians' action appeared more than just grandstanding. They disabled the SAM missile launcher and removed the torpedoes and anti-submarine rocket launchers.

The seizure of the ship was met by Ukraine's National Security and Defense Council's recommendation to the country's president to deploy 10,000 troops to the border.

THE ROCHAMBEAU BRIDGE

"Better to talk inside," Heath told Reilly. "Come on over."

"I'd love to, but cars aren't being allowed anywhere near here."

"I'll send a car. Where are you exactly?"

"Just off the bridge. South. Traffic isn't moving, but I'll hike up to a place where you can have me picked up." It ended up being more than a mile away at the Marriott in Crystal City.

"Mr. Reilly?" the CIA driver asked when he pulled up some thirty-five minutes later.

"Yes."

"If you wouldn't mind, your identification."

Reilly produced his ID. The driver checked the picture against the man standing outside his Town Car. He also called in his Illinois driver's license number. Three minutes later, Reilly was on his way to the Langley, Virginia headquarters of the CIA, checking the news on his cellphone.

En route, Reilly's phone rang. He had half-expected the call earlier.

"Hi, Marnie."

It was Marnie Babbitt, a Barclays Bank vice president calling from London. He had recently gotten involved with the international executive. Extremely involved.

"Aren't you in D.C.?" she asked in a panic.

"Not exactly. Virginia."

"I heard—"

"You heard right. But I'm fine. Following the reports myself now." Less information was definitely best.

"And New York and St. Louis."

"Yes," he said.

"Be careful. Stay out of the city."

"I don't think that will be an issue. I can't get across."

"Well don't even try, mister."

"I won't."

"Promise me."

"I promise."

"And meanwhile, trouble here, too."

She explained what he already knew. Gorshkov was making NATO spread its assets, perhaps to ultimately reclaim the old Soviet satellite nations.

She then asked when he was heading to Europe.

"First Chicago, if I can get a flight out."

"Keep me posted. I want to know wherever you go. And I want to see you when you get here."

They said goodbye without an *I love you*. That hadn't been spoken yet, but was surely to come soon. That was the trajectory they were on.

His next call was to corporate headquarters, first to have Brenda Sheldon, his assistant, book a flight out. Then a call to activate his company's crisis team and trigger the highest threat level at all the KR—Kensington Royal—properties throughout Eastern Europe.

4

Bob Heath greeted Reilly in the lobby. Security was heightened, even more than normal. Visible weapons out at the ready.

"You picked a hell of a day to travel," the CIA officer volunteered. Reilly allowed himself a needed laugh.

"Seems to be a habit of mine." Heath gave Reilly a bear hug that made him gasp. He was two years younger, thirty pounds heavier, and solid. A brick. A tall, bald brick.

The two men had history. They'd met on a mission out of Kabul. Reilly was the CIA man's regional Army intelligence contact, his eyes and ears, and the reason he was alive today. They were on patrol when their convoy stopped to help a young boy alongside a supply route. It was a diversion that immediately cost the lives of six Americans and the boy, who held a detonator. More servicemen were taken down by Taliban soldiers hiding behind roadside boulders. Total American casualties: 19.

Reilly made a break for the door. Heath followed, but as soon as he cleared the transport, he took a bullet in his left leg, shattering his femur. Reilly caught him as he fell hard. With all his strength, he dragged the operative to a gulley and away from the line of fire. They settled behind a boulder out of sight. Reilly kept pressure on Heath's wound, covered his mouth to mute his cries, and waited. They waited for hours. Ultimately a pair of Sikorsky UH-60 Black Hawk helicopters flew over the kill zone and rescued Reilly and Heath, the only survivors. The experience left Heath with a limp and Reilly with a friend for life. It also marked the beginning of the end of Reilly's military career. Four months later he resigned, after a one-star general covered up the fact that he had knowingly sent Reilly's convoy into harm's way.

Thanks to this connection, after his discharge Reilly had taken a job with the State Department. Upstairs, Heath briefed Reilly on the developing crises and the White House response.

"Taking care of business at home. No comment on Latvia and Ukraine. The White House is leaving that to NATO for now. Meanwhile, major metro arteries are in lockdown. Subways, trains, bridges and tunnels. Flights are still going out, but governors are sending the guard to bolster TSA. Here, it's the Marines to Dulles and Reagan."

"What do we know?" Reilly asked.

"Next to nothing. The usual suspects are stone silent. The only claims are from groups that couldn't possibly pull all this off."

"So back to my point—a coordinated diversion."

"No proof," Heath offered.

"If you're waiting for proof it might come too late." Heath poured two cups of coffee. Black for both of them.

"Have a seat, brother." He pulled a file from a drawer and slid it across the desk.

Reilly looked at the cover. Plain, brown, and not labeled. He opened it and didn't need to go past the cover page. He knew exactly what it was.

O'HARE INTERNATIONAL AIRPORT
CHICAGO

Reilly barely made it to Dulles in time for the United 12:45 p.m. flight to Chicago that his assistant, Brenda, had reserved. As he approached the TSA security check, he received a text from Brenda about a car service pickup at O'Hare and the particularly worried property managers phoning from Eastern Europe. He texted that he would call them before takeoff or email from the air.

Then another text appeared: she wrote that a man named Vincent Moore urgently wanted to see him. Reilly didn't know anyone by that name. He responded in all caps:

WHO???

She instantly wrote back:

FBI.

Reilly took another of those long breaths. Like the one on the bridge.

While passing through the heightened TSA check he overheard grumblings from passengers, complaining about the delays. Reilly appreciated the added security but wondered if flights had been cancelled given the threats. He imagined the conversations going on in the White House, and landed on the ultimate decision not to create more panic. *But…* he thought.

"Reagan's backed up, but not so much here," the young woman TSA Officer noted. "However, Homeland Security is not allowing inflight Wi-Fi. Part of a pre-established emergency directive." That made sense to Reilly, but for two-and-a-half hours he would be out of touch with his office and most of his worried European GMs.

By making the reservation, his name went into a national database, the Passenger Name Record (PNR), authorized by 49 U.S.C. § 44909(c)(3). The law required airlines operating to, from, and through the United States to report passenger information to the Department of Homeland Security. Reilly's name worked through the system in the same two-and-a-half hours, enough time for DHS to coordinate with the FBI in Washington, which in turn notified the Chicago bureau. Enough time for FBI agents to meet Reilly at the United Airlines gate at his destination.

The plane stopped short of the terminal. The pilot got on the PA and gave a friendly update.

"Sorry folks, we're just on hold for a bit waiting for a tow in. Shouldn't be long."

But with every passing minute, principally because of the events of the day, passengers showed their impatience to the flight attendants. Reilly just sat back in his seat, suspecting what was to follow. After thirty minutes and a hook up, the plane moved forward and was brought in line with the jet way. Reilly, sitting up front, was among the first to deplane. He immediately heard his name called.

"Mr. Reilly. Daniel J. Reilly."

The voice was deep and with the kind of authority Reilly instantly recognized. *Government.*

Two square-jawed men in their thirties wearing dark grey suits, loose enough to hide their standard-issue Glocks, stepped forward, blocking him.

"You're Dan Reilly?"

"Yes," he replied. But he thought, *You know I am. My photo is on your phone.*

"This way, please."

The *please* was not out of kindness. Reilly didn't move. They produced their FBI identification.

"Good enough?" the lead agent asked sarcastically.

"Good enough," Reilly replied.

Agent One led. His partner walked behind Reilly. They went through a door away from public view, along a series of narrow corridors into a stark white room with a table and two chairs bolted to the floor. Agent Two pointed to a seat for Reilly to take. It faced a mirror. The mirror wasn't for reflection.

"Sit." This time there was no *please* attached.

Reilly complied, as he knew he should.

THE UKRAINIAN-RUSSIAN BORDER

The Russian forces were assembling at eight locations: Yelnya, Klintsy, Valuyki, Boguchar, Millerovo, Persianovskiy, and bases identified as Rostov-1 and Rostov-2. All short distances from the border.

They included two brigades of the Russian First Guards Tank Army, elements of the 20th Army, the 28th Motorized Rifle Brigade, the 49th Army, and 2,500 paratroopers. Everyone was there to fight, to take Ukraine. Fifty-thousand strong, more than twice the number of troops they faced.

For years NATO had kept trying to build off-ramps to avoid war. But for all the talk, these men and women on the line understood what was in the heart of command—in the soul of their country: to take back what was theirs. This would be a battle of honor. Justified by history, and likely ignored by the West.

At least that's what they were told.

KIEV, UKRAINE

Stephan Lazlo had five calls into Chicago, each more urgent than the last. He was general manager of the Kensington Royal Hotel in Kiev. While he waited for Reilly's instructions, he reviewed the new color-coded corporate threat assessment directives. Blue was normal: no apparent threats. Some training, which the hotel was woefully behind on. Next, Yellow: this was an actual alert level that would be triggered when intelligence returned unspecified threats to US citizens and US businesses in hot spots.

Lazlo put a check mark next to it. The procedures were to remove any American flags; review evacuation plans; increase security in public areas; require positive ID photos of guests; remove all large containers like waste receptacles; limit roof access; keep meeting rooms locked when not in use; tow any abandoned vehicles; and restrict all engineering and electrical areas. All good ideas, but more applicable to a terrorist threat than an invading army.

Orange, the third threat level: everything under blue and yellow, plus. Another check. Nothing remains in storage; all arriving packages are to be inspected; no vehicles allowed in any parking lot unless registered and cross-referenced to guests; barricades up to restrict parking close to the building; all suspicious boxes to be removed; and all shift changes checked by department heads.

Finally, Red. The highest level. Adding to Blue, Yellow, and Orange, Threat Condition Red adds mandatory hotel entrance through metal detectors for all guests.

"As if that will stop Gorshkov's troops," Lazlo muttered.

He continued to read the directive set forth a few months earlier by Dan Reilly and his advisors. No cars parked unattended within fifty feet; cement bollards deployed to prevent full vehicular access to the hotel; visibly armed security; and dogs. Bomb-sniffing dogs.

"Der'mo!" Shit! Definitely Red.

Lazlo paged through the thick spiral-bound procedures until he came to "Evacuation." As he read the procedure he thought, *Where the hell is Reilly?*

NATO HEADQUARTERS
BRUSSELS, BELGIUM

The 179th Military Committee, NATO's highest military command authority, were behind closed doors that were constantly flying open with new reports, all grave.

Present: the Allied Chief of Defense, General Robert "Rocky" Rockford; Supreme Allied Commander Europe (SACEUR), General Elias B. Turnbull; Supreme Allied Commander Transformation (SACT), NATO Secretary General Carlos Phillipe; and Chairman of the European Military Committee, General Jules Rother. Together the team represented NATO's command structure, with no shortage of plans and no end to their worries.

"Risks and results," General Rockford demanded.

Pens scribbled on papers, hands rose. But before a strategy could take form, the command assessed the situation. Nothing provable; everything worrisome. Across the board, Canadian, Czech, Polish, Italian, Albanian, and Slovak troops stationed in Latvia were on alert. Limited American forces were also in country; most had been transferred out after training exercises concluded. What remained were merely 750 men and women and only 115 armored units. A first line, hardly defensible.

American firepower was available, but far from Latvia. The 7th Bomb Wing assigned to the Global Strike Command Eighth Air Force was stationed at Dyess AFB, outside of Abilene, Texas, and the 28th Bomb Wing operated out of Ellsworth Air Force Base, ten miles northeast of Rapid City, South Dakota. At this moment their B-1B Lancers were not in the air. The United States was dealing with its own problems now. First-term President Alexander Crowe was a man without any immediate answers and certainly no solutions. For now it was a game of "watch and wait."

"Watch and wait" was propitious, for the moment. But NATO command wondered how long the moment would last. To make matters worse, if Crowe invoked Article 5 now as America had after 9/11, NATO's resources would be severely divided, which very well might be what Gorshkov intended. Moreover, no one in the NATO situation room really knew what or where to target, short of the Kremlin itself.

FIVE YEARS EARLIER

The *Man Gyong Bong*, a four-story, 9700-ton cargo/passenger ferry chugged though the night, hugging the coast of the Sea of Japan. It had sailed quietly from the port of Rajin-guyok in the Democratic People's Republic of Korea to Vladivostok, Russia. A normal route—though not a normal night.

The ship had berths for 193, but through the nine-hour voyage only eight paying passengers were aboard. Seven had jobs as high-rise construction workers; they were all legitimate and going no further than Vladivostok. Those seven would send more than half their income back home. But not actually to their homes—to the government. The North Korean government. Their salaries, along with those of the tens of thousands of other North Koreans working in and around Vladivostok, went to government coffers, for decades helping to offset crippling Western sanctions.

Seven of the eight. The eighth was different. He was a bright and talented 29-year-old with tremendous potential—potential developed by North Korea's National Intelligence Service. Potential recognized by Russia's SVR, *Sluzhba vneshney razvedki*, the foreign intelligence service. Unlike the other seven onboard, with whom he had nothing in common, this young man was going to get special training that would take years. He was a spy.

In North Korea, spies had the status of generals. Their families enjoyed the perks that came with loyalty: better housing, a car, first choice of food off the barely-stocked market shelves. They had these benefits so long as the spying member of their household remained loyal. And there was the small print: if captured by an enemy government, they had standing orders to commit suicide. If they didn't, the regime would punish all family members still living in the country. It wasn't pretty and it often wasn't quick. But it was ultimately final, a time-honored incentive for the spying member to stay in line for the sake of his extended family.

This eighth man understood this. He was committed, an officer of few words and many special skills. In school he had excelled in math and science, which earned him an engineering degree. On the soccer field he distinguished himself as a never-give-up scoring champion. In the army, he proved himself smart and fearless. He had the highest marks in sharpshooting and little regard for people who didn't measure up to the job. That attitude and natural ability brought him to the attention of North Korea's intelligence service, and in turn the Kremlin, which had a special long-term mission planned.

The man would train in a secret city with second- and third-generation Koreans whose families had lived in Russia since the Korean War. It would take years and tremendous coordination, but ultimately they would be serving the cause of the Russian Federation and the Democratic People's Republic of Korea against the West's imperialism. That imperialism was manifest through NATO's post-Cold War expansion.

At 0625 Pak Yoon-hoi stepped off the gangplank. Two men in business suits and trench coats approached. They were intelligence operatives of the Russian SVR.

"Pak Yoon-hoi?" the taller of the two men asked in Russian.

"Yes," the North Korean replied in their language. Another one of his skills.

No identification was required.

"Come with us."

That was the extent of the conversation. Yoon-hoi didn't need to talk to them anymore than he had. They were just his transporters.

Pak Yoon-hoi looked around. The first light of the morning illuminated the Vladivostok skyline. He was in Russia, but he had also just taken the first step towards becoming an American.

* * *

At the same time the SVR handlers were waiting for the North Korean, another person was surreptitiously watching the ship dock through his camera's telephoto lens. Leonid Kaminsky had three jobs: teach photography in the humanities program at Far Eastern Federal University in Vladivostok; complete his own post-graduate requirement with an after-dark photo essay titled "Vladivostok, the Pulse of the City;" and stay alive. The staying alive part had nothing to do with his teaching or most of his photography work, though some of tonight's photos might find their way into an academic presentation. Some, not all. Definitely not the shots through the long lens aimed at the arriving passengers.

Ordinarily, the *Man Gyong Bong* offloaded nearly two hundred North Korean passengers. This morning, just a handful. Kaminsky considered that odd. *Eight. Only eight?*

Seven looked like day workers in the kind of clothes that conformed to North Korean regime standards—black denim was allowed; blue jeans were not (the government had proclaimed that they embodied Western imperialism). White shirts were expected; no shorts or revealing skirts; no trousers on women rolled above the knees. Flats for women and nondescript black shoes for men. No dyed hair, no long hair. Fashion enforcers patrolled the streets of the Democratic People's Republic of Korea, writing citations for people who failed to follow prescribed rules.

But through his telephoto lens, Kaminsky photographed a lone man with commanding posture and a self-assured mien, wearing clothes few North Koreans could afford. Kaminsky clicked twenty photos from his high hide on the roof of a warehouse facing the dock. *Five-ten*, he thought. *Military or ex-military*, which in either case made him active in some branch of the government. He wore a yellow t-shirt, blue jeans, black lace-up boots, a black leather jacket, and a baseball cap. *Interesting. Maybe significant.* He opened the aperture to get a clearer view of the man's face just as he was met by a pair of official-looking Russian government goons. Kaminsky revised his thinking: *extremely interesting; worth exploring.*

Leonid Kaminsky would get his photos to his supervisor. Not his university Chair or Dean—his boss in Langley, Virginia at the Central Intelligence Agency. That was the part of his job he took most seriously—staying alive.

6

PRESENT DAY

JUNE 5

HENDERSON, NEVADA

Some things worked correctly. Almost simultaneously, Richard Harper's cell phone rang and he received an incoming text and an email; it was Homeland Security emergency protocol kicking in. Not a test this time, but a warning to step up enhanced security.

Harper had heard the morning news more than three hours earlier, and actually thought the alert should have been triggered sooner. But now he followed procedure: additional eyes on security cameras; check on all vehicles for under-carriage explosives; no parking within 100 feet of the building. Overtime was automatically authorized for regular guards to patrol outside, and additional day hires were called in to take up posts at the River Mountain Water Treatment Plant.

But most part-time help wouldn't be familiar with the operation of the plant, or even its layout. Most except for four—they'd studied the plans and came with extra gear.

O'HARE INTERNATIONAL AIRPORT

Reilly figured that his absence would be noted. He counted on Alan Cannon, the company's vice president of global safety and security, to inquire on his whereabouts. For the time being, he'd simply see what the FBI wanted and try to determine what they knew.

The lead agent asked for Reilly's phone and wallet. He dubbed him *Good Cop*, anticipating how he was going to conduct the session.

"Cell phone and wallet," demanded the second agent as he noted Reilly's disheveled clothes. He crossed to Reilly's side of the table and made his order all too clear.

"Now!" This one Reilly determined to be *Bad Cop*.

Reilly complied. They put his items in a large brown envelope and wrote Reilly's name and the time on the outside. After that, the room fell quiet. Reilly suspected they were waiting for someone else to arrive. Someone more important than the pair who brought him to the room. Likely the man Brenda had texted him about.

At minute six, Good Cop, trying to be nice, remarked, "You must know why you're here." It wasn't delivered as a question.

Reilly believed he knew, but instead said, "Why don't you tell me?" Bad Cop laughed.

Reilly recognized what was going on, the pressure they were applying. He'd been on the other end of this kind of interview numerous times in the service. *No,* he corrected himself. *Not interview. Interrogation.* So, he decided to lighten the mood.

"Gentlemen, you obviously know who I am. And you're having a very busy day. So am I." He gestured to his dirty clothes. "I have responsibility for my staff and American citizens at my company's hotels in Latvia and Ukraine. So let's get going. This isn't a friendly conversation."

Neither FBI agent responded. Reilly filled the void, more for the benefit of the people on the other side of the glass. He stared at them.

"I've called a crisis team together. They're waiting for me. Lives are in the balance, people."

No one on either side of the one-way mirror responded. Then the two agents heard a command in their ears over their wireless. They stood. A moment later the door opened.

"I'll take it from here," said an obviously senior FBI agent, who entered carrying a thick file folder.

"Special Agent Vincent Moore, Mr. Reilly." He produced his identification. Moore was six-four, African-American, imposing, and authoritative. This was the agent who had phoned his office. He had all the means to find out where Reilly was.

Reilly reasoned his time with Good Cop and Bad Cop was over. Now for Really Bad Cop.

The two agents took positions on either side of the door. Moore, a block of a man with short-cropped hair, wearing a rumpled suit jacket he didn't care about, took a seat directly opposite Reilly.

"You don't appear surprised that you're being detained, Mr. Reilly."

"I've traveled a great deal to some pretty bad places. This is nothing new."

"But in your own country?"

"This isn't a normal day. I don't expect normal things on days like this." Moore ignored him. He tapped the stack of files he'd placed on the table.

"Then you understand why we intercepted you."

"Why don't you just tell me, Agent Moore?"

"Three reasons so far, but the day is young: the Lincoln Tunnel, the 14th Street Bridge, the Musial. They're right out of a State Department Red Team threat report, Mr. Reilly."

Moore removed a spiral-bound folder from the top file and turned it around so Reilly could read the bold letters on the cover.

"It was prepared for the National Security Council and DHS," Moore said. Reilly said nothing.

"Highly sensitive. A report, more of an inventory on critical assets ranging from dams to hazardous material sites, nuclear power plants, local festivals, crucial urban highway overpasses, and bridges and tunnels."

Reilly remained silent, but anticipated Moore's follow up.

"You're familiar with such a report?" the FBI agent said.

"I think you know the answer to that."

Reilly nodded to Moore's hand. Moore smiled, but it was anything but friendly. He slid his hand off the paper, revealing one other bit of type. Reilly's name as author.

"Mr. Reilly, the three attacks today were carried out in precisely the manner you described."

"Researched. Warned," Reilly responded.

"Described," Moore repeated, invoking a new, more accusatory tone. "In detail. Explicit detail."

"That was my assignment, Agent Moore. I went further than previous analyses, if that's what you're referring to as *detail*, because I was instructed to."

"Whatever you want to call it, it makes you a person of great interest in today's events."

CHICAGO
KENSINGTON ROYAL HOTELS HEADQUARTERS

"He was confirmed on the flight," a worried Brenda Sheldon told Kensington security chief Alan Cannon. "But he didn't show up for the driver. And he's not answering his phone."

"His phone is registered with the company. I'll do a Find My Phone search. In the meantime, keep dialing."

Cannon tried tracking the phone. Nothing came up. He phoned the airline to confirm that Reilly had been onboard. He had been. *So,* he said to himself, *somewhere between getting off the plane and reaching the baggage claim, he disappeared.*

Alan Cannon, a former FBI agent himself, made a call to his old boss.

"Sorry, Mr. Cannon. Director Mulligan is not available right now."

Not available. This had multiple meanings, from 'in the bathroom' to 'at the White House.' A meeting with the president was most likely, given the morning's events.

"It's urgent," Cannon replied.

"Everything is right now. I'm sorry, Mr. Cannon."

Cannon placed another call. This time to a direct cell phone number, no handler in between, to the TSA chief at O'Hare.

"Kenny, Alan Cannon here. I know you're underwater, but I have a problem." Kenny Green listened attentively. The TSA supervisor put Cannon on hold for three minutes before returning with a single sentence.

"An FBI team is questioning him here at O'Hare."

"Why?"

"I don't know. They went around us. But an agent, some big shot, flew in from National on a private plane to meet him. An FBI honcho with real stripes. That's all I have."

"Not good enough. I want to see him."

"I don't know, even for you," Green said. "I've already told you too much."

"You never talked to me today. And considering that's the case, how about you also don't tell me exactly where Dan Reilly is."

MOSCOW
THE KREMLIN

Nikolai Gorshkov was having a good day. NATO was surely scrambling. The U.S. was preoccupied and Latvia was now in his crosshairs. Soon, Ukraine. All Gorshkov had to do was issue the order, but he had a longer game to play: one that would give him everything he wanted, with minimal casualties.

Before that, there was another bit of business to deal with. Most displeasing. And when President Gorshkov was displeased, people usually paid dearly.

"Send in the first," he told his aide.

Waiting in the corridor were four paunchy men who enjoyed the spoils of the good life, and one tall, beautiful, early-40s blonde in a brown military uniform. They had been sitting absolutely straight for the past hour. Though no one spoke, the men—two deputy directors of the FSB, Moscow's Mayor Victor Markovich, and a general from the eastern border of Latvia—gave one another suspicious looks. Each likely pondered whether they'd be sold out by the others. The woman appeared self-assured, but on guard. The FSB officers knew her by reputation, and her rumored association with the president.

One by one, the men were called in. Before marching into Gorshkov's office, each straightened his uniform and sucked in the fat. One by one they exited after barely two minutes. Each ashen, looking ahead at an uncertain future. Uncertain by the hour.

Then it was the woman's turn. Col. Martina Kushkin stood. She took confident steps forward. Undoubtedly President Gorshkov had staged the waiting time: political theater. He wanted her to be reminded of his power and how he dealt with people who had failed him. But there would be another reason. She was anxious to find out.

7

NEW STANTON, PA
MOTEL 6

A man of blended Asian and Eastern European heritage sat in the motel room with his four operatives, all loyal but privy to only pieces of the plan, not the whole. For that reason, he knew each of them by name, but they knew one another solely by number. The men were identified as THREE, FIVE, SIX, and SEVEN. The leader was TWO; it would be presumptuous for him to have taken ONE. In his mind, that was reserved for his country's leader. No one had the designation FOUR—culturally it was considered bad luck, equivalent to the number 13 in the States.

Like TWO, they all wore jeans, loose-fitting t-shirts, and sneakers. No hoodies. They had arrived separately in rented cars, drawing no attention from the motel staff. Small talk was not allowed. Nothing personal either—they were a team, but not friends. If ordered, they would kill each other without hesitation. They accepted this. They were also reminded it would be for the good of their families, and the point never had to be explained further.

Each had unique expertise in explosives, electronics, and computers, as well as martial arts. They were in Pennsylvania for business. A planned follow-up to what other compatriots had already accomplished in Washington, New York, and St. Louis: the business of disruption. Highly visible attacks against multiple targets.

This group had entered the country under fake passports through airports. Other mission teams had parachuted in above the Canadian/U.S. border and secretly docked on fishing boats. Nothing on paper could trace them back to their native country. Yet, if captured, they would end their lives immediately by their own hand or at the hands of the enemy—*for the good of their families*. They were all North Korean nationals.

TWO had chosen each man for his expertise and by the way they could slip in into American society. His operatives were recruited from active military, the children of mixed marriages, and single. All spoke perfect English. All were unquestionably loyal.

The TV set was on when they arrived. It was tuned to a soccer match on an American sports channel. Uzbekistan was playing Italy; Italy was ahead. The audio masked their conversation to any passersby outside the room. Their own country had lost the day earlier, news they only heard from the play-by-play announcer during a recap.

TWO gathered them around the queen-sized bed and unfurled a city map. It had no specific markings. He'd memorized every important detail. He required the same from his men.

First, the assignments: SIX and SEVEN would retrieve supplies from a local storage facility on Hunker Waltz Mill Road. TWO had purchased the necessary electronics from a Walmart outside of Hudson, NY and a Fry's in Downer's Grove, IL. The more lethal items had been smuggled in from Canada in compartments, hidden in the undercarriage of five pickup trucks and transferred to a 16-foot U-Haul truck driven to New Stanton by TWO.

THREE and FIVE were in charge of renting a new fleet of vehicles from five different locations and preparing them for the mission.

Next the exact schedule, accounting for traffic issues and weather: as with the first attacks, coordination was critical to both success and escape. As he spoke, TWO looked at SEVEN. He stopped.

"Is something wrong?" he asked.

"No, sir."

TWO tipped his head to SEVEN's crossed leg. Right over left. The man looked down. The right was twitching. SEVEN automatically tightened his muscles.

"It's nothing." But SEVEN recognized his superior's concern. Another cultural superstition: it was believed that by shaking a leg, a person shakes all the good fortune out of them. He uncrossed his legs and squeezed his toes inside his American Nikes. He looked at the others who had picked up on the observation.

"I'm ready."

TWO returned to his map. For the next thirty minutes he reviewed the operation, from precise structural weak points to surveillance camera positions, from the approach roads to the specific targets, to their own exfiltration routes. The briefing concluded with him notifying the group that they had 24 hours to make ready.

They casually left one at a time, each certain not to make too much of the departure. Their training had taught them to take in the surroundings, but not to act suspiciously. Their orders were to move through the day in a leisurely fashion, return to their respective motels, watch TV, and then proceed to their assigned destinations at the appointed times. Along the way, they were to obey every stop sign, traffic light, and pedestrian crosswalk. If pulled over by police for any reason, they were to act polite and responsive, produce their fake or stolen IDs—they had multiple choices—accept the ticket, and get on their way. They were after all posing as American citizens, and blending in wasn't hard anymore.

8

MOSCOW

THE KREMLIN

Colonel Martina Kushkin stood when summoned by Gorshkov's lieutenant. She had survived meetings like this before and was certain she would again. But she never really knew what the president might do if provoked.

A new assignment? Activate a sleeper under her command? Or a goodbye for good without a pension, a dacha on the Black Sea, or a last kiss? She set aside the last thought. No words could save her if that was Gorshkov's intent. *So*, she thought, *new orders that likely involved one of her trainees*—a pupil from the special school she taught in, modeled after the Andropov Institute of the Cold War Era. *Which one?* She had twenty especially talented and field-worthy sleeper spies. Among them ten star pupils, but fewer than five whom she would trust with top assignments.

The Russian colonel steeled herself as she entered Gorshkov's office.

No, she said to herself. *I will not end up as my foolish comrades in the waiting room. This is my time to shine. To do whatever Nikolai Gorshkov requires.*

She stood at attention before the president. The former KGB and FSB officer rose. A positive sign.

"Martina, you look well," the Russian leader said.

"Thank you, Mr. President. You as well."

It was the truth. Flattering, but the truth. Gorshkov was as fit at 67 as he had been forty years earlier at the end of the Cold War. Not an ounce of unwanted fat, nor any trace of kindness or humility.

"How did those traitors look to you as they left?"

"Defeated, Mr. President," she quickly answered.

"As well they should. And to be in their company?" the president asked.

"I am not in their company," she declared.

"Of course. To be waiting in their presence?"

"You wanted me to see their expressions, coming in and leaving. A reminder, perhaps a warning."

"Not a warning. Never for you, Martina. I trust you too much to question your dedication."

She knew that wasn't true. Gorshkov didn't trust anybody completely; even his spies were spied upon.

"But you are right about a reminder. There is no room for mistakes. They made mistakes and each will suffer the consequences."

"Yes, sir."

Gorshkov motioned for Kushkin to take the seat in one of the wide, red jacquard Louis XV chairs. Comfortable. She imagined the men who had been in his office minutes before, but not invited to sit.

The president pressed a button under his center desk drawer, which closed and locked his office door. He opened a gilded lacquer liquor cabinet from the same period, and removed a bottle of Minskaya Kristall vodka and two glasses.

"May I?"

"No thank you, Mr. President."

"Perhaps later," he said lasciviously while pouring a glass for himself.

Kushkin nodded. Gorshkov had taken her before. She hoped this was not going to be one of those nights. But the decision was not hers.

The president walked around his desk and sat next to her in a matching chair.

"Now, to one of the reasons for your visit."

Visit. An interesting term. Not one of her favorites.

"Yes, sir."

"Given the identity of the individuals who preceded you, what can you assess? Strictly from an intelligence point of view?"

Less than a year earlier, the Russian Federation was forced to stand down from Latvia. Additionally, rumors circulated that the FSB had recently lost an agent in Brussels, an agent long connected to Gorshkov. She considered that Gorshkov could be cleaning house, particularly in light of current operations to the West. She began strongly.

"Sir, General Titov was poised to storm Latvia. He suddenly stopped at the border. Perhaps that was not your wish. Perhaps if he had moved earlier—" Kushkin saw Gorshkov purse his lips, an indication that she had made a correct assessment. But which? She continued, "At the same time, as I understand it, the FSB did not provide enough backup for an operative in Brussels, a legend in KGB and FSB annals. A friend of yours. The agent was killed on a mission. Mayor Markovich may have provided information that contributed to the agent's death."

"Not may, did."

"And you are holding him and the two FSB deputy directors responsible. You're correcting those internal mistakes."

"Very good, Colonel. And beyond that? Your purpose today?"

"I can help you right things. Undoubtedly through my assets."

"Quite correct."

"They will do as I order. As you order. Good rising stars. Ready."

"One of them you call *Polunochnyy*. Why?"

"You've read my reports on them, Mr. President?" she said, feigning surprise. He gave a hearty laugh.

"Of course I have."

"I name them for many reasons. In this case, the time of day when much can be accomplished."

Polunochnyy. Midnight. Kushkin smiled.

"The asset is one of my best. Dedicated. Extremely capable. Adept.

Well-placed. Rising in influence."

"Loyal?"

"Completely. Beyond reproach."

"Recent communications?"

"Limited, of course. Selective updates on active measures. The current assignment is—"

"I'm aware, Martina. Any personal meetings?"

"Recently no. But as I said—"

"Eighteen months ago. Christmastime in Paris," Gorshkov stated.

Kushkin showed no surprise. *Even spies were spied upon.* As in the old Soviet Union, the new Russia had its eyes and ears in hotel rooms even in the West.

"Yes, sir. We met at a hotel bar. Pre-arranged."

"And then to your room, Colonel."

"Yes, sir. One night. Debriefing." Gorshkov laughed.

"I suppose that will suffice."

Colonel Kushkin straightened in her chair and declared, "Mr. President, I use all of my skills to instill loyalty and personal faith."

Gorshkov smiled knowingly.

"Well then," the president said, "here's what I require." He explained.

When Gorshkov finished, she was ready to leave and make arrangements. He had other ideas.

"You look radiant tonight."

"With a little more warning," she regretted the word immediately. "I mean, time…"

"You never disappoint."

That was what she had been trained for, and what she had trained others in—the art of seduction, manipulation, and all kinds of pleasure. After all, women who pleased him could advance. Those who didn't were given to the oligarchs for their pleasure before being banished to the streets. The men had challenges as well. In fact, all her recruits had to be willing to perform in any manner spying required, with either sex.

"Neither do you, Mr. President," she lied.

As she unzipped his pants, Gorshkov removed her tie and worked his way down Kushkin's buttons. He opened her shirt and stood back to admire her breasts.

"Beautiful. But before we begin, assurances, Martina."

"You will scream with joy."

"No, my kitten. Assurances that your assets will follow through. Do what is necessary. What you order."

The FSB colonel smiled.

"Without hesitation." Martina Kushkin unhooked her bra without taking her eyes off Nicolai Gorshkov. "Without *any* hesitation, Mr. President." She wet her lips and glanced at his crotch. "Trust me."

She saw Gorshkov flinch. A *faux pas*. Trust was something Gorshkov never did. Kushkin would have to work harder. Now…and later.

9

O'HARE INTERNATIONAL AIRPORT

"It's about the specificity, Mr. Reilly." Reilly leaned forward.

"If you have a question, Agent Moore, I'd like to hear it."

"Oh, I've got a whole list, and I've just begun to dig into you and your storied career." Reilly tipped his head to the side. A direct challenge. The FBI agent opened the top file containing summaries of Reilly's background.

"Kind of a bratty kid growing up in Boston. Mother worked a 911-call center. Even got the word when you were in trouble one time. Care to discuss that?" Reilly sat expressionless.

"In high school you did some work with the Boston Police Department. I assume it was some easy fix to work off time. Developed a proficiency on the gun range."

Reilly folded his arms.

"You went to Boston University, worked as a part-time rent-a-cop. I'm curious about that. Why not stay with the police? Authority issues, Mr. Reilly?"

Reilly leaned back, his arms still folded.

"Army. Some special schools redacted in my copy." Moore pointed to the blacked-out portions on the second page. "Spook stuff?"

The question went nowhere.

"Well, I can find out. Then Afghanistan and an incident with a general. He stayed, you left. I guess it was those authority issues again. Signs of growing discontent with America? I don't suppose you'd want to—"

Reilly said nothing.

"I didn't think so." Moore glanced at the third page. "Then the State Department as an analyst where you had access to enough high-level intelligence to prepare your report." He tapped the top of the spiral bound report. "And plan. And your latest career in, what do they call it, the hospitality business," the agent said snidely. "Are you hospitable, Mr. Reilly? Or have you used the job to develop relationships with foreign leaders? We have you recently at the Kremlin, in Brussels during an aborted bomb attack, in Tehran meeting with government officials, talking with Mexican cartels, and who knows what all over Asia."

Reilly leaned into the table and now put his arms down, one over another. Neither defiant nor challenging. Moore tried to read him. He couldn't.

"Factually correct? That is all you, Mr. Reilly." Dan Reilly smiled and finally spoke.

"The locations, yes, but your assumptions are all wrong."

"Then correct the record."

"I don't need to correct any record. But, please, I'm eager for you to get to your real point."

Moore flipped the report on the desk around. "Let's talk about this." He read the full cover aloud.

A REPORT ON CRITICAL UNITED STATES
INFRASTRUCTURE VULNERABILITIES

SUBJECT TO FOREIGN AND DOMESTIC ATTACK

PREPARED FOR

UNITED STATES NATIONAL SECURITY COUNCIL

THE OFFICE OF INFRASTRUCTURE PROTECTION

DEPARTMENT OF HOMELAND SECURITY

Daniel J. Reilly

United States Department of State

TOP SECRET

"Your blueprint."

"My report, Agent Moore." Reilly replied without raising his voice.

"Which distinctly outlines specific targets, detailing opportunity, means, and timing. Specific bridges, tunnels, overpasses, airports across the country."

"And more."

"Access and likely escape routes. Time of day traffic flow. Locations of surveillance cameras and security posts. An evaluation of security at those locations. Comprehensive, including the 14th Street Bridge, the Lincoln Tunnel, and the Stan Musial Veterans Bridge."

"Among many others. But I'm still not authorized to discuss it." Moore jammed his finger on the file.

"As of six hours ago that might have been true. Now it's in my hands. And for that matter, so are you, Reilly."

"I will only confirm to you that I researched, wrote and delivered a white paper with that title for the National Security Council whose members are the President of the United States, the Vice President, the National Security Advisor, my then-supervisor at State, now Secretary of State Elizabeth Matthews, and cabinet heads for State, Defense, Treasury, and Energy. I will assume, which is something I don't like to do, that at some time since my departure from government service the analysis was distributed more widely. Undoubtedly it, or elements of it, wound its way through the inter-agency pipeline including members of Congress. While I have maintained strict confidentiality, which I continue today—here and now in this room—I do not know if the report has been declassified or worse, leaked."

Moore's eyes shifted left. A classic tip-off to Reilly that at least one of his statements struck a nerve.

"My opinion, Agent Moore?"

Moore shot Reilly a neutral look.

"Director McCafferty sent you out without a thorough briefing," Reilly stated sharply. "You've come loaded for bear believing I have to be your leak. Based on your cursory read of my background, you've already decided I'm a traitor, traveling the world selling secrets, masterminding an attack on the United States, perhaps in support of Russia, while Gorshkov is threatening the Baltic and Ukraine."

Now Moore leaned back, opened both hands; a gesture for Reilly to continue.

"So, yes, for the record of whatever's being observed or recorded, I'll assume what you have is my white paper, Agent Moore. The one thing you got right is that it is a blueprint for what's gone down today, and more that could go down tomorrow. Beyond that you're wrong. If you're even slightly suggesting that I've gone off the rails—"

"You wouldn't be the first," Moore said.

Reilly looked beyond the FBI agent, directly toward the mirror.

"I suspect there are one or two others behind the glass. So this is for everyone: any of you know where I was this morning?"

"D.C."

"Excellent guess, since you tracked me through the airline database out of Dulles. But where? Really where?"

Moore waited for Reilly to answer his own question.

"I didn't think so. On the 14th Street Bridge, heading into Washington," Reilly continued. "And if you think I was responsible in any way, why would I be a few cars behind the explosion? Why would I have helped people to safety?"

A surprised reaction from Moore.

"Oh yes, check the surveillance cameras. I'm sure you have the authority to do that. It's cheaper than the fuel you spent getting here to interrogate me."

Reilly noted the tab on another file Moore brought: his redacted military service record.

"And since you referenced my Army record, I recommend you follow up with the Pentagon. And not to tell you how to do your job, you might want to cross-check the name of a man I pulled out of a Humvee under attack in Afghanistan. Give him a call. His number isn't registered, but with your contacts I'm sure you'll be able to track him down."

Reilly stood and collected his personal items.

"Now if you don't mind, I have a crisis committee to meet with in town and a staff in Europe to protect." He walked purposely to the door. The two FBI agents blocked his way. He knew they wouldn't move without approval from Moore. He waited. Five seconds. Ten. Fifteen. Reilly breathed in deeply.

"Now, Special Agent Moore. We both have work to do." Moore nodded to Good Cop and Bad Cop to let him out.

"You know, this isn't the end of it."

"Far from it," Reilly replied. As he walked out he heard his name called again, this time by someone familiar.

CHICAGO EXPESSWAY

In normal traffic, if there ever was such a thing, the drive from O'Hare to the Kensington Royal headquarters could take anywhere from 32 minutes to two hours. But because downtown bridges were closed due to the nationwide alert, Alan Cannon had to work out an alternate route: up. He booked a helicopter out of Vertiport, located in the Illinois Medical District. It was a twelve-minute flight on the Sky Share and another fifteen to the United terminal.

Cannon was eager to know what had happened. Reilly explained as they returned to the helicopter pad. He kept the conversation general, short on specifics.

"Jesus, Dan. You really stepped in it, right up to your waist."

"Higher. Choking level. Like I'm Person of Interest One."

"And where'd you leave it?"

Reilly said, "At the door when I got up and left."

"I'll make a call," Cannon replied.

"Trust me, as soon as I'm back at the office I will, too." Reilly's was going to be to Bob Heath to launch a little interdepartmental conversation.

While they waited to board the helicopter into town, Reilly checked his texts and voicemail. He had waiting updates on the crisis committee assemblage and urgent calls from London. Four. Each with more worry.

"Hi, Marnie," he began calmly when the woman answered.

"It's been hours. I've been leaving messages—"

"Got them all. I'm fine, sweetheart." He decided not to go into any specifics. "Just landed in Chicago. On my way to the office."

"You should have called me."

"I know."

"Damned right you know. No excuses." He smiled.

"You're right. I'll be jumping into a crisis team meeting as soon as I'm in."

Cannon caught the PA alert announcing their flight back into town. He tapped Reilly on the shoulder. He nodded.

"Look, I've got to go. I promise to call you later. Might even see you tomorrow night."

"Really?" She sounded more than pleased. Excited. "Please. I need you."

Need was just one confession short of commitment. Neither had used the word yet, but Reilly felt it was coming. He ended the call assuring Marnie he would phone with his travel plans. On board, he buckled up, leaned back, closed his eyes, and pictured the dangers certain to come.

10

CHICAGO

KENSINGTON ROYAL CORPORATE HEADQUARTERS

Reilly walked into his scheduled international crisis team meeting with his head of security, Alan Cannon.

In attendance were Kensington Chief Operating Officer Lou Tiano; Senior VP of Legal Chris Collins; newly appointed International VP under Reilly, Scott Allphin; VP of Human Resources Mark Pilarski; and marketing chief Patricia Brodowski. On the phone were two consultants, retired Army General BD Coons and former FBI Director Tom Reardon. Others were scheduled to arrive over the next four hours.

"Sorry I'm late," Reilly volunteered. "What do we have?"

"Fear and worry," Allphin reported. "And not just in Kiev and Riga, but at all our properties that border Russia. We've elevated them to Red status. Going Orange in Germany, France, and Poland."

"Lou," Reilly said, "We should consider moving our major U.S. domestic operations up to at least Yellow. IDs and key cards required to enter the elevators."

The COO agreed.

"Mark, you and Pat should get on it with the regional teams." Tom Reardon jumped in.

"So far they've targeted infrastructure," the former FBI chief offered.

"Strategic, like straight out of a handbook." The phrase echoed in Reilly's mind. He forced himself to focus.

"General Coons, any thoughts?"

"Listening now. But if you're considering action in Europe, you should do it quickly."

"To that point, is Klugo coming online?" Reilly asked. Donald Klugo, a private security consultant working with Kensington Royal, had special contacts who could act quickly. Very quickly.

International VP Scott Allphin replied, "He'll be with us in ten."

Reilly heard the answer but couldn't shake Reardon's comment. *Like straight out of a handbook.*

BRUSSELS
NATO HEADQUARTERS

NATO command worked through the early evening. They reviewed the latest field reports and aerial surveillance footage of Russian Federation troops on the Latvian and Ukrainian borders.

"Probably forty thousand troops now facing Kiev. About half that number up against Latvia. Ukraine looks like their first move," General Rochemont speculated.

"How will they go in?"

"From all directions," the NATO military commander stated. "Not so hard when you plan for it. Especially with paratroopers dropping in overnight. Based on Russia's training exercises, which they take very seriously, I'd say they're ready to deploy at any minute. However, now that the cat's out of the bag and we know, and Gorshkov knows that we know, I expect he'll bolster with more force. That would mean a few more days, maybe a week. That also gives him more time to psychologically fuck with us."

Another update came in. An aide distributed it. Rochemont finished reading first.

"Like I said, more force. Another 500 armored divisions. And he's testing our patience with his bombers flying low and even closer to the border."

The report had nothing new on Latvia, but that didn't mean it wasn't coming. Secretary General Phillipe leaned forward to address that point.

"I've spoken briefly with Secretary of State Matthews. She assures us that America will meet its commitments to NATO, but..."

No one liked a *but* from Phillipe.

"...politically and militarily, from America's perspective, NATO comes second."

Left unsaid was what that meant for Ukraine's future. Ukraine was in third position (or further back) since the country still wasn't part of NATO—a longstanding concession to Russia.

CHICAGO

The Kensington Royal team turned on CNN International during a coffee break. News feeds from Riga, Latvia showed massive confusion: traffic out of the city snarled, thousands lined up at airline ticket counters, people heading west on scooters, bicycles, whatever means they had. The London-based news anchor described it as an 'uncoordinated evacuation.' A member of the on-air panel used a different word: Escape.

The anchor read a Kremlin statement declaring that Russia was merely engaged in scheduled military exercises. But these simultaneous, seemingly coordinated exercises on both the Latvian and Ukrainian borders were creating panic. Russia wanted its satellite states back, noted one analyst. It appeared as if Gorshkov was prepared to take two at once.

The newscast broke for a commercial and Reilly's team returned to work. Klugo, the security consultant, was now on the line from Brussels, briefed and ready with information.

"Don, thanks for joining in. We don't have a lot of time. How quickly can we get teams out?"

"Your first concern is Kiev. Thirty hours," Klugo reported, "with a squad from Jordan to coordinate the exfil and get civilians to the airport and out. Total time on the ground—six hours. Five if everything goes well. If it doesn't..." He left the notion hanging.

"Not Riga?" Pat Brodowski asked.

"Kiev first." Klugo repeated. General Coons nodded agreement.

"And how large is your team, Don?" Reilly probed. "How many people can you get out?"

"They're outsourced. Experienced. Fourteen, heavily armed. Two-eighty comfortably in our Airbus, three hundred plus if we're not interested in comfort and you forgo all but essential carry-ons. So, go or no go?" the security consultant asked.

Reilly looked at CEO Lou Tiano, who was texting furiously. Reilly suspected he was communicating with the company's founder, EJ Shaw. Tiano held up a finger. Seconds later he received a reply.

* * *

Reilly excused himself after twenty minutes discussing logistics, money, and timing. According to texts from Brenda Sheldon, he had to get on his way. Again. But waiting in her outer office, pacing the floor, was a surprise visitor.

"Special Agent Moore. Twice in one day?" Reilly said sarcastically. "To what do I owe the honor?"

"You apparently have a friend in..."

"High places," Reilly didn't acknowledge that he'd phoned Heath at the CIA. Word had undoubtedly gone up the chain quickly.

Moore shook his head. "That doesn't excuse you from being a pain in my ass."

"And you in mine," Reilly replied.

He extended his hand. Moore accepted the gesture.

"Got any coffee?" the FBI agent asked. "It's been a long day."

"For both of us."

"Coming right up," Brenda offered.

"Meanwhile, let's talk inside. Oh, just so you know, in this building the mirrors only reflect."

Vincent Moore chuckled as they both sat down at Reilly's table.

"I want to talk more about your report."

"First a question for you," Reilly replied.

"Now you're asking the questions?"

Reilly studied Moore for a moment.

"Milk? Sugar?"

"What?"

"Do you want anything in your coffee?"

"Do I look like a milk and sugar kind of guy?" Now it was Reilly's turn to smile.

"No, I suppose not." They volleyed small talk for a few minutes until Moore got to his point.

"Back to your report."

"Like I said before, I can't discuss anything." Moore opened his briefcase and removed the report.

"Your friends have released you from your obligations. You can talk to me." Reilly stood, walked to the entrance, and closed his office door.

"I haven't been told that. So for now, same rules. But it's not such a good idea to be walking all over town with a copy of it," Reilly said.

"Really, I wouldn't worry about this one." Moore slid the material across the table. "Take a look."

Reilly turned it face forward and opened it up. Beyond the first page, the rest were blank.

"You know, you're a son of a bitch."

"So I've been told," the FBI agent replied. "Now tell me what you can, and what we need to be worried about."

Reilly glanced out the window before replying gravely, "Everything."

11

TWO YEARS EARLIER

Pak Yoon-hoi lived in an American town, ate American food, watched American movies and TV shows, and read American newspapers. All of these in Russia.

Nicolai Gorshkov had resurrected the idea of secret American towns from past Soviet regimes. During the Cold War, Russia trained spies to pass as Americans, to infiltrate society, business, academics, politics, and the press. They were schooled to look and sound like natives. They had to be able to fill out mortgage applications, go to supermarkets, buy without haggling, and speak openly without fear of anyone watching.

Over the years, many sleeper spies were discovered and expelled by the FBI. However, with the fall of the Soviet Union, others imbedded in American society decided to just blend in and live the rest of their lives comfortably in the west.

Then Putin came to power. And Gorshkov rose in influence.

Nicolai Gorshkov never forgot that President Gorbachev and the last of the Communist regime folded. In his mind, they gave up. Surrendered. Abandoned Russian ideals and the Russian people.

In the years since, it became his goal to ultimately turn back the clock, one deliberate rewind at a time. To do that, Gorshkov determined he needed new sleepers to slip into U.S., UK, and EU society. However, compared to the height of the Cold War, there was an interesting difference in today's spycraft. Contemporary spies didn't have to look like the typical white westerners, or even sound like them. In the intervening years, immigrants from around the world became commonplace in cities throughout the United States and Europe. Foreign accents were everywhere: in schools, in businesses, on TV and the radio.

So, slipping spies into America's infrastructure was easier than ever. Invariably, some were discovered. But for every one that was, there were dozens who were never detected.

Gorshkov recruited from Russian ranks. He also pulled in talent from outside, North Korea included.

Pak Yoon-hoi began his training with a singular purpose: to be the best. He became proficient in English; studied American popular culture, sports, and politics; developed a taste for Western cuisine; and, most importantly, learned nearly one hundred ways to kill. In fact, by the end of his first year of studies his fellow students avoided fighting him. Broken arms and legs were the least of what could happen: he'd killed two opponents. But Pak Yoon-hoi had no regrets—as far as he was concerned, those fallen sparring partners had been too weak to survive.

The Russian president watched videos of his star pupil and received monthly updates. He had natural charisma that gave his men confidence and assurance that their own contributions were honored. He encouraged them to go further, train harder, be better—though they would never be the best. Yoon-hoi was. He'd progressed so quickly that Gorshkov expanded the scope of his plan.

Not wanting him to become bored, Gorshkov gave his North Korean recruit special assignments—internal assignments. Eliminating dead wood in the Russian Federation: men and women, oligarchs and journalists. Burned spies and washouts who wouldn't make it. In each case he performed admirably, without hesitation or remorse.

A slit throat. A car bomb. A choking in the height of passionate sex. A sniper shot from 600 meters. A poison pellet shot at close range from an umbrella. A gas explosion at a dacha. A fall from a bridge.

All unexpected. All quick—except when it was necessary to extract confessions, apologies, or simply pleas for forgiveness that usually came from traitors or incompetent bureaucrats.

Pak Yoon-hoi was exceptional. A born assassin, Gorshkov thought, who might actually defy statistics and make it to age forty.

Yoon-hoi was told he was on loan from the Democratic People's Republic of Korea to prepare for the most secretive assignment the Supreme Leader had ever envisioned. The Russians would prepare him and with the Russian-Korean team, he would bring honor to his motherland. And Yoon-hoi, a follower and true believer, had no reason to question authority.

12

SUMMERLIN, NEVADA

Richard Harper consulted on the new security plans for the Southern Nevada Water Authority's Intake Station No. 2. Recommendations, changes, patrol routes. He understood that Lake Mead itself would be an unlikely, wasted target for anyone intent on introducing chemical or biological poisons: it was far too big. It would take hundreds of trucks loaded with chemicals or bio-toxins to have any impact. Detection would be easy and, once discovered, the supply would quickly be cut downstream.

The hard target—the physical structure—Hoover Dam was itself too hardened. The road across the structure now prohibits heavy commercial vehicles, making a truck bomb attack difficult. A jumbo jet on a crash course from the south could impact the dam, but heightened air defense systems after 9/11 vastly reduced the possibility of success.

But there were other vulnerable spots along the water supply route to Las Vegas, and Harper knew them all.

Above-ground sections of the Southern Nevada Water Authority's system were more than 60 years old and in serious need of attention. Harper considered those areas Target One. Since the World Trade Center bombing, no one was permitted to fish, land boats, or even hike along the southern two-thirds of Lake Mead's Saddle Island, where intake pipes were located. Security guards and cameras covered the area, but the pipes could be Target Two: more difficult to hit since they were underwater, but vulnerable to experienced divers with explosives.

Target Three: the entrance to the treatment plant. Patrolling duties were transferred from Metropolitan Police to a private security agency after 9/11. But should a terrorist cell infiltrate the security force, they'd have an ally on the inside. Cyber threats made the internal computer system Target Four. The delivery pipes and smaller downstream reservoirs were Targets Five and Six. Target Seven: Train tank cars loaded with chlorine gas. Chlorine gas is classified as a toxic inhalation hazard. It's hazardous and deadly in its purest form, though used judiciously in treatment plants to purify water. However a chlorine train spill, as deadly as it might be, was still highly localized.

So he focused on the impact of explosions inside the treatment plant. Not just one plant—multiple plants. Security assumed that it would be impossible. Richard Harper believed otherwise, and knew that even bomb sniffing dogs could be thrown off.

It would take patience and time, training—exceedingly specific training—and access. Truly inside access, trusted and unquestioned. The foreign national working under the assumed name of Richard Harper had all three.

13

CHICAGO

Reilly took one of the yellow pads from a credenza behind the conference room table and removed a simple ballpoint pen from his suitcoat pocket. In the center of the top page he drew three slightly overlapping circles aligned as a triangle: a variation on the Olympic logo. One at the top, two at the bottom. He wrote a word inside each circle. Infrastructure in the top circle, Transpo and Comm in the two overlapping bottom circles. Then he enumerated.

"Three key areas from my report: first, infrastructure. Electrical grid and power plants, highways, bridges, government buildings."

"The Internet," FBI agent Moore noted.

"Correct," Reilly said. "And overlapping with natural intersects— transportation. Airplanes, cars, trucks, buses, subways and trains, and the feeder routes they use."

"All of which we've considered at the Bureau."

"I'm sure you have, along with the third, Comm. TV, radio, cell phones. Even GPS satellites. Not an immediately likely target, but you don't need a missile to affect transmission. As you know, GPS signals can be blocked on a small scale by spoofing gadgets and mobile phone jammers, and on a larger scale drone jamming equipment can send planes off course. And one step beyond: computer viruses or false commands sent to GPS satellites. That kind of tech can take satellites offline or reposition them to render them useless."

"Terrorists have that capability?"

"Individuals? Not necessarily. Rogue states, most likely. Major technological nations." Reilly now shaded the overlapping areas of each circle with his pen.

"Okay, Moore." Reilly got to his bottom line. "Was the main target transportation?

"Yes."

"Are you sure?"

"Well, yes. The attacks disrupted transportation in D.C., New York, St. Louis and other hubs."

"But it also tied up infrastructure—emergency procedures for government. Homeland Security, you guys, let alone protection for facilities, services, and people."

"Yes," the Agent conceded.

"And what about communications?"

"Not this attack. Nothing disrupted."

"Disrupted, no," Reilly offered. "Because the enemy wants to spread panic, publicize the chaos. Undermine faith in the government."

The last observation resonated. Vincent Moore saw where Reilly was leading him.

"The attacks have become the top story on the news. America first, edging out everything else."

"Precisely. Edging out Europe," Reilly declared. "Communications was the real target." He paused for a teachable moment; he wrote down two words and turned the paper around. Moore read silently at first, then aloud.

"Diversion = Deception."

"Absolutely. And right now, I'm willing to bet that the president is having a hard enough time wrapping his head around our own problems—forget Europe."

"So Russia attacked us," Moore wondered.

"Possibly, but what do I know? I'm just a hotel guy who travels a lot."

"A hotel guy who knows people in high places, and who wrote a shopping list of today's targets."

"I think I've told you all I can, but you haven't asked me the most important question, Agent Moore."

"Which is?"

Reilly spread his arms wide, a gesture that conveyed the enormity of what they didn't yet know. "What's next?"

WASHINGTON, D.C.
THE WHITE HOUSE

President Alexander Crowe had had an entirely different day planned. Meeting with 4H students, signing a new international climate initiative, and then a flight on Marine One, the Presidential helicopter, 62 miles north-northwest of Washington, D.C., to a secluded wooded area in the Catoctin Mountain Park. To Camp David, and two days of golf, and hopefully a break from global concerns.

All plans for that day were abandoned with the first explosion. It escalated with the second and third attacks. And then came the satellite images and intelligence from the Baltic nations and Gorshkov's latest gambit.

Beginning with the report of the initial attack, it had been briefing after briefing; Pierce Kimball, the National Security Advisor, was by his side for each session. In and out of the Oval Office came the heads of Central Intelligence, the FBI, and NSA, the Secretaries of Homeland Security, Defense, State, and Interior, and lastly, Vice President Ryan Battaglio.

This latest meeting had everyone crammed into the basement Situation Room. It was a 'quiet room' where neither cell phones nor recording devices were allowed, but ideas and solutions were welcome. The president's team examined a photograph on a monitor.

"A diversion," Pierce Kimball said. "Brutally elegant."

Kimball had been decorated for valor in Iraq, and had served as commander of the Combined Joint-Inter-Agency Task Force—*Shafafiyat* in Kabul, Afghanistan. He was then moved inside the Pentagon as Vice Chief of Staff for the U.S. Army, and completed more than 35 years of service as a four-star general. As a civilian, Kimball then accepted a senior-level appointment at the State Department before opening his own political consulting firm. President Crowe had then brought him back inside, appointing Kimball National Security Advisor. No longer in uniform, the bald, six-four, two-fifty Kimball still commanded attention. He used his voice effectively, punctuating adverbs and adjectives for impact.

"What kind of diversion?" the president followed up.

"The kind a magician uses. Look at the pretty lady to hide the deceptive moves. In this case, the lady wasn't so pretty."

"You've got that right." Kimball knew he did. He recognized the operation.

"Any chatter?" Crowe asked the CIA chief.

CIA Chief Gerald Watts peered over his tortoiseshell glasses. His 25-year intelligence career began as a summer intern at the CIA. Since then he'd worked the Asia desk, was assigned to Moscow, and served in other posts, none of which were on any resume. Watts' four years as Deputy Director for the previous administration made him the natural pick for Crowe as Director.

"Aside from noise on the Internet, no."

"What kind of noise?"

"Conspiracy theories. Everything from domestic terrorists to you, Mr. President."

"Me?"

"Wag the dog, sir. Create havoc against slipping poll numbers. Not real, but believable in some fringe quarters and pushed out automatically by bots. They began popping up within a half-hour after St. Louis. Timed and programmed to trigger."

The President opened his hands, his signal that he needed more explanation.

"We're looking into the usual suspects: Russia, Iran, North Korea.

Possibly China. But we haven't completely ruled out ISIS or Al Qaeda and other groups."

"Any digital fingerprints?" Crowe asked.

"None yet."

Next, Crowe turned to FBI director McCafferty.

"Anything, Reese?" the president asked.

"Only assumptions. Highly coordinated," the former New York City Chief of Police said. He had handled terrorist threats and attacks in New York and took bombings especially personally. He'd lost his fiancée at a London café when a suicide bomber took a seat, had three relaxing sips of coffee (all caught on CCTV cameras), and then opened his jacket revealing a chest packed with explosives. He stood and pressed a trigger. Crowe had been told the story before meeting McCafferty. He could never look at him without thinking of the trauma and memories his director brought to the job.

McCafferty continued: "And very well-financed. We're already looking into bank transfers and screening camera footage along the bridge and tunnel, running license plates, and checking on the Kawasaki Jet Ski rental on the Mississippi. And something else."

He paused. The kind of pause that invited a reaction.

"Too soon to comment, sir. But there's a State Department report that bears some attention."

McCafferty shot Pierce Kimball a look. Kimball cocked his head to the side in subtle acknowledgment. Vice President Battaglio took it all in. He was anything but quiet and reserved, but he had nothing to contribute. Not yet.

"What kind of report?" Crowe asked as he loosened his tie and rolled up his sleeves.

"Prefer not to say, Mr. President."

"Well, I prefer you do, Reese."

"I'll take that, Mr. President," Secretary of State Elizabeth Matthews volunteered. Alexander Crowe turned his attention to Matthews, his most trusted cabinet secretary.

"A blueprint, Mr. President. A step-by-step blueprint for what occurred today. Prepared for me when I worked at State. Detailed beyond belief."

CHICAGO

"You're a bit of a mystery, Reilly," the Agent Moore admitted.

"Not to my friends," Reilly replied. "Maybe if you get to know me—"

"I bet there's a lot your friends don't even see."

"My job just requires me to worry about things. Like you."

"Which means you get sensitive information. What do you give in return?" Moore asked.

Reilly shrugged his shoulders.

"My point exactly."

At that moment Reilly's assistant stepped in.

"Your flight, Mr. Reilly," Brenda Sheldon announced. "But you should change first." She held up a hanger with pants, shirt, and sports jacket.

Moore looked surprised.

"Another flight?"

Reilly checked his watch and stood. "Yup. London. Gotta go."

Brenda rolled in his suitcase and handed Reilly his boarding pass.

"Everything's inside." That meant his crisis committee update and reports from Kensington Royal General Managers across Europe.

"Thank you, Brenda." He took the suitcase and began heading toward the door.

"But we're not through," Agent Moore called out.

"We are for now," Reilly said, waving back with the pass in hand. "Unless you're interested in returning to the airport with me."

"Traffic's still nuts," Moore said.

"Not if you're over it." Reilly smiled. "Think of me as your captive audience. Closest you'll get to really detaining me."

WASHINGTON, D.C.
THE WHITE HOUSE

"Let me get this straight. We've got terrorists following a game plan that *we* wrote?"

"I wouldn't call it a plan, sir. But essentially, yes," Matthews replied, "a comprehensive assessment of weaknesses to our infrastructure. Expertly researched and written in plain English."

"Jesus," Crowe said. "How the hell did it get out?"

"Three possible ways: leaked, stolen, or sold."

"And you commissioned this?" Crowe asked.

"Yes."

"Well, you should have burned it right away."

"Actually, sir, it's helped us tighten security in many locations. But Congress has not been a cooperative partner. Money."

Matthews now addressed the FBI Director.

"Reese, I'm curious. How did you get hold of the report?"

"Sources."

"You had eyes inside State?"

Reese McCafferty said nothing.

"Okay, Elizabeth," the President said, redirecting the conversation. "What about the author? A source of the leak?"

"It isn't him. He wouldn't. I can vouch for him." FBI Director McCafferty was working under a different assumption.

"Put a pin in that, Mr. President. My best field agent is with him now."

CHICAGO

The ride to the heliport in a KR Town Car provided the perfect time to talk.

"Game theory," Reilly began. "Ever hear of it?"

"No," the FBI agent replied.

"Essentially it's an explanation of how players in a game employ cost-benefit scrutiny of both their actions and the reaction of the opposition—the enemy. Probabilistic risk assessment, PRA for short. A means to determine if the positive outweighs the negative, and the probabilities of succeeding. It's how governments consider protecting high-value targets, making terrorists aim for less protected ones. Flipped around, it's how state-sponsored terror, as opposed to individual terrorist cells, choose their objectives and plan their attacks." Moore listened closely.

"In 1993, ten Islamist extremists, some connected to the World Trade Center bombing that year, planned to bomb the Manhattan Federal Building, the United Nations, the Lincoln and Holland Tunnels, and the George Washington Bridge. An FBI agent infiltrated the group and stopped the attack. Ten years later, an al Qaeda plot against the Brooklyn Bridge was foiled. Terrorists hoped to bring down the bridge by cutting the suspension cable. The leader was arrested in Columbus, Ohio. In 2006, an attempt to bomb a PATH train tunnel between New York and Jersey was flagged on the Internet. Eight conspirators were arrested by Lebanese police on tips from the U.S. Their downfall was open research on Google, traced right back to them. Not smart," Reilly noted, "but typical of your garden-variety terrorist."

He glanced out the window at the city bustling below them, and took a deep breath before laying out even more recent cautionary tales.

"A Long Island native schemed with Al Qaeda to bomb a Long Island Railroad train that served the community where he grew up. Pakistani police arrested the American training in the country in 2008, before he returned to carry out the plot. In 2012, a Kosovo-born Islamist extremist conspired to plant bombs in a Tampa, Florida Starbucks, a police center, and a bridge. He was arrested by undercover FBI agents after he obtained dud weapons from them."

"All intercepted," Moore confirmed.

"Yes," Reilly said. "Great work from the FBI, and in each case the terrorists were likely willing to die for the cause. Now add a higher level of planning to the game playing. Instead of fringe groups, substitute plots hatched by well-organized governments. Professionals with real training."

"What makes you think that's what occurred today?"

"One reason: professionals operate to penetrate, attack, and escape. To live another day. Suicide is not part of their mission." Reilly again breathed deeply. "None of the attacks appeared to be suicide missions. Right?"

"Are you assuming that these attacks weren't carried out by terrorist groups?" Moore asked incredulously.

"I am. They have the earmarks of a government mission. Four factors point against anything but: one, we have counterterrorism measures that deter radical groups; two, and you'd know better than me, we have a positive track record of intercepting or infiltrating their operations; three, perceived structural soundness discourages them; and four, money matters. It takes a great deal of money to evaluate, buy, conceal, and transport equipment. And even more to actually execute a plan like this. All of this, the facts, the figures, the conclusion and the worry—it's all in my report. You should read it," Reilly summarized.

Moore smirked. Reilly leaned back in his seat and closed his eyes, but continued his explanation.

"Well-financed teams, Moore. State-sponsored with all the ways and means. Our tunnels and bridges make for valuable cultural icons. They cost millions of dollars to build and will take billions to repair. Three targets so far, and I don't think you'll find terrorists in the rubble."

Reilly saw that they were now a few blocks from the Veriport pad on South Wood Street. He looked back at Moore.

"Do you know how many bridges there are in the U.S.?"

"I don't know. Say two hundred thousand."

"Triple that. Six hundred thousand," Reilly said. "I identified approximately one thousand that, if disabled or destroyed, would lead to significant deaths or injuries, economic disruption, and societal disarray. Now on top of that reality check, throw in the nearly three hundred and forty major highway tunnels, and another two hundred-plus transit tunnels, many under rivers and bays. Just think about the Lake Pontchartrain Causeway: for eight of its twenty-four miles, you can't even see land. Then there's Seven-Mile Bridge to the Florida Keys, and the seven-mile San Mateo Hayward Bridge crossing San Francisco Bay. Ninety-three thousand vehicles a day cross it. And don't forget the Chesapeake Bay Bridge Tunnel, seventeen point six miles shore to shore. I worried about all them," Reilly admitted. "You should, too."

They sat quietly until they got to the heliport and boarded for O'Hare.

"We don't have enough resources, Reilly," Moore said, once they were again in the air.

"Tell me about it."

Twenty minutes later, after landing at O'Hare, they approached TSA security. Reilly offered Moore his hand.

"Can't say you didn't make the day more interesting." He produced his ID and boarding pass to the officer who scanned it on his device.

"Sir, you're Daniel Reilly?"

"Yes."

"I'm afraid there's a problem."

"Oops," Moore said. "I forgot to mention you were flagged for detaining."

"Still?"

"Easy to get on a no-fly list. Harder to get off. I'll clear this up."

"You do that," Reilly said. Moore produced his identification and pulled Reilly aside.

"Give me a few minutes."

He dialed his cell and spoke softly, waited for a response. Two minutes later he hung up, thanking whoever he had spoken with. Then he returned to the TSA officer.

"Mr. Reilly should be good to go. Try again."

Reilly was cleared to board.

"I have to admit," Reilly said, "it doesn't hurt having an FBI agent tag along to help circumvent TSA lines."

"One of the perks of being my suspect," Moore grinned.

As they approached the scanner, Reilly had a request.

"I want my report. Blank pages don't do me any good, I need to refresh myself with—"

"I'll see what I can do."

"I need it."

Reilly waved goodbye without looking back. He continued to the gate, and walked right onto the plane, ready to relax in his first-class seat. Halfway down the jet way, Reilly felt a tap on his shoulder. Not a hand, but a thick business envelope. He turned to face Vincent Moore again.

"You forgot this."

Reilly shot a curious expression.

"Don't give me that look, Reilly. You've got nine hours of reading time to get caught up."

Reilly smiled. He was beginning to like Moore.

The FBI agent leaned in and whispered, "Oh, and you didn't get it from me."

"Of course I did." Reilly motioned above. "There are cameras to prove it."

NEW YORK, NEW YORK

"Who the hell is that?" The *New York Times* investigative reporter froze the image on her computer. "That guy." Savannah Flanders pointed to the video from the 14th Street Bridge.

"Him."

"Don't know," replied co-byline reporter Mike Blowen. "But he's been popping up on a bunch of the videos."

Flanders rolled through the Facebook and Instagram cell phone uploads until she found an even better frame than the previous one. She grabbed a snippet and printed it out. It was a little soft, out of focus. She tried other frames until she had something sharper.

"Some kind of good Samaritan?" Blowen suggested.

"More than that. Watch." She hit play again. "He was on autopilot," the front-page reporter surmised.

Flanders went to a saved link containing another survivor's footage.

"Again. Moving toward the action. Who does that?"

"Military? Someone in law enforcement?" Blowen proposed. "ATF? Capitol Police? Hell, it's D.C., take your pick. But plainclothes or off-duty."

"Whatever, the guy has seen action. He knows what to do. He's not afraid."

"How do you know?"

"My dad was a first responder. I saw a lot of what he did."

Flanders watched another posted clip. Her subject was further in the background.

"You think he's a story?" Blowen asked.

"I do. And a good one for us. What's your guess on his age, Mike?"

He rolled his chair closer to her computer.

"Late thirties. Or a really fit early forties. Hard to tell."

Flanders grabbed more screenshots. She uploaded them into a FaceRec tool installed on the *Times* computers. The system mapped coordinates of a subject's face, but in this case, all the footage was shaky and most of the actual images were soft. So Flanders uploaded inexpensive Movari video-stabilizing software on her computer. The program would reduce bouncing and she could then select better images and hopefully find a match in an open source Vis.js library. Though not as reliable as the FBI's more robust technology, it allowed newsroom editors and reporters a shot at narrowing down a person's identity. And a shot was all she needed.

Flanders waited while the program ran through millions of images culled from news stories and photo archives. Nothing. Even the best of the video wasn't good enough for the newspaper's version of facial recognition to produce a match.

After more than an hour trying to enhance the images herself, she sent the footage to the *New York Times* graphics department.

"Need better," she was told.

Flanders took that as a challenge. She'd find better by tracking down Mr. Late 30s to Early 40s herself.

OVER THE ATLANTIC

Dan Reilly read his six-year-old report on the plane. Most of his conclusions came right back to him. What differentiated his analysis from other Homeland Security and most government reports was the way he portrayed America's vulnerability. He'd not only identified targets, he painted vivid descriptions of what things would look like the day after an attack, and more days, weeks, and even months later. He described faces of parents as they carried the bodies of their children away from horrific blasts, and children who had to be torn from their mothers and fathers by strangers and would never be able to forget the anguish.

Reilly had gathered pictures of terrorist attacks in mosques and cafes, explosions in hotel lobbies, and the aftermath of gunmen in movie theaters. No one above him understood why he needed this kind of research to prepare what was supposed to be a clinical white paper about America's vulnerability. At least, not until they read his report. It was impossible not to be moved. Reilly's paper gave government readers a visceral reason to fortify infrastructure and identify vulnerabilities.

Its emotional tone was a sharp warning, and dramatically different than previous studies. That's why it was broadly circulated, and apparently leaked. On top of the human toll, Reilly's full report identified nearly 77,000 targets that could strategically hurt America, and some 600 that were so critical that life could be turned upside down. "If attacked in the manner outlined," Reilly noted, "the United States should brace for a catastrophic loss of life as well as catastrophic economic losses."

He remembered writing those words, stopping at the keyboard, and envisioning the horror to America's infrastructure. Dams no longer holding back mighty rivers and huge lakes; nuclear utilities adjacent to major cities leaking radioactive materials; airports, bridges, and tunnels shut down. He detailed smaller targets as well, from local gas stations and county fairs to petting zoos. The common denominator: places where people congregate, where press coverage carried weight, and where normal routines could be disrupted.

Reilly's report flagged oil refineries, which produced in excess of 225,000 barrels per day; electrical grids that, if pulled offline, could affect upwards of 35,000 citizens; and mega-corporations where immediate losses would be in excess of 10 billion dollars. Reilly's research carried dire individual warnings about Washington, D.C.'s Metro area, the entire San Francisco Bay Area Rapid Transit system, New York City's 472 separate subway stations, and Los Angeles's most important interconnecting freeway overpasses.

Midway through reading, Reilly put the report on his lap. He closed his eyes and went back to his harrowing escape from the 14th Street Bridge. The fire. The smoke. The screams. The dead. His thoughts turned to his experience in Afghanistan: bombs and snipers. More dead. And then he saw himself walking through the rubble of the terrorist attack on the Kensington Royal Hotel bombing in Tokyo a few months ago: the smell, the godawful smell. The images were seared in his consciousness. The absolute loss. *Not the building*, he thought. *Buildings can be rebuilt.* But all those lives. And now that horror had come back to the U.S., just as he'd predicted.

Reilly was tired, but he forced himself to read on through the list of likely targets by category. His paper rightly suggested that America could more easily recover from individual attacks. But as multiple locations were hit in a coordinated effort, the impact would echo through small towns all the way to Wall Street and Pennsylvania Avenue.

Reilly expected there was already a run on ATMs for cash, a record number of guns and bullets sold, and the hoarding of supplies, especially water, sanitizers, and toilet paper.

After another thirty minutes of re-reading, he came to his recommendations:

- Further review of significant targets and development of strategic, coordinated crisis plans to better secure them.

- Provide state homeland security offices with directives as they evaluate vulnerabilities and defense measures.

- Prioritize needs and risk assessments, analyzing human and vehicular traffic flow, access to airports, and critical stress points on bridges and within tunnels.

- Develop budgets with state homeland security administrators and the Department of Homeland Security to support local private businesses with basic, visible deterrents such as bollards, security cameras, and secured entrances.

- Establish a review timeline to correct immediate deficiencies.

What Reilly didn't know was whether anything positive had been done. Very little, he suspected. What he'd intended as a study to lead to proactive defensive measures had instead, apparently, become a shopping list for—

For whom?

Thinking about what he'd told Moore, governments were top of the list. Strategically, Russia. Economically, China. Politically, North Korea and Iran. Reilly wrote each down along with homegrown domestic terrorists as a category, which he quickly crossed out. *Too complicated. Required too much expertise,* he reasoned.

Al-Qaeda and the Taliban were within the range of possibility until it came to the autonomous driving cars in the Lincoln Tunnel. *Out of their realm.*

China? *No,* he reasoned. *Too many self-inflicted economic wounds. They need American trade.*

Iran? *Too risky given their own internal instability.*

Two left.

North Korea. *No known sleeper structure inside the United States to carry out an operation of this size.*

One suspect remained: Russia. But even Russia might need cover. He thought for a moment. *Who better to enlist than the Democratic People's Republic of Korea? Russia could maintain deniability. If discovered, then Moscow denies everything yet creates further instability with a U.S./ North Korean conflict.*

He closed his eyes and adjusted his First-Class seat into a full recline. *Russia. Russia and North Korea.* He had an idea that lacked all proof. He had nothing to make a convincing argument.

Reilly soon fell asleep. He slept through the president's televised press conference, watched live by others en route.

WASHINGTON, D.C.

"Good evening." President Alexander Crowe sat stoically at his desk in the Oval Office. He looked tired and somber. His voice was low.

"Today America was attacked. Brutally and cruelly. Without warning, hundreds of citizens—men, women, and children—died at the hands of terrorists. Hundreds more were injured. Thousands of families are directly affected, and many will never hear the voices or feel the touches of loved ones again. Many are tonight looking at empty beds or across the dinner table for missing children."

The camera slowly zoomed in.

"Tonight, we remember Jean Seymour, a mother and schoolteacher on her way to work. A victim of the bombing on the 14th Street Bridge here in Washington."

The video cut to a photograph of the victim lying face down, and then pictures of others Crowe referenced.

"LaMarr Brown, his wife Justine, their two children Raff and Diana, killed in the Lincoln Tunnel explosion. Miguel Carrera, returning home from his overnight shift as a guard at Walmart, his body just recovered and identified after his car went into the Mississippi in St. Louis. You'll hear about more in the days to come, hundreds more. Read about them, remember them. Mourn them."

The president came back on camera. His tone changed.

"I promise you, as President of the United States, that we will honor their deaths by tracking down the criminals who attacked America. We will bring them to justice or bring them to their deaths. No matter what cracks they crawl into, no matter where they run. And if they're watching tonight, as they probably are—" the camera zoomed in tighter, "you will suddenly find the world is too small to escape from this hunt. We will find you."

Crowe read off the teleprompter, but he could have given the address without one. Anger fueled him. And although he didn't talk about revenge, Americans heard it between the lines.

"For those who seek to break us, we will not be broken. For your cowardly acts of terrorism, you will suffer. And if we should determine that you have acted under the authority of another government, that government, its leaders and its military will face the consequences with extreme prejudice."

Crowe wanted his message to hit near and far. He ended it in under three minutes with "God Bless America," but no mention of NATO's worries or invoking Article 5 of the NATO Charter.

15

NATO HEADQUARTERS

Representatives of the twelve Eastern European nations that had formerly been part of Soviet Russia's buffer zone from the West watched the American president's speech live. There was nothing in it for them: no words of consolation, no offers of protection. The Russian Federation was threatening two of the twelve. If two could fall, all could fall. The clock would be reset to Cold War standard time. Each of them knew their own country's brutal history, and that of their neighbors: invasion and oppression. The past suddenly appeared all too present.

After the fall of the Soviet Union in 1991, the world seemed a safer place. Many of the nations turned to the West and opened their previously closed society to democratic elections. The threat against the existing North Atlantic Treaty Organization countries lessened. Moreover, as NATO redefined its mission, it pushed eastward, signing former Soviet satellites into the alliance.

Assurances were made that the NATO-Russia Founding Act of 1997 was not an attempt to undermine the Kremlin. The agreement stipulated that NATO would not permanently place combat forces in Eastern Europe or deploy nuclear weapons in new member nations. Nevertheless, the fact was that Russia's thousand-mile protective border was gone. It was a map that Nikolai Gorshkov's predecessor, and now

Gorshkov himself, vowed to redraw.

And why wouldn't he?

Years earlier, the West did little after the Kremlin took back two former Soviet territories, Georgia and Crimea, by force. American and European leaders had ruled out any direct military response then, and now Latvia and Ukraine were in Russia's crosshairs.

"Gentlemen, I move that we invoke the Readiness Action Plan," NATO military commander Jules Rother stated. The plan, established in recent years, acknowledged that the Russia of today was acting differently than the Russia of the mid-1990s. The Baltic States were increasingly anxious about Russia's nation-grabbing appetites. During a NATO summit in Wales, the alliance had even approved a rapid-reaction force that would include 4,000 troops.

"Four thousand against—?" the Secretary General Phillipe asked.

Rother sighed.

"Forty-thousand. A suicide mission."

16

THE WHITE HOUSE OVAL OFFICE

AN HOUR LATER

"Copycats. Completely predictable," FBI Director McCafferty said as he slid three summaries across the coffee table to the President.

"They're coming out of the woodwork. Lone wolves across the country, disenfranchised sickos. We caught one on the Seven Mile Bridge to Key West. His car died and his bomb was shit. Another at Allentown, Pennsylvania's Dorney Park. That could have been devastating. The guy's gun wouldn't fire. But they're upping security anyway. And LAPD really got lucky, damned lucky taking down a guy with a box of flares. His plan was to light up the Hollywood Hills."

"God Almighty," President Crowe exclaimed. "What a world it's become."

"They're out there, Mr. President. Inept, but deadly. We've notified local police to put every mall and theater and other large gathering places on high alert, and to constantly surveil bridges and tunnels. There'll be lots of overtime. But big events empower little people."

"Little people who want to kill."

"Yes, sir."

Conversation stopped while the President considered his options. After a deep breath, which he audibly exhaled, he said, "Time for

General Chase to activate the Guard."

Crowe referred to General Ellis Chase, Secretary of Defense. "He can notify the Governors on my order. I want them visible everywhere." Of course, in reality he knew that *everywhere* was impossible.

He made the call and returned to Director McCafferty.

"Now tell me you have some leads, Reese."

The FBI chief shook his head.

17

Julia Jackson had one room left to clean—one room until she could finally take a break after a long day as a housekeeper at the Quality Inn on Old Stage Road. But her day would not be over. She still had to study for a test at John Tyler Community College, where she was pulling straight As in the school's nursing program. Another test and one step closer to her dream job at Richmond's Johnston-Willis Hospital.

She didn't really care about her housekeeping job. She worked for the money and the tips that were all too infrequent. That didn't mean she wasn't diligent; Julia Jackson was good at it. She'd be good at anything, and even better as a nurse.

The routine never changed; order was important. Turn on the TV, usually daytime talk shows, but today the news. The awful news. She watched for a few minutes and imagined what D.C. hospitals were dealing with—what she'd be doing if something like this occurred when she was on nursing duty. Could she even handle it?

Yes, she said to herself. But she was not a nurse. Not yet. So the 22-year-old housekeeper returned to her routine: vacuum. Clean the toilets. Put out new glasses with pleated paper covers (something not everyone did). Bag the old towels and replace them. Strip and make the bed. Dump the trash cans. This took 20 minutes. She ended with the rubbish. The bedroom trash can was filled with cardboard and plastic wrapping. She'd seen the same in the bathroom container.

Julia Jackson was a good student. She remembered something her day manager had mentioned during training her first week on the job; he'd said it more as a required throwaway line, a list he was told to read. One of many. Most didn't seem important. Even this one, until today.

She turned back to the news coverage. The bodies on the bridge. Cars still hanging precariously over the edge. The helicopters whirling overhead, the last of the ambulances leaving. She heard the death count. Higher in the last hour and with only estimates on the numbers of those who'd drowned.

The smoke had cleared, and the live footage showed investigators working the scene into the late afternoon. This wasn't a world away. The 24th Street Bridge was a direct shot north on 95. Less than two hours away.

Then Julia looked down.

The trash can.

Jackson thought about dialing the front desk, but stopped inches from it. She remembered another thing. *If you see something, say something.*

She backed away from the phone. *Don't touch it. Don't touch anything.* She left the hotel room, placed a "Do Not Disturb" sign on the door, and took the elevator to the security office.

"Hey Alfredo, I need your opinion," she said to the front desk clerk. "But first let me borrow your computer."

"Oh?"

Julia hadn't talked much to Alfredo Jimarez, but she was always pleasant to him. Like a nurse would be.

"Nothing personal," he said. "You'll get me in trouble."

She was already typing key words into Google and not focused on his comment. Her search took her from one extract to another.

"Did you hear me?"

"Uh huh." She continued to type.

"Rooms all done?" he asked after a minute.

Julia Jackson shushed him.

"Really, if anyone sees—"

She leaned back, satisfied with what she found.

"There," she exclaimed.

"There? There what?"

She stood.

"Come with me. Room 312."

In the room, Jimarez looked into the wastebasket filled with AAA and AA battery wrappers.

"It's just trash from some tourist. Dump it." He began to reach down.

"No!" she shouted. It was so loud and so unusual a command from the typically quiet housekeeper that Jimarez froze.

"Who uses so many batteries?" she asked.

"I don't know. Tourists. Photographers."

"Right, but who else?" she asked.

"Julia, enough! You're going to get us both in trouble."

"I'll tell you." She pointed to the still turned on TV set. Now she wished she hadn't touched the remote. *Fingerprints*, she thought. Jimarez still didn't get it.

"The attack, Alfredo. They say terrorists need batteries. That's what I Googled."

"I don't follow."

Jackson stood eye to eye with Jimarez.

"For bombs, goddammit."

"Jesus, you've been watching too much crap. Just clean the room."

She ignored him. "Depending on what they planned, they'd need lots of batteries. That's what I see."

"No way. We're not anywhere near...."

"Wrong. We're close to Washington. Now go look up who was in this room last night and what time he checked out."

Jimarez shook his head in disbelief.

"This is nuts."

"Do it. And don't touch anything on your way out!"

18

LONDON

HEATHROW AIRPORT

Dan Reilly cleared British customs and exited with his baggage. A Kensington Royal driver met him and as they prepared to depart, Reilly stopped. A CNN International telecast on a terminal monitor caught his attention. The anchor ran through a list of the copycat attacks occurring in the United States; video B-roll showed scenes in Knoxville, San Francisco, Los Angeles and other cities.

"I suppose it was inevitable," the young woman chauffeur said.

Reilly shook his head.

"Anything here?"

"London's been quiet. Nothing else on the Continent."

Reilly didn't think it would remain that way.

NATO HEADQUARTERS

BRUSSELS, BELGIUM

An aide to NATO Secretary General Phillipe entered the command center.

"A message from President Gorshkov, sir."

Phillipe took the communiqué, read it himself, then aloud. "In the interest of peace and as expression of goodwill, the good peoples of the

Russian Federation, through its leadership seek to convene a meeting to discuss current tensions and this government's sovereignty eight days hence in Stockholm, Sweden. This will be the only invitation proffered. A response is required."

Members of NATO's 179th Military Committee shouted simultaneously.

"What's his game?"

"He's playing us."

"Only invitation? Response required? Then what?"

There was more grumbling and rumbling until General Turnbull, the Supreme Allied Commander, Transformation (SACT) raised both hands in the air.

"Okay. Quiet, everyone. We'll run the language through intelligence for nuance and intent. But as I see it, Gorshkov wants to gauge what he can achieve through threat."

"We know what he wants," blared NATO Secretary General Phillipe. "And in a year, or less, he could have it all if we don't stand firm."

"Or sooner," Turnbull argued. "It comes down to what Crowe will do. And right now, that's nothing."

Phillipe sighed deeply. He dialed his secretary on a landline at the table.

"I need to talk to the following people in this exact order: the British Prime Minister, the French President, and the President of the United States."

As they came through, Phillipe put each call on speakerphone for the benefit of the team. Coleen Waring, the British Prime Minister, expressed concern but no real outrage. His conservative government had pulled back from NATO just as a past American president had.

"I will want to hear what President Crowe says," Waring concluded. "But it seems to me that Gorshkov is merely dipping his toe in the water again. Not a great deal to worry about."

French President Paul Reims was more outspoken, but equally noncommittal.

"France is not about to start a war over what could just be sabre-rattling exercises. It was before. Probably it is again. Besides, from what you have indicated, his communication clearly suggests his willingness to sit and talk."

"Read between the lines," Phillipe countered. "He's warning what would happen if we don't talk, Mr. President. 'To discuss current tensions and this government's sovereignty.' Good lord, he wants his border nations back. And this time, he's at the front door with his own troops in plain sight."

"Gorshkov can't possibly believe…." the French president began before trailing off.

"Believe it," Phillipe snapped.

"Mr. Secretary General, perhaps if the American president took a firm position," Reims said, echoing Prime Minister Waring's reply. "Then we'll talk again."

The call ended with no more support than when it began. The French and British leaders might say something different to the press, but right now NATO command knew they had little or no support from key member nations.

"So Riga will have to fall before anyone acts?" Phillipe quietly asked his advisors and command.

"New fears whip up the same old sentiments that Hitler and Stalin so effectively employed," General Jules Rother offered.

"Must history repeat itself?"

"Monsters sleep. Monsters awake," Rother continued. "Gorshkov offers protection against NATO. A continent-wide realignment seems all the more likely. Intimidating Latvia and Ukraine just speeds up the clock."

"So meeting with Gorshkov won't make a difference," Secretary General Phillipe concluded.

No one had a reply.

WASHINGTON, D.C.

President Crowe expected the NATO Secretary General's call. He should have initiated it himself, but there was too much to deal with domestically.

"Yes, Mr. Secretary General," Crowe answered. Vice President Ryan Battaglio listened on an earpiece along with National Security Advisor Pierce Kimball. "Of course, we've been following the developments in Europe."

"As we have in your country, Mr. President. Our thoughts and prayers are with the families."

Crowe hated the expression. It was a convenient go-to response. But in truth, anyone subjected to disaster whether natural or manmade, accidental or intentional, needed more than *thoughts and prayers*. And for that matter, so would Latvia and Ukraine if Gorshkov advanced. But Crowe accepted the expression of sympathy in the manner it was offered: sincerely.

The President listened attentively to the Secretary General who finished with, "It looks bad."

Crowe had a thought, more political than military.

"The communiqué was directed to NATO. There was no mention of the United States?"

"No, Mr. President."

"Then a reply from me would be unexpected?"

"It would be."

"And it would likely make him reconsider his next move."

"Possibly," Phillipe replied.

"Definitely. Because he thinks we're too busy with our own troubles—which we are, but it could throw him off. First, to show solidarity, even though I'd be seriously criticized at home for any military action; and second, to let Gorshkov know that NATO resolve remains strong."

"It could escalate the situation, Mr. President. Quickly. We have eight days. I'd like to use that time to consider other alternatives. It gives you some cover, too." Crowe agreed and proposed another idea.

"Okay. Accept the invitation, but do so publicly. Restate Article 5."

"Without guarantee of member support?"

"You don't need to prove it, Mr. Secretary. Just state it."

The two leaders ended the call. Crowe saw that his Vice President was upset.

"You don't agree, Ryan?"

"No, Mr. President. This is not our fight."

"Good lord, our allies have to know we support them!" Crowe thundered.

"With what's going on here? The press will have you for dinner. Focus on America first."

President Crowe folded his arms across his chest. His Vice President was not with him, but this wasn't Battaglio's decision to make. He turned to Kimball.

"Inform Gorshkov that we have spoken and despite what he sees in the press, the United States stands by NATO. Furthermore, the Russian Federation is advised not to take any hostile action in Europe."

Battaglio stood and went to the door. Shaking his head and with his back to Crowe he quietly muttered, "Fool."

* * *

The Kremlin responded ninety minutes later with a statement dictated by President Gorshkov:

"The peoples of Latvia historically and economically are linked to our brothers and sisters in the Russian Federation. We have long heard their call for unity. This is our final offer to meet with NATO. A reply is expected within 24 hours."

Phillipe read the reply. He walked over to a map of Europe on his wall. Everyone watched as he stared at it. Then he took a step forward and silently mouthed the names of NATO's member nations on Russia's eastern border. Estonia, Lithuania, Belarus, Moldova, Romania, Bulgaria, Montenegro, Ukraine. *A new Russian Federation,* he thought. *A resurrection of the old Soviet Union.*

19

Dan Reilly caught four hours' sleep, took a shower, and walked into the Kensington Royal corporate offices conference room to meet with his Europe crisis team. It was a similar composition to his group in Chicago, but with additional regional expertise.

Reilly knew each committee member by name. He'd worked with them on the kidnapping and rescue of a KR General Manager in Berlin, and their follow-up after a recent bombing attempt at a property in Brussels. As he looked around the table, he acknowledged an ex-Royal Marine Commando, a retiree from Great Britain's famed domestic security agency MI-5, a Middle Eastern mercenary who was associated with Donald Klugo in Chicago, and Kensington Royal's chief corporate counsel. Each looked stern. Chris Collins, the company attorney, appeared the most worried, which was nothing new. On the phone from the U.S., General Coons. It was time to drill down, further into the details and closer to the danger.

"What are we looking at?" Reilly asked.

"Helicopters are out of the question. Given what's going on in the square near your property in Kiev, it will be too dangerous to put down," said Kalib Hassan, Donald Klugo's outside contractor. "As Mr. Klugo told you, we'll have to get your civilians to the plane. Then there's the challenge of getting past friendly guards or invading forces. It will come down to money or guns. We have to be prepared with both."

"How much money?" Reilly asked.

"Enough to grease wheels, open doors, create traffic lanes, and guarantee take-off."

"How much?" Reilly asked again.

"I'll make some calls," the Middle Eastern mercenary said.

"Make them now."

Kalib Hassan rose from the conference table and went into the hall to find a private room.

"What's the latest news?" Reilly asked. Brian Crance, the ex-MI5 officer, answered.

"My contacts tell me NATO is going to accept Gorshkov's offer to meet in Stockholm. Not that there's much of a choice. No location picked yet, but—"

The *but* hung in the air.

"The Russian delegation has stayed at our hotel before. I'll find out if that's their intention again."

Reilly typed a text to his office. He narrated what he was doing.

"Checking to see if there's been any inquiry to block rooms in the next week. High-level clearance."

"The meeting would buy more time to extract people from Kiev and perhaps Riga," Crance said. "Takes some immediate pressure off."

They discussed the point for another two minutes until Reilly held up his finger as he read an incoming text from Brenda Sheldon in Chicago.

Confirmed. Request to block rooms. High security.

"From?" Chris Collins asked.

Reilly began to type but stopped mid-sentence. The answer was in a second text: Russian Federation Travel Office.

"Bingo," Crance concluded. "How many?"

Reilly typed again. The reply came seconds later. "Three."

"Rooms?" Collins wondered.

"Floors. Three floors."

Reilly suddenly felt torn in three directions. Riga, Kiev, and now Stockholm.

"Jesus," he blurted. "Any sense of how Gorshkov will act, or react, during this conference?"

"Just an opinion," Crance, the former British spy offered. "If past behavior is anything, he could grandstand then suddenly bolt, claiming there was no give. Then he'd invade."

NEW YORK

Savannah Flanders found more user-submitted footage of the 14th Street Bridge attack, most of it shaky. She stabilized the footage with her editing program and fast forwarded through everything.

"Okay," she said to her monitor, where she was screening a clip off the MSNBC website. "Show me something good."

Flanders rolled through it with the sound down. It depicted panicked people staggering forward, away from the cloud of smoke and explosions. Zoomed in tighter, she saw victims coughing, some crying, and many bleeding. Uniformed personnel assisted those they could, but it was too late for others. A pan of the bridge focused on boats beginning to encircle the area just under a gaping hole in the span.

Flanders turned up the sound. She heard the anchor's interview with a freelancer who was either at the right place at the wrong time, or the wrong place at the right time. He called MSNBC, and minutes later uploaded his footage to the network's portal from his DSLR. The interview continued over the raw footage. He described the scene as best he could above the sound of sirens, helicopters, and bullhorns.

Pulled out wide, Flanders felt the full impact of the attack: hundreds injured, lives destroyed and the nation's capital at a standstill. But she was looking for one man. Already, it was almost an obsession. That's what made her one of the best on the *Times* staff, what had earned her a Pulitzer Prize for her investigative series on the Russian mob's ties to New York borough politics.

But at this moment, she wasn't thinking of awards. Just an interview with a man, Mr. Late 30s to Early 40s.

She paused the footage, smiled and leaned back. She had found her man. He had turned directly towards the freelancer's camera. Full face on. A wide shot, but enough pixels to work with. She grabbed the still frame, then another.

Flanders studied the images. She began writing down her first impressions. Despite the chaos, her man was absolutely in control; someone who knew how to act with authority in a crisis.

She loaded the best images in the FaceRec program and waited for a match. "Let's see who the hell you are. I bet you have some story to tell."

LONDON

Reilly and Marnie Babbitt met for dinner at The Wolseley in Piccadilly. They made their toasts to one another over Kir Royale, clinked glasses, and decided on just three appetizers to share: wild mushroom soup, Atlantic prawns with a lemon aioli, and a dozen oysters. The oysters spoke the loudest to them. The only time they took their eyes off one another was when they each checked and responded to text messages and emails. Marnie finished first and declared, "Enough!"

Reilly agreed.

"But not enough of you!"

"You have that right, Mr. Reilly."

Thirty minutes later, they fell into each other's arms in Reilly's Kensington Royal London Towers suite. They made up for lost time, ripping at clothes, and not waiting until everything was off. They were noisy and didn't care, especially Reilly. He longed to feel her warmth, taste her tastes, and be held tightly—everywhere. Marnie Babbitt took him in and with every move demonstrated that he was wanted, needed, and greatly desired.

They breathed as one; intertwining, merging, and flowing. Satiated, Marnie leaned on her side facing him. She gently stroked Dan's hair, but had a distant look.

"You're in deep thought," he said.

"I don't know. I guess I just enjoy the quiet."

"I like that," he replied.

She nodded, kissed him lightly and pulled back. Reilly sensed there was still something else on her mind.

"What is it?"

Marnie nodded. She sat up.

"How close were you to the explosion?" It was the question he had assumed would ultimately come, and now he had to answer her.

"Not that far away."

"Dan," she chided.

"Fairly close." Marnie moved across his body. Her breasts pressed against him.

"How close is fairly close?"

"Very. About like this." She gave his ear a gentle nibble.

"Come on. Really, how close is very?" He turned his head, lowered his chin and faced her eye-to-eye.

"I was on the bridge."

Babbitt closed her eyes and rested her head on his chest. She whispered, "Tell me more."

Now Reilly stroked her hair as he recounted his experience, all that he'd been through. All that he'd seen.

"You could have been…." Marnie held him close but didn't finish the thought.

"I wasn't."

"And now where do you go? Into more trouble." She lifted up. "Latvia next? Ukraine?"

He didn't answer, but his deep sigh confirmed everything she suspected.

"Why?"

"It's my job."

Marnie pulled away. He reached out and touched her. She tensed.

"There's too much I don't know about you. Will you ever trust me?"

Reilly sighed. He just didn't know.

20

MOSCOW

THE KREMLIN

Nicolai Gorshkov didn't place much value in trust. Loyalty was another thing. He rewarded it when it was freely given, and punished anyone who didn't show respect or conspired, openly or privately, against him. He described it as his management philosophy, a philosophy developed during the waning days of the Cold War.

Gorshkov was a young Lieutenant Colonel in those days, carving out a reputation as a man not to cross. He had served the KGB by luring, engaging, and manipulating foreign journalists, academics, scientists, politicians, and executives. When compromised, they'd do his bidding— Soviet Russia's bidding—stealing whatever there was to steal. State and military secrets, corporate plans, research findings, think-tank studies.

During his time in East Germany, Gorshkov and his aides had successfully entrapped thirty high-level officials. But when the Berlin Wall fell, it quickly became apparent that a divided Germany would become whole without Russian influence. He was thus ordered to burn all of his records and drop his remaining assets. And so, in the last hours of his time in Potsdam, he burned box upon box of intimate reports, titillating audio tapes, and salacious 16mm film—everything he had used to control his network.

However, all the smoke that rose up the chimney into the frigid December night sky back in 1989 did not prevent Gorshkov from seeing beyond the end of Communism, and beyond *Perestroika*.

President Mikhail Gorbachev was intent on purging the old ways and making way for the new. The Kremlin had sold Nicolai Gorshkov out. He vowed no one would ever do that to him again. He would be the good soldier, so long as it served him. But he was determined to rise in power. To the top. He would build a network of people loyal to him and only him, and ultimately eliminate those who had abandoned him and the system.

Following his return to Russia, Gorshkov quickly advanced in the ranks of the KGB and its successor spy agency, the FSB. He parlayed his ever-expanding position into political circles, which ultimately brought him inside the Kremlin. Decades later, exhibiting the patience of Job but loyal only to his own aspirations for power, Nicolai Gorshkov became the natural heir to the Russian Federation presidency.

On his way to the top he amassed billions, and felt no remorse for eliminating rivals and threats. They included the KGB officers in the chain of command who had reduced his Potsdam work to ashes, and politicos who failed him now. The press, which he now controlled, acquiesced to his *re-shuffling*. They reported the news as he dictated— the recent sudden deaths of an incompetent Moscow mayor, a very replaceable general, and several valueless FSB officers.

He had learned how to survive in the classic Machiavellian manner, with special emphasis on swift, decisive action. It was the old Soviet Union reborn, but so far without the Eastern Bloc countries. So far. Today his minions were doing his bidding with active bots and bullets in the chamber. Like the old days, he had "influencers" in his pocket advising their bosses in corporate America and on Capitol Hill to stick to their own knitting and stay out of Europe's affairs. By every account, it was working masterfully.

His aides reported that public sentiment over the terrorist attacks in the U.S. was putting America first and the rest of the world a distant second. MSNBC, CNN, and Fox News had echoed and amplified the point. Moreover, President Crowe appeared to be ignoring the buildup on the Russian Federation border. And NATO was, by all accounts, floundering.

Gorshkov's campaign to take back neighboring countries—as he described it, "Russia's historic destiny"—would be his crowning achievement.

Crowning. Now that was a new idea. He liked it.

21

LONDON

THE NEXT MORNING

In an empty office at the London Kensington Royal Hotel, Reilly faced a fresh legal pad that wouldn't be blank for long. He turned it sideways and wrote three city names: Stockholm, Riga, Kiev. In the left column, he enumerated immediate dangers and immediate decisions. He tackled Kiev, then Riga. Both lists had virtually the same items:

- Upgrade to Red Status

- Arrange for €100,000 cash

- Finalize timelines for evacuation

- Book commercial airlines and backup private jets

- Rent seaworthy boats

- Rent buses, hire drivers

- Order 250 yellow shirts for immediately delivery

- 25 yellow flags for immediate delivery

- Deliver 25 analog phones with backup batteries

Next, Stockholm, site of the upcoming summit:

- Security demands

- Upgrade threat to Red status

- Food checks

- Street closures

- Advance team meetings

- Close down guest parking

- No parking within 100 feet of building

Reilly brought his notes into the morning meeting. He began with a question for his experts.

"What's the chance everything will go to shit before we're ready?"

Kalib Hassan spoke first.

"High degree of probability. Escalation could be imminent."

"And if that occurs?"

"There's an old Arabic saying," the mercenary offered. "Do not stand in a dangerous place expecting miracles."

Reilly didn't dare say it, but he thought, *Too many crises, not enough people.*

The London team had laid out the potential priorities for him.

Crisis One: Kiev. Crisis Two: Riga.

Both read like worst-case scenarios: Invasions. Thousands dead. Possible all-out land war.

Crisis Three: Stockholm. But, for now, that was more about business logistics and operations.

For now.

NEW YORK

THE SAME TIME

Daniel J. Reilly.

Savannah Flanders read the name and the brief—the extremely short brief.

Daniel J. Reilly. President of Kensington Royal Hotels, International.

US Army Captain, retired. Former State Department officer. Divorced.

"That's it?"

"He keeps a low profile," Blowen explained. "That's from his company bio."

"Nothing on LinkedIn?" Flanders asked.

"Same."

"Well, I was right about one thing," Flanders concluded. "He was field ready. Trained. But now that you know his job, find me some clips, Mike. He can't fly completely under the radar with such a high-level job."

"Got some already. Clips from recent Congressional hearings. Ready to screen." He hit play. Flanders circled around to his computer and watched an archived C-SPAN session where Reilly was questioned by several Senators she had interviewed in the past. One cantankerous, the other friendly. *No surprise there,* she thought. *Right down party lines.* She made a note to call both. Blowen played the more substantive friendly testimony.

"Mr. Reilly, thank you for joining us today."

"You're quite welcome, Senator."

"Following up on the Chairman's line of questioning, you recognize that the U.S. cannot provide complete protection for American citizens traveling abroad."

"I do. That would be impossible."

"Then what are you proposing?"

"Terrorism is our new reality. Radical terrorism is responsible for virtually all of the attacks against hotels, most of which are owned or managed by American companies. We considered ourselves lucky in the 1970s when the Irish Republican Army phoned pre-attack warnings. Those days are over. Modern terrorists aren't polite *or* politic. Their goal is to kill as many innocent people as possible. Unannounced and unabashed. Terrorism is no longer just a political threat, it's a corporate business threat as well. In order to be prepared, we have to be armed, armed with information. Armed with timely, credible intelligence."

"At what cost, Mr. Reilly?"

"Well, information gathering and sharing comes with a price tag, but so does the failure to invest in preventative measures."

"I remember this," Blowen said. He stopped the playback. "Reilly was asking for raw intelligence."

"More than the online State Department advisories?"

"Right. It's coming up."

Senator, members of the committee, there have been terrorist attacks against hotels virtually every year since 9/11. Thousands dead. Tourists and first responders. Children. Christians, Jews, and Muslims. The bombs have not discriminated. Nearly half of these terrorist attacks used VBIEDs—Vehicle Born Improvised Explosive Devices. Kensington Royal is examining ways to increase our security perimeters to help guard against such attacks. But that has not thwarted VBIEDs from getting up to barriers at hotels and restaurants, or suicide bombers and gunmen from checking in at the front desk or sitting down for one last meal.

The clip ended. Blowen found another, but Reilly's testimony was interrupted when he received word that his company's hotel in Tokyo had just been bombed.

"He left, just like that. It was a horrible attack."

"And once again, he ran *toward* the danger," Flanders observed. She pulled away from the computer, thinking.

"I need to meet this guy."

LONDON

A statuesque beauty turned heads as she walked out of the revolving doors into the London Kensington Royal Towers. She was dressed in a slinky red dress cut way above the knees and strappy high-heeled sandals. She noted the stir she caused, but didn't react. It was all intentional. Her outfit was something of a uniform, provoking the intended reactions.

She stood to the side of the check-in queue, looking like she was engrossed in a phone call. She wasn't. Though she held her cell to her ear, she was actually waiting for a particular front desk clerk she had her eye on to finish with a guest.

When the young man was ready he smiled.

"I'll take you."

Oh yes you will, she thought.

He held up his left hand, warmly waving her forward. The woman smiled, wrapped up her fake call, and instantly engaged the handsome clerk whom she judged to be in his mid-twenties. *The perfect age. Open, inexperienced and impressionable.*

"Good morning," he began warmly.

"Good morning." She read his nametag and said in an appealing manner, "Jonathan."

Jonathan responded perfectly to her. Based on his age, exceptional good looks, and first-blush reaction, and the fact that he had no ring on his left ring finger, she decided he probably did all right with some of the women guests he personally checked-in.

"My first time at your lovely hotel," she offered in Russian-accented English.

"Well, I hope I can help make it a comfortable stay for you."

She smiled.

Jonathan was about to ask for her identification and credit card. She beat him to it and handed over her *Yellow Sberbank of Russia* Gold MasterCard and her Russian Federation passport in the name of Maria Pudovkin—not her actual identity, but one that worked for international business. Her real name was Colonel Martina Kushkin.

"Ms. Pudovkin, let's see now." He pulled up her reservation. "We have you for two nights."

"Perhaps more," she replied.

Jonathan read into the reply what he wanted, then looked into her portfolio.

"Well, good news. I can upgrade you to an executive suite." It was his personal change, not the hotel's.

"You can do that for me?" He smiled. "Thank you. That would be wonderful."

They chatted casually about her stay. Some meetings, museums, and restaurants. Nothing she had to get to on any schedule.

"I'm pretty open."

Jonathan swallowed hard and completed the check-in process.

"Alright now. Would you like any assistance to your room?"

Not to the room, but in the room, she thought. Pudovkin would undoubtedly give the young man an experience he would never forget. Now she just smiled.

"No, thank you. But if I need anything, I'll be sure to call you, Jonathan."

"Please do." He programmed two plastic electronic key cards and placed them in her hand.

"Here you go. You're all set. Fifth floor."

She leaned in and whispered, "Why don't you keep one for yourself? For later."

She pressed the card back in his hand. He casually palmed it, hiding his excitement behind the check-in desk.

Pudovkin sighed deeply, allowing her ample breasts to visibly rise and fall. Then she turned to the elevator thinking, *An inside contact is always worth a good fuck.*

WASHINGTON, D.C.

President Crowe returned to television to calm the country, but it wasn't working. Not this time. Not this President.

Opposition radio hosts had been fueling talk of retaliation for days. Across the dial there were rants about "the Arabs, right-wing extremists, left-wing radicals, socialists, MS-13 gangs," and by nationality, "The Saudis, the Russians, the Chinese, and the Mexicans." But there was no consensus of opinion. And commentators who routinely trolled in conspiracy theories claimed the attacks were President Crowe's own doing, so he could establish martial law and solidify his power base.

More sympathetic hosts warned the White House to avoid another Iraq. Another Afghanistan.

Crowe opened with a middle-of-the-road approach which was immediately met by raised hands and shouts from reporters wanting to be recognized. He braced for a hostile press conference.

"Mr. President, do we have any intelligence on who is responsible for these terrorist attacks?" asked Washington PBS reporter Stan Deutsch.

"No. But we are committing the full resources of the FBI's Joint Terrorism Force, Homeland Security, and Central Intelligence, as well as law enforcement agencies across the country."

"Since there are multiple attacks that are obviously well-coordinated and require a significant investment," began CNN's Deborah Ball, "is there a money trail to follow?"

"That will be part of the investigation."

"Will be or is?" Ball countered.

"We're following every possible lead."

Crowe took a drink of water, wishing he had given a stronger reply. He returned to the CNN reporter.

"Deborah, to be clear, we are investigating all aspects. The identity of these killers, where they're from, the money behind them."

John Rantz from Fox News cut in.

"If it's a foreign government, will you ask Congress for a declaration of war or order a punitive strike on your own?"

"We are not there yet, John," Crowe replied. "But I will not remove any option from the table at this time."

"Mr. President," shouted a reporter from InfoWars, "It's been said that your administration itself could be behind these horrific acts. Can you categorically deny that charge?"

Crowe shot a critical look at the agitator and moved on.

"Next question."

Hands shot up. The press pool shouted more questions. MSNBC, Fox, and CBS the loudest. But Crowe suddenly held up both hands, signaling for quiet. He returned to the Infowars reporter he had ignored.

"Wait. I categorically deny your assertion. And you, sir, bring shame to your profession. That's assuming I can even call you a professional among your peers."

It was a sharp retort that would lead most newscasts that night.

"Next."

The shouting resumed. The president recognized Jack Casey, a WERS-FM news reporter from Boston.

"Mr. President, are the attacks on the United States related in any way to what's occurring in Europe, because—"

"We have no evidence to support that."

Casey jumped back in.

"Excuse me, sir, but following up on an earlier question, according to a NBC/*New York Times* poll, Americans, by a margin of 85 percent to 15 percent, do not want the United States to have any involvement in a war in Eastern Europe. Can you explain the administration's position at this moment? Your position, Mr. President?"

Crowe hesitated. This was the question he definitely didn't want to answer.

"We're studying the situation."

More hands. More reporters yelling out.

22

NEW YORK

Figuring Savannah Flanders had worked through the night, Mike Blowen came to work the next morning prepared. He put a nonfat vanilla latte to the side of her computer, within easy reach.

"Full strength," he said.

"Thanks." Flanders barely looked up from her typing.

"How's it going?"

"It's going. You?"

"I'll tell you one thing: almost everyone I interviewed said they'll move before they go under or even over the river again."

"Same kind of reports out of D.C. and St. Louis. But that will change. We all go back to our old routines."

"Like lightning never striking twice in the same place?" Blowen suggested.

"More like we have to just go on living." Flanders handed her latest printouts to Blowen.

"This is for the file now. They want us on background for a Sunday lead story. Vulnerabilities to infrastructure. I said we'd do it, but I want time on another angle."

"Did you tell the desk what it is?"

"Not yet. Gotta get more. Hopefully in person."

"What if someone else gets to him first?"

"Let's just make sure that doesn't happen." Flanders paused to refocus, then asked, "Okay. Anything new?"

"The State Department would only confirm he had worked there. Not what he did."

"What about the Army?"

"Sealed, according to my contact at the Pentagon. Trying to find out. No one's opening up yet. I'll call in some favors."

"Do it." Savannah Flanders concluded, "There's more to Reilly than meets the eye."

LONDON

THE SAME TIME

Reilly and Marnie Babbitt talked over lunch at The Ledbury. Marnie complained that her upcoming travel was as harried as his. Washington and Philadelphia, then on to Cairo and maybe Moscow. The uncertainty in Eastern Europe was making her work as a Vice President of Development and Finance for Barclays Bank ever more challenging. Projects in all three Baltic nations were on hold. The same for Ukraine.

"Tell you what, I'll trade with you," he mused.

"How about we meet up?"

"I can't promise anything. Not for a while."

Marnie nodded. "But you'll keep me posted. Every day," she implored, reaching across the table.

"The best I can."

"Your best is better than anyone else's."

Reilly smiled at the intended double entendre.

"Okay," she continued. "You can start now."

"With?"

"Your schedule. Where are you going first? And when?"

* * *

The hotel clerk was off duty. Col. Martina Kushkin, presently Maria

Pudovkin, was on. She had taken him places he'd never been. And now lying in bed, she ran her left hand through his hair, kissed his neck softly, while her right hand gently caressed him where he most wanted. Through the foreplay she knew this was a perfect time to pump him in an entirely different way.

The Russian spy got the young hotel employee to talk about his family, his life, and his aspirations. She praised him for his professional manner and predicted he would have a tremendous career. Not to rush pressing for information, she slid her head down and let him enjoy her warm lips. This aroused him, but he was not fully ready again. So she came up above the covers and kissed him deeply before resting her head on his chest.

"You must get to meet a lot of beautiful actresses and famous women. Have you ever made love with any?"

"Oh, no."

Time for more flattery.

"Well, they don't know what they're missing." She touched him again.

Jonathan sighed. She had more questions, but they could wait.

* * *

"Paris," Reilly offered.

Paris. This was news, Marnie thought.

"Why Paris?"

"Nothing serious," Reilly said, shrugging it off. "A quick intermediate stop. Security upgrades to check on." He didn't indicate they were real needs based on actual threats. "Chunnel over in the morning. With luck, just one night."

"Okay, so let's steal some time after."

"Can't. Stockholm. The NATO talks. The Russians have block-booked our property."

"Just what you need. So, when will I see you again?" She sounded disappointed.

"As soon as possible."

"You'll be staying at the Metro Tower in Paris?"

"No, the Paris Kensington Rêve."

"Classy," she joked. "I could make it more memorable for you."

"You sure could," he said. "But not this trip."

She pouted and suggestively ran her fingers over the stem of her wine glass.

* * *

The Russian agent, an expert in the explicit art of *Sexpionage*, was patient. More talk, then his reward would come. Kushkin got him to boast about the company computer system and its firewalls. He explained things carefully, the way someone would to a child, but in detail. She pretended she hardly understood, so he went further. She'd pass everything she learned onto Moscow. It might prove helpful there, in Stockholm, or later.

Next she asked about the organization, "—which you're obviously going to be an important part of."

He liked that, which led to questions about the operation and the management. She worked her way up the ladder as her fingers worked their way down his chest.

"And who's that guy who was on TV talking to senators a while back? The executive from Chicago? Seems important."

"You're talking about Mr. Reilly."

"Right, that's him. I can see you in that kind of job in a few years."

"Really?"

"Really."

That opened him up to share everything he knew about Dan Reilly, which was limited, but it included his immediate travel plans—to the Paris Kensington Rêve.

* * *

"Listen," Reilly said, "you should really steer clear of Washington. Transportation in and out is going to be bad for a while. And for that matter, Moscow too. You don't want to get stranded there if Gorshkov makes a move."

"I don't, or you don't want me to?"

"Both," he admitted.

Marnie replied, "I like way you say *both*. It's been a long time since that sounded good coming from a man." Marnie reached across the table for his hands. "Both. Yes. Both."

"So, no Russia trips?"

She withdrew her arms.

"Now who's asking? Dan Reilly, my lover, or Dan Reilly, international business competitor? You know I can't talk about what we have going." Reilly gritted his teeth.

"Sorry. Out of bounds."

"Well, here's the deal," she proposed. "I'll tell my lover as long as he doesn't tell anyone else."

Reilly smiled slyly. "Really, I'm sorry. I shouldn't have asked."

"It's okay. No state secret. We've sought assurances from Moscow that our business agreements in Latvia will be honored."

She stopped at that.

"And?"

"We're waiting." She decided to turn the question around. "You?"

"Same," Reilly said. "Both."

"Both. That word again. We're both worried?"

She looked away. Reilly saw worry, but there was something else which he couldn't quite place.

* * *

Jonathan said he should go. The Russian FSB officer wasn't ready for him to leave. Not quite yet. He was better than most his age and she was enjoying that. But there might be more she could gather, particularly about the most recent topic, Daniel J. Reilly. She continued in earnest, nibbling his ear and stroking him lightly.

* * *

This time Reilly reached across the table and took Marnie's hand.

"How about no more business. Just pleasure."

"My thoughts exactly. Your place or mine?"

"Mine. But not now. Back to work."

"I suppose I have to as well."

Marnie picked up her glass of water and raised it in a toast.

"To *both*," she offered with a smile.

He raised his glass and was about to clink but stopped. He examined it.

"What?" she asked.

He tilted the glass slightly, tipping the contents from side to side. It created a small wave.

"What is it?"

"Nothing."

"That's not a nothing response."

"Really?"

"It's a glass of water. You drink it."

"Unless," he returned the glass to the table, "...you can't."

He took out his phone and quickly sent a text message.

23

CIA HEADQUARTERS
LANGLEY, VA

Heath sat at his desk with the door closed, with Reilly's original terrorism assessment report he'd gotten from the Director. He rolled up the sleeves on his blue button-down shirt and loosened his tie. He'd told his aide not to disturb him "at least until dinner." At 6 p.m. he revised the request. "Ten o'clock." An hour later he was alone with a sandwich.

He was particularly interested in a three-word text he'd received hours earlier from Reilly.

Let's talk WATER

Without indicating what Reilly wanted, it was soon apparent he was referring to America's water resources. More than 151,000 independent water systems in the United States. An impossible number to fathom. Obviously, Reilly wanted him to narrow the scope. And so, he read into the night.

He made notes in the margins and highlighted key sections in yellow. He came to the same conclusion that Reilly had in his report: with open reservoirs supporting most communities, a hundred thousand miles of aging underground pipes, unpatrolled open-air aqueducts and canals, and only moderately guarded treatment plants, the nation's water infrastructure was impossible to completely secure.

Reilly had outlined the threat of toxins that could be introduced at key distribution points. While this was more of a localized issue, Reilly noted it could cause wider panic if multiple coordinated attacks occurred. Reilly's paper pointed to another threat: terrorists targeting a major distribution hub that serves a large region, a major city, or a network covering states. He cited the Dam Safety and Security Act of 2002 that recognized the importance of enhancing safety to the nation's 77,000 dams. The problem was the federal government had oversight of only five percent of those dams whose failures could result in significant loss of life. The remaining structures were owned or controlled by local or state governments, or private entities.

Even more revealing, Reilly's report spelled out in detail how a coordinated effort aimed at multiple small dams could cripple farm communities. And on a far larger scale, Shasta and Folsom Dams in California, Grand Coulee Dam in Washington, Glen Canyon Dam in Arizona, and Hoover Dam, located between Nevada and Arizona, which feeds water to the Southwestern U.S. Each had weaknesses and Reilly had pinpointed them. All five were operated by the U.S. Bureau of Reclamation and considered "critical infrastructure," meaning their impairment or destruction could seriously impact national security. Heath viewed that as one gigantic understatement.

Reilly concluded the section with a warning: "Dams are loaded weapons with the safety off."

It was a *holy shit* moment for Heath. But that was not the worst of it. He re-read another section which troubled him just as much: Bridges.

They were targeted in the East and the Midwest. What about the West? There were five bridges that came to mind. *The Astoria-Megler Bridge over the Columbia River in Oregon, the Vincent Thomas south of Los Angeles, the Coronado Bridge in San Diego, the San Francisco-Oakland Bay Bridge, and——.* He stopped in mid-thought and quickly dialed Reilly.

"What's up?" the hotel executive answered from bed.

"Your goddamned paper. That's what. Got a few minutes?" Heath asked.

"Yes."

Heath shared his concern: dams and bridges on the West Coast.

"Bingo," Reilly replied.

"Okay. Bridges first. Give me your risk assessment."

Reilly stood and began to walk naked around the room. "Rule out the Astoria-Megler over the lower Columbia River. It's a magnificent span, the longest continuous truss bridge in North America. But as horrible as it would be, it's a 24-hour news story to the rest of the country. Same for the Vincent Thomas in San Pedro. A link to the harbor, but most people in LA don't even know it exists. Probably never even seen it. The San Diego-Coronado would be an impressive take-down, but nowhere near the impact of targeting the Bay Bridge between Oakland and San Francisco or the Golden Gate."

"My thoughts exactly. The Golden Gate would be number one. It's virtually a national monument," Heath concluded.

"But hardened and harder to attack. It's patrolled more just because it's so iconic. No, I'd pick the Bay Bridge. At this moment it should be on a super-heightened state of alert with Coast Guard patrol boats every fifty yards on either side. If possible, every twenty-five yards. I'd slow traffic down. Squad cars everywhere. It will piss off everyone, including the bad guys. And that's the point. Visible deterrents deter.

"I evaluated the targets on the basis of probability distributions: how much damage a truck bomb can do and at what pressure points. A pre-stressed concrete beam, a continuous steel-plate girder, or the deck cantilever truss."

"Saw that," Heath said. "Didn't quite understand it."

"$R=CVL$," Reilly said from memory. "R is for Risk, defined as the potential loss to a system. C represents the consequences of an event occurring. V stands for vulnerability, and L is the likelihood of an attacker succeeding. That's where the probability rests. At this point, V is a given: the bridges, as we've seen, are extremely vulnerable. But it takes a great deal of effort. As far as the Golden Gate and Bay Bridge go, I'd rule out an attack by water. An oil tanker could do real damage, like the one on the Mississippi, but get the Coast Guard in place and you take away the water route. An air attack is possible. Load up a private jet, maybe two or three, and aim for the supports."

"Jesus, Reilly. You're right. Little or no TSA interference. Take off and aim."

"Except," Reilly said over the phone from England, "that's a suicide mission and each of the prior attacks were walk-aways. So, no. Not now. The teams are too valuable to the cause. They act like mercenaries, not martyrs. It's a sophisticated organization that has undoubtedly promised its team real-world rewards, not virgins in heaven."

"So, we're back to truck bombs? But that still means they have to abandon their vehicles to escape."

"Yes."

"I'll add a letter to your equation: F. F is for *we're fucked*," Heath declared.

"Not with visible defenses on either side of the 8,980-foot span. Remember what scared off *jihadists* who had taken handheld video footage of the Golden Gate after 9/11? Police patrols. Coast Guard vessels in the sea lanes. And the governor made the threat public, which took Californians by surprise, but also made terrorists nervous. That's the goal of safety at our hotels: make the targets unattractive. Too difficult. And the bottom line, the best course of action, the counter move against a terrorist attack is to let terrorists know that we know what they're planning. That we're ready. That they can't succeed. But it may be too late for that.

"To my thinking, focus on The Bay Bridge over the Golden Gate. Less attention is focused on it which makes it more attractive a target. The bridge had been retrofitted and rebuilt, making it the world's largest Self-Anchored Suspension Span with a single, almost mile-long main cable supporting the weight of the bridge. Terrorists armed with significant timed explosives could take out sections of the concrete roadway. Loss of life would be significant. A strategic attack could close the bridge down for weeks or months, if not longer, crippling the California economy."

He visualized the 4.5-mile span that carried more than 270,000 cars a day between Oakland and San Francisco. A potential for disaster far worse than the 1989 earthquake.

"So, what are you recommending?" Heath asked.

"Talk to Moore at the FBI. Tell him we should think big or go home."

24

NEW YORK

Flanders stared at the phone. *Enough time waiting,* she thought. She dialed the number for the Kensington Royal corporate headquarters.

After being connected through the switchboard and put on hold for two minutes, she heard a warm but authoritative voice. Protective.

"Mr. Reilly's office, this is Brenda."

"Hello, Brenda, my name is Savannah Flanders. I'm a writer for the *New York Times.*"

Flanders heard typing on the other end. The woman was taking notes. *Good. Well-trained. Efficient. Like her boss.*

"Ms. Flanders, if you're calling about an interview, I have to refer you to our communications department. Pat Brodowski. Her number is—"

"Actually, I was hoping that I could speak to Mr. Reilly more off-the-record."

The typing stopped.

"I'm afraid—"

Flanders was very used to the pivot, the transfer, the brush-off.

"Please, Ms.—"

"Sheldon."

Good. She still's talking.

"Ms. Sheldon, Mr. Reilly performed incredible heroics in Washington.

He saved lives at the risk of his own. He was the first to act and directed others to help. Military officers. First responders. He acted like someone in command."

Flanders waited for push back. There wasn't any.

"Ms. Sheldon, ten minutes with your boss on the phone. Please. I'm certain the Kensington Royal Corporation is proud of him."

"We are."

An admission. Good. Still engaged.

"There are people who are alive today because of him."

"It's not the first time," Brenda volunteered.

Another admission. An opening.

"I can believe that." Changing gears now, Flanders tried for the closer. "How's tomorrow. I can fly in from—"

"I'm sorry Ms. Flanders, he's currently out of the—."

Sheldon stopped short of explaining where. Flanders filled in the sentence herself.

"Of course. Will you at least let him know I phoned and I'm able to connect with him wherever he is?"

Flanders gave her cell and office numbers and heard Sheldon's typing again. She concluded with, "Thank you for your help, Ms. Sheldon. I'll call back tomorrow."

"That won't be necessary. I'll get back to you."

Savannah Flanders hung up knowing three things. Brenda Sheldon would pass along the request. Dan Reilly was already out of the country. And he was the real deal.

"Mike," she said. "Pull up the list of the KR properties in Europe."

"Gotta be about twenty," the reporter said.

"Then we're going to check all twenty and see where this Daniel J. Reilly is staying."

LONDON

Reilly looked at the incoming text message from Bob Heath. One word; one word that showed Heath had come to the same horrible possibility

Reilly considered. A president's name, but not a president. A location, but more than a location. A facility, but beyond most comprehension. A modern marvel nine decades old.

Hoover.

25

HENDERSON, NEVADA

LATE THAT NIGHT

Harper parked in a lot adjacent to a Denny's on West Warm Springs Road. He went to the restaurant every eighth day at precisely 2 a.m. and always ordered a Grand Slam—two pancakes, two eggs over easy, two bacon strips, two sausage links, and a side order of hash browns. Part of a routine. Never fully eaten, but enough to bide his time for an hour. Just an hour. Never longer.

He sat at a table in the far corner, which was usually open. If it wasn't, he took seat at the counter and placed his coffee cup upside down. A signal.

So far, he'd been met twice, but only when he was at the booth. On both occasions it was the same person. The first time was five months prior. The second just a month ago. He didn't know if tonight would be another one of those nights.

It was.

Harper saw the oncoming car lights reflected in the restaurant window. A vehicle slowed, rolled into the lot, and parked. Then nothing for two minutes. Two minutes exactly. When the door to the restaurant opened, Harper caught sight of a dark-haired man. Medium height. Blank face. Mixed ethnicity. He wore a tight-fitting black t-shirt, black jeans, black laced-up boots, and a Los Angeles Rams cap.

The man ignored empty seats close to the entrance, taking a booth where he would be back-to-back with Harper.

Harper was a third of the way through his Grand Slam. The other man ordered an egg white omelet.

"You've taken to the food," the man whispered after five minutes of silence.

"I've learned to like it," Harper replied softly.

"The smell is offensive." Harper ignored the comment.

Another minute passed.

"Be ready," the man finally said.

"I am. When?"

"When I tell you." A chill went through Harper. He felt the time would be soon.

And that was the end of the discussion.

Angie Peterson, the young waitress on the graveyard shift, came by the two tables and offered coffee. Harper nodded politely. The other customer waved his hand over his cup indicating *no*.

Peterson remembered him and how uncomfortable he made her feel, then and now. Not because he looked like a foreigner of some sort or that he was a terrible tipper. It was his manner: cold, calculating, dangerous. He always took the seat that backed up to her regular. And they seemed to trade conversation in whispers. *What was that all about?*

Peterson had another passing thought. Not so strange considering she lived in the land of conspiracy theories. All around were people caught up in UFO intrigue, mind-altering government microwave blasts, black helicopters, spy satellites, and ghosts. But she let the idea fade away. *No one needed another wild idea.*

She smiled at egg white man and put the check down, expecting little back.

TICONDEROGA, NEW YORK

THE SAME TIME

Some fifty-two hundred people lived in the small town in the Adirondack Mountains, where Lake George and Lake Champlain converge. Citizens welcomed the 100,000-plus tourists during the warm weather months and mostly kept to themselves as the thermometer dipped down in winter.

The historic importance of Fort Ticonderoga during the American Revolution was not lost on the community. It had been strategically built between the Hudson River, controlled by the British, and the French-controlled St. Lawrence River. At times it was under the French rule, then British. The patriotic Green Mountain Boys took it back, then sent fort cannons to Boston to help repel a British attack, but in June 1777 it fell into British hands again. In 1781, the British abandoned Fort Ticonderoga; thereafter it lay unused until bought by a family, and ultimately restored and turned into a tourist attraction.

Today the fort represents the indefatigable American spirit. Individualism and patriotism. Politics in the area have been traditionally bluer than red, but the voices are a blend, colored by the rich history of the area. The region was home to people plugged into the news and others who lived off the grid. Ticonderoga was also home to Franklin W. Wrightman, a national talk-radio host who broadcast out of his home, yet influenced the narrative across the nation.

"Frank Talk Today, America. The country is under attack. And left or right, center or fringe, this is time to test our mettle. Our infrastructure has been hit. What are we to do? Our citizens killed. What are we to do? Our nerves frayed. What are we to do?"

Wrightman loved stirring the pot. His listeners counted on it.

"It's been days since Washington. Days since New York. Days since St. Louis. And so far, we've heard nothing but platitudes from the president. I ask you, is this the president we want at a time of crisis? Is silence the response we deserve? I don't see the skies filled with military jets. Do you? I don't hear our phones beeping with national alerts. Do you? I can't feel the ground shaking with our boys' boots on the ground.

Can you? We might as well just say it. Killers, welcome to America. Take what you want, roam the country, because we're not going to do a damned thing to stop you!"

Frank Wrightman was like so many others on the radio: a rabble-rouser and an entertainer. Far more noisy than newsy. He hadn't voted in years but complained about the electorate. He spoke for the *everybodys* and the *nobodys,* but lived the life of a phenomenally wealthy *somebody*.

He claimed he used the airwaves to responsibly inform. *Incite* was more accurate. And the news of the past few days gave him enough to fuel the fire for weeks, maybe longer. He went after President Crowe, stoking fear and anxiety. He also made it very clear this was not the time to get into any problems in nations we couldn't spell, couldn't point to on a map, and had no real use for.

"I've got frank talk. But I'll tell you one person who probably won't listen. The man in the White House. He's got nothing and he's running on empty. Now, let's take some calls."

"Hello, Franklin. First time caller, long time listener."

Wrightman rang a bell.

"Go ahead, newbie."

"I live up north in Maine. Should have brought this up at the time. Kind of figured it wasn't anything, but now—"

"Uh huh, uh huh," Wrightman said, seemingly either not interested or otherwise distracted.

"Well, I'm a trucker for…" he paused. "I don't think I should say the company."

"Okay. Where are you going with this?"

"Right, right. I'm sorry. Little nervous. But Maine, New Hampshire and Vermont's my territory. Nighttime hauls for morning deliveries. And a few months ago, I was driving along Maine State Highway 1 in Aroostook County and I could've sworn I saw something."

"This isn't a UFO show, caller. I can recommend—"

"I'm not talking about that. And it's only because of the news that's out. I just don't know what to do."

Wrightman was getting impatient.

"You've got a minute before I have to go for a commercial."

"Okay, okay. Sorry. I was driving along Maine State Highway 1."

"We have that."

"It was dark, but against some northern lights, damned if there weren't black parachutes floating down."

"Hold on," the talk show host said. "Parachuting into…?"

"Not into, but near Limestone. Limestone, Maine. I'm just sayin'—"
Franklin Wrightman seized on the declaration.

"Let me get this straight. You think—"

"Not think, I saw parachutes," the caller demanded. "Now who parachutes in the dark near the border with Canada? I mean if Limestone was still an Air Force base, I'd get it. But they shut that down years ago. Never should have, but they did. You know what I think, Franklin?"

"Say it."

"Maybe they were some of those terrorists who attacked us. That's what I think. They had to infiltrate somehow."

"Stay on the line. We need to talk more."

26

LONDON

THE NEXT MORNING

Marnie Babbitt rose and showered before Reilly. Reilly sat up in bed admiring the beautiful woman who came out of the bathroom naked, but fully made up. Now, for his pleasure, she sensually slipped on a green high-neck ribbed midi dress that she'd stashed in her Coach tote bag. It accentuated her curves perfectly.

"Sure you don't want to take a later train to Paris?" she asked demurely.

"Can't." Reilly's legs were stretched out—the sheets covered him, but didn't hide his interest. "I wish. But can't."

"Too bad."

Babbitt folded her previous day's dress in her bag and came to the side of the bed.

"Bye, sweetheart," she said. She lingered over him for a moment, inhaled the scents from the night before and kissed him. It was a nice kiss, but hardly the kind of kiss that really reinforced *'too bad.'* Reilly sensed something was wrong.

"What's the matter?"

"Nothing. Everything," she said. "It just gets harder leaving you."

"Me too, you."

"I worry. And I wish… I wish you would let me into your world more."

He closed his eyes and smiled, but didn't answer. Marnie brought her fingers to her lips, kissed them and placed them on Reilly's. Then she left his hotel room.

Thirty minutes later, Reilly was also downstairs and in the lobby checking out.

"I hope we'll see you again soon, Mr. Reilly," said the young man on the desk who completed the process. Reilly recalled meeting him but had to look at his nametag.

"Jonathan. Of course, I'll be back. Thank you. In the meantime, keep our guests happy."

With exciting memories top of mind, Jonathan smiled. "Yes, sir. The most important part of the job."

Jonathan diverted his eyes, looking across the lobby to the woman sitting alone at a table sipping a latte. Maria Pudovkin. She caught his smile. By force of habit, Reilly naturally followed his eye contact. He turned and looked over his shoulder. Some twenty feet away was a woman of unparalleled beauty who was looking in his direction. Perhaps at Jonathan.

Reilly smiled inward. *A striking woman in a hotel. Things happen.* He'd been there, too. In fact, that's how he met Marnie Babbitt—in a hotel in Tehran. *Yup, things happen.*

Reilly took a cab to London's St. Pancras railway station. He arrived with forty minutes to spare before his scheduled 10:24 a.m. Eurostar train. The two-hour-and-twenty-three-minute ride through the Chunnel was due to put him in Paris's Gare du Nord station at 1347, or 1:47 p.m. After that, a quick €15 cab to the hotel.

Reilly grabbed a coffee from a kiosk just as he heard the first call to board. Halfway to the Business Class car his phone rang. He rested his paper coffee cup on his suitcase and read the display identifying the incoming call. A 202 area code with a prefix he recognized: the FBI.

"Let me guess," Reilly began. "Agent Moore."

"Expecting my call?"

"Disappointed if you hadn't. What's up?"

Moore avoided the question. Instead he asked, "Where are you?"

"On the way to Paris. About to get on the train."

"Got ten minutes?"

"Sure. Talk while I walk." He chucked the nearly full coffee cup in a nearby trashcan, pulled his suitcase and listened.

"No, find a place that's quiet," Moore said.

"Really?"

"Really."

Dan Reilly left the station altogether, certain he'd miss his scheduled train to Paris. He settled on a park bench at neighboring St. Pancras Gardens.

"Okay, Moore. Thanks for making me miss my train."

"Don't worry. There's another in, what, an hour or so?"

"You know, you suck."

"Been told. But enough about me. I need your advice on a couple of things."

Reilly was actually surprised. He leaned back, watched children running with unbounded energy, pigeons pecking for whatever crumbs they could find, and squirrels chasing each other through the grass.

"Go," he said.

"What's your experience tell you about how the perps entered the U.S.?"

Between Heath and Moore, he was beginning to feel like the man who memorized all the secrets in Alfred Hitchcock's *The 39 Nine Steps*.

"Probably more your strong suit, Moore," Reilly said. "And DHS."

"Just give me your top-line thinking. You're a bad guy and want to come into the US. How would you do it?"

Reilly audibly exhaled.

"Multiple ways. Land, sea, and air. On land, I guess I'd be a sleeper, hiding in plain sight and waiting. Maybe legitimately moving up through the system; better jobs, more responsibility. Classic Cold War stuff. Probably with a seemingly legitimate reason for being here. By sea, possibly at night on fast cigarette boats from Cuba or Haiti or…" he thought for a moment, "Daytime. Connect with a fishing boat. Meet in international waters. Bribe someone. A lobster catch off New England. A blue marlin craft along the Southeast. Not so difficult. Or small subs in areas not patrolled by the Coast Guard. That's pretty much thousands of miles of shore. They might come in on a tanker, lowered at night, approach submerged, drop off operatives, and return to the mother ship. Completely possible."

"And air?" the FBI agent asked.

"It's fairly easy to come in on commercial flights under real or stolen passports. But why take the chance of ICE taking me out of the game with false papers? So, I'd pose as a student or a foreign businessman."

"Okay, think more out of the box now. Movie shit. How would you sneak in?"

"Come on, Moore, you've got better minds than me to work this out."

"I've got *you*."

"Movie shit?"

"Right."

"Okay. Large stretches are unpatrolled even though we have a radar bubble that covers almost everywhere. The Mexican border is blanketed with commercial and military radar. Canada, too, but—"

"But what, Reilly?"

"Denser woods, ways to drop in."

"Meaning?"

"Low flying planes under the radar, rising quickly, for a short, fast parachute jump, then out of there."

"Bingo."

"Bingo?"

Moore read from a transcript of a caller on an overnight radio show. "We're questioning the guy today."

"So why did you even need me to go through all this?" Reilly asked.

"Affirmation. Because you think like them."

"Which doesn't mean I'm one of them."

"You're off my list."

"Well I can sleep easier."

"That's one thing I bet you don't do. But there's something else."

"Oh?"

"We got a call from a woman who lives about an hour south of D.C. Chester, Virginia. She was passed from one agent to another, right up the ladder. Ultimately to me. Smart. Hard working. Apparently juggling a few jobs to pay for school. One of them is at a motel where she's a housekeeper. Following me so far, Reilly?"

"Completely, and you're about to tell me she found something."

"Yes I am, and yes, she did. Wanna take a guess?"

"Hotel room. Housekeeping. Something in the room trash. Packaging, wire shavings. No, probably batteries."

"Jesus," the FBI agent declared. "Close."

"Battery packaging."

"Damn right."

27

KIEV, UKRAINE

THE SAME TIME

Three thousand of Kiev's citizens crammed into *Maidan Nezalezhnosti*, or Independence Square. They stood on the six fountains dedicated to legendary brothers Schek, Horiv, Kie, and sister Libed, who, according to Ukrainian legend, chose the location for the town's foundation and named it in honor of Kie. Others hung onto Independence Column, adorned with a statue of Archangel Mikhail, viewed as the patron saint of Kiev.

Under Soviet control, protests were not permitted in what was then called October Revolution Square. It was expanded after World War II with ample room for Ukrainian troops under Russian rule to parade and display their military hardware—purposefully staged to keep people mindful of the authoritarian rule.

That changed with the overthrow of Communist leader Mykola Plaviuk in 1992. But even since then, independence has meant different things to different people. There were handmade posters warning of the proximity of Russian troops, fascist banners with varying versions of a "Ukraine for Ukrainians" slogan. College-aged activists from the left called for the president to resign, while the right-wing working class demonstrated for lower gas prices. Gay and lesbian protesters had their chants. Women's groups, theirs. Everyone was nervous.

More people poured into the square by the hour. Speakers shouted through bullhorns in different quadrants. On the fringes, jeers turned into shouting, and innocent scuffling devolved into shoving. Still, things might have remained calm had it not been for the pro-Russian protestors that entered the square from three different directions.

Bottles and rocks flew. Molotov cocktails exploded. Protesters scattered as best they could, but there was little room to run. Some made it to the Trade Union Association Office, others flooded into the square's cafes and shops. Those who could stormed into the hotels along the square, including the Kensington Kiev International.

No one knew where the first bullets came from, but they came, and people fell. A student with no real political position who went just to be part of the protest with her boyfriend. An Uber driver who advocated for lower gas prices, a liberal priest, a pregnant teen, a German newspaper reporter. All dead within the first minute. The police moved in, but not soon enough, and without enough firepower.

The screams fanned through the buildings and shops. Cries for help in multiple languages were drowned out by helicopters, sirens, explosions, and gunshots.

People around the world watched amateur livestreaming footage on YouTube, Instagram and other portals. International news organizations picked up a feed from 24 TV, a Ukrainian news channel. Telecasts from Europe to the United States ran title cards reading "Breaking News," "Riot in Ukraine," and "Independence Square War Zone," as anchors waited for facts to follow. Russian TV added another: "Russian Loyalists Killed in Kiev."

* * *

Dan Reilly returned to St. Pancras. He bought a sandwich, a new cup of black coffee and a copy of the *Guardian*. For thirty minutes he bided his time in the waiting room, looking up from the paper to a TV monitor. Considering the number of times a day CNN ran "Breaking News" title cards, the words had relatively little meaning. Reilly, like most people, was desensitized. But when he saw video of rioting in what he recognized was Kiev's Independence Square, and then read the lower third descriptions confirming the fact, he tossed out his sandwich and his second untouched coffee and walked closer to the monitor while pulling his overnighter.

One camera panned the square. Reilly saw his company's hotel in the background, the Kiev International, undamaged but clearly in the danger zone.

He pulled out his phone, found a number in his contacts and dialed. His call to Stephan Lazlo at the hotel went to voicemail. Reilly left a message and followed it with a text. That's when the boarding announcement came for his second train to Paris. He began walking toward the platform when his phone rang. It was a specific ringtone that only sounded when Edward Jefferson Shaw called: the first eight bars of the Grateful Dead's classic *Truckin'*. He'd chosen it because Shaw often called with an urgent change of plans.

PART TWO

TRIP WIRE

28

KENSINGTON RÊVE HOTEL

PARIS, FRANCE

1915 HOURS

"*Bonjour, monsieur,*" the doorman said to the well-dressed man walking up to the hotel entrance. He carried a folded copy of the day's *Les Échos,* the city's business newspaper.

He returned the greeting, "*Merci,*" and nodded politely. Before entering he waited for a departing guest to come through the revolving doors. All polite. The mark of a gentleman.

Inside, he casually took in his surroundings. Louis XIV. Polished oak walls, marble floor, mirrors and chandeliers. Regal. Luxurious. He also noted the locations of surveillance cameras at the far corners and a dome in the middle. He was in plain sight of the guards, a sign of the heightened security across the continent.

The man looked like he belonged at the Kensington Rêve. A visitor checking in on a nice summer afternoon. Paris had been quiet for nearly a year. No terrorist attacks. The dangers on the Russian border must have seemed a lifetime away to the other patrons.

He relaxed at a table in the lobby. A waitress asked if he would like anything to drink.

"*Café au lait,*" he said. When it came, he let it sit without touching it. He wouldn't. Fingerprints.

The man alternated leafing through the pages of his newspaper with watching people milling about at the front desk, waiting for elevators, and crossing to the lobby bar. His main focus was on the entrance some 20 meters away.

Twenty-five minutes after he sat down, a tall businessman emerged through the revolving door and caught his attention. *A bit under two meters tall. Approximately 82 kilograms. Muscular. Black hair closely cropped.*

Four mental boxes checked.

Aware of his surroundings. Purposeful. Certain of his steps, where he was going, why he was there.

Three more boxes checked.

Now closer scrutiny as the man approached.

Tailored dark business suit. Crisp dark shirt. No tie.

The man he was waiting for, the American hotel executive, typically wore a tie. *But apparently not today*, he thought. Anyway, it didn't matter. He still checked three more mental boxes.

Confirmed.

He casually folded his newspaper in half and in half again. Now he smoothly slipped his holstered Sig Sauer 9mm pistol between the pages and deftly screwed on a suppressor. In one move, he rose and scanned for anyone who could get in his way. *No one.*

Calculating a direct twelve-step intercept, he crossed the lobby and advanced. *Ten seconds.* Just as he had practiced.

At step eleven, with a friendly, unassuming voice, the man said, "Reilly? Dan Reilly?"

The executive turned, smiled and began to respond.

The gunman lifted the newspaper with his left hand, his finger on the trigger with his right.

"Excuse me—"

The assassin smiled. Something he liked to do. It made it more interesting.

Pop, pop, pop. He put three bullets point blank into the man's heart. Three shots that entered and exited so cleanly that they lodged into the oak wall thirty feet away almost in a row.

The suppressor cut down the noise, but didn't eliminate it. Predictably, cell phones went up and began to record the scene. But in the confusion, within the four seconds it took people to react, the assassin—his mission completed—stepped outside the field of view and was through the manual door, politely held open by the same doorman who had welcomed him in. No one captured his image.

29

NEW YORK

TWO HOURS LATER

"Christ!" Blowen exclaimed. The reporter pulled away from his computer terminal.

Savannah Flanders was on a phone interview. She shushed her colleague.

Blowen gave her a cut sign and gestured for her to hang up. Flanders cradled the phone between her head and shoulder and mouthed, "I can't."

"Yes, you can," he whispered. He pantomimed "Goodbye."

Flanders had another follow-up question but said, "I'm sorry, Senator Davidson, I've been flagged into an urgent meeting." She flashed a dirty look at Blowen. "I'll reschedule with your office."

After her obligatory thank you, she hung up and began chastising Blowen.

"You know how long I've been trying to get him on the phone for a statement about Reilly's appearance at his committee."

"This is more important. Reuters just broke a story about your boy."

"What boy?"

"Reilly."

"What about Reilly?"

"He was shot in Paris."

Her eyes widened. Her jaw dropped open. Suddenly she wasn't concerned about getting a sound bite from the U.S. senator Dan Reilly had sparred with in a subcommittee hearing. Flanders rolled her chair around to Blowen's computer as he pointed to his screen.

"In the lobby of one of his own hotels."

Flanders read the headline and shook her head.

INTERNATIONAL EXEC KILLED IN PARIS HOTEL LOBBY

CHICAGO

THE SAME TIME

CEO Lou Tiano's secretary answered the call from the Paris Rêve general manager.

"This is Richard Korn," the French executive began. "I need Mr. Tiano."

"Mr. Korn. Mr. Tiano is in conference." She didn't explain it was the Chicago Crisis Committee discussing domestic procedures. But she did hear some urgency in his voice.

"It's about Mr. Reilly."

"Certainly, but he can call you back at the Réve when he's free."

"Now, for God's sake!"

"If you can give me more information."

"Good lord, woman! There's been a shooting at my property."

Up to this point, Leigh had been writing on a call sheet. She stopped and stuttered.

"Wh…what if I get Mr. Reilly for you in the meantime? I think I can—"

"You don't understand! It was Reilly! Reilly was shot! Now get Tiano!"

Carol Leigh gasped. "Yes, sir. Hold please." She tore down the hall as best she could in heels, knocked on the door of the large conference room, barged in, and signaled for her boss to come.

"Excuse me," he said to the team. He rose.

"Carol, we're deep into…"

Leigh said breathlessly, "Mr. Korn is on the phone from Paris. He's calling about Mr. Reilly. Something horrible has happened. He's been shot."

Tiano ran to his office, faster than he'd moved in years.

PARIS
THE SAME TIME

The Police Nationale took control of the crime scene and began to take statements from eyewitnesses. They were joined by a team from the Direction Générale de la Sécurité Intérieure, the General Directorate for Internal Security, and representatives from France's other intelligence and military agencies.

Investigators were already reviewing CCTV videos from security computer hard drives. The police believed that the attack was premeditated. Witnesses claimed the assassin sought out a man named Dan Reilly. The killer waited for the opportunity and fired point blank. Three shots.

Within a half-hour of the shooting, the French teams had reviewed clear video of the perpetrator, pulled still frames, and emailed them to law enforcement databases around the world.

30

In the minutes immediately after the assassin left Kensington Rêve, he walked into Hema, a department store four short blocks away on Rue Rambuteau. He made his way to the men's room, chose the middle stall, locked the door, and in order he took off his jacket and tie, his holster, and his white dress shirt, leaving on a short-sleeved black t-shirt. One part of his identity erased. Next, he turned his coat inside out, taking it from black to blue with arm patches. He removed his black hairpiece revealing a shaved head, put on tortoiseshell glasses from an inside jacket pocket, and from the same pocket extracted and extended a collapsible cane. He bundled his white shirt under his arm, tucked his wig in his back pocket, put his holster and jacket back on, flushed the toilet, and unlocked the door. He was now a different man, a good fifteen years older.

Before leaving the men's room, he took off his gloves and stuffed them into his jacket pocket. Outside he gave people something to ignore: a man with a limp. No one paid attention to him; people were wondering about all the sudden police activity in the 4th *arrondissement*.

* * *

Surveillance cameras showed that the killer never took his gloves off. No fingerprints. He ordered a drink, but didn't touch it. No DNA. He was given a check but failed to pay it. No signature on a credit card. The initial conclusion was a hit: planned, calculated and personal. But the more the Paris police and French intelligence examined the crime scene and took statements, the more they adjusted their thinking. A hit gone bad.

* * *

Around the corner, the assassin retrieved a late-model Peugeot that was parked exactly where he was told it would be. He found the key in a metal box, attached to the driver-side wheel-well. Three days' worth of clothes needing washing were in a suitcase in the trunk. A backpack held more clothes and a receipt from Hotel Bastille Spéria, under the name Markus Visser, a Dutch teacher on holiday. His current identity. He left it all earlier before he donned his businessman disguise. Now, as he merged into traffic, he was certain his work was already leading the news. He began whistling a Russian folk song his parents had taught him, and headed to the A1 toward Belgium. Two hours and fifteen minutes later, he would say goodbye to his short-lived Visser identity, become somebody else, and return to his isolated home in Norway.

31

LONDON

HEATHROW AIRPORT

The phone rang.

"Hello."

"Well, you sound damn good for a dead man."

"What?" Dan Reilly asked.

"You don't know?" Kensington security Chief Alan Cannon asked.

"What? Know what? Just got to Heathrow. Shaw rerouted me to Caracas. It's the long way around to Kiev, where I should be going."

"Christ, Dan. You really haven't heard."

"I'm about to board. Just tell me."

"A few hours ago, a man who was taken for you was shot and killed at the Rêve in Paris."

"Oh my God!" Reilly stepped out of line. "I was supposed to be there."

"Right, and somebody counted on that." Cannon went through the details of the attack, working up to the victim.

"They haven't released his name yet. Unfortunately for him, he fit your height, your build, your hair color, your basic look, and the time you were due in. The killer brazenly walked up behind the guy thinking he was you. He called your name. The man automatically turned, as most people would to explain the mistake, and tap-tap-tap, three shots through the heart. The assassin escaped during the confusion. So, Dan," Cannon summarized, "who wants you dead?" He had a second, more pressing question ready when Reilly didn't immediately answer.

"And who knew where you were going?"

* * *

Who? As he stood in line to board his flight, he considered the list. Not many people knew his immediate travel plans. Certainly he was in the KR computer system, but with recent security upgrades hacking was infinitely more difficult. Not impossible, but definitely more difficult.

Reilly thought about everyone who would have known. *Brenda Sheldon. Members of the London crisis committee. Agent Moore at the FBI, but only shortly before he was due to go. Korn and his staff in Paris. Lou Tiano in Chicago. Who else knew? The corporate travel department? The London crisis committee. ...Who?*

The gate attendant announced his flight was ready to board. He stepped forward and rolled his suitcase alongside. Reilly suddenly stopped. People maneuvered around him.

There was another.

32

LONDON

News spread quickly and Brenda Sheldon was tasked with fielding calls from inside and outside the KR corporate community, including Dan's ex-wife, Pam. Sheldon told everyone the same thing.

"I don't know anything more than what you've probably already heard. A gunman in the lobby. The police are investigating." She held it together as best she could, even through a second conversation with the *New York Times* reporter, who dialed in on her way to JFK.

Sheldon was exhausted. She didn't think she could handle another call. But the phone was ringing again. It had a caller ID that shook her. Her voice trembled.

"Yes?" Not hello.

"Brenda."

Her heart skipped a beat.

"Dan? Dan, you're—."

"Alive. Yes."

Sheldon burst into tears. Reilly consoled her.

"Look, I don't have a lot of time. I'm about to take off for Caracas. Shaw rerouted me. It saved my life."

"Thank God."

In the minutes that followed, he explained that he had only recently learned what happened. He expressed true regret that someone had died in his place. That made his next question all the more urgent.

"Think carefully about this, Brenda. Who knew where I was going? Who did you tell?" She didn't need time to think.

"No one on the outside. Corporate had your schedule. There's a reporter trying to track you down, but you know I don't disclose any information like that without your permission."

"What's her name?"

"Flanders. Savannah Flanders. She's probably gone onto another story."

Reilly didn't think so. He could be more newsworthy now. Especially now.

"No one else?"

"No."

They talked about the calls that had come in after and those she made proactively. Colleagues, friends, and Reilly's ex-wife.

"Has Marnie called in?"

"Ms. Babbitt," Brenda replied, more formally. "Not yet. What can I do?"

"Call people back. Let them know you heard on the news that it wasn't me. But you haven't heard why. Also, you don't know where I am. Just keep a list of who phones and why."

Reilly thanked Brenda again and hung up, debating what he'd say to Marnie. He had to call her. Their relationship was growing. But...

* * *

As he thought about it, Reilly's life was filled with "buts." *But I have to cancel dinner tonight. But I have a late meeting again. But my flight is in two hours. But the office is on the other line. But I know I promised.* Each had cost him another part of his marriage. Each had cost him relationships since.

Marnie Babbitt also lived out of a suitcase. She logged hundreds of thousands of air miles a year. They met up in exotic locales. They ate in five-star restaurants. They tumbled into beds in grand hotels. And with it all came another *but*. There was nothing in their relationship that had any semblance of normality. And now with the assassination attempt, he feared he could put her life in danger. All of this was on his mind as he dialed.

"Hello," she shivered, looking at the caller ID.

"Marnie, it's me."

Utter silence followed. Two seconds. Three, four and five.

"Marnie, I'm okay."

"What? How?"

"I was expected in Paris but didn't make it. Lucky, I guess."

More silence until she finally said, "God, Dan, up until a half-minute ago—" She let the words trail off. Babbitt sounded as if she was crying.

"You could have called sooner."

"I only found out a few minutes ago. After all, who would notify a dead man that he was dead?

"Don't you dare joke!"

"I'm sorry."

"So, where are you?"

He decided to make up an answer. He wasn't even sure why.

"I'm not supposed to say."

"Says who?"

"Not supposed to say that either."

"It's me. Where are you? I want to come see you."

"Marnie, someone knew where I was headed." He stopped before asking the hardest question. "Did you tell anyone?"

"Dan..."

"Did you discuss my schedule with anyone?"

"No. No, of course not. Why would I?" Reilly had no reply. Just a nagging thought.

"I'm sorry, honey. It's probably the same questions police will ask. And I'm asking everyone."

"Are you in London?"

"Can't say."

"Even to me?"

"I'm sorry." He heard a long, exasperated breath.

"Then call me. Every day. Every single day. Promise me."

"I will."

There was another long pause.

"Be careful," she said softly. "Promise."

"I promise."

33

SUMMERLIN, NEVADA

"Mr. Harper, have a seat. Some people want to talk with you."

Richard Harper nodded to his supervisor and acknowledged the two suits in the office.

"This is FBI Agent Ronald Brown and Homeland Security Agent Nancy Sugarman."

Brown stood six-two. He looked like a man who had been beaten up a number of times and vowed never to be taken down again. Sugarman was younger. Not quite a rookie, but still learning the ropes. She remained a half-step behind Brown.

Richard Harper studied them both. They looked the part. *Intent. Grim. Armed, at least Brown. No, both.* Nonetheless, he forced a smile. It didn't seem appropriate to shake hands.

"We're not just here for a visit," Brown said. "We're putting this facility on high alert."

"Good," Harper quickly volunteered. He exhaled a silent breath of relief. "Considering the news back east, I'm grateful."

"We'll need a walk through, Mr. Harper. All the ways in. Vulnerable operational points."

"Of course."

"Richard knows the facility like the back of his hand," the supervisor said. "Ask him anything."

"Absolutely," Harper said. "We can start at the control center."

"Thank you," Sugarman replied.

Harper led them out. There were places he definitely wanted them to see and others he purposefully would keep off the tour.

WASHINGTON, D.C.
WHITE HOUSE SITUATION ROOM

President Alexander Crowe entered last. He took the seat facing the largest of the four mounted television screens in the secure basement facility that was wired to the rest of the world. The Situation Room was relatively small, not at all as depicted by most Hollywood productions. Tight quarters where presidents before him had watched real-time, live video attacks against Al Qaeda, monitored riots in the US, and made fateful decisions about North Korea's submarine fleet.

"Ladies, gentlemen."

Facing Crowe around the long table were FBI Director Reese McCafferty, CIA Director Gerald Watts, National Security Advisor Pierce Kimball, Secretary of State Elizabeth Matthews, and Homeland Security Director Runetta Adams. The greetings back were equally formal.

"Mr. President."

"Reese, start us off."

"Thank you, Mr. President." FBI Director McCafferty stood to the right of the largest monitor in the room. There were many. He pressed the remote and a PowerPoint title card appeared.

Federal Bureau of Investigation

Preliminary Findings in the Attack on US Infrastructure

It was dated and marked Top Secret.

McCafferty thanked Director Watts for the CIA's cooperation, and noted the speed at which everyone in the investigation chain moved. As he narrated, he clicked through the slides.

"Here's what we've determined to date. Multiple teams, working off one coordinated game plan, which indicates this was complex at every level. From start to finish. And we have no reason to believe we are at the finish.

"Beginning with D.C. We've raised the trucks from the Potomac and pulled VIN numbers. They were rented in Wheeling, West Virginia two weeks ago. Plates switched. Stolen off trucks in long-term parking in Salt Lake City. That speaks to the reach of the organization. Not so coincidentally, the cameras at the rental office went out the day before. No video of the renters. Another indication of the scope and sophistication. The credit card used for the rental was stolen from a man in hospice in Tampa and not missed by the family. Thanks to a heads up from a housekeeper, we're working on evidence that placed the team in a motel in Chester, Virginia the night before. That's where we believe they wired and armed the bombs. We pulled fingerprints from discarded battery packages found by the housekeeper. They're being run now. We're also running the packaging to see where the batteries were purchased and if there were active CCTV cameras at that location. Given the numbers of batteries, we're hoping they came from a single store but if not, we might still be able to pick up the trail."

NSA Advisor Kimball raised his hand.

"Can we hold questions for now, Mr. President?" McCafferty requested. I want to cover our initial findings, then Director Watts and I will answer everything to the best of our knowledge after."

Crowe nodded and Kimball dropped his hand.

"Next, the St. Louis attack. The Kawasaki Jet Ski used in the escape was discovered upstream. Burned. We were able to trace it to a vacation rental in Miami. According to the field report, a man took it out for an hour and never returned. The credit card used was stolen from another hospice patient at the same facility as the first. Pretty damned smart. We're looking at sign-ins at the facility and having all patients and their families account for their credit cards. If this is their MO, we might get lucky and be able to flag a purchase as it's happening. We've also contacted all hotels and motels within a 100-mile radius of St. Louis to check on discarded battery packaging like those recovered in Virginia. Navy divers are looking for bomb parts. But the Mississippi is still muddy from spring rains and, as we know, it flows extremely fast. Confidence is low that we'll retrieve much there.

"Three, the self-driving vehicles in the Lincoln Tunnel. They were running on Chinese software."

"China?" the president interrupted. "A connection?"

"Not necessarily. The system used is on the open market, sold to car manufacturers in Italy and Germany and already showing up in the aftermarket. The guidance could have come from there or been bought and sold many times over. We'll be tracing whatever we can. Of course, we're looking for forensic signatures including latent fingerprints, traces of perspiration or other natural secretions on the steering wheel, the doors, the radio, wherever. We're also examining security footage at restaurants and stores in Chester, Virginia, developing composite sketches from motel eyewitnesses, reviewing CCTV footage in the target areas, and we have another important lead."

Everyone hung on McCafferty's next words.

"Director Watts, you can take it from here." The CIA chief rose and began in a deliberate monotone.

"We now believe a team parachuted into the United States more than two months ago. Northeast Maine at the Canadian border. A trucker spotted them, but only reported it well after the attacks. We're backtracking now with air traffic control, but we can definitely confirm that a private flight out of Edmundston, Canada went below radar on the Canadian side as it approached the town of Limestone, Maine, then quickly rose high enough for a short drop. The plane returned to the field. The pilot walked away. We're working with NAV Canada on identification. We have blurry CCTV images from Edmundston of the passengers, who claimed they were on a fishing trip. They never returned. They also intentionally avoided looking directly at security cameras and were not subject to CATSA, the Canadian version of TSA, search. We can't tie them to the attacks, but it makes the hairs on my back go up. It also suggests that more teams may have infiltrated the US in similar ways or come in through other soft entry points."

Crowe nodded.

"It's the opinion of the Agency that this was not domestic terrorism. This has the hallmarks of a deeply financed, well-prepared foreign operation. As Director McCafferty noted, the attacks were expertly coordinated and carried out. We're talking about a major international player; smart, with a bigger endgame than just creating havoc."

PITTSBURGH, PA

The assassin drove the route, checking for possible problems. So far, none. America was still an open society. *Fools,* he thought. It's the one thing he really couldn't comprehend. There was security, but no one seemed really worried. Even despite the earlier attacks, people were anxious for life to return to normal. Unlike in his country, in the U.S. trouble always seemed to happen to other people farther away. *Maybe it was because the country was diverse. Maybe because people didn't understand real suffering. Hunger. Poverty. Maybe because they didn't respect the rule of law. The rule of one. The rule of the leader.*

Well, he thought, *in a short time it will come home to millions of people here. What do they call it? City of Bridges. But not for long.*

SUMMERLIN, NEVADA

The FBI and Homeland Security agents finished their walkthrough of the Southern Nevada Water Authority's Intake Station No. 2 at the control station.

"Anything else?" Richard Harper asked.

"Nothing right now," Agent Brown replied. "Your security will be on duty 24/7?"

"We are a 24/7 facility, sir. We're never without eyes and ears, both human and—" he pointed up to a surveillance camera, "—electronic. No one goes in or out without being monitored."

"Including your hired security?"

"Including."

"We'll want everyone's names and Social Security numbers," the Homeland Security agent added.

Harper smiled. "Of course, but everyone has been vetted."

"Then we'll vet them again. Is anyone having marital difficulties? Financial problems? Drug or alcohol issues?"

"Not that I'm aware of, Agent Sugarman."

"Become aware. They're more susceptible to recruitment through blackmail. Notify us of anyone who shows unusual tendencies, a change in work habits, not making a shift, sudden illnesses, or interest in areas beyond their scope. They're all signals."

"Yes, sir," Harper replied. "But because of the operation here and the impact on Las Vegas and beyond, we maintain the highest possible standards."

"Raise them higher," Brown declared.

"Is there something you're not telling me?" Harper asked. "Do you suspect a problem here?"

"Just raise those standards higher. Oh, and we're going to augment your security detail."

Harper forced himself to nod approvingly. "Of course. Whatever you feel is necessary."

The agents left, and Harper was grateful they didn't know enough to ask to see some of the more sensitive areas of the facility.

34

PARIS, FRANCE

Savannah Flanders's French was good, thanks to the eighteen months she spent at the *New York Times*'s Paris bureau. Her time in the city also gave her entrée to police circles. She recognized an inspector talking to his officers at the Kensington Rêve.

"Chief Renard," she said walking up to him. "May I have a moment?"

The French police officer glanced at Flanders. He instantly recognized her and held up a finger. Flanders stepped back and patiently waited.

"My goodness, it's been…" He calculated how much time had passed. "Two years?"

"More like three," the reporter replied.

"We let time slip by too easily."

"We surely do."

"And so, a crime brings you back to Paris. Is there something you can share with me?"

"That's my question for you, Paul."

"No comment."

She filled in her own answer. "I'm inclined to think international. Reilly was in Washington on the bridge when it was bombed. He helped in the rescue. Days later he's shot in his company's hotel. That just doesn't happen."

Renard tilted his head to one side, taking in the information but saying nothing.

"Paul, you're holding back."

He still said nothing.

"Come on. Show a little love. Any leads on Reilly's killer? What does your surveillance video show? This has the feel of a calculated hit with a quick escape plan. That raises two possibilities: he crossed somebody in organized crime, and this was payback, or it's a government hit. But what government? In either case, it makes me wonder why anyone would have a contract out on a hotel executive, unless he was more than a hotel executive."

"That's a big jump, Savannah."

"Or not. Come on, show me a little love, inspector."

Renard looked left and right before stepping forward to whisper. "Give me your number."

Flanders fished out a business card from her back pocket. She said, "I want the story first."

"And piss off everyone in Paris?"

"You owe me. Remember I came to you about your department's collusion in the Louvre theft. I gave you a two-hour lead before breaking the story. Time for you to make your arrests."

"You're calling in the mark?"

"I am. Time to collect," Flanders said with self-assurance.

"Okay. Keep your phone handy."

"Always is."

Inspector Paul Renard waved *adieu.*

Savannah started for the exit but paused at the chalk outline on the floor. She'd seen them before, dozens of times. It always left her with the same queasy feeling. She walked around the gruesome outline. Arms flailed out; body crumpled. Dried blood on the left side, where his heart had come to a stop. She made mental notes for her article. Grim depictions of a crime that had taken a hero. Flanders wished she had met him.

She headed for the door. Time to check into a hotel. Not this one. And shower.

* * *

Flanders heard the phone as she was about to step into the shower. Blowen from New York. She inserted an iPod earpiece in her left ear.

"Hey there. What's up?" She turned the shower off, put on a hotel bathrobe, and crossed to a desk in the bedroom.

"Good news, bad news, interesting news."

"Bad news first," Flanders replied.

"Bad news it is. Most of Reilly's record is sealed."

"We knew that," she replied.

"Lt. Reilly's Army record, that is," Blowen continued. "But on the good news side, I've got bits and pieces from a source and even earlier history from a few calls I made to Boston, including the Boston Police."

"Police. He's got a record?"

"No, he got into a summer teen program at the Police Academy. His mother was a 911 operator. Apparently beloved. So, he had an open door to seeing how departmental branches worked, from the ballistics unit, to juvenile, harbor patrol, and the mounted unit. By the time he was through with high school, he'd earned a reputation as a crack shot."

"Was his father a cop?"

"No. Killed on a land mine while serving in the Army."

Flanders nodded. Blowen continued. "While in college in Boston, Reilly took a job as a security guard at the Prudential Center, a local office, apartment and shopping mall. Uniformed and all. I'm getting pictures. There was an entry that the Boston police had during his senior year. Reilly interrupted a robbery at the mall. Three men. He tried to take them on. A clobber on the head took him out of the fight. Another security officer found him and called 911. Here's a timely coincidence: his mother was on duty. He got help damned fast.

"Reilly gave a detailed description of the robbers. They were caught. He went back on the job, finished school and enrolled in the Army. Thanks to letters of commendation from the Chief of Police and his bosses, he was admitted into the twelve-week Officer Candidate School in Fort Benning, Georgia. After that, the Army sent him to the US

Army Intelligence Center and NETCOM, the U.S. Army Network Enterprise Technology Command at Fort Huachuca, just north of the Mexican border in Arizona. Secret shit. And because of that, I didn't get much of what goes on there. Then Reilly went to the Defense Language Institute at the Presidio in Monterey, California, for Russian and Farsi immersion classes. After that, Afghanistan. Whatever he did, most of it's sealed. But I tracked down one detail."

"Oh?" She was taking notes but feeling she'd be writing Reilly's obit instead of a feature article.

"He was decorated for valor, then he retired unceremoniously."

"Unceremoniously?"

"Picked a fight with some general, don't have the full story yet or his name. But it was bad enough for the general to go down and for Reilly to have to watch his back. So, he left, but went right into a State Department job. According to my source, he did bigtime research on potential terrorist attacks."

At that moment her phone vibrated. She looked at the caller ID. It was from a French cell.

"Hold, Mike," Flanders said to her colleague. "Call coming in." The reporter switched over and went from English to French.

"Flanders," she began.

"Because I like you and we're not having this conversation, you have thirty minutes before this goes out to wider."

"Thirty minutes? I gave you two hours. I can't do much in that time, even online."

"The world moves much quicker today, Savannah. Thirty minutes. Write fast."

Flanders turned the volume up on her earpiece. "Go," she said.

"Reilly," he paused to make sure she would follow him.

"Yes," She wrote Reilly's name on her pad and circled it.

"…wasn't the victim."

"Say that again."

"Mistaken identity. We're absolutely certain. The deceased is an

American businessman. But not Reilly."

"How long have you known this?"

"Long enough, but I couldn't tell you before. Had to wait until we notified the family in Connecticut, which we've done. I've called a press conference in thirty, now twenty-nine minutes. You have an anonymous source, so go write your story. If you want more, come back to the hotel and ask your questions with everyone else."

"One more question, Paul."

"One more."

"Where's Reilly now?"

"You're the reporter. Find out. We'd love to talk to him, too."

With that Flanders returned to Blowen with her news.

"Now I've got a bulletin for you."

35

CARACAS, VENEZUELA

THE NEXT AFTERNOON

EJ Shaw's mission for Reilly was urgent and in two parts. During his call, the company founder had not minced words.

"Given the political turmoil in Venezuela, we're ready to close down the Caracas Kensington Royal properties and arrange for the management to move to the Bogotá Hotel."

It had been Reilly's recommendation a month earlier, but now Shaw was prepared to pull the plug—and no matter how much Reilly objected, Shaw insisted that he go. Reilly asked if there were others who could go instead; Shaw said no.

"People trust you, Dan. It's your plan. Set it in motion."

The general managers at both hotels had been informed of the decision. Caracas was getting too dangerous for Chicago to guarantee the safety of guests, even if they upgraded to full Red Hotel status. It was the right decision, and was reinforced for Reilly by the military presence at the airport and the third-degree treatment he got at customs.

"Name."

It was clearly printed on his passport, but Reilly answered with no emotion.

Less is best. There was a time when he would have chatted up the officers on duty, but not today. Venezuela had slid further into Bolivar-esque autocratic rule; the United States was not a friend of the current administration (Russia, China, Cuba, and North Korea, however, were). The fundamental shift in alliances against the U.S. made the armed officer approach Reilly with intense suspicion. The feeling was mutual.

"Daniel J. Reilly."

The customs officer, probably 35 and politically indoctrinated (or just power-hungry), studied Reilly, his photograph, then Reilly again.

"Occupation and purpose of your visit," he said accusingly. If the officer was trying to throw Reilly, it didn't work. Reilly smiled politely and kept his eye contact directly on the man that separated him from his job and getting to Kiev, where he was really needed.

"Executive with the Kensington Royal Hotels. I'm here to visit the Kensington Caracas Vista."

The company had decided to remove the name *Royal* in the Kensington name. It didn't sit well with the ideology of the socialist regime.

"To visit? We struggle every day because of your sanctions, you seek to overturn our government. And yet you want to visit?" Reilly waited a beat before answering. It was his interrogation training; experience told him to respond in a non-threatening manner.

"A company visit, sir. To meet my general manager."

"I asked for what purpose. You answer with who. Again, what is your purpose at this critical time in our history?"

"Upgrades," Reilly said. It was a safe word. And it was true. Upgrades for security's sake, like the ones he hoped were working now in Ukraine.

"For whose benefit?" The customs officers waved his American passport but showed no sign of handing it back.

"For travelers, our guests. For local employees. For their safety. It's my job to check on our hotels around the world. We have two in Caracas."

"Not to spy on *República Bolivariana de Venezuela?*"

Reilly remained focused on the officer but still friendly, not challenging. Challenging could put him in jail.

"To meet with management and staff."

"After that?"

"On to Colombia to do the same in Bogotá." He considered adding that he'd just come from Europe but stopped. Again, *less is best*.

The guard realized he had no reason to hold the American and he wasn't even having fun taunting him. Running out of questions he asked, "How many days, American?"

"No more than two."

"Two," the custom officer responded. "You are to stay in your hotels, do your work, and leave. Two days. I will note that on your passport and in the system. Do you understand, Señor...?" He stumbled over his name.

"It's Reilly."

"Señor Reilly. Two days. No more. We will be watching."

He stamped Reilly's passport with the force that could have broken the stamp. It told Reilly two things: he had won this round, and he'd better be careful. A pissed-off man on the frontline could make trouble in the backfield.

"Thank you, officer." He stopped short of saying *have a nice day*—there weren't many nice days in this struggling dictatorship, he imagined.

Reilly flagged down a cab and realized that, as in Russia, it was probably driven by a government employee. He pretended to fall asleep for the ride into Caracas.

First, the Kensington Caracas Vista on *Av Venezuela con Calle Mohedano*. He'd check in and immediately meet with General Manager Raul Gonzales-Espinosa. His goal was to keep the briefing short, positive, and to the point: to provide protection for guests while beginning to close down in phases over the next month. Gonzales-Espinosa, a Venezuelan-born executive with twelve years of dedicated service, listened intently.

Reilly outlined the immediate needs that needed attention that week. Next, the harder requirements over week two. The portly forty-four-year-old general manager nodded as he took notes. Then Gonzales-Espinosa outlined the safety measures he'd recently implemented.

"We check all deliveries before trucks are permitted in. Likewise, the identity of the drivers. Bags are scanned and we have two dogs on the property."

"How long do you work them?" Reilly asked.

"Four hours on, four hours off. Round the clock."

"No good," Reilly responded.

Gonzales-Espinosa looked confused. "I thought—."

"They're good for forty-five minutes, then they have to rest. Their attention to scents fades. You'll need a kennel with at least ten more Belgian Malinois through the shutdown."

"Belgian what?"

"Malinois. They're the best."

"This is Venezuela. We have one Basset Hound and one Beagle."

"Can you get more?"

"Eventually, maybe."

"What about your security team? Do you trust them? All of them?"

The general manager snickered reflexively. "This is Venezuela."

"And we have procedures to follow," Reilly argued. "What about the rest of the staff?"

"Loyal and dedicated. I know them and their families."

"Good. I want to thank them going and coming at the shift change, and explain that we'll be hardening the hotel for everyone's well-being."

"That will mean a lot, Mr. Reilly."

"And we'll provide severance. Six months."

"Our people will be very grateful."

The general manager then dropped his gaze.

"What is it, Raul?"

"I've been worried for my family. My son is sixteen. The army could take him any day. And my daughter. She's fifteen. They could—"

He didn't have to explain. The Caracas streets were dangerous day and night. More dangerous for girls.

"How long will it take for them to be ready to leave? And will they be willing?"

"With convincing, a week." He shook his head. "Teenagers. They think they're invincible."

Reilly remembered his own early years.

"Yes. Invincible. But get them ready. We'll get you and your family out."

Over the next three hours, Reilly briefed the security officers. After that he addressed the staff as their shifts ended or began. Raul Gonzales-Espinosa was correct, they were dedicated and extremely grateful.

Reilly remained in the hotel that night. He heard gunshots. Single-fire weapons he expected were from civilians, answered by more serious automatic fire from the army. No wonder Raul wanted to get his family out of the country.

The next day he took another cab to the more luxurious Kensington Bolivar on *Av Luis Roche* and gave virtually the same message to the general manager and his team. Ricardo Levy, a Venezuelan-American and an old friend of Reilly's, was equally cooperative and supportive. But he really wanted to get out. He thought Shaw had him in the wrong place.

36

MOSCOW

Nicolai Gorshkov's displeasure usually ended with staff changes. Permanent change, without retirement or pension. Sometimes his decisions came with a warning; when that happened, the accused never had time to plead their case. They never knew what lay around the corner, in their homes, or when they started their cars.

Tonight would be one of those nights. Gorshkov summoned two FSB officials. Only one, a man, could make it in person. Lt. Colonel Boris Belkan stood smartly at attention before him. The woman called in on a secure line from the London embassy. Gorshkov addressed them both sternly.

"Lt. Belkan, Colonel Kushkin, I'm certain there's an explanation," he began sternly.

"Yes, Mr. President. A simple case of mistaken identity," Belkan explained.

"There is nothing simple about this! Colonel Kushkin, would you describe it in the same manner?" Gorshkov yelled.

"No, Mr. President. This was an unauthorized mission," she replied sharply. "The order was to observe."

"That was not my understanding," Lt. Belkan countered.

Now Kushkin was furious. "Then you understood wrong! That was not the plan."

The call went painfully quiet for ten long seconds. At the eleventh second, Gorshkov smiled uncharacteristically.

"I think we can move beyond this."

The answer surprised Martina Kushkin, until it didn't. She recognized the tone. She'd heard it before and seen where it had led.

Gorshkov, now speaking in a soft, conciliatory tone, said, "I understand. Mistakes happen. Excitement of the moment. Mixed signals. An opportunity arises and your man takes advantage of it. Would you describe it that way?"

Belkan hesitated. His gut told him he was being baited. But to disagree might be worse than to walk into this conversational trap. He decided another approach: a non-answer.

"I can fix this, Mr. President. This will never happen again under my command." Gorshkov smiled again.

"Fixing it. Yes. My thoughts exactly. And your thoughts, Colonel Kushkin, since this was also your responsibility?"

"I clearly communicated the order. But I will stand by any decision you make."

"Sir, if I may?" Belkan said, still at attention.

"Yes, lieutenant?" Gorshkov asked.

"We are continuing to track the subject."

"Oh? And where is he?"

"Well, I don't have that at this moment. I'll find out."

"Actually, I have that information already," Kushkin said. "He was spotted leaving Heathrow on a flight to Venezuela."

"Sir," Belkan continued, "We have assets in Caracas. I can easily find out why he went there instead of Paris."

"Thank you, lieutenant. But I believe Martina understands her charge."

Gorshkov employing Belkan's FSB rank, but Kushkin's first name, chilled the junior officer.

"Unless there are any last thoughts, I think we're done here," Gorshkov said.

"Certainly, Mr. President," Kushkin replied.

"Yes, Mr. President," Belkan added, now worried about Gorshkov's unusually calm manner and his phrasing of 'last thoughts.'

"Well then, there's one more thing."

Gorshkov pushed his chair back from his desk and opened the top right drawer. Belkan remained at attention. Kushkin was silent over the phone. She sensed what was coming.

The Russian president removed a loaded PSS SP-16 7.62x43 mm pistol from his desk. It was the FSB weapon of choice for covert operations and assassinations. He admired the gun, turning it from side to side, appreciating its design and marveling at how light it was in his hand.

Belkan stiffened. He knew the weapon well. It had no manual safety, and though it was low-powered, the PSS SP-164 was especially effective at short range. Twenty-five meters was its maximum effective distance, but he was barely two meters away. He imagined the wedge-shaped bullet in the chamber. Gorshkov casually waved the gun in the air.

"There are so many reasons one chooses a certain gun. There's weight. Ease of operation. Handling. Of course, effectiveness. But I find it more emotional than physical. In my hand, the right weapon, this gun in fact, becomes an extension of my whole being." He laughed. "I'm probably not making any sense."

"You are, Mr. President." Boris Belkan had heard about the mind games Gorshkov played. He worked hard to hide his fear, though his voice gave him away.

"Of course, this isn't the best weapon to keep in a shoulder holster, but a desk drawer? Six rounds. It's always ready."

"Yes, sir."

"They tell me at the firing range that my marksmanship is in the top one percent. But people are always flattering me." He laughed again. "Sometimes I think they switch the targets out and let me take home ones only filled with bullseyes. Truthfully, I should be better, and they should be truthful. But people are people." Gorshkov lowered the pistol. "What do you think, lieutenant?"

A trick question? Belkan quickly thought. *How to respond?* Gorshkov demanded loyalty. But loyalty didn't depend on truth; it depended on faithful obedience, which often conflicted with truth. The only truth that mattered was Nicolai Gorshkov's truth.

"Sir, you are president. I serve you."

Gorshkov smiled. "Of course you do."

Belkan relaxed his shoulders. Gorshkov had used his full rank. *Better?*

"Lieutenant, you're dismissed. Colonel Kushkin, please stay on the phone. You'll want to hear this."

Belkan hadn't focused on Gorshkov's last statement. He turned on his heels, an exact military about-face, at which point Gorshkov raised the silenced gun and shot Belkan twice through the left side of his back, shots perfectly aimed to puncture his heart.

Kushkin heard the pair of pops over the phone.

"Martina?" the president asked. "Still there?"

"Sir."

"Continue as planned and get Belkan's officer back home. I'll talk to him in the same manner," Gorshkov said, returning his pistol to the desk drawer.

BRUSSELS

"Nothing changed overnight," NATO Secretary General Carlos Phillipe reported when the command team reconvened. "No advancement at the borders. No increase in troop movement. Quiet for now, but Russia is ready and able to pounce on two fronts simultaneously. The U.S. is preoccupied; we're not unified. Gorshkov knows that. Maybe he even planned that. I'm going to Washington to try to convince President Crowe that he needs to stand with us despite his own problems. Without visible U.S. engagement, Russia will have a cakewalk into the Balkans, let alone Ukraine. They're days away from taking two nations. We can fight, but we won't win without American buy-in."

The NATO command grumbled its agreement.

"We have seven days before Stockholm. Each of you needs to canvas our members—what level of support can we realistically expect?"

"Article 5. A visible provocation," General Rockford replied. "It should be everyone."

"Should, but won't," Phillipe admitted. "And Latvia hasn't even asked for help yet—and Ukraine's not a member."

"So we take the initiative. Troops on full alert and E-3 Sentries flying round the clock. Russia can't possibly miss our readiness."

"What about reactions from members? Latvia will be jumpy," Rockford said.

"I'll handle them and we'll ask for forgiveness later." He paused. "If we need to."

VENEZUELA

One more stop. One more delay before Reilly could return to Europe. One more element in the potential evacuation plan in Venezuela: a strategy session with the KR staff in Bogotá, Colombia. Then Reilly would attend to the impending threat in Ukraine.

He was tired. When he got too tired, he was inclined to get sick. But in the midst of multiple crises, there was no time for exhaustion or illness. So, he started the morning with a Z-Pak of antibiotics he kept in his bag. Despite his globe-hopping and dabbling in international affairs, it was a reality check that under his job title, he was a regular man. *No James Bond. No Jack Ryan*, he thought. *Just Dan Reilly.*

At Simón Bolivar International Airport he boarded an eight-seat Gulfstream 150 twin-engine jet charter. He preferred big planes; the bigger the engines, the better.

"Good afternoon, Mr. Reilly," the young flight attendant said. She greeted him in the charter lounge. "I'm Roxanne Castro."

"Hello," he said. "Are we ready?"

"On time. May I take your bag?"

"No, thanks. I'm fine."

"I'll run you through the safety procedures before we take off. Just follow me, please." Castro's English was as perfect as he suspected her

Spanish was. And probably Portuguese, too, considering the South American charter routes the company flew.

"We'll have a short flight, a little over ninety minutes. First west along the coast, then south," she said.

"Short and sweet."

He rolled his suitcase on all four wheels, followed Castro out to the plane, up the portable steps, and into the all-white cabin with white leather seats. He chose one on the starboard side, three rows down.

The captain stepped out of the cockpit and introduced himself.

"Michael Tuxhorn, Mr. Reilly. Welcome aboard. We'll have you there in no time."

Reilly figured his pilot, an American, was either a Navy, Air Force, or Marine vet. He asked.

"Where'd you serve?"

"Two tours on the *USS Carl Vinson*. Flew enough F-35Cs off the deck, I think I could land this on a dime."

"I'm hoping you have longer runways these days," Reilly joked. "Just in case." Tuxhorn smiled.

"No worries. Sit back and relax. Roxanne will take care of you."

With that she arrived with a mimosa, cheese, and crackers.

Ten minutes later the Gulfstream lifted off effortlessly, rose and banked to the north. Reilly settled comfortably into his seat, reclined the seat back, and figured he'd get at least an hour's rest. That was until he felt a sudden sharp bump—not the kind of bump that occurs with sudden turbulence. This was an impact.

The plane shook. It pitched right and dipped. His half-consumed drink spilled. The cheese plate that Roxanne Castro had delivered just minutes before seemed to float for a moment. He heard an alarm from the cockpit. The engines—or at least one of the engines—seemed to race.

Reilly checked his safety belt. It was secure. Then he called out, "Roxanne, are you okay?"

She said she was. He knew she wasn't.

As quickly as the chaos began, the flight normalized. The pilot leveled the jet and climbed. Reilly unfastened the clip to the safety belt and walked up the aisle. He sat across from the flight attendant and buckled in again.

"I think we're out of it," he offered.

She nodded and relaxed her grip on the arm rests. "Right."

She was about to get up and check in the cockpit when the pilot announced, "Sorry about that Mr. Reilly. All's good. Seems like we had an encounter with a bird just before cracking a thousand feet. I'd say we did better than our feathered friend. But we're checking out our systems."

"Ever experience that before?" Reilly asked the flight attendant.

"No, but I saw pictures of what a bird of prey did to a Cessna near Simón Bolivar. It wasn't pretty." She unbuckled and stood. "I'm going forward. Stay buckled, Mr. Reilly."

Five minutes later she returned.

He asked, "Everything looking good up there?"

She hesitated. "Mostly. They're still working it out."

"Shouldn't we turn back?" They were now fifteen minutes on the established route along the coast.

"The captain says we're okay."

Thirty minutes more proved the captain was wrong. Reilly heard another alarm and then the plane shuddered rapidly. An order, not a request, came from the cockpit.

"Mr. Reilly, Roxanne, we're going to have to put down. The nearest airport is Maracaibo; La Chinita International. It's a full-service airport and a Venezuelan airbase. It could get bumpy along the way, that bird did more damage than I initially thought."

Reilly wondered what kind of damage, but it didn't matter. This was Captain Michael Tuxhorn's plane. His responsibility. His call. For the next eighteen shaky, tense minutes, Dan Reilly put his trust in the former Navy aviator.

Ten minutes into the increasingly bumpy flight, the Gulfstream banked left over the Gulf of Venezuela and crossed low over what appeared to be a very active naval port with battleships and transports. He spotted Chinese and Greek flags on the ships. Nothing unusual, but interesting to someone with a keen eye. China had stepped up its trade with the regime. Especially food and durable goods. *But off-loaded at a navy port?* Reilly wondered.

The thought vanished when the jet vibrated violently and dropped at least one hundred feet. Roxanne automatically shouted, "Brace, brace, brace!"

Reilly bent his body forward and put his head down. The plane continued to rattle. His suitcase, wedged in across the aisle, slid out. Reilly stopped it with his left foot and dragged it under his feet.

The engines seemed to struggle. The plane continued to shake. He peered out the window. He calculated they were less than five hundred feet over the port, now the city. The airport had to be less than a mile ahead.

A half-minute later they landed hard and fast, which told Reilly the situation was even more dire than imagined. The jet braked, made a speedy right turn off the runway, and rolled to a stop.

"Roxanne, prepare the cabin to exit," the pilot commanded over the PA.

Tuxhorn said *exit*. Reilly heard *evacuate*, which he was more than willing to do.

Once the plane stopped and the door opened, Reilly thanked Roxanne and safely stepped away. He looked at the Gulfstream 150. From the left it seemed fine. He walked around the front and saw exactly why the pilot had to put down so quickly. The lower part of the nose, not visible from the cockpit, was torn apart. Much of the avionics likely destroyed. Feathers were embedded in the smashed metal and more of the bird was probably inside.

Any crash you can walk away from... he thought.

The sun beat down on Reilly as he stood on the hot tarmac. He heard the plane's engines shut down.

Reilly got his bearings; they were on the edge of the commercial side of the airport, adjacent to Rafael Urdaneta Air Base. One hundred yards away, he saw the kinds of activity he'd expect at a military airbase. He took inventory: helicopters, four MI-17s, a pair of two-seat MiG 29s, and nine one-seat MiG 29s. Further away, he counted three other fighter jets, likely Sukhoi SU-30MK2s.

All in all, Russia had a strong presence at Rafael Urdaneta.

Soon a fire truck and a tow arrived. The tow hooked the Gulfstream while the airport's fire team assessed the damage, took photographs of the outside, and climbed the gangway.

Reilly stood with his bag a safe fifty feet from the plane. A van approached. It slowed to a stop and a mechanic wearing an orange vest waved him in. Reilly said hello. When that didn't get a reaction, he tried *Buenos Dias*. Except it wasn't a really good day. The driver simply nodded. *Just as well*, Reilly thought. His stomach was uneasy, and his ears were clogged due to the rapid descent.

Because of the ground traffic, the van took a circuitous route to the main terminal. This put them on peripheral access roads around the main runways. The driver said something in Spanish and pointed to a route ahead; a military aircraft needed to pass, so the van veered left, closer to a pair of Rafael Urdaneta hangars full of activity.

Reilly saw trucks rolling in and out, supervisors barking orders. He rolled his window down. A blast of hot air caught him. So did the conversation; it wasn't Spanish. Asian. *Mandarin?* he wondered.

As they approached, Reilly determined the people in charge were definitely Asian. So were the non-uniformed workers under them. He strained to place the language. He held his nose, closed his mouth, and blew hard. His ears unclogged. Conversations came with the warm wind. *Korean. Definitely Korean.* He considered taking pictures from his cell phone but thought better of it. A wise decision because moments later, a Venezuelan MP noticed the unauthorized vehicle. The soldier shouted a command and pointed, then pulled a walkie-talkie from his belt.

"Uh oh," the driver said.

The reaction needed no translation. He stepped on the gas and drove as fast as he could along the access road. It wasn't fast enough. A military style Humvee intercepted them within 100 meters. The driver stopped. Soldiers with arms at the ready jumped out and surrounded the van.

Reilly heard shouts of *"Intrusos! Conseguirlos!"* He knew enough Spanish to recognize 'Intruders! Get them!' The drawn guns were the exclamation points. The driver pointed to the crippled jet across the airport. He tried to explain, but he was a mechanic sent to pick up a passenger, not a negotiator.

Reilly slowly got out of the vehicle. He raised his hands and figured it would take some doing, but they'd let him go once the MPs or the airbase command talked to La Chinita air traffic control.

At least that's what he hoped.

* * *

It took forty minutes before an English-speaking officer entered the cramped trailer office where Reilly was being held. For all intents and purposes, it was now an interrogation room—sweltering with a non-functioning air conditioner.

Reilly removed his jacket and rolled up his sleeves. He was certain his driver would be questioned in the same manner. His account would support Reilly's. So, for now, he considered this just theater. But a misstep here, like in customs, could cost him.

The Venezuelan lieutenant held Reilly's passport and wallet. He was overweight, on first blush ten years older than Reilly, and undoubtedly sent in unprepared by a commander. Reilly expected he would try to prove himself.

"You have made a terrible mistake, Señor Reilly. This is a secure facility. You can be shot on my order alone."

Reilly said nothing.

"Your confession will make it much easier."

"Lieutenant…" Reilly read his name on a tag above his left pocket. "…Monagas. I'm an American hotel executive on my way from Caracas to Colombia. My plane hit a bird. We had to put down quickly. You can easily confirm that with the tower or my pilot."

"They are not here. You are. You trespassed."

"My driver made a wrong turn."

"Purposely."

"By mistake." Reilly looked sincere. He lowered his shoulders to show contrition rather than defiance. "My identification in my wallet will confirm my work."

"I've examined it. No doubt it is your cover. You're an American spy."

Reilly remained calm.

"A phone call to my office in Chicago or my hotel in Caracas can quickly clear this up. I encourage you to—"

"They will lie as you are. You're spying."

Reilly decided to push some.

"What is there to spy on?"

This threw the Venezuelan. He couldn't answer without revealing what was happening at the facility. So, he fumbled through Reilly's wallet.

"Please, sir. Examine the jet. You'll see the damage. Speak to the pilot and the tower. All I want to do is rebook and leave. This is all a mistake, and not my doing."

This went on for another ten minutes. Same questions, same answers, with the inexperienced officer trying to trip Reilly up. Frustrated, he finally left.

Reilly stood and listened to a loud conversation through the wall. Different than his: emotional, full of shouting. His driver was being questioned. They'd have the same story, but Reilly wished he'd remained calm.

After another half-hour, Monagas returned with a black hood that he put over Reilly's head.

"Wait. What? No!"

"Shut up. Do what I say."

Hooded, Reilly was led out of the trailer. The lieutenant barked some orders and answered one himself. He pushed Reilly into a jeep, sat him down and drove off without a word. At what Reilly calculated was a mile with some sharp twists and turns and the sounds of aircraft taking off and landing, Monagas stopped and pulled off the hood.

"Out now!"

Reilly looked around. They were at the commercial side of La Chinita International.

"My passport, my wallet."

The lieutenant pulled them out of his pocket and tossed them on the ground.

"Take them, spy, and leave!"

Reilly nodded but decided not to respond. What he wanted most was a shower, a drink, and no more airport run-ins.

39

PITTSBURGH, PA

THE SAME TIME

Six 18-foot U-Haul trucks rolled onto Pittsburgh's Three Sisters Bridges spanning the Allegheny River to and from downtown. The Roberto Clemente, the Andy Warhol, and the Rachel Carson. They were just three of the city's 446 bridges, more than any other metropolitan area in the world, including Venice, Italy.

These three bridges were identical. So were the trucks' approaches: three from downtown, three from the opposite side, each pair converging within minutes in the middle.

In a choreographed dance, the drivers all proceeded onto the spans and positioned their trucks perpendicularly across the clogged lanes. Then they each stopped, turned off their engines, got out, and threw their keys into the river. Like the vehicles they drove and the bridges they blocked, the men looked identical; they all wore Steelers' caps, dark sunglasses, beige jackets, black turtlenecks, blue jeans, and black sneakers. Once out of their vehicles, they each walked in the direction they came from.

Honking started almost immediately. Another annoying morning rush hour tie-up. *Typical.*

A passenger in the taxi behind the inbound truck on the Roberto Clemente Bridge opened his door and yelled at the driver as he walked by.

"Hey, what the fuck!"

The driver ignored him.

"Hey, you! Stop!"

He didn't. Ten seconds. Fifteen. Then a realization. Now out of the taxi the passenger screamed, "Run! Clear the bridge!"

Twenty seconds. Others began opening their doors as reality set in. *Not typical.*

Twenty-five seconds. Panic was spreading in both directions.

Thirty seconds: mass confusion. People struggling with their safety belts. Car doors opening quickly and hitting people as they fled.

The scene was the same on the Warhol and on the Carson. A Pittsburgh police officer on his way to morning duty watched a man purposely march toward him. The cop opened his door and stood.

"You, stop!"

The truck driver ignored the order. He checked his digital watch: thirty seconds. *Fifteen seconds more.*

The officer, sensing trouble, ran after the man.

"I said stop!"

Instead of heeding the order, the truck driver began to run. He reached under his jacket, turned without slowing down, and fired an unbalanced shot from twenty feet. It missed. The officer's return fire didn't; the truck driver, shot in the chest, went down.

Forty seconds.

The policeman kicked the man's gun away from his body. He looked back toward the truck, then ahead to the end of the bridge. He calculated quickly. The span was roughly four hundred feet in either direction. He'd been a sprinter in high school—at top speed with obstructions, he might make it in thirty seconds. *But,* he thought, *that was years ago. And now—*

The first truck exploded with a deafening howl. The cop went down, barely avoiding shrapnel. He didn't even hear the second explosion, but its searing heat scorched him. He picked himself up; he was still alive. He saw that others, in burning cars, weren't.

Pittsburgh shut down. Bridges, traffic and railroad tunnels, pedestrian tunnels, bicycle tunnels, subway tunnels all closed. Pittsburgh was dependent on its tight-flowing infrastructure; close even one traffic tunnel and the city is paralyzed. Close them all and tens of thousands of vehicles and hundreds of thousands of citizens are isolated.

In less than an hour, Pittsburgh, Pennsylvania became a war zone gripped by panic.

40

Reilly's flight landed early in the morning at Dulles. As soon as he came into the lobby he noted people crowded under TV monitors. They were clutching their loved ones and shaking their heads. Crying. The lower third banner below the CNN anchor read "Pittsburgh Under Siege: Bridges Attacked."

He joined the crowd and felt utterly responsible. Multiple calls to make. He told Bob Heath to meet him at Langley; then he phoned Marnie Babbitt in London.

She opened with, "Finally. I haven't heard from you in days. No texts. Nothing. I've been worried sick. Where the hell are you? I hope it's not Pittsburgh."

"No, and I'm sorry," Reilly quietly offered while walking through the airport. "Still traveling. I've been keeping a low profile."

"I get that. But it's me."

"Okay."

"So where are you?"

"Just landed. In DC now."

"You say that like's it just a stopover."

"Well, yes. A few stops in Venezuela. Then Bogotá." He avoided any mention of rogue players.

"What are you *not* telling me?" she asked.

"Only what I can't."

"You've got to do better than that. I don't know what's going on, but you owe it to me."

Reilly apologized again. Marnie asked when he'd be back.

"Can't really say."

"Can't or…"

"Can't, Marnie."

"Well for God's sake don't do anything stupid," she said. "But Stockholm is still on, right?"

"Yes, eventually."

Reilly was definitely dodging her questions. *Dammit,* he thought. He hated feeling this way. They hung up with some sweet talk that missed the mark.

41

In another part of the day Reilly failed to share with Marnie, he took a cab straight to the CIA. Bob Heath greeted him downstairs, then took him to his sparsely furnished office. They skipped the small talk.

"I've got something, but first fill me in on Pittsburgh."

"It's bad. Really bad." Heath summarized the initial FBI assessments, which were culled from eyewitnesses and local police.

"Right out of the report. I should have seen it. I'm sorry."

"We should have, too. Same with the Bureau." Heath admitted. "They're cleaning up. But the three bridges are structurally at risk. The death toll is rising, Pittsburgh is in total lockdown. Police are overwhelmed. The National Guard is posted throughout the city. There is one bit of positive news, though: a police officer took down one of the terrorists."

"Alive?"

"No."

"Then where's the good news?"

"Forensics. The FBI is working on everything from dental work to tattoos and any surgical scars that might support a national signature."

"It would be a lot more positive if he were alive."

"Well, that's not an option. So what's next? You're the expert."

Reilly didn't hesitate. "Hoover."

"The Bureau doesn't think so. They made a thorough search of the dam, the pumping stations, right down to the filtering stations and pipelines along the delivery route. According to them, there's no imminent danger."

"Was there any sign of danger in Pittsburgh before the bridge bombings?" Reilly asked.

"No."

"Then they're wrong. It was a potential target in World War II, it's definitely a more important target now."

Heath vaguely recalled learning some of the history. Reilly explained in more detail.

"A month after World War II started in Europe, U.S. intelligence got a tip through our embassy in Mexico that two German agents intended to blow up the intake towers and destroy the high-voltage lines. They planned on posing as fishermen, boating up to the Lake Mead towers, and planting bombs. One of the operatives made multiple trips to scout the location and take photographs. The plot was foiled. The government buried the details to prevent any scare. But as a result, the dam and lake were closed to everyone but the most essential personal. When people noticed that no one was allowed to fish or boat on the lake, rumors spread. The Bureau of Reclamation later released a press statement that the dam was safe, and the plot was a merely a rumor."

"But it wasn't," Heath noted.

"Not if you consider that defensive measures were proposed including stringing a huge net over Lake Mead to catch air dropped bombs and torpedoes. They also drew up plans to camouflage Hoover and even build a three-quarter scale model downstream from the actual dam as a decoy. But they didn't."

"So they did nothing?" Heath wondered.

"No. The Army installed floodlights near the dam to blind pilots, and laid out a wire net which prevented boats from coming within 300 feet of the dam. After Pearl Harbor, a gun turret pillbox was constructed above the dam. It's still there. So, Hoover and its greater network was a serious target then and is even more so now."

"Would they target the water supply or the electrical grid?"

"In terms of target effectiveness the real impact is water. The *they*, whoever *they* are, have been going for news that creates scary pictures. Shutting grids down means TV's won't work. You can't watch cable news if there's no electricity. So to my mind, this is about video impact. Turn off the faucets off in Las Vegas in mid-summer and it's a threat that says, 'Pay attention to us. We can get you anywhere, America. Anyway we want.' And if *they've* truly paid attention to my report, and they have so far, that's their real message."

Reilly paused to allow this to sink in.

"Now I have something for you, something to take all the way to the top: I just came from Venezuela. You're going to need to get eyes on what I saw."

He described the shipments he identified while flying over the port of Maracaibo. He gave his detailed observations once on the ground— who and what he saw at Rafael Urdaneta Air Base, how he was held and questioned for nearly two hours before being blindfolded and released outside the commercial airport. Finally, his opinion about the nationality of the actors.

"Koreans. More specifically, though they weren't uniformed, North Koreans. Anything you know about that?" Reilly asked.

Heath stood and paced. He pulled his thoughts together.

"I do know the Venezuelan military took control of three civilian ports in recent months. One of them was Maracaibo. And Pyongyang offered," he paused to recall the exact phrase, "'…socialist solidarity and cooperation' with the Venezuelan regime."

"This looked like more than solidarity."

"Could be food and durable goods. They need it."

"Bullshit," Reilly declared. "Not the way they were concerned about me and what I might have seen."

42

WASHINGTON, D.C.

THE WHITE HOUSE

The Secret Service agent led the NATO Secretary General straight from his helicopter into the Oval Office. President Crowe immediately stood from behind his desk as Carlos Phillipe entered.

"General Phillipe, good to see you."

"And you, Mr. President. My condolences for America's losses. We've heard the latest." President Crowe came around and hugged his guest warmly.

"Thank you, Carlos. Hard days for all of us. May I offer you coffee or tea?"

"Coffee would be wonderful."

Crowe went to the silver urn, set on a colonial sideboard originally used by Thomas Jefferson, and began pouring coffee into a blue cup bearing the Presidential Seal.

"This thing holds 25 cups but recently we've been refilling it every few hours. Milk or cream?"

"Milk, please."

Along with Phillipe's coffee, Crowe brought a plate of madeleines to the table in the center of the room.

"I've asked Pierce Kimball to join us, he's on his way from a

Pentagon meeting. But let's begin."

"Thank you, Mr. President. I'll get to the point: we are invoking the Readiness Action Plan to respond to Russian forces lined up against Latvia. We are poised to support Ukraine as well, but as you know, it's a different situation there."

"Troop strength?" Crowe asked.

"Four thousand troops. Vehicles, weaponry, and munitions in support." Phillipe opened his briefcase and handed Crowe a folder. "It's detailed in the order."

"Kimball believes such a move will further provoke the Russians," Crowe replied. "Gorshkov's been trigger-happy since early spring when he was first ready to move."

"I respect his opinion, but to be perfectly frank, the United States has shown little interest in our current situation," Phillipe said. He took a sip and flinched; the taste was not to his liking. He quickly slid the mug back onto the table.

"We live on the razor's edge, Mr. President. There is no trust between NATO and Russia. The alliance's protective shield is viewed by Gorshkov as an encroachment on nations he considers within his sphere of influence, either culturally by language or historically by fiat."

At that moment, Pierce Kimball walked in.

"I'm sorry I'm late. As you can image, we're quite busy here."

Phillipe stood.

"As are we, Mr. Kimball."

"Help yourself to some java, Pierce. The Secretary General has advised me that they are deploying troops to Latvia under the Readiness Action Plan."

Kimball turned halfway toward the seating area as he poured his coffee.

"A miscalculation, Mr. Secretary General, at great peril to peace. Your move could bring the crisis to the boiling point."

"It's already at the boiling point, as you call it. The Russian Federation is threatening a member nation and its intention is to bring Ukraine back under its domain. Gorshkov has never hidden his view that at the end of the Cold War, NATO's expansion amounted to a cancerous tumor on the Russian body politic. He believes the way to cut it out is by surgically removing NATO. Consider: Crimea, Georgia, they were the easy ones. NATO has no relationship with them. But the rest of Ukraine, they think it's theirs. And Russia has a nationalistic view of Latvia too. Mr. President," the NATO chief addressed Crowe directly, "I implore you take a stand now."

Kimball interrupted before the President could respond.

"Right now, Americans want us to focus on the threats at home."

"Because they don't know where Riga is!" Phillipe shot back. "Well, they damn well better learn, because Kiev, Warsaw, Bucharest, and Sofia are next. And given the changing political climate in Germany, who's to say Berlin won't be the capital in a new Russian alliance! We face a fundamental redrawing of the Eastern European map—it's imminent. Our command has been meeting with our European leaders and we're trying to build a consensus, but we want America in the lead. Without your support, the alliance will be absent of actual political strength, let alone greater firepower. And without that, Gorshkov will take advantage of the situation unless we make it very clear that the United States of America, you, Mr. President, will support Article 5."

The Oval Office fell silent.

"Mr. President, Dr. Kimball, I can see it's time to go. Thank you for the coffee. However, like your position, it was weak."

Crowe fixed his eyes on Phillipe. A smile began to form.

"Mr. Secretary General, another moment please. I have an idea." Pierce Kimball gave the president a surprised look.

"It won't be everything you want, but it may buy some time without costing me impeachment."

Carlos Phillipe took a step toward the president.

"Go ahead. I'm listening."

* * *

Fifteen minutes later, President Crowe's secretary acknowledged that the Russian President was on the phone and the appropriate members of the administration and intelligence community were listening in.

"Thank you. Put him through."

A moment later, Crowe was on with Gorshkov.

"Mr. President, thank you for taking my call on short notice."

Alexander Crowe waited for the English-to-Russian translation in Moscow and, in turn, the reply from Nicolai Gorshkov to be translated back to him.

"It's a rare occurrence these days that we should speak," Gorshkov said. "To what do I owe the pleasure?"

"I take no pleasure in calling you under such circumstances. As you know, the United States has been brutally attacked. Civilians in four of our major cities have been killed. America's armed forces are at maximum alert." He waited for the translation. When no reply came, Crowe continued.

"And yet, Mr. President, there is another crisis in Eastern Europe. A crisis of your creation. As pre-occupied as we are with our own national interests, I assure you we are just as committed to our NATO allies." Following some whispers over the phone, Gorshkov spoke.

"Mr. President, you speak of your national interests. Do you deny the Russian Federation its own? Of course, you do. The United States has been party to NATO's expansion. Right to our very borders, and in the process your North Atlantic Treaty Organization has violated agreements, abrogated its promises. NATO is a lie to us. So do not speak to me of your commitment."

"Mr. President, English, please. We will save each other a great deal of time. And time is apparently not on our side."

"Very well," Gorshkov replied.

"Soon you will be convening in Stockholm. I urge you to act with restraint. The world will be watching."

"Don't lecture me about the world when Latvians are crying out for freedom, when a reunited Ukraine will lead to peace. No, Mr. President. Do not talk about the world watching me while your own people are watching you. I read your press accounts, I see your television broadcasts. Europe is as far away as the Vale, the Stormlands, and the Reach."

Kimball didn't understand the reference. Crowe whispered, "Game of Thrones."

"You do not know the resilience of the American people, Mr. Gorshkov."

"And you do not understand the centuries-old plight of Russians. Mongols, Napoleon's army, Hitler, we fought them all and we survived. But Russia was most secure when we created a defensive alliance against the West. Since we've lost that, you and your allies have given us no reason to feel safe. We *will* be safe again."

"Don't underestimate me or our history either," Crowe said forcefully.

"There is a Russian expression, Mr. President," he said in English, "'You cannot pull a fish out of a pond without effort.'"

"Ah yes, we know it as 'No pain, no gain.' And I have another well-meaning Russian proverb for you. 'If you like to sled, you have to be willing to drag it.'"

Gorshkov laughed. "Close enough, Mr. President. You never fail to surprise me."

"I believe I can say the same about you. The fact is, I know your history. You should learn ours."

They ended the call politely, but without resolution. NATO Secretary General Phillipe and National Security Advisor Kimball looked drained.

"What just happened?" Kimball asked.

"We played chess Russian style," Crowe said. "Fast."

Phillipe nodded. "Very. And that proverb you quoted?"

"It means it can be fun going down the hill, but going back up, not so much. In other words, be prepared to pay for what you enjoy."

"I'm not sure I understand in this context," Phillipe replied.

"But Gorshkov did."

43

MOSCOW

"Your best assessment, General?"

Gorshkov's Chief of General Staff, Army General Boris Dubynin, stood at attention in Gorshkov's Kremlin office. On the spot where a young lieutenant had died, but only after the carpet had been replaced.

"Masterful, Mr. President."

"Not me. Crowe."

"Crowe? Crumbling in the chaos around him. Grandstanding, but with no audience. Stymied. Bewildered."

Gorshkov nodded, and smiled to himself.

WASHINGTON

"What's Gorshkov thinking, Pierce?"

"Calculating what you'll do next. You threw him," the National Security Advisor told President Crowe.

"He doesn't get thrown off. Besides, whoever listened on the call is showering Gorshkov with praise. Now he's strategizing, feeling he's got the best of me." Crowe turned and looked out the window toward the Rose Garden, turning over the conversation in his mind. He came to a worrisome conclusion.

"And you know what, maybe he does."

MOSCOW

"America is nothing more than a spectator to the unfolding global events."

Gorshkov furiously paced as he talked. The more he wound up, the faster he paced. General Dubynin dutifully watched him cover the office, back and forth.

"Like England and its self-inflicted wounds over Brexit and the EU, America has lost its compass. It no longer has a true north, a purpose as a major power. Its democracy would have failed eventually, we have just advanced the clock with our intervention. And now Crowe is consumed with threats to America's infrastructure and, if he makes the wrong decision, politically or militarily, his administration will fail. But we may not need to wait for that to happen."

"He's totally paralyzed," Dubynin replied without picking up on the last comment.

WASHINGTON

"Phillipe was right. Gorshkov knows that NATO has no muscle unless we're engaged. Without confirmation that we're all in, he will exploit our indecisiveness to move. Four thousand troops won't deter him. The only way to stop Gorshkov—"

The president returned to his desk and begin writing.

"Sir?"

"I'm ordering the *USS Harry S. Truman* Carrier Strike Group to the Baltic from the North Atlantic. The Pentagon can make the announcement tonight."

Pierce Kimball said, "Yes, sir," but he didn't agree with the decision.

"Find out how long it will take for them to deploy, then speed them up."

"A deterrent, Mr. President."

"We can hope."

MOSCOW

"Crowe said we should know their history." Gorshkov ran through what he remembered. *Colonization, Revolution, the Civil War, westward expansion.*

"Where is Crowe from?"

"I don't know."

"The state they call Arizona," the president said, answering his own question. The Chief of General Staff didn't make the connection.

"He's a cowboy, General Dubynin. A cowboy and I will knock him off his high horse."

44

HENDERSON, NEVADA

Harper sat at his usual Denny's corner table, at the usual time, ordering his usual Grand Slam with two pancakes, two eggs over easy, two bacon strips, and two sausage links, from his usual waitress. He also waited for his sometimes-usual visitor.

Halfway through his 2 a.m. breakfast, the sometimes-usual man entered. And as usual, which suddenly hit the waitress as highly unusual, he wore the exact same dark clothes as he had on his previous visits. And, like always, he ordered his juice, egg whites, and dry toast and looked straight ahead, a dismissive signal for her to leave.

The usual, she thought.

After placing the man's order, Angie Peterson busied herself at the counter. She heard nothing except the soft rock music that was always on. But in the mirror, behind the pie display, she caught a reflection of the customer. His lips were definitely moving. He was talking, more whispering to the man whose back was to him—the only other person in the restaurant. The only person he ever sat near: the regular.

Peterson finally accepted the obvious. *It's a meeting. Or more than a meeting. A rendezvous. Sex? Drugs?* She continued to observe. *Gangsters from Vegas?* Her mind raced as she focused on the lips. Moving some. Stopping as if listening. *Definitely listening.* And moving again. *Obviously secretive.*

The trouble was, what was obvious through the mirror to Peterson was also obvious to the man at the table. He saw her reflection and caught her curiosity. And the moment their eyes locked in the mirror, she looked away.

Five minutes later, Peterson brought the man his egg whites, toast, and juice.

"Here you go, sir."

She placed the food on table. He lifted his head and smiled. Not a friendly smile. A cruel smile. *A warning?* She forced a question to break the tension.

"Will there be anything else?"

"Just the bill."

Angie Peterson placed it on the table. Seven minutes later he was gone. But he wasn't gone. He waited across the street in the dark, through the dawn, and morning's first light.

At seven she walked out into the sunshine, got in her car, and drove to her 700-square foot home on Gray Fox Way.

The man followed her in his vehicle and waited again. Patiently. He waited for her to sleep. It would be easier once she fell asleep. It always was. No need for her to suffer. She just wouldn't wake.

His Russian handlers and his Korean generals might not be so sympathetic. But the man known as Pak Yoon-hoi at home, and in the U.S. as Billy Park, was on his own. The woman took too much interest in him. She could describe him to police or worse yet, pick him out in a lineup.

Yoon-hoi quietly broke in, calmly walked through her living room, down the hall, and slowly cracked open the door to her bedroom.

Funny, he thought. *She lives alone, but she closes her bedroom door as if she has roommates. Old habits die hard.* He smiled to himself. At least she'll die easily.

He removed his knife, a 6-inch folding blade bought for cash without a problem at a Walmart in Las Vegas. He'd use it only once. That's the way he worked: once and gone, like his burner phones. And once was now.

45

LONDON

THE NEXT NIGHT

Reilly returned to the London Kensington Royal exhausted. He desperately needed a good night's sleep, alone. Which is why he didn't call Marnie.

In the lobby he surveyed the expanse. No matter how tired he was, Reilly never simply passed through. Like a battlefield officer, this was terrain to evaluate, to identify who looked like they belonged and who didn't. He watched people coming and going and others milling around. He saw couples and families heading to pre-theater dinner, and a woman talking with the concierge, trying to secure tickets to a play in the West End.

He overheard conversations in English, French, German, and Chinese. All normal, except—

As he approached the check-in desk, Reilly caught sight of a particularly striking woman in a black leather jacket, black slacks, and high black boots. *A businesswoman? A tourist waiting for a companion? No.* She had eyes on him.

Noting Reilly's glance, she turned a page in a book she wasn't reading and smiled.

Reilly widened his view as he walked forward. He was aware of her lingering look. He casually circled the lobby, warmly greeting roving staff members who were wearing wireless earpieces and welcoming guests. Peripherally, he kept the woman in view.

Reilly, no longer feeling tired, was now on alert. She was doing surveillance. Not good in one of his hotels. But what was worse—he felt he was her subject.

He went to the front desk, retrieved his room key and turned to see if the woman was still there. She was. Reilly asked the desk clerk to have a bellman take his suitcase up to his room—he had something else to do.

"Hello," he said with the same manner he'd been talking to his staff.

"Hello," the woman said, with a slight accent he quickly placed as Russian.

"How's the read?" he asked, peering down and seeing she was paging through Thomas Piketty's influential book on economics, *Capital in the Twenty-First Century*. Reilly had read it on a flight to Beijing.

"Deep. I don't understand most of it."

He smiled. *Or any of it,* he thought and he was willing to bet the book was on the seat and she just picked it up before sitting. A handy prop.

"Are you a guest? I'm with the hotel, I'd be happy to help you."

"Thank you. I'm on holiday—heading out in a few minutes. But it's kind of you to ask."

"Well then, have a nice day," Reilly said. "Do let me know if there's anything you need. I'm Dan Reilly, you can ask for me by name."

"Thank you, Dan Reilly," she said again before looking down.

"*Pozhaluysta, madam—*" You're welcome, Madame.

"And I'm Maria Pudovkin," replied Col. Martina Kushkin.

"Your English is very good, Ms. Pudovkin."

"Your Russian," she laughed, "is very poor, Mr. Reilly. But thank you again for your hospitality. Perhaps we'll meet again."

"I have a feeling we will."

Pudovkin, he mused. *Not even a chance that's her real name.*

46

HENDERSON, NV

The Denny's night manager never knew Angie Peterson to be late. So, when she hadn't shown up an hour after her shift began, he called her cell. Peterson's voicemail picked up. He left a concerned message. He did the same thirty minutes later, and another thirty minutes after that. Now three hours without word from his employee, he called the Henderson Police Department.

A deputy was dispatched to Kansas Avenue at 1:40AM. Her dented Ford Galaxy was in the driveway of the single-story home. He felt the car's hood: cold. He knocked on the locked front door: no answer. He peered through the front window. Nothing.

With his duty flashlight in hand, the deputy walked around the structure, peering into each window. The small dining room and the kitchen: nothing. Next, fifteen feet away, the bathroom window with fogged glass: nothing. Now a dark bedroom with an opened shade. He shined his light, first illuminating a closed door at the far end. Then across the wall to a six-drawer dresser, to the middle of the room, and then the opposite side, to the bed: nothing.

He continued around the corner of the house, finding another bedroom window. His flashlight beam flooded the room. He slowly panned from the door to the open closet, past the bureau and TV, to the bed; a blood-soaked bed with the body of the thirty-three-year-old woman face up. Her throat was slashed.

Deputy Waldo Sheridan hadn't known her by name, but he recognized her from the restaurant. Always chipper and refusing tips from police, always there with free coffee and refills. He liked her and wished her well the last time he had seen her. Looked like it hadn't turned out that way.

Sheridan radioed for backup and a medical examiner. People would have to be woken up. The only way to help her now was to secure the crime scene and look for evidence.

*   *   *

By 6 AM ET, details of Angie Peterson's murder were circulating through the National Crime Information Center, NCIC, the database shared among federal, state, and local criminal justice departments and the FBI. A seemingly local matter wouldn't have been noticed some 2,421 miles away from Henderson except for the proximity to a keyword already flagged by the bureau: Hoover Dam. Vincent Moore's work had been deliberate; he'd requested that anything and everything that came up from the area be sent to him.

At 8:35 AM in Washington, Moore read the report. He'd eaten at the Henderson Denny's just days ago. At night, too, probably served by the murder victim. Moore tried to picture her: early thirties, sandy brown hair pulled back in a bun. Friendly and chatty. He downloaded a series of photographs attached to the file; it was her.

The preliminary NCIC report described the cause of death. Brutal, but apparently no rape involved. Or theft.

So, Moore wondered, *why did someone kill you? Why you?*

47

LONDON

The next morning Reilly was on his way to his next flight. He finished checking out and quickly headed through the hotel lobby. Suddenly a woman with a rolled-up *London Times* took three steps directly toward him.

"Mr. Reilly?"

Dan Reilly automatically lifted his head. The woman smiled.

"Dan Reilly?"

Almost simultaneously, a man the size of a refrigerator appeared from near the entrance along with two security officers with weapons drawn and aimed. Safeties off. From behind, Refrigerator Man locked both of his arms inside hers. Her newspaper fell to the ground. With his right foot he slammed the back of her leg just behind her knee. The woman crumbled to the ground. Guests in the lobby scattered. Refrigerator held her still, not that she could have moved against his weight.

The guard to Reilly's left swept him behind and held his gun three feet from the surest part of his target, the woman's chest.

The other guard kicked the newspaper away. Sections separated. But there was no weapon.

"I can explain," she said.

"Shut up!" the security officer protecting Reilly replied, now slipping her purse down her arm and nodding to the man to loosen his grip so the third guard could take it.

"I'm—."

"I said shut up!"

The security officer opened her purse and rummaged through the contents. Wallet, paper, keys, passport. No weapon.

"Clean," he said almost disappointedly. Then he checked her wallet and found her identification. He stepped back and holstered his pistol. Refrigerator Man took that as a cue to loosen his grip.

"Are you happy now?" She rose, giving all three guards an incensed look. "I'm a reporter for the *New York Times*." She held her arm out for her purse. "My name's Savannah Flanders. Who the hell did you think I was?"

Reilly stepped around his protector.

"I'm sorry, Ms. Flanders. We've had some issues."

"That's why I'm here. And to tell you the truth, you're a hard man to find," she said. She glared at Refrigerator as she rubbed her arm. "Even harder to talk to once found, apparently."

"Well, you found me. But I have to admit, you gave me a scare."

"You? The gun was on me!" Flanders declared. "That's a first. I don't want a second."

Reilly felt like saying, *Can't guarantee anything if you stick around me.* He didn't. Instead he announced to everyone in the lobby, "All's fine." And to Flanders he offered, "I hope you understand. You approached…."

"Stupidly. Just like the assassin in Paris. Totally my fault. I should have realized." She now addressed the guards. "No issue from me, gentlemen. You were doing your job."

The first guard to act picked up the newspaper and returned it to Flanders.

Reilly looked at his watch and told the security team, "We're fine. Thank you. I owe Ms. Flanders a conversation." To her he added, "I presume if we don't chat now…?"

"I'll find you again."

"Now it is, then." Reilly led her to an office behind the check-in desk. Once settled, Flanders removed a reporter's notebook and opened to a blank page. She sat, he stood.

"I phoned your office and spoke with your assistant," she began.

"I got your messages. Brenda told me you were passed along to our public relations department."

"I don't talk to PR people. I write investigative articles for the *Times*, Mr. Reilly. We develop stories on our own."

"And I'm your story?"

"You were because of what you did in Washington."

"Oh?" he asked, not acknowledging anything.

"Yes and the story only got more interesting because—"

"I'm not anyone's story, Ms. Flanders."

"Before you decide that, let me explain. From all the video I watched of the 14th Street Bridge attack, one man stood out. One man who helped people. An elderly couple, women, children, disoriented victims. I lost count. This man risked his own life, getting people out of their cars before they exploded. All of this before others acted. We searched for this man, Mr. Reilly. Calls everywhere, some facial recognition programs, and then a simple match to testimony at a Senate hearing. Your testimony, Mr. Reilly. We discovered you are."

"Persistent."

"Like I said, Mr. Reilly, tenacious. I wanted to interview you about the morning. What you did. What you saw. Whether you sensed anything beforehand." She smiled and added, "Who you are."

"I wasn't the only one—"

She interrupted. "You were the first."

"I'm afraid I can't help you with much," Reilly stated. "I was just a guy who wanted to help."

Flanders smiled. "Who could help…who was even trained to help. That's you, Mr. Reilly."

Reilly checked his watch. "I really have to—"

"Two more minutes. If after that you don't want to talk, I'll do the story on my own."

He sighed. There was no easy way to get out of this. "Okay, two minutes."

"Well, maybe three, but stop me at two if I haven't engaged you," she replied lightly.

"Go."

"You see I was so intrigued by your accomplishments that we dug deeper into your background. What we could find of it. We were able to piece together early history. Growing up. Your father's death. Your mother's work with the Boston police. It gets foggier after that. We have some of it. Special military training, an assignment abroad and an incident with a general in Afghanistan. All of that might not be of interest had you not acted in the moment in Washington and then just the other day in—"

"Paris," he volunteered.

"Yes. The assassination attempt against you. In my line of work, I've never believed in coincidences."

Reilly gave a half-smile. "You're not alone." He decided to sit, signaling she'd just bought more time.

"Ms. Flanders, I have no doubt that in time, with your resources, you could dig far and wide to put together a compelling piece. But simply put, my actions in D.C. were in the moment. I had a choice. I stepped in."

"Not everyone would."

"You're right. But your research must have shown that I'm in charge of my company's international business. And internationally, we face threats that we have to prepare for. We've been targeted at times. Even attacked. So we've developed comprehensive security plans that rate the risks. It's my responsibility to implement those plans." Reilly didn't go so far to say he was the father of the Red Hotel strategy, which ranked the level of threats and outlined the necessary security procedures to accompany each assessment. "All of this means, lives matter to me. I did what I could on the bridge."

Flanders thought for a moment. "So, are you asking me to forget writing about you?"

"I'd prefer that."

"But I haven't gotten to my most important questions."

Reilly tilted his head, fully expecting the reporter wouldn't give up. "Which are?"

"Why did someone want to kill you? And do you have any idea who it was?"

Without hesitating, Reilly lowered his voice. "I can't comment."

"That says a lot."

"It says I can't comment."

The reporter realized she was no longer just interviewing—with still nothing on paper—a business executive. He was much more than a man helping others in a crisis. He was in the middle of one himself.

"We're through, Ms. Flanders."

"Actually, I have one more question." Reilly blinked. "There's a rumor circulating about a State Department study that details terrorism soft targets across America."

"Oh?"

"Targets that have been hit in the past few days in just the manner outlined in the report."

"Have you seen it?"

"No, but I thought a former member of the State Department might know something about it."

"Look, Ms. Flanders, I don't respond to rumors based on something that may be years old. And I can't comment on anything about my past government work, which you've obviously been looking into. I'm in the private sector now."

Flanders smiled. "I never said it was an old report, Mr. Reilly. Thank you for confirming that."

48

LONDON

HEATHROW AIRPORT

Reilly fastened his seatbelt in advance of takeoff. He was in a bulkhead row adjacent to the door on the port side of the commuter plane.

The Austrian flight attendant knelt beside him.

"You're capable of assisting in case of an emergency?"

Please, no more emergencies, he thought.

"Yes. Definitely."

He was told they'd have good flying weather. However, based on the most recent State Department advisories he read on his phone, landing in Kiev could be a problem.

Just as the pre-flight announcement began, Reilly's cell rang. It was Alan Cannon.

"About to take off," Reilly whispered.

"This won't take long. I've got an update for you on Paris."

"Oh?" The flight attendant wagged her finger good-naturedly at Reilly.

"Got an admission from one of the KR London staff. A young man on the front desk. Very guilty sounding. Apologetic."

"Over?"

"You…and the man in Paris. He told a guest where you were headed.

Pillow talk," Cannon explained.

"Jesus," Reilly said.

"Yes, I talked to him myself. He confessed that a woman came on to him when he checked her in. A Russian businesswoman. Named...."

"Maria Pudovkin," Reilly interrupted. He was greatly relieved it was the fake Russian tourist, not Marnie.

"How did you know?" Cannon exclaimed.

"She was in the lobby yesterday. Stalking me."

49

KIEV

Landing at Boryspil International Airport was hard enough; getting through the mass of people in the terminal was another thing entirely. Thousands without tickets were waiting for planes out of the country, but not enough planes were coming in.

Reilly pushed through the crowd. He hailed a cab, expecting an expensive ride into Independence Square.

"Eight-thousand-five-hundred UAH," the driver said in English. Three hundred US dollars.

"You've got to be kidding. It's usually 900 UAH."

"Nothing is usual right now. Today it's eighty-five hundred. You want a ride or not?"

"Independence Square," Reilly said. "The Kensington."

"Can't get you all the way in," the driver said.

He looked over his shoulder and smiled. It didn't improve his looks. He had a scar on his right cheek. Reilly figured it was from a knife fight. His grey t-shirt was rolled up to his shoulders, revealing a tattoo of a bat over a parachute atop two crossed swords. Distinctive. Memorable—the shoulder sleeve insignia of the 3rd Spetsnaz Regiment, signifying his service in the 3rd Special Purpose Detachment of Ukraine's Special Forces Command. Reilly didn't acknowledge it.

"I saw the rioting on TV. How close?"

"From the hotel? Right there. Bad time for a tourist."

"Uh huh," Reilly replied.

"Do you know your way around?"

"I do."

As they left the airport perimeter, the driver showed he was up to date on all the developments.

"The fucking Russian Southern Military District has 50 formations and military units aimed at us. The Black Sea Fleet, the Caspian Flotilla, and whatever planes they have ready to drop bombs on us. Gorshkov accuses us of violating Article 19 and 21 of the UN Convention. Blaming Ukraine for encroaching on his maritime security and provocative actions in the shipping lanes. Bullshit."

"Doesn't Russia have the right to inspect any vessel sailing through the Sea of Azov?"

"More bullshit. A bullshit treaty from 2003 and they're abusing it. Using it as bullshit provocation. They ram our boats; they attack our sailors. They parade them before the cameras and make our boys recite memorized texts that they knew they were in Russian waters. It's all a lie. They supply their pro-Russian thug separatists with arms and so we live under martial law. But for how long? They say forty-thousand troops are ready to invade. And what will you, the West, do? Nothing. The same nothing your country gave Crimea. We are not NATO. We're not France or England, or even Poland. I bet you can't even spell Ukraine right."

"I can spell it just fine."

The driver snickered.

"Who are you, man? Nobody wants to go to Kiev. Everyone wants to get out."

"Yeah," Reilly said under his breath.

"On business?"

"Yes."

"Hard time to get business done. Better act fast."

"You've got that right," Reilly replied.

The driver smiled. "If your business involves getting out alive, I know the best routes. It won't be Boryspil."

Reilly cocked his head. The driver saw the look in his rear-view mirror. They were sizing each other up.

"Ah, I have your interest."

"Keep going, mister…." Reilly waited for the driver to give his name.

"Volosin. Ilya Volosin."

Reilly played a hand.

"Lieutenant Colonel Volosin?"

The driver laughed. "Major." He reached back and offered Reilly a hand to slap. "Very observant. So again, who are you?"

"Someone who will need those routes."

"It'll cost," the former special forces officer joked.

"If you're for real, that won't be a problem."

* * *

The CNN video Reilly had seen didn't tell the whole story. Tanks blocked vehicular traffic to some streets in the city center. Troops gave long, hard looks to cars passing by. Looks that could kill.

Volosin made twists and turns, adding more time to the drive. "You worried?" he asked his passenger.

"Worried enough to make plans."

"Spoken like an experienced officer as well. U.S. Army?"

"Retired."

Volosin looked at his fare again in the rearview mirror. He watched him evaluate the roadblocks and the infantry.

"Ah, you're surveying. And planning." Reilly said nothing. The Ukrainian smiled.

They passed shops that should have been busy with tourists but were deserted, street vendors whose wares were covered in canvas, not just for the night, but perhaps for a long time. And the famed National Museum of Science, typically filled with children, boarded up. Reilly spotted school buses certain to remain locked in an adjacent parking lot until after whatever was going to happen happened.

"Can't get you much closer," Volosin said.

Firetrucks blocked Independence Square. Hoses were hooked up and manned, not for fighting fire, though that might be necessary if Russia bombed the square. For now, they were being used as water cannons.

"Get out and walk like you know what you're doing. Be prepared to show your passport ahead. Don't look so interested in what's going on, my friend. Turn right, your hotel is two blocks down."

Reilly thanked the former commando and paid him as agreed.

"One more thing," Volosin said. He wrote his cell phone number on a scrap of paper and handed it back over the seat. "You're going to want to call me."

Reilly took the paper.

"I just may."

The ground was wet from the spray of hoses and the blood of rioters. Guards stood every hundred feet, checking IDs and questioning protestors stupid enough to invite trouble and pedestrians brave enough to venture out of their hotels. Armored personnel carriers slowly maneuvered across the cobblestones, breaking up groups larger than ten but getting pummeled with rocks and bottles from demonstrators.

Dan Reilly worked his way through the mayhem. It took twelve minutes to get to the hotel, now more of a five-star sanctuary. He was met by security officers at the door.

"No entry," said one of the biggest rent-a-cops Reilly had ever seen. He held the palm of his hand up. Reilly pulled his suitcase close and produced his identification. The guard radioed a supervisor inside. Five minutes later, a well-dressed man emerged from the lobby.

"Mr. Reilly! Thank you for coming."

"Stephan," Reilly said gratefully. General Manager Stephan Lazlo gave the guard a signal. Reilly could pass.

The lobby was as much a war zone as the exterior; it was filled with guests and people off the street seeking shelter. Someone was attending to a young woman's head injury. Others, already bandaged, were resting on the couches, chairs, and floor.

Reilly stood in the center of the lobby and did a slow one-eighty turn. The cacophony of outside sounds was drowned by wailing inside.

"It was relatively calm until the pro-Russian protesters moved in. I watched from the ballroom. Seemed very coordinated. They marched in, ramped up the rhetoric, starting fighting leftists, and then there was gunfire."

"Where did your guards come from?" Reilly asked.

"Mostly local bar bouncers. I had their phone numbers in case of an emergency."

By this time they'd worked their way to Lazlo's office. Reilly parked his suitcase and the general manager offered him a scotch, which he gladly took.

"How much cash do you have on hand?" Lazlo was thrown by the question.

"Cash? Well, about the equivalent of $15,000 U.S. Maybe more."

"I'll need more." He knew where he could get it, but didn't say. "Stephan, take me through the security measures. Don't skip a thing."

"We have five hotel vans."

"Vans, not buses?"

"Buses are a problem. Drivers are a problem. Anyway, we can't get them into the square. The closest access is three blocks down Borysa Hrinchenka Street. And that's still dependent on traffic and the time of day. Early morning would be best. 0500."

Reilly settled into a chair. He didn't see what he wanted.

"You don't look happy," Lazlo noted. He wasn't.

"How many people to exfil?" Military talk—he corrected himself. "To evacuate?"

"Two-seventy, two-eighty. We're getting a count. But the situation escalated faster than we anticipated. People didn't want to leave, then flights began getting cancelled. And then dealing with all the luggage. I told everyone one bag each," Lazlo said, thinking he had made a good decision.

"No suitcases," Reilly insisted, "except what they can carry. Maybe not even that."

"People aren't going to be happy."

"Start preparing them." Then he asked for a whiteboard, something large to write on.

"Catering has them. I'll have one brought up."

"As big as possible. And markers." As Lazlo opened his top desk drawer and pulled out several thick markers, Reilly looked at the wall.

"Nevermind catering."

Reilly took the markers, walked to the wall, cleared a credenza and removed a painting.

"What are you doing?" Lazlo asked.

"Giving myself writing space."

He wrote in block letters, IMMEDIATE PRIORITIES. Under it three columns: Buses; potential routes out, labeled Evac Corridors A, B, C, and D; and a large dollar sign. Next, Reilly removed his cell phone from his suit jacket pocket and dialed the newest number he'd entered. It rang three times.

"*Pryvit*," a man answered. *Hello.*

Reilly decided to give the man respect.

"Major Volosin, this is Dan Reilly, you drove me...."

"Ah, hotel man. Good. You got in safely."

"Yes, and now I want to make a deal with you about leaving," Reilly said. "With about 300 of my closest friends."

50

KIEV

The buses weren't the problem. Nor the men. Ilya Volosin had both. But getting everyone to safety would be the real challenge. Through roadblocks, past protesters—and there was another unknown: *what if the Russians moved in?*

Volosin quoted Reilly a price. It was high. But it was a seller's market.

* * *

There are two kinds of phones to use in many crises: a traditional land-line or a charged satellite phone. Digital phone less so, because digital towers can be shut down or blown up.

Lazlo handed Reilly the sat phone.

"You can use my office," the general manager said.

"No. The roof. I need line of sight with the Globalstar Net."

Lazlo showed him to the roof and left, partly to give Reilly privacy, partly because he didn't want to know more than he already did.

Reilly checked for a signal. Green. His first call was to Alan Cannon. He found his head of security in Riga. Cannon listened to the plan that Reilly presented.

"Complicated."

"Complicated times."

"And you want my approval before going higher?"

"You got that right."

"OK. You've got it."

One.

Reilly's next call was to Chicago and Chief Operating Officer Lou Tiano.

"How much?"

Reilly gave him the number.

"God almighty, Dan. Does anything come easy to you?"

"You want an international business, you get international problems."

Two down. The third call would be the hardest.

"EJ," Reilly began when the KR chief came on the line. "Got a few things for you to greenlight."

There was nothing in Reilly's voice that indicated he'd take anything but a yes.

"Why do I think this is going to be an expensive call?" Edward Jefferson Shaw wondered out loud. Reilly permitted himself a chuckle.

"Because you know me."

* * *

As always, Reilly took a room on the fourth floor, hook and ladder accessible. Near a stairway exit, but not directly next to it. He ordered a club sandwich with fries, coffee, and a glass of local red wine. While waiting for his food he showered. Over the past week, he'd had far too little sleep—both travel and Marnie Babbitt were to blame, as well as friends and enemies tracking him. And now he was in Kiev, possibly at ground zero in a matter of days. Maybe hours.

But there was more on his mind. *What am I missing?* he thought. *Things that you miss will kill you. What is it?*

It was a question he couldn't answer today. Not for the next thirty-six hours. Not for the next week. But it was a question he had to answer and it was about Marnie. *Why can't I commit to Marnie? What's holding me back?*

Reilly finished his sandwich, transferred his coffee to a cardboard to-go cup, and returned to the roof. He had two more calls to make. The first to Jordan. If that went well, then he had a second to make to Dubai.

A man answered. He said, "Speak," with a cultured English accent. Reilly knew him to be a former SAS commander who grew richer outside the service as a mercenary operating in Amman.

"Reilly."

"I know a bloody thousand Reillys. I hate the name Reilly. Too many different spellings. That's why I never write their names down. I'd rather do business with someone named McCarthy or Sullivan, or O'Rourke. Actually, forget O'Rourke. Too many spellings, too. Which Reilly is this?"

The irascible attitude assured Reilly he was talking to the right person: Reginald Thompson. Hating both *Reginald* and *Reggie*, he always went by Thompson.

Reilly gave him a one-word clue.

"Thompson, remember Yogyakarta?"

"Oh, that fucking Reilly."

Reilly had referred to an operation in Indonesia that utilized the services of the mercenary and his men.

"Yes, that one."

"Two els, correct?"

"Hasn't changed, Thompson."

"Same company?"

"Same."

"What can I do for you, Reilly two els?"

"More of the same. Details to be worked out. Closer to your neighborhood this time. Transportation. Protection. Exfil."

"Numbers?"

"Two-eighty-five, maybe a few more."

"Doesn't sound good," Thompson said. "Location?"

"From Whiskey5." It was the pre-established code for Kiev set by Thompson. "To Alpha." Alpha meaning London.

"Pass," the mercenary declared.

"Cash," Reilly replied. There was a pause on the line.

"Keep talking," Thompson instructed.

"I have a local to do the heavy lifting. Credentialed. You fly in, pick us up and take off."

"Primary airport is negative."

"Agreed," Reilly said. "My local is looking into an alternate."

"How soon?"

"Your soonest, with a window to back in to your arrival."

"I'll need cash." He quoted an amount. It was actually under what Reilly had asked Chicago for. Reilly quickly agreed.

"Deal," said Thompson. "Depending...."

"Yes?"

"Speed. It's going to go to shit there any time. Wheels up and out of Whiskey5 in forty-eight hours."

"We can be ready faster."

"Are you in Whisky5 now, Reilly?"

"Affirmative."

"Okay. 36 hours. Terms are cash, two hundred fifty thousand in my hands before the plane leaves here. One hundred on delivery at Alpha."

"Deal," Reilly said.

"Call me in three hours," the British ex-special forces officer said. "By the way—"

"Yes," Reilly replied.

"Bring enough *Nalysnsky* for my team. They'll be hungry."

Without the next phone call to Dubai there wouldn't be the thin fried pancakes stuffed with cottage cheese, raisins and berries, let alone a safe way out of Kiev. Reilly dialed. It rang three times, then a man answered in Arabic.

"Marhabaan."

Reilly responded in Arabic.

"Marhabaan. Al-salam 'alaykum. Hdha Reilly." Hello. Peace be upon you. This is Reilly.

"Some syntax issues, but good enough," Hadem Nami replied with a chuckle. "*Wa Alaikum-Salam.* And unto you peace. But English will do. It's good to speak with you again, my friend."

"Likewise, Hadem."

Dan Reilly had done business with the Dubai banker twice. Not for corporate building transactions—it was always fast cash that wouldn't transit into or out of the United States. American dollars were preferred, but Nami could provide required funds in euros, Russian rubles, English pound sterling, Saudi riyal, Mexican pesos, Jordanian dinars, anything. He was the president of a bank without a street-front entrance, only a phone number which often changed, and the means—never openly discussed—to fund special operations at an interest rate, never to be negotiated. Tiano and Shaw approved the amount and the terms: four hundred fifty thousand in U.S. dollars.

"How shall we handle this transaction?" the banker asked.

"An associate will meet you in two hours. You may set the location thirty minutes prior by texting me. I will respond within one minute confirming the site."

Reilly gave his regular cell phone number for the text communications and the sat phone as a backup.

"Two hours. Rather sudden, my friend."

"Time is not on my side. Besides, you're used to putting shit together quickly."

Nami laughed again. "Normal terms?"

"Normal terms," Reilly said. Nami's money would return 30 percent profit, paid in full within thirty days. Expensive, as Shaw noted. Necessary, as Reilly explained.

"I'll send you the location. It will not be difficult for your courier to find."

"Thank you, Hadem."

"One more thing, Reilly," the banker said.

"Yes."

"Advice." Nami's voice flattened.

"With a price?" Reilly asked.

"This comes free. An old Arabic saying: 'Be wary of your enemy once and of your friend a thousand times, for a double-crossing friend knows more about what harms you.'"

"I'm not sure I understand, Nami."

"Things I hear. Whispers."

Hadem Nami conducted business with governments and crime syndicates, oligarchs and mercenaries, banks and corporations. Reilly wouldn't learn more no matter how much he pressed. It was a warning. A very specific warning.

"You will receive my text in ninety minutes. I hope we can do business together again." He ended the call with the Arabic "*Ma al-salamah.*"

It wasn't the "Goodbye" that stayed with Reilly. It was the previous comment. *I hope we can do business together again.* It underscored his warning.

Precisely ninety minutes later, Reilly received his text and replied as planned. He immediately texted his courier in Dubai, ready and waiting thanks to Alan Cannon's long-distance work. The courier confirmed receipt of the location and the precise time. He responded with a simple "K."

* * *

At 1900 hrs. Kiev time, four Russian Sukhoi Su-57s from the 6950th Airbase in Saratov Oblast overflew Ukraine's eastern border, approaching Kharkiv. Ukrainian Armed Forces responded, firing S-300PS ground-to-air missiles. They missed. The invading stealth jets, the latest and most deadly in the Russian Air Force, deployed defensive measures. Then they targeted the launch sites with Kh-38M air-to-ground missiles. Seconds later, they took out the six launch sites and instantly killed 34 men and women.

Twenty-two minutes later, Ukraine's president, Dmytro Brutka, put his nation on war footing. He notified his United Nations representative in New York to convene an immediate session of the Security Council. But Russia had already lodged its own complaint against Ukraine's provocative missile launch against its fighter jets, which the Kremlin insisted had not crossed the border.

Brutka phoned the President of the United States, who listened attentively. As America's problems were growing worse, so were Crowe's. But he promised to call President Gorshkov and put the 86th Airlift Wing at Ramstein Air Force Base, Germany, on alert. It was not enough for Brutka, who ended the conversation angrily.

By 2240 hrs., Ukraine's National Security and Defense Council asked Parliament to declare a state of martial law. That very act forbade strikes, protests, rallies, and mass congregations. Forbade, but didn't prevent, especially those organized by pro-Russian sympathizers and sleeper spies. They began to form and, according to plan, converged again on Independence Square outside Dan Reilly's hotel.

Reilly woke to the commotion. The escape window suddenly looked tighter. He hoped to God nothing else would happen, but he wouldn't have bet the house on it.

51

THE KREMLIN

As most Gorshkov press conferences went, this one was unfolding as pure theater. The Russian premier acted shocked at the suggestion that Russia was invading a country.

"Invading? Invading a nation whose people have cried for recognition? Invading a country that denies rights for our brothers and sisters, historically and ethnically Russian nationals, yet living under the yoke of oppressive, despotic Ukrainian rule? We hear their calls for freedom!"

He played the wounded party when a woman reporter from the state-owned daily, *Rossiyskaya Gazeta,* asked about the Russian buildup on the Latvian border.

"Sofia, I really don't understand how you can ask that."

But, of course, he did. He'd written the question himself and hand-picked the reporter, a woman whose sexual charms impressed him more than her writing.

"Year after year, NATO threatens us at our Baltic borders. Estonian, Lithuanian, Latvia—what are we to do, Sofia? Let them in without so much as an alarm bell going off? At the same time, half the population in Latvia considers themselves Russian!"

His figure was on the high side by a large measure, but neither Sofia nor any of the other reporters noted the discrepancy.

"I get thousands of letters each week from desperate cousins in Latvia." Another lie. "Help us, President Gorshkov. Protect us, President Gorshkov. President Gorshkov, please come for us. My heart goes out to them. But the heart is a muscle and it works in partnership with other muscles that must be flexed to be recognized," he said. "Through diplomatic channels we've sought that Russian nationals, long living as second-class citizens, be able to vote; to be counted as equals after decades of political servitude; to have their birthright recognized. We've asked. We've petitioned. We've been denied as NATO grows stronger."

Gorshkov looked disapprovingly at the reporter. He wasn't finished. She would have to endure more. But after the press conference she would be rewarded with a diamond necklace to match the bracelet she wore. Gorshkov had a bureau full of them. When they ran out, he'd buy more.

"I suggest you get your facts right, Sofia. As I stand here, NATO has more than 50,000 troops on a so-called exercise pointing very live missiles at us. At us, Sofia, our homes. Where millions of peace-loving citizens live. NATO has made the world more dangerous, and America's support of NATO and its demand for more compensation from NATO members has created a great imbalance. In sheer numbers, America has limited borders to patrol—two, Canada and Mexico. The Russian Federation has 20,139 kilometers of border and fourteen countries that must each get our full attention." He rattled them off by heart. "Norway, Finland, Estonia, Latvia, Lithuania, Poland, Belarus, Ukraine, Georgia, Azerbaijan, Kazakhstan, Mongolia, the People's Republic of China, and the Democratic People's Republic of Korea. Fourteen. I will not ever compromise on our safety. Never!"

Sofia sat. Yakov Sokolov stood. The senior reporter for Russia's English-language TV channel that played on American cable systems had another Gorshkov-written, well-rehearsed question. He asked it in both English and Russian.

"Mr. President, Yakov Sokolov, RT. Do you have any words of support for the people of the United States, given the series of terrorist attacks over the past two weeks?"

"Yes, thank you, Yakov," he said after the question was repeated in Russian. Gorshkov lowered his eyes from the cameras and paused. More theater.

"I have spoken with President Crowe, expressing our sympathy for the victims and offering our assistance in tracking down the killers," he said, another lie. "Good people were merely trying to lead their lives, going to work or home to loved ones. But cowards struck them down. It is unconscionable. Yes, of course I expressed my sincerest concern. And in this difficult hour, he should do the same for us."

Then Gorshkov doubled down. He went for one more prepared line, designed to resonate across the Atlantic.

"The United States should pay attention to its own threats and stay out of Russia's business."

He stood and stared at his close-up camera. It was a look that could kill.

52

HENDERSON, NEVADA

Vincent Moore walked into the Denny's accompanied by Henderson police deputy Hank Sheridan. Sheridan had picked Moore up at McCarran International Airport in Las Vegas. On the drive to the restaurant, their first stop, he filled the FBI Agent in on where they were with the investigation, which wasn't very far.

Two truckers were at the counter when they arrived. A couple sat side-by-side at a window. A mother and son were deeper in the restaurant, and an older man was just leaving. A new waitress was on duty.

"We'd like to speak to Winston," Sheridan said. He knew the night cook fairly well.

"He's in the kitchen. This way."

She led them through a swinging door. Sheridan handled the introductions; Winston Chambers, a fifty-something African American, wiped his hands on his apron and offered a greeting to Moore.

"FBI," he noted. To the local cop Chambers said, "This is bigger than you thought, Hank?"

"We're trying to figure that out, Winston."

Moore took over.

"Mr. Chambers, what do you remember about Angie Peterson last night? Nothing is too insignificant to mention."

"Well, I've already gone through it with Hank. But whatever you need, Agent Moore."

"Did you see anything unusual?"

"No. Just a few regulars, but I mostly know them by their orders. And honestly, I don't see much from in here except when I grab orders through the window." He pointed to the rack of order slips clipped up above the steel window.

"Anyone acting suspiciously?"

"Like I said, I don't see much."

"You have CCTV cameras," Moore said.

"One." Chambers leaned through the portal and pointed to the corner. "Not working. Hasn't for months."

It was a problem that existed in too many establishments: the equipment was up but not running. Totally useless.

"Okay, back to that night. Can you describe anyone she waited on?"

"Like I said, I don't see much. But yes, we had a rush at around midnight. Might have been a concert crowd coming home from Vegas."

"And Ms. Peterson was on duty then?"

"Yes."

"Credit card transactions?" Moore asked.

"I handed everything over to the deputy."

"Well, we've talked to everyone we could identify from the charges," Sheridan admitted. Winston thought for a moment.

"Locals were out by around 1:30. Then it was quiet until a couple of guys rolled in. Angie knew one of them, he was a regular. She called him Mr. 2 a.m. Grand Slam. That's what she wrote on the order. After him, a guy I never saw, but I remember his order. Always egg whites, and he never finishes."

Moore needed more than what they ate. "Anything else we could use to identify them besides their orders?"

"Well, maybe yes. I did look out. Have to crane my neck to see the corner. That's where they sat. Grand Slam was turned away from me. So was the other guy, sitting back to back with him. But I caught him leaving. Not full on, but I saw him. I think an Oriental guy."

"Asian," Moore corrected.

"Right, Asian. Well, maybe not Asian. Don't really know. More American than Asian. A mix."

"And the other guy. The semi-regular?"

"He stayed a bit longer. Polite, quiet, cash customer like the Asian, um, the Asian American. After that it was pretty quiet through the rest of the night. A truck driver came in around four, ate at the counter. Another credit card customer. Hank, you have that one, too." Sheridan acknowledged this with a nod.

"Back to the two before, Mr. Grand Slam. Have they been in since?"

"No, sir."

"Show me their tables?" Moore asked.

Chambers led them to the far end of the restaurant, to the corner and the table adjacent to it. As they walked, Moore considered the questions he asked himself in Washington. *Why you, Angie Peterson? Why you, why that particular night?*

"You know," Chambers volunteered, "I think 2 a.m. Grand Slam never sat anywhere else. And neither did the other guy. Back-to-back. Odd for strangers to do that since the restaurant was empty."

Moore took a seat at the corner table facing the wall. It was certainly secluded. He got up and went to the table next to it. A woman and her young son were finishing their meals. He introduced himself and showed his badge, which impressed the boy.

"Would you mind if I sit where you are, young man? Just for a moment. You'd be helping me with an important investigation."

"I really don't know," his mother said nervously.

The boy overruled his mother. "Sure." He was excited.

"Thanks. Just for a bit."

Now Moore had a clear view of the entrance, the hallway to the bathroom, and straight down the counter to the cash register. He pulled his gaze back along the counter and focused on where Deputy Sheridan was standing, pouring himself some coffee. Moore's face reflected in the mirror behind the pies. Sheridan caught his gaze and nodded.

Why you, Angie Peterson? he thought again. Then he understood why: Peterson had had a perfect view of the two men talking. She became suspicious, and her suspicion was reflected in the mirror by the man facing out. The man who didn't want that suspicion to interfere with—what exactly?

What? he wondered. Suddenly, it came to him: *exactly what Reilly had warned them about.*

53

WASHINGTON

Alexander Crowe couldn't drop the Chamber of Commerce conventioneers from his appointment calendar. They'd come from all over the country, scheduled well before the events that had so suddenly grabbed the news. Some of the participants knew one another, but most did not. For entry into the White House (the Oval Office to be exact) to meet the president, they had provided their Social Security numbers ahead of time. Everyone was cleared.

There was one slight change, however: Michael Lu. The real Michael Lu, the representative from Chino, California had looked forward to meeting the president. He supported him, had voted for him and believed in his economic policies. A Presidential photo-op for his son was what he really wanted.

Michael Lu was a second-generation South Korean; his parents had immigrated legally to the U.S. Like many others, they started out working in a grocery store in Brooklyn. But the family had ambition and they'd come with some money. After understanding what it took to run a business, they decided they were ready to own one. But not in the cold—they moved to a Southern California town called Chino where both English and Korean were spoken and they could build a new life.

By the time Michael was born they owned two markets. By the time he graduated from high school, they had seven; before he finished college, it was up to eleven. With his business degree Michael joined the family firm, eventually succeeding his father as principal owner. A few years later, he was voted president of the Chino Chamber of Commerce. That position earned him a place at the national convention, which led to a White House invitation and the promised photo for his son.

The only problem was that Michael Lu never made it to the Capitol. He was met in his hotel room by a man who looked a great deal like him. He had been sent to replace Lu temporarily—just for the White House visit. It was a clean kill at Lu's door: a dart to the heart. No blood, no mess. Five-foot-seven Michael Lu 1 was folded in two and stuffed in a large duffle by five-foot-seven Michael Lu 2. Michael Lu 2 put the body on a luggage dolly he'd brought to the floor. He rolled the dolly to the elevator, down through the lobby, and out the door to a waiting cab—an associate—never to be seen again.

Meanwhile, Michael Lu 2 skipped all the Chamber of Commerce events, except for going to see the President of the United States. He stayed in the middle of the pack as he entered, then slightly off to the side as Alexander Crowe spoke.

"Ladies and gentlemen, it's a pleasure to have you here," President Crowe said to the excited executives and one intruder.

"American exceptionalism has many colors, many stories of achievement. You represent the spirit of American business and the very foundation of our economic success. You create businesses and businesses create jobs. Without you we have no America. I'm proud to meet you."

The national Chamber president spoke. "Mr. President, we are honored, and your time is short. Allow us a few photographs and we'll be out of your hair."

"Thank you," Crowe said. "We're ready and I'm all smiles," though that was far from the truth.

Nineteen of the lucky twenty squeezed in for a photograph. Michael Lu 2 remained off to the right side where he knelt and quickly removed a miniscule item from his left vest pocket. It was barely a half-inch wide.

Paper thin. Metallic. Flat. He deftly transferred it to his right hand and placed it on the carpet's edge at the wall just behind the drapes. Next, as people continued to jockey in line, a planted White House coaster slipped down his left sleeve. It matched the other brass coasters in the Oval Office, with the presidential gold seal, with one major difference: it contained a thin heating element. His final step was to place the thin metallic sheet directly atop the fake coaster. No one noticed. He then stepped aside, away from the group photograph.

The White House photographer snapped a quick series of shots. *Historic,* Michael Lu 2 thought. *Soon even more history would be made.*

* * *

Michael Lu 2 left the Oval Office. He passed on taking the chartered bus back to the conference. Instead he walked. Minutes later he sat on a park bench across Pennsylvania Avenue. He took out his cellphone— just another tourist checking his messages. Except, of course, he wasn't.

He mused over the fact that the most anachronistic function on the device he held was the telephone itself: everything else it did was beyond the realm of whoever invented the telephone. With his fingerprint he could make banking transactions; with a swipe he could find a hookup for the night. He could text, email, or videoconference around the world. He could watch videos and play mindless games. But now, he was about to play a war game with a remarkable, deadly device.

Michael Lu 2 pressed an app on his phone. It was programmed with a snarling face. *Appropriate,* he thought. He followed a prompt to remotely turn on the mechanism. The so-far unnoticed flat sheet, warmed on the fake coaster and silently formed into a tiny, self-driving square with a single small point sticking out. Ingenious. Something out of science fiction, but very real.

An image appeared on Michael Lu 2's phone from the onboard camera. But it was dark and unfocused. *The curtain.* He pressed a command. The device inched forward into the open. The image improved. He saw the American president on his telephone at his desk. He couldn't hear the conversation; audio capabilities would have added more weight to the gadget. Video sufficed.

He panned the whole room; the American president was alone with an origami robot.

When the robot was first developed only a few years earlier, its activation required close operation; not so for the latest generation. It was amazingly simple for a complex object: a cubic neodymium permanent magnet that the robot folds itself around, a tiny battery, and ultra-thin electromagnetic coils that allow the robot to operate from a magnetic field.

Lu 2 got his bearings and steered the origami robot ahead. It silently moved under Crowe's desk toward his right foot, and stopped when it reached his right shoe. Lu 2 double-checked his immediate surroundings. No one paid any attention to a man playing with his phone. He returned to his assignment and executed the robot's most difficult maneuver: extending a point. He directed the robot just above the president's shoe. Now more slowly, carefully, so as not to tickle the president. He took a deep breath and entered another command. The tip extended. It contained a toxic cocktail of ricin and VX. A scrape of the skin would do. A puncture would be even better, like a mosquito bite, but immediately worse.

Contact. The president reacted, reflexively twitching his leg. The tiny robot fell, righted itself under Michael Lu 2's guidance, and provided a view upward. President Alexander Crowe's fingers attacked an itch on his ankle under his sock. *Confirmation.*

Some four feet away, near the bay windows, was a plastic water bowl that belonged to America's First Dog, Chipper, a Jack Russell Terrier/ Chihuahua mix—a true immigrant. The tiny origami robot moved toward it. A straight shot. Lu 2 guided the robot up the side and into the bowl. An instant later, the video went to black as the parts, including the battery, began to dissolve. Thirty seconds later there was nothing.

54

KIEV

Standing in Lazlo's office, Volosin looked more formidable than he had in the driver's seat. He was the same height as Reilly but broader, more muscular. He was unshaven; his hair was short and grey. He dressed in leather, like a biker, and yet he spoke with a friendly, assuring voice.

"Short window for everything to work," observed the former Spetsnaz officer.

He turned away from the rough map of Independence Square that Reilly had drawn on the general manager's wall. Lazlo watched, unsure of the man Reilly had chosen to engineer their escape.

"If I had just picked up another tourist, my life would be much easier."

Reilly laughed. "Yes, but this beats tips."

"As long as you don't get me killed. Twenty-four hours?"

"Starting now. This time tomorrow."

They paused long enough for the sound of Ukrainian jets to clear the sky. They overflew the city every few minutes, each time seeming like they were lower and more numerous.

"Lots of moving parts."

"Lots of them already moving," Reilly added. "Now show me the best way to get to your buses."

"You'll have the money?"

"It's on the way."

"My men will need to see it."

"I need to see the buses."

"Money first."

"Your money when everyone's on board the plane."

Volosin laughed. "Dealt like a true Ukrainian, ok. Twenty-four hours. We will be ready. Now show me your plan."

WASHINGTON, D.C.

Five minutes before the president was due to meet with the Speaker of the House, Crowe's chief of staff, General Lou Simon, opened the door to the Oval Office. He smiled at the familiar scene: the president catching a power nap over his desk. His dog Chipper doing the same beside him on the floor.

A few feet in, Simon cleared his voice. Crowe didn't stir. More surprisingly, neither did Chipper.

Walking further in, Simon repeated the guttural sound. Nothing.

Almost to the desk, the dog was still not stirring. Simon switched on his booming four-star general voice.

"Mr. President!"

No response.

He leaned over and shook Crowe. He didn't wake. Simon ran around the side, inadvertently tripping over the white dog with brown ears. The dog remained motionless. He leaned the president back in his seat. Crowe's eyes were open but showed no awareness. His mouth was covered with a spongy white foam. Simon thought he detected labored breathing, but he wasn't certain.

He reached under the left side of the desk, felt around for a small button and pressed it hard. A high-pitched siren blared loudly. Any other time it would have sent Chipper barking and awoken anyone in the West Wing. Everything that happened next happened fast.

Four Secret Service agents, members of the Presidential Protective

Division (PPD), poured into the Oval Office, their Glock 19s out. Simon backed away and pointed at the president. A second agent shouldered his service weapon, whipped Simon around, spread his legs apart and forced him face first against the wall while a third agent held him at gunpoint. The fourth Secret Service agent radioed, "Eagle down. Eagle down. Home base. Medic!"

Simon attempted to turn his face and explain. Agent Two would have none of it. Simon didn't try it again; there would be time to explain later.

Within a minute the president's doctor, Kay Balue, rushed in with a black leather medical bag containing more than the basics. Twenty seconds later, staff nurses followed with crash carts including oxygen and a defibrillator. Balue, dressed in a blue pantsuit and loafers, bent down and administered to the president. She'd been the Crowe family primary care physician long before he became president. Now his life was in her hands. No one spoke as she worked.

She found his pulse, but pursed her lips at the sight of white foam dripping from his mouth. The oxygen was ready, but first she needed to clear his throat. She bent over and quickly swabbed his mouth. Another fifteen seconds—fifteen seconds she didn't know if she had. A nurse bagged the swabs.

"We need to airlift him!" Balue commanded. It was her decision to make. The President required care beyond the capabilities of the White House Medical Unit (WHMU). A gurney arrived by minute two. If the White House drills proved effective, a medical helicopter would be on the lawn in three minutes. Three critical minutes.

Balue looked at the president's dog.

"Dead," said Secret Service Agent One.

"I want a necropsy," she told the nurse with the gurney. She saw the dog dish on the floor. "And take that," she indicated with a downward nod of her head.

"What do we know?" Balue asked the room.

"I found him," Chief of Staff Simon said, straining to turn his head.

Secret Service Agent Two released his grip. "Just as you see him. I thought he was napping. He has…had a conference coming up with the Speaker."

At that moment they heard commotion in the hallway. The Speaker of the House had arrived. The Secret Service detail barred him. There was shouting.

"Quiet!" Balue yelled. "And?"

"I pressed the alarm. I have no idea what happened."

"I do," Balue said gravely. "Poison." She motioned again to the dog and back to President Crowe.

By minute five the president was wheeled out to the medevac helicopter for the short flight to Walter Reed National Military Medical Center. Dr. Balue accompanied him, along with a contingent of Secret Service agents and armed Marines.

Minute six, the Director of the Secret Service called Vice President Ryan Battaglio and Supreme Court Justice Justin Shultz to come to the White House. He instructed, without further explanation, "Now!"

KIEV

Volosin finished studying the map of Kiev with Lazlo's four routes.

"No," he said.

"No? No what?" Lazlo replied.

"These routes won't work. We'll get bogged down in minutes." He took a marker and wrote a new route. "This way, and we'll need extra cash," Volosin said. "We're likely to be stopped by soldiers or gangs. Good, bad, they'll all be on the take. A caravan of buses offers appealing possibilities."

"Done," Reilly said. He looked at Lazlo for confirmation. Lazlo blanched.

"How do we know your men won't be any different?"

"Really?" Major Volosin replied. "Alright, a fair enough question." He smiled.

Reilly recognized the tone. Polite. Patient. The kind of smile he had often used trying to explain something simple to a general who couldn't comprehend a field decision called in the moment that contradicted orders. It was the kind of smile that said, *I'll tell you, but you still won't fucking understand.*

"There are many dangers, Mr. Lazlo. But I'm not one of them. Mr. Reilly was fortunate to meet me. I know the streets, I know the gangs. I know who to pay and how much. Right now you have no better friend."

"Well, I just met you," Lazlo said dismissively.

"We meet new people every day. Some are good. Some not so."

Volosin addressed Reilly now. "You just met me, Reilly. What am I to you?"

"My new best friend."

"Well then, we understand one another."

At that moment an ear-blasting jet flew over. It set off alarms on the few cars that were in the area. Next, sirens in the square blared, followed by an explosion.

It was no longer a matter of even twenty-four hours.

WASHINGTON, D.C.

"Mr. Vice President, we have to do this now," Chief Justice Justin Shultz declared. So far, the president's National Security Advisor, Secretary of State Elizabeth Matthews, the Speaker of the House, two cabinet members, and three Secret Service agents were present for the swearing in ceremony. Unceremonious, but necessary. Others were informed and would either arrive in time or not.

Also present was Chief of Staff Lou Simon. The Secret Service had released him—no one really believed that Simon, a trusted friend of the president's, would attempt to assassinate him, let alone his dog. Crowe and Simon had known each other since Simon, a nationwide radio host, first interviewed Crowe. In the years since, he became a member of Crowe's staff in Congress, moving up to press secretary, and now the president's powerful Chief of Staff.

They assembled in the Cabinet Room since the Oval Office was now an active crime scene.

"Wait." The vice president was still working on understanding the gravity of the news. "Alex is still alive," Ryan Battaglio said. He somehow felt that using the president's first name would help him make it through the crisis.

"He's in a coma," Pierce Kimball said. "At this moment, the nation is without a president. Accept your responsibility, Ryan." The first name helped the National Security Advisor as well.

The vice president was visibly shaken, unprepared for his ascension. As a second-term Florida senator he had run for president in the primaries, but only hoped to win a cabinet position. But Crowe picked him as his running mate to help bring in southern votes and now, at forty-eight, five years under the average age of a newly inaugurated chief executive, Ryan Battaglio was about to become president—or more precisely, Acting President of the United States.

"I want my wife and kids here," Battaglio said.

"Sir, I understand, but we can't wait," Simon implored.

"They have to be here before I put my hand on the Bible."

"Yes, sir."

For the next twenty minutes the country had no leader. Finally, Carolyn Battaglio and the Battaglio teenage twins, Samantha and Sydney, were led into the Cabinet Room, unaware of the situation. It quickly became apparent.

"Okay, now, Mr. Vice President?" Chief of Staff Simon asked.

"Give me another minute."

Battaglio explained what had happened to his family, what was going to happen. The children were excited. His wife was nervous.

Battaglio walked forward to stand next to the Chief Justice. He straightened to maximize his full five-eight for the cameras. He wore a dark blue suit, white shirt and red tie. At the last minute, President Crowe's secretary stepped forward. She tearfully attached a flag pin to his lapel and withdrew.

"Alright. I'm ready," Battaglio said. But he clearly wasn't. He was nervous, unprepared, and at this moment, everyone could see it.

55

WASHINGTON, D.C.

Section 4 of the 25th Amendment to the United States Constitution, ratified after the assassination of President John F. Kennedy, stipulates the process. President Crowe was alive, but incapacitated. Now the law dictated what had to be done.

> Whenever the Vice President and a majority of either the principal officers of the executive departments or of such other body as Congress may by law provide, transmit to the President pro-tempore of the Senate and the Speaker of the House of Representatives their written declaration that the President is unable to discharge the powers and duties of his office, the Vice President shall immediately assume the powers and duties of the office as Acting President.

White House photographers memorialized the moment. Battaglio's wife to his left, the twins flanking him. The Speaker of the House, the President Pro Tempore of the Senate, majority and minority party leaders, Lou Simon, Pierce Kimball, and the four cabinet members who made it in time spread out in both directions, all wondering how they would work with the new commander in chief.

Battaglio raised his right hand and placed his left on the Bible. The Chief Justice of the Supreme Court read thirty-five words from the

United States Constitution. He concluded with, "So help me God."

Thirty photographs, but no handshakes. It didn't feel right. As people were beginning to leave, Acting President Battaglio cleared his throat.

"Of course, Mr. Vice President," Secretary of State Elizabeth Matthews replied.

Battaglio shot a stern look to the forty-three-year-old cabinet secretary. "It's Acting President Battaglio," he said sharply.

"Apologies," Matthews couldn't quite say the words. "Yes, sir."

Now he had everyone's attention.

"As of a few minutes ago President Crowe was reported in critical condition." He paused. "President Crowe has given so much to this country. I pray that will not include his life." Heads bowed in agreement. Battaglio continued, "I'm going to Walter Reed on Marine One to see him and talk to his doctors. When I return I want a briefing on how the hell this happened. And call in the president's speech writers. Have them get me something profound to read." He swallowed hard, realizing he had just made the same mistake the Secretary of State had. He was president for the moment—and possibly for longer.

56

WASHINGTON, D.C.

Phones rang around the globe. Bulletins set off alerts. The cable news channels cut in with Breaking News graphics and hot musical cues. Dan Reilly got word in Kiev, Marnie Babbitt in Madrid. Bob Heath in Langley. Vincent Moore in Nevada. Nikolai Gorshkov in Russia.

Dan Reilly used his sat phone to contact Heath. The CIA officer had little information, but what he did know he shared.

"Poison, Dan. That's what the White House doc thinks. Unknown who or how."

Reilly didn't say anything. He was thinking. This wasn't in his State Department report, but it should have been. He should have seen it.

Inspired, tactical, impressive.

* * *

"What kind of poison?" Acting President Battaglio demanded. "And how does a president and his dog get poisoned in his own office?"

FBI Director Reese McCafferty stood facing the new commander in chief with Pierce Kimball and Lou Simon to his right, and the Director of the Secret Service to his left. No one had either the time or the desire to sit. Battaglio wanted precise answers. McCafferty only had possibilities, not even probabilities.

"According to the log, the last group in was from the Chamber of Commerce. Everyone cleared. That was at 1530. Lou found him twenty minutes later at 1550. Dr. Balue is working with President Crowe's physicians at Walter Reed. They're running toxicological test so we'll know more soon. In the meantime, agents have been dispatched to each of the chamber members who met with the president."

"To talk with them?" Battaglio asked.

"To detain then."

"What else do we know?"

McCafferty stood. He looked pale, like one of the statues at a Washington memorial. The former Denver chief of police and twenty-year FBI agent was widely recognized for never leaving a stone unturned. But now he was stymied. At this hour, with the country under attack and President Crowe poisoned, McCafferty was in charge of the biggest investigation of his life.

"Calculated. Coordinated. Expensive."

"A fringe group or a nation?"

"Too early to determine," he said.

"Well, then you have nothing," Battaglio said acidly.

"Mr. President, we will find out but we have to do this systematically. Do it wrong and it's the stuff wars are made of, sir." Battaglio shrank into his chair in the Cabinet Room and looked around.

"When can I get into the Oval Office?"

"A day, maybe two. We're pulling prints, checking for DNA, anything that might be in carpet fibers."

"I want the office by tomorrow."

It was an unreasonable request, but the director didn't push it. Battaglio was nervous; overwhelmed. He wanted answers. McCafferty switched gears.

"Some news I was due to give President Crowe today, sir: we are tracking operatives who crossed the border from Canada."

"Crossed?" Battaglio asked.

"Parachuted into Maine, likely to carry out the attacks. Others slipped in, possibly by sea. The Northern borders are porous, especially for those with real money to fund operations. Of course, some might have been here legitimately—sleepers, waiting. And we can't discount others on work or student visas. We have teams working on parts of the explosive devices recovered in the Potomac, the Mississippi, the Lincoln Tunnel, and on the Pittsburg bridges. We could get lucky yet."

The director wished he hadn't said lucky. He had to give this president, this acting president, concrete information to settle him down.

Battaglio, once Chair of the Senate Intelligence Committee, picked up on McCafferty's usage.

"Mr. Director, thinking like a terrorist, why would we have chosen these targets?"

The FBI Director took in a deep breath. His cheeks puffed out. He exhaled audibly and looked at CIA Director Watts. Watts took the cue and stepped forward.

"Actually, we did choose those targets. Each of them and more." Battaglio blanched.

"What?"

"There was a study," Watt continued, "A joint paper that bubbled up from State, with Homeland Security, CIA, and NSA input. Classified. Top Secret. SCI." Battaglio understood the designation: Sensitive Compartmented Information.

"And?"

"Under lock and key, never to see the light of day," the CIA director explained.

"Let me guess," Battaglio said, "Somebody broke the lock."

"Quite possibly, yes."

"Director McCafferty, not to state the obvious, but you are talking to the paper's authors?"

"Author. Single. And yes. He's out of government now, works in international."

"International what?"

"Hotels. President of the Kensington Royal International chain."

Secretary of State Elizabeth Matthews cleared her throat. Battaglio automatically turned to her.

"Mr. President, I can add some clarity. He worked for me in the State Department. He's dedicated and thorough. I can assure you the leak was not his doing."

"Are you absolutely sure?" Matthews began to respond—but McCafferty interrupted.

"We have questioned him thoroughly."

"And?"

"Questioned and released."

Battaglio shrugged off the answer.

"He passed all the tests," Matthews interrupted. "A decorated vet. A State Department resource. Now an international player."

"Players play," Battaglio insisted. "Money talks. Offshore money talks the loudest."

Here Battaglio spoke with some knowledge. He was familiar with Senate intelligence committee reports on Russian spies operating in the U.S., who curried favor with political parties and members of Congress.

"What is this so-called research paper of his?" the acting president asked.

"Major targets. Many are fairly obvious—it wouldn't take a stolen paper to put them on terrorists' lists."

"And other targets?"

"Right out of his research. Chapter and verse."

"Where is he now?"

"Ukraine, Mr. President," Watts said. "He's working on getting people out of Kiev. We're in touch."

"Christ. Is he a hotel exec or some sort of State operative?"

No one volunteered an answer. Battaglio looked disgusted with the team he had just inherited.

"Sir," McCafferty finally said, "under the circumstances, we must limit your exposure. The Bureau's best recommendation is that you remain in the White House, meet only with those with the highest security clearance, and have us test everything you eat. No matter where you go, White House chefs will either cook your food or supervise its preparation. More than usual, you're in lockdown."

More silence until the FBI Director's phone buzzed. McCafferty looked at the display: FBI agent Moore's name came up.

"Excuse me for a moment." The FBI chief backed away and answered. "Yes," he said quietly.

"We have all of the Chamber of Commerce members who went to the White House except one."

"Who?"

"A man named Michael Lu. Mid-thirties, from Chino, California. New to the national conference. He cleared his security check but now he's disappeared. Not at any functions, not answering his phone which, by the way, was in his hotel room."

"Family?"

"Concerned," Moore said. "His wife talked to him last night. She said they have a standing evening phone call. He missed it today. But here's the real rub."

"Go on."

"According to a hotel bell captain, Lu was last seen leaving the hotel, rolling a large duffle bag. The bellman asked if he wanted a cab. He didn't. Instead, he walked down the street. Later he was seen at the convention center where he met up with his group and boarded the scheduled bus to the White House. No one reported him traveling with a duffle."

"You're about to propose a theory, Vincent."

"Yes, sir. My team believes we'll locate the duffle bag, probably in a dumpster. Inside will be Michael Lu. The real Michael Lu. Dead. We're looking for someone who assumed his identity for the sole purpose of gaining access to the president."

"And what do you base this on?"

"Stuffed animals."

Battaglio raised an eyebrow, not understanding.

"Sir, we found two expensive stuffed animals in Lu's room. His wife said that was his routine whenever he traveled. Toys for his children. That's not something someone does who intends to disappear. He bought them, fully planning on seeing his family. The Bureau does not believe he is the assassin."

*　*　*

"Ladies and Gentlemen, it is with a heavy heart that I address you tonight, as Acting President of the United States," Ryan Battaglio began. He was on a head-to-toe shot in the Lincoln Room. He wore a dark blue suit, a white shirt, and a black tie. The camera slowly zoomed, stopping at the two-button medium shot. His voice was steady; his demeanor, at least for the camera, was commanding. "I was sworn in three hours ago, soon after President Alexander Crowe was found unresponsive in the Oval Office. The cause of his illness is being investigated by the FBI. We have not ruled out the possibility that he was poisoned."

Battaglio lowered his eyes and shook his head to let the word sink in. *Poisoned.*

"At this hour, President Alexander Crowe remains in a coma at Walter Reed National Military Medical Center here in Washington, D.C. He is alive, but the Constitution is clear: if the incumbent president becomes incapacitated," he didn't continue to quote the other conditions, "then the succession order must be invoked. According to the 25th Amendment, it became my duty to assume the job as acting president. The oath of office was administered by Supreme Court Justice Justin Schultz. While I serve you tonight as Chief Executive and Commander in Chief, I pray that President Crowe will make it through his greatest challenge to reassume his post. Over the coming days many theories will fill the airwaves. I urge you not to let fringe conspiracies or what you may perceive as silence from the White House lead you to false conclusions. We will share information as we can, but we will not compromise our investigation—an investigation already underway by the FBI."

Battaglio did not point to the suggestion of an international plot.

Now was the time to speak with expected presidential confidence as his writers had crafted.

"To the people behind this heinous, criminal act, listen well: America's voters determine the direction of the nation. You do not. Elected officers, chosen every two, four, or six years set the course of our great country. You have no power over us. You may grab headlines, you may even create chaos, but the United States of America will not be brought down by your cowardly actions."

Battaglio leaned forward, as if to talk directly to the perpetrators. It was a cold, unmistakable look. "And you better pray along with us that President Crowe lives."

The new president nodded slowly. It further emphasized his determination to viewers. Most of the country had never heard Ryan Battaglio speak; now they would never forget him.

"America has suffered this month. The lives of hundreds of loved ones have tragically been taken. Admittedly, we must gird ourselves against greater threats. And while we will not live within the shadow of fear, we cannot afford to be complacent in the sunlight. Not in our house. Not in the White House. God Bless America, and have trust that all quarters are at work while you sleep."

Acting President Ryan Battaglio delivered the prepared speech perfectly. He held his gaze until the stage manager called, "Clear." In those two seconds he decided he would be a visible, confident presence for the American people. He would rise to the responsibility and, believing that he had the power to change things, he decided his next act as president was to set up a series of international telephone calls. He was determined to emerge as a leader on the world stage.

57

KIEV

Reilly always seemed to be crossing one hotel lobby or another—watching, judging. This time it was all the more urgent. He checked the security measures, all active and manned. The scanners were overseen and operated by security officers in blue jackets, white shirts, and black pants. Weapons—Glocks, metal batons, handcuffs and pepper spray—were all visible. The guards were charged with scanning all incoming suitcases and packages, but there was nothing to scan. People were simply milling about, no one leaving and no one entering.

Reilly noted that guests at the elevators were, per heightened security procedure, being asked to show their room keys. They were also required to sign a register, and before entering their names were wirelessly communicated to the front desk for verification.

He stepped outside through the revolving door into sheets of driving rain. In the last few hours, a heavy downpour had taken the fight out of most protestors, patriots and scoundrels, free Ukrainians and Gorshkov's paid thugs. *Keep raining*, Reilly thought. Rain could do him good tomorrow; it might even delay what seemed like the inevitable. But just as the rain drove away the crowds, any comfort he felt was drowned out by the roar of more low-flying jets.

Back to his survey.

Vehicle-stopping bollards had been drilled into the cement, probably unnecessarily considering cars and trucks were already blocked from Independence Square. Moreover, they wouldn't stop tanks—certainly not Russian tanks.

Reilly nodded to the private guards at the main entrance. They were a bigger version of the security team inside, just as Lazlo had explained. But none of them carried guns, per Reilly's orders; guns could escalate a situation and put guests and staff in further jeopardy.

Reilly returned inside. Things were as they should be…except for the woman in a green hoodie and black jeans. He'd missed her before. Her back was to him. Now she confidently walked toward the elevator, rolling her suitcase with an attached computer bag, and clutching her purse. Reilly walked forward.

"Ms. Flanders," he said. "What a surprise."

The *New York Times* reporter stopped and smiled. She shifted the room key in her right hand to her left and offered to shake Reilly's hand.

"Just following my story, Mr. Reilly."

THE KENSINGTON ROYAL NORDISKA HÔTEL

STOCKHOLM, SWEDEN

THE SAME TIME

Another city. Another hotel. Another woman.

She wore all black. A designer leather jacket, low-cut black silk blouse, tight jeans, and chic over-the-knee boots. She held back in the check-in line, waiting for the right station to open up. She let two businessmen and one couple pass as she eyed a handsome blond twenty-something hotel clerk.

"*Nästa,*" he said. Next.

She acknowledged the attention with a shy smile. A deception; there was nothing shy about the woman now facing the young man. The clerk smiled the kind of smile that hardly hid his interest.

"Hello," she replied softly in English, with a distinct Russian accent. He switched from Swedish, immediately captivated by her sensuality.

"May I assist you?" He forced himself to maintain eye contact and not drop his gaze to what he wanted to see.

She read his nametag and replied, "I certainly hope so, Herr Karlsson."

Karlsson smiled. She had him.

MADRID

THE SAME TIME

And another city. Another hotel. Another woman.

Marnie Babbitt hailed a cab outside the Marriott where she was staying, her business successfully wrapped—a new 980-million-dollar construction loan signed with Vista Superior, one of Spain's biggest office developers. She had the fully executed papers in her Coach attaché case. Photocopies went to her Barclays London team; they'd generate seed funds within forty-eight hours.

She undressed, took a robe from the closet, and lounged on the bed. A much better way to talk with Dan, if he was available.

She dialed.

"Hello." Reilly answered on the third ring.

"Hi darling."

She heard loud noise in the background. Rumbling, like at an airport.

"Did you just land, sounds like…."

"I'm not at the airport, in the city now. Kiev—" A formation of fighters drowned out the rest of what Reilly was saying.

"You okay?" she asked.

"As along as those jets are Ukrainian. But can I call you back?"

Marnie heard what she thought was another person saying, "Here you go. Two *Lillet on the rocks*."

Marnie realized she wasn't going to have a sexy conversation.

"Sorry, I guess I caught you at a bad time."

"It's okay," Reilly said. "I'm with a very persistent reporter."

"A *she* reporter?"

"Yes," Reilly declared.

"I hope *she's* ugly as sin," Marnie said.

"Sure is," he chuckled. "I'll get you later."

"You better. And you sure she's ugly?"

"Very," he lied.

 Marnie Babbitt hung up, frustrated.

58

WASHINGTON, D.C.

Moore reviewed the latest results from the FBI labs at Quantico with disappointment. No matches on the prints that came back from the batteries discovered by the hotel maid. No fingerprint matches on the rental car signatures. Negative as well on pieces recovered from the trucks in the Potomac: the perpetrators were either foreign with no record, or they slid in under customs and had been hiding in plain sight.

The lab was still working on tracking down the origin of the electronics in the autonomous cars. The parts were not standard for any commercial models, which made it all the more difficult.

Nothing was coming easy, including how the poison was administered to the president. Yet, this is where Moore shined. It was all a process of elimination: consider all the possibilities, discard the obvious, place high value on the unlikely because it just might turn out to be true. Follow every lead. Listen to others, but don't doubt yourself.

The obvious facts: The attacks were well-funded, well-rehearsed. That meant they needed places to train without being observed. Or, he reasoned, where observations were controlled. That meant a secure location, one with bridges to practice on. He ruled out Americans off the grid: planning at this level required a foreign base.

Moore, a former New York detective known for his

obsessive-compulsive nature, shifted his focus from the attackers to their targets: America's infrastructure and the presidency itself—a blow to America's emotional resolve. His thinking brought him to a conclusion that the attacks were intended to inflict more psychological damage than their physical toll. Certainly, they were crippling, but what was the impact? A transportation standstill, yes. But more than that: political gridlock.

Focus, his inner voice told him. *Focus harder.* Then he realized the inner voice wasn't his. It was Reilly's.

* * *

CIA Director Gerald Watts entered the Oval Office accompanied by his lead investigator, Bob Heath.

"Good morning, sir," Watts said.

"Let's reserve the adjectives until we see how the day goes," the acting president replied.

"Sir," Watts said, "I want to introduce you to Case Officer Heath."

Battaglio nodded. The acting president, known for his economy of words, proved himself true to his reputation. "Help yourself to coffee and then let's have it."

They passed on the coffee.

"What do you have and how bad off are we? Even more important, how they hell did they get to Crowe? And why the damned dog?"

"We're working with Bureau to find out who they—"

"On that point, Case Officer Heath, who the hell are *they*?"

"*They*," Heath said, "are a skilled team. Military-trained. Tech-savvy. Loyal. Willing to obey orders, work as a unit to achieve their goal and get out. That's key. They're trained to walk away alive. In fact, time after time, that's precisely what they've done: walk away. That means they're confident, duty-bound. Soldiers. Foreign, able to pass as Americans, as evidenced by making it all the way into the Oval Office. Therefore, proficient in English. Skilled in explosives and electronics. Make that expert in both. Able to communicate without exposing themselves.

Smart enough to use stolen credit cards to throw off investigators. And probably as deadly in hand-to-hand combat as mass murder."

Battaglio showed his impatience. "Again, the *they*, Heath? Names, countries."

Heath glanced at Watts. He hadn't made up his mind on Battaglio, but his first impression was not positive.

Battaglio rose and walked to the windows. He pushed the gold curtains to the side and peered out onto the garden. Flowers moving gently in the summer breeze. Orioles and robins on the lush trees, oblivious to the Secret Service snipers on the White House roof. Two squirrels chasing each other and scrambling up a tree. Nature doing its thing while terrorists did theirs.

"Well, this is a total waste of time," Battaglio said side-stepping Heath. "This meeting is over."

Something bothered Heath. It was the same thing that gnawed at Vincent Moore and Dan Reilly. Battaglio wasn't seeing it, but he did.

Distraction.

59

FBI LABORATORIES

QUANTICO, VIRGINIA

Ruth Ann Joslen loved solving puzzles. She'd been honing her skills for more than thirty years: a Rubik's cube at age nine, the *New York Times* Saturday crossword puzzle, the hardest of the week, beginning in middle school. In high school she turned to chemistry, which presented her with new and more complex puzzles. Molecular, cellular, right down to atomic levels.

Joslen lived for it. Colleges competed with offers of a full ride. She chose the University of Rochester, where she excelled as an undergraduate in biology. She earned two more degrees in quick succession: a Masters in Biological Engineering from MIT, and a PhD in Molecular and Cellular Biology from NYU. FBI recruiters were at graduation to meet her. Now three decades later, she was still solving puzzles as Unit Chief, and often consulting with HAMMER, the Hazardous Agent Mitigation Medical Response team run by the Secret Service Technical Support Division (TSDF). Her present assignment was to determine how President Alexander Crowe was poisoned, and send her findings as quickly as possible to the White House Medical Unit.

The best clue was the dead dog. Whatever the president ingested, Chipper did, too. *But why poison the dog? And how?* Joslen was stymied.

She hated being stymied. Stymied didn't solve puzzles. Clear thinking did. Somehow Crowe was poisoned. Somehow the poison ended up in the dog's bowl behind his desk. There were no traces of poison in the water glass on Crowe's desk. *And yet, somehow…*

A pill? A poison-tipped pen? Neither possibility would explain the dead dog.

The timeline: Crowe was fine before the visit by the Chamber of Commerce. He collapsed onto his desk sometime between the time the photo op was over and when the Chief of Staff found him.

She paused. *The photo op.* The White House photograph documented the session.

Joslen wove her shoulder-length gray hair into a bun. Her husband loved the look, but he hadn't seen her since this new assignment began. She kicked off her flats, sipped a fresh cup of black coffee—she lost count of how many she'd had at six—and called for the photographs from the White House. It took twenty minutes, but she got them via email. Photographic analysis wasn't her skill set, but eliminating possibilities was another way of getting to the possible.

Two hours squinting at the computer proved nothing. A series of wide shots had been snapped as Chamber of Commerce members were getting into place for the actual photo of record; the visitors gathered in two rough lines of the twenty with Alexander Crowe front and center. One picture. Then another few with ever-better smiles. She examined the photos and automatically counted: twenty including the president.

Joslen stopped. *Twenty people including President Crowe. Twenty?* She counted everyone again. Three times. Each time, twenty. But the White House log indicated there should have been twenty guests *plus* the president. Twenty-one with the Secret Service agents out of camera view.

Someone was missing.

The FBI agent's heart pounded. She reviewed the sequence of photographs more carefully, identifying each participant on her screen by number. In a corner of one of the first photographs in the sequence, she spotted a man at the side of the group turned away from the camera, kneeling to tie a shoe. *Or as if to tie a shoe.* She'd taken him as Secret Service at first. She now realized he wasn't.

She blew up the photograph 300 percent. The man, one of the Chamber of Commerce delegation, wore loafers—there were no laces for him to tie.

60

KIEV, UKRAINE

Savannah Flanders offered her hand. "Agreed," she said. Reilly took it and sealed the deal. A compromise. Not what the *New York Times* reporter originally wanted, but a first-person story of some sort—still front page news. Reilly would allow Flanders to chronicle the hotel evacuation as long as she didn't ID or photograph him or the Ukrainian team members. The reason, security. Same for the identity of their plane out and the crew on board. But in that case, his company's security. He failed to explain that the crew was actually comprised of hand-picked mercenaries.

She further agreed to hold the story until everyone was out, on the plane, and clear of Ukrainian airspace. No tweets prior. She would have to follow orders, without argument, as if she were one of the regular hotel evacuees which, for Reilly's purposes, she was.

Reilly had positioned them at a table along a wall in the lobby, facing out. Their conversation had taken them through forty minutes, two pours of their drinks and the only appetizers still available: *Varenyky*, moon-shaped dumplings filled with pickled fish and cream cheese. Before the food was cleared away, Reilly's phone rang.

"Hey, buddy," Reilly said, careful not to identify Bob Heath by name. "What's up?"

Reilly turned away from the reporter as Heath told him. It was a short talk. He hung up and his mind raced.

"Important?" Savannah asked.

"Just a friend."

"You look worried."

"Worrisome times, Ms. Flanders."

"You look more concerned now than you did before." It was a probing reply, but Reilly didn't take the bait.

"Beyond what we've agreed to, I have no other information for you."

"I'll protect everyone's identity," she replied. "But I came to Kiev to find out more about you. And it seems like there's a lot to discover."

"I'm just an employee, and right now I need to be as good at my job as I can."

"You're more than just an employee, Mr. Reilly. And from what I've already seen from the bridge and in your travels, you're very good at what you do. In fact, I bet you can describe the entire scene here in the lobby. Right down to faces and clothes. Is that part of your job as a hotel executive, or the part of the job that made you a target in Paris?" she pointedly asked.

Reilly leaned in across the table. "Ms. Flanders——"

"Savannah."

"Ms. Flanders," he repeated. "I have contacts, like you. It is my responsibility to gather the most information I can. You've undoubtedly seen my Congressional testimony."

"I have."

"Then you should also know that what I do for my company, others do for theirs. Global politics requires global assessments. That call was one of them. It's going to get worse before it gets better."

Reilly stood. "We'll be leaving early. You better get some rest."

"How early?"

"Don't unpack. Be in the ballroom at 4 a.m. Two hours earlier if you want to be up with me."

"I'll be there at two."

It was now early evening, seven-thirty. Flanders thanked Reilly and left the table. He remained, watching her walk to the elevator, show a security officer her room key and identification, and head upstairs. Reilly would hit the roof for final sat phone calls to Jordan and Dubai and then reconvene in his general manager's office for a meeting at 8:30. From there it would be a countdown.

FBI LABORATORIES
QUANTICO, VIRGINIA
THE SAME TIME

"There's this guy in the photos," Joslen reported to FBI Director McCafferty. "He intentionally ducked away from photographs in the White House, and—"

"We know, Ruth Ann. We're on it."

"Jesus, Mac, you sure could have saved me a lot of time."

"Sorry. But it helps to have independent confirmation."

"Who is he?" she asked.

"No leads. An enigma."

"An enigma who bent down to tie a shoe."

Reese McCafferty said, "Okay. So?"

"In the corner of a picture. He went to lace his right shoe. He turned slightly to the side, near the drapes in the Oval Office."

"And?"

"Ever know anyone trying to lace a loafer?"

This gave McCafferty pause.

"I thought you'd like that," the chemist said proudly. "It's not on camera, but while he was down on a knee, I think he put something on the floor. I looked at all the other photos after that, nothing in any except one: there's a flat round object, an inch or two across. Hard to really see even with it blown up, but it appears to be a coaster. Right where the guy's shoe was. And it wasn't in the shot of him bending down. Mac, find that thing. Maybe the cleaning crew picked it up. I want to analyze it. It's given me an idea."

KIEV, UKRAINE
THE SAME TIME

The meeting began contentiously.

"No reporters!" Yuri Volosin demanded. The hotel general manager agreed with his countryman.

"The city is closing down. We all have family. We can't afford being exposed if the Russians move in."

"Not if," Volosin interrupted. "When. And when is anytime. Now, tonight, tomorrow morning."

"I have her assurance," Reilly stated, "no one will be identified. Your men will be blurred in all of her photographs."

Volosin stood three feet from Reilly and showed his anger. "My men may bolt. We've been burned by American press before. She puts them all at risk."

"I have to get her out. She'd be writing about it anyway. I negotiated protections."

"She's a journalist. Let her cover the fucking invasion."

"Major," Reilly said without a real reason to believe what he was about to say was true, "I trust her. And I trust you. Let's focus on what we must do together."

Volosin let his objection settle in with the look of a seasoned combatant judging an uncertain ally.

Reilly fixed his eyes onto his new associate. Five seconds. Ten seconds. At twenty, Reilly cleared his throat with an inviting, "And?"

The corner of Volosin's lips curled. He had seen what he wanted from Reilly: determination.

"I'll be watching her," Volosin replied.

"That makes two of us."

"But the price goes up."

Reilly expected as much. The price always goes up with complications. "What is it now?"

"Ten thousand more. You can get it. It's probably already on the way." Volosin proved himself a shrewd player. "We can pick it up together when your plane arrives."

"Agreed."

With his new price settled, Volosin's manner changed immediately. "Now trust me," he said with a cold stare. "You will not take off until I'm paid."

Reilly responded in kind. "You'll get it. My promise. And the buses?"

"They'll be at the loading point at exactly 0400. My men have the route, but I'll have sentries posted along the way in case we need to detour."

"Good." Reilly now turned to his general manager. "Stephan, you have everything I asked for?"

"Yes, in boxes. Everyone gets yellow t-shirts to put on in the ballroom. The flags go with us on the buses."

"Alright. At exactly 0315 cut the landlines and the Wi-Fi. At 0320 sound the fire alarms. And over the hall PA, announce in English, Ukrainian, French, and German for everyone to come to the ballroom with just their essentials. No more than one carry-on each. That should take 30 minutes. Then room checks. Once settled, they get their t-shirts to identify themselves to one another and to us. Take a head count going out. Head count at the buses. Again, at the plane. We'll march to the pickup point at 0350. Tight formation. Have wheelchairs available, too."

Lazlo wrote everything down. He would pass the schedule onto his security.

"Numbers?"

"Two-sixty-five including staff."

Volosin cut in. "The bouncers stay."

"They're our security," Lazlo replied.

"I'm your security, your protection, your army."

At that moment the sky lit up outside Lazlo's east-facing window, more brightly than in a thunderstorm. Explosion bright. Reilly automatically counted the seconds after the first glow appeared. At twenty, a booming sound. Twenty seconds. Roughly four miles out as sound travels—1,125 feet per second, 747 miles per hour, 4.7 miles per second.

The warning Reilly had heard on the phone from Heath had been correct: Russia was on the move.

FBI LABORATORIES
QUANTICO, VIRGINIA

Ruth Ann Joslen wasn't ready to share her suspicion. At this point it was unsubstantiated and maybe too wild for the FBI, but not too wild for someone with the right degrees and contacts.

She called an engineering professor in Cambridge, a former lover—a geek who'd been building geeky things ever since his teens. His name was Lincoln Towers. An odd name for a person, but he lived up to it—very tall at six-seven, with a thin, bearded face.

Joslen woke him up.

"Lincoln, it's Raj." His nickname for her.

"What?" he whispered. "Shelley's sleeping."

"Put something on and go to your desk. I'll call you back in five."

"Jesus, Raj, can't it wait until…never?"

She laughed.

"Your country needs you." She hung up, waiting exactly five minutes before dialing again.

"Okay what is it?" Implied was, *this time*.

"I want you to tell me how you would try to kill the president."

She explained the problem. The poison, the dog, and the victim. Traces of the poison in the dog's bowl. The same poison in the president. But no visible means to dispense the dose.

"You've obviously woken me up because you think there's a mechanical solution."

"Maybe."

"And you wonder why there's no evidence other than the dog's bowl."

"There was a coaster on the floor. The kind that you put drinks on, gold leaf with a presidential seal."

"How I'd do it?"

"Yes, with your most diabolical thinking," Joslen replied.

"I'll make this quick so I can go back to sleep."

"You mean you already know?"

"You asked how I'd do it, here it is: google 'origami robot.' *Popular Science*, *Popular Mechanics*, online videos, lots of stuff on YouTube. It was developed by MIT. The most practical applications are medical."

Medical. Saving lives, ending lives, Joslen thought as she entered the topic in her computer. Lincoln continued to explain, but Joslen was already reading on her own.

"Are you there?" he asked, after a minute of no replies.

"Yes! You're a genius."

"We both know that."

"Thank you. I love you."

"No, you don't, but you're welcome anyway." He hung up.

Her next late-night call was to FBI chief Reese McCafferty.

"Mac, I know how he got to the president."

61

THE KENSINGTON ROYAL NORDISKA HÔTEL

STOCKHOLM, SWEDEN

Marnie Babbitt flew to Stockholm knowing that Dan Reilly would also be heading there soon. Rooms were hard to get, but Reilly's name opened doors at the Kensington Royal even with the Russian/NATO summit just days ahead. She had her own business to conduct: people to meet, deals to set up. And some shopping, for things she could more easily get in Stockholm than bring with her.

The negotiations, if the leaders went so far as to negotiate, were still five days out. So, she'd be well rested before Reilly came.

Babbitt noted the changes at the property. Operations moving to what did Dan call it? Red Status. Windows were reinforced with new wire netting made by a British firm. People could see in and out, but the thick metal weave would dampen the impact of outside detonated bombs. Bollards were up at the entrances. Bomb sniffing dogs on forty-five-minute drills patrolled with their handlers. Security was everywhere. When she went to the elevator, she learned that rooms on the third, fourth, and fifth floors were already blocked off, undoubtedly for the Russian delegation.

Dan Reilly's systems were taking hold, and they were comprehensive and expensive. She admired what he had accomplished: it was above domestic or regional politics or national divides. It was a solution to a global problem—terrorism. Reilly had set the standard in the corporate world. No building would be totally impregnable, but now his hotel in Stockholm would surely be a harder target.

Getting the Russian contingent in and out presented more challenges, but once beyond the hotel perimeter they wouldn't be Reilly's concern. That worry fell onto the shoulders of Sweden's police and military, NATO command, and Russian Federation officers, some of whom were already checked in.

Once in her eight-hundred square-foot room, Babbitt unpacked, undressed, and showered. She considered making a spa appointment, but instead decided to call it an early night, order a Caesar salad and a glass of wine, and try to reach Reilly. A relaxing conversation would do them both good.

KIEV

Reilly's phone rang. He smiled seeing the number.

"Hi sweetheart. A little busy right now."

"Oh, you're no fun."

"Won't be for a while," he replied.

"Then store it all up for me." Reilly laughed. She heard commotion over the phone. Loud sounds. Explosions.

"Mind telling me what's going on?" More explosions and the whopping of low flying helicopters.

"It's heating up here in Kiev. But I'll be leaving soon. I'll call you when I'm out."

"I'm in Stockholm. Come soon." Reilly told her to sleep well. Before they hung up, she told him to do the same, but expected he wouldn't.

Sleep was definitely not on Reilly's agenda. The night was going to be long and the escape dangerous. He regretted not getting to Kiev earlier, but EJ Shaw insisted on his Venezuela trip. The regret intensified when his phone rang.

"Reilly, Volosin. Bad news."

STOCKHOLM

Colonel Martina Kushkin was back on the job. Her latest subject was most willing: front desk clerk Nils Karlsson had accepted her key, her advances, and her bed. He was easy and hard at the same time. Karlsson didn't object to anything, which was a great deal more than he usually received. And when the woman he knew as Pudovkin asked if she could take some video selfies of them to remember him by, he agreed.

Who needs hidden cameras to catch compromising sexual acts, she thought, *when this generation shamelessly puts everything out on social media anyway?*

She'd wrapped her new subject around her fingers and between her legs. But so far there was no need to make him feel compromised. He willingly shared house gossip.

It was a job for Pudovkin, but a job with gratification. She felt satisfaction when she allowed herself to give in to the sex, and ultimate satisfaction that came when she manipulated men, and on occasion, women, to talk.

KIEV

"What?" Reilly asked the former Ukrainian SAS officer.

"You have to reroute your plane. Zhuliany is out now, too."

Zhuliany, also known as Igor Sikorsky, was Kiev's secondary airport. It was named for the famed Ukrainian aircraft designer.

Reilly repeated his exclamation: "What?"

"The roads are jammed. Choke points everywhere. And gangs. Even with my men, I won't risk it. But we have an alternate site to the west, a smaller airport."

"How much smaller?" Reilly asked over noise outside.

"Smaller. I don't know. Not big fucking jets."

"We have a big fucking jet coming in. An Airbus 320. It needs runway length. Christ! Hold on."

Reilly opened his laptop and asked Volosin for the spelling of the airport. He typed in *Z-h-y-t-o-m-y-r Airport* followed by *runway length*. He read it aloud. "1,650 meters."

"What's that?" the Ukrainian asked.

"End to end, the total length of the runway." Reilly did a fast calculation on paper. "About 5,400 feet."

"Okay, that's good. Basically, one of your miles."

"Wait!"

Reilly then did a Google search for the Airbus 320 airport requirements.

"Shit!" he declared. "Too short."

"How short?"

"By a thousand feet." He did the math again. "1,917 meters."

"Fuck. A good pilot can brake fast," Volosin said.

"Maybe," Reilly replied. "But a full plane taking off, short by that much? Find another possibility."

"No time. The Russians are crossing the border."

Reilly knew that, though he hadn't told Volosin.

"Call your contact," Volosin declared. "Get that plane rerouted to Zhytomyr."

* * *

Articles 102 and 106 of the Constitution of Ukraine gave President Dmytro Brutka powers to govern, protected by the law unless removed by resignation, election, health reasons, impeachment, or death. Right now, the most pressing concern for the first-term president was death. A bullet in the head by pro-Russian nationalists taking the capital, an attack from a Russian bomber, misguided friendly fire from Ukrainian troops, or an assassination attempt by some crazed citizen.

The fifty-four-year-old former Channel 5 television news anchor-turned Minister of Commerce-turned head of state had no real political ideology. This was particularly true with Russian troops knocking on his door. Serving somewhere in absentia was a possibility, maybe Paris or London. Resigning was an even more attractive option.

"Get me a way out of here!" he ordered Viktor Lytvyn, his Chief of the General Staff and Commanding Officer of Armed Forces of Ukraine.

Here was the presidential residence at Mariyinksy Palace. The problem was how and where to go, given the quickening events. Word came that the Territorial Directorate North and Western Operational Command air bases were beginning to take fire. That meant the home of the 40th Tactical Aviation base at nearby Vasylkiv and the 7th Tactical Aviation housed at Starokostiantyniv were too dangerous.

"Then where?" Brutka demanded from his secure basement communications center, which suddenly seemed less than secure.

"A civilian airport, Mr. President. We'd fly in low, board you on a private jet. You'll be out of Ukraine airspace within thirty minutes. Safer than helicoptering all the way to the border. You can govern remotely."

Brutka really didn't give a damn about governing. He just wanted out.

"Certainly not Boryspil or Zhuliany. So where? And when?" The president sounded panicked. "And how soon?"

"Zhytomyr, Mr. President. A short flight. But first we have to sequester a corporate jet."

"Well, goddamn, do it!"

* * *

Reilly returned to the roof to phone his Jordanian contact. He checked his watch. He was late for this next scheduled call. He dialed and Reginald Thompson picked up on the first ring.

"Thompson, it's Reilly."

This time there was no good-hearted banter.

"What the fuck's going on? In another two minutes I was going to cancel on you."

The explosions in the background were evidence enough of what was occurring.

"Change of plans."

"No shit, Sherlock. We've got eyes overhead. I see what's going on."

Reilly didn't ask and didn't want to know how the mercenary tapped into satellite imagery or communications. But it was good that he knew.

"Whiskey5 is out. I need you to reroute west to another airport. A regional field. Zhytomyr.

Thompson replied. "Zhytomyr? Never heard of it."

"Find it. It's on the map. But it has a shorter runway."

"By how much?"

Reilly read the numbers.

"You're crazy. Do you have any idea how—?"

"I do."

"The problem is the math, Reilly. The math doesn't work."

"Come on, Thompson. You've done more with less."

"Fully loaded on the way out? Find me another otherwise I turn the plane around."

"I can't. My transportation options are limited and I'm relying on friends on the ground here to make this work."

The ex-British commander said nothing. Reilly dared to use his first name.

"Reginald?"

"I'm here."

"Well?"

"We're talking a different deal."

"Let's have it," Reilly said, expecting as much.

"The price just went up with the risk: 25 percent more. I'll need the additional money within twelve hours of clearing Ukrainian airspace."

"Okay on the first. After we land, give me twenty-four hours on the extra."

"Twelve, otherwise I'll be coming for you," the mercenary countered.

"You'll have to get in line."

"What?"

"Nevermind. Eighteen hours."

"Deal. But there's another problem."

"I'm listening," Reilly replied.

"If you want to take off, you'll have to solve a serious weight problem."

Reilly knew exactly what he meant.

"I'll have it figured out. Just make it to Zhytomyr."

62

National Security Advisor Pierce Kimball briefed Acting President Battaglio, who was trying to get comfortable at the president's desk—now his desk. Live satellite images fed a monitor. The president's team viewed the northeast border between Ukraine and Russia from above; motion was on the Russian side, forward motion. Battaglio listened first to Kimball, then to CIA Director Gerald Watts, and then to Chairman of the Joint Chiefs, General Robert Levine. Lou Simon, President Crowe's Chief of Staff, followed along.

"Options?" Battaglio asked, not immediately certain what was possible.

"Limited," General Levine said. "Like before." *Before* was Crimea. "Because Ukraine isn't in NATO, we have no formal reciprocity agreement."

"There's another consideration," Watts said. "We've intercepted internal communications. Brutka is working on his exit plan, he could be in exile by early morning Ukraine time."

"What about Americans? Gorshkov would have to guarantee their safety," Acting President Battaglio stated.

"Based on what?" Kimball was serious. "He's still claiming it's a humanitarian effort in support of Russian nationals."

"Same bullshit Putin used," Battaglio declared. "The world can see what's going on."

"But Americans don't take the time to understand or care," General Levine argued.

"Lou? What's your take?" The Chief of Staff, an associate of Crowe's since the senate and never more than lukewarm on Battaglio, shook his head.

"You do still work here," Battaglio said, acknowledging their differences and suggesting changes to come if Crowe died.

"Sir, General Levine is only reporting on the polls and the commentators."

Battaglio felt he needed to say something strong. He proposed a call to Gorshkov, asking him to temper his actions.

"President Crowe did that. It went nowhere," Pierce Kimball interrupted. "Without some concrete action, you'll appear weak. If anything, you need to step it up."

No one disagreed. No one spoke.

"Then I'll face him in Stockholm. It's time he met the new President of the United States."

Simon almost blurted out, *Acting President.* He assumed the others likewise held their tongue

As people were standing to leave, the president's secretary called on the intercom.

"FBI Director McCafferty is here to see you, sir. He says it's urgent." Battaglio told everyone to stay.

McCafferty entered and Battaglio immediately sensed his urgency.

"Sir," McCafferty sat opposite the acting president. He removed a single sheet of paper from his attaché case and passed it across the desk to Battaglio who quickly read the three-paragraph missive. It included photographs.

"You can't be serious, Reese," he said after a minute.

"Completely," McCafferty replied. Battaglio handed the paper to the National Security Advisor. Kimball read the summary. He was used to briefings on nuclear stockpiles, troop deployments, terrorist threats, Russian flyovers into domestic airspace, security breaches, and government computer hackings. But not poison dispensed by a self-dissolving... He said aloud, "Robot?"

"Who's going to believe this?" Battaglio stammered.

"It's real," McCafferty stated. "We have a partial photograph of the operative who deployed it and..."

McCafferty removed a coaster from his pocket. He manipulated it through his fingers like a close-up magician would a coin.

"And what?" Ryan Battaglio asked.

"This is what powered it. We recovered the disc..."

Kimball interrupted. "It's just a fucking—"

"To be accurate, a charging station for an origami robot."

"A what?"

"Origami robot. The coaster is actually a sophisticated electromagnetic charging station made to look like a common White House coaster. It's quite ingenious."

McCafferty produced a sample from his case. A folded flat sheet that he placed on top of a thin metal platform.

"Watch."

In seconds, the paper slowly transformed into a multi-sided origami that began moving.

Everyone was stunned.

"It's made of 1.7 cm PVC sandwiched between laser-cut layers of dissolvable polystyrene. According to developers, it can weigh as little as 0.31g. Once on the pad and activated, the PVC contracts, and on the edges where the structural layers had been, it folds into itself. Our lead investigator gave the problem to an MIT expert who confirmed that with a minute camera and the right upgrades, the robot could be radio-controlled by cell phone or tablet. Cutting-edge technology, sophisticated enough to also contain a dart to deliver poison to the President of the United States—all within a miniature device like this that unfolds, walks, does what's instructed, then dissolves in water."

"It's crazy," Battaglio concluded."

"It's absolutely real," McCafferty said.

"But why the dog?"

"The dog's death was purely coincidental, but it's what led to our conclusion. The origami robot dissolved in the dog dish, the dog drank the water, the dog died."

"My God!" Pierce Kimball said incredulously. "A fucking paper robot. Nobody's going to believe it."

"We have proof," McCafferty said, pulling a last item from his folder: a photograph. He gave it to Battaglio. Kimball walked behind the acting president and peered over his shoulder. The photograph showed an Asian man kneeling near the drapery. He had a flat item in his hand: the coaster.

"Although the perpetrator tried to remain off to the side, out of the photographs, the White House photographer caught him in this picture. He was a member of the Chamber of Commerce delegation, a man named Lu from Chino, California. But we believe it wasn't Lu. Someone assumed his identity. The real Lu is missing and presumed dead."

"Why?" the acting president asked.

"To create further instability. Confusion. Disarray," Kimball proposed. "But maybe much more. Maybe to add to the chaos on top of the attacks we've seen. To demonstrate they can get to anybody anywhere, including the president."

Ryan Battaglio slumped into his chair. President Alexander Crowe's chair. It suddenly didn't seem to fit him.

63

KIEV

To most, the evacuation was not a surprise. Lazlo's staff had given advance warning calling every room. That didn't erase the shock of the blaring alarm in the middle of the night and the public address announcement that recycled for ten minutes. No suitcases, only essentials. One small handheld bag each. Guests quickly dressed, packed their essentials—identification, medications, tablets and phones, and whatever clothes they could stuff in their carry-on, and made their way down the stairs to the 2nd floor ballroom.

By 0350, all 247 guests and 35 staff members assembled in the spacious room where weddings had to be booked more than a year in advance, companies competed to have their Christmas and New Year's parties, and Ukrainian businesses held annual board meetings. No one took much notice of the 18th Century crystal chandeliers, the dark crimson carpet which matched the floor to ceiling curtains, or the *trompe l'oeil* depictions of the Ukrainian countryside.

As the street-facing windows vibrated with blasts miles away, wives and husbands clutched each other's hands, and strangers who spoke different languages huddled together.

Savannah Flanders stood off to the right against a wall below a painting of a woman lounging on a divan without a care in the world.

Flanders made a note that the painting, by contemporary Ukrainian artist Irene Sheri, offered sharp contrast to the uncertainty in the room. It was just one of many observations she recorded in her notepad

Reilly saw a printed poster on an easel with photographs of a woman and man.

Vitayemo, Yulia I Zelay.

He found a young woman employee and asked what it meant.

"*Congratulations! Yulia and Zelay.* Yulia is the daughter of the Minister of Commerce. Tonight was to be their wedding. I guess someone forgot to take it down."

Reilly did it himself.

"Make sure there are no obstructions anywhere. Signs, flowerpots, chairs. We'll need to move quickly. The more room the better."

Once everyone was assembled, Reilly climbed up on a chair.

"May I have your attention please!"

Reilly waited for translations in Ukrainian, French and German.

"My name is Dan Reilly." He told them his position with the company and what the next few hours held. People were nervous. Some cried. He offered assurances.

"We're going to get you out safely. You have my promise. We're working with a team of very experienced soldiers who know the city and will get us to an airport. Before going downstairs, you will be given a number. Remember it. Follow your group leaders holding flags. Keep them in sight. Stay behind the person in front of you at all times until we board the buses that are just a few blocks away. With Independence Square closed we'll walk in the groups of twenty to our buses on a nearby street. We will do our very best to ship everything left behind to you, but our primary concern is your safety."

Now came grumbling, groans, and complaints. Loud and angry complaints. Reilly raised his hands insisting on quiet.

"They're just things," Reilly said. "Things can be replaced. But you have friends and family who are waiting for you. Worried about you. And if we don't move quickly as a group, then we will miss our window to leave."

He looked at his watch while the translators caught up. Reilly nodded to staff members at each corner of the ballroom to begin handing out the bright yellow t-shirts with the hotel logo that Reilly had ordered before leaving London.

"Put the t-shirts on over your clothes. We're passing out felt-tip markers. Write your name and city on your shirt. Think of it as a nametag."

There was a more practical worse-case reason to have names on the shirts, but Reilly didn't state it aloud.

"There's no need to trade up or down for sizes. They're all extra-large. Just take one and help those around you. This way we will be able to keep everyone in sight and together and you'll be clearly identified as civilians, not combatants."

Reilly remained on the chair as the shirts were distributed. At 0355, he saw Volosin and ten armed men enter. Each carried a small white flag on a pole. Reilly acknowledged them with a wave and clapped his hands loudly.

"Ladies and gentlemen, our escorts have arrived. We will begin departing in fifteen minutes. Keep the flags in sight at all times."

He advised people to use the bathrooms now because there would be no stops.

"Also, no phone calls, emails, or texts en route." An Italian businessman asked why. "Phone calls might be monitored. We want to move through the city without drawing any attention. That means we'll be walking through Independence Square quietly."

Reilly finished with his thanks and a word of comfort.

"You are my responsibility and I promise you: I'll get you out of the country."

A flurry of question followed.

"Is Ukraine being invaded?"

"Will the Russians kill us or use us as hostages?"

"When did you say we'll get our suitcases?"

There was no time to answer them.

"Please, just follow the procedures."

Reilly stepped off the chair and was speaking with Volosin when a young woman interrupted.

"Mr. Reilly, my name is Deborah Ball. I just want to let you know I can help. I just graduated from college with a hospitality degree and decided on a vacation through the Balkans. Some vacation," she said forcing a smile. "Maybe this will turn into a good learning experience."

"Deborah, thank you," he said with a smile. "I'd love your help. You can definitely take lead in one of the buses and make sure everyone is accounted for. Keep an eye out for anyone needing assistance."

Reilly made a mental note to talk to the woman when they made it out; she'd just earned herself a corporate job at the end of this harrowing vacation.

Four seniors asked for help. Ball immediately assisted. Stephen Lazlo went to a woman in a wheelchair. Reilly put them in the first group: they'd leave with a little head start.

As people began to move out, Savannah Flanders shot video on her iPhone. She watched Reilly break away from the group, talk to Lazlo, and take two thick envelopes from him. Payoffs to get to safety, she concluded.

* * *

Volosin's team parked four school buses on Prorizna Street, two blocks from the Kensington. *Rented, bought, stolen?* Reilly didn't know and didn't care. Fully loaded, each could seat 72 with another twenty or so standing. They had to load 96 or 97 onto each bus; it would be tight and uncomfortable.

The Ukrainians, likely military trained and long reporting to Volosin, led the groups, flags held high. Their weapons were shouldered and holstered. Reilly recognized them: Israeli-made ITI Tavors, 5.56x45mm assault rifles that could be used in either semi-automatic or fully automatic fire mode and Fort-14TP 9x18mm handguns; standard Ukrainian Army issue. The men were big and tough, killing tough.

Bearded and tattooed, with scars and broken teeth worn as badges of honor. Some spoke English better than others. They were direct and polite. They kept the evacuees moving while scanning the buildings above Borysa Hrinchenka Street on the way to Prorizna. Reilly wished it had been a shorter walk, but this was Volosin's call. He wanted easier access to roads west.

More explosions. These seemed closer. Still outside of the city, but closer. Planes and helicopters screamed overhead toward the action. Volosin was right: they'd never have made it to the main airports.

Reilly alternatingly ran to the front of the assemblage and held back to make certain no one got separated. Deborah Ball was doing as promised, as was Stephen Lazlo. Flanders shot more video and photos, avoiding Volosin and his men. Reilly rounded the corner with the last group to the spot where the buses were supposed to be waiting. He exhaled a grateful chest full of air: they were all there.

At the door of each bus was a driver, armed and aware, helping people board and throwing items too large to load to the side. The door to the first bus closed fully loaded, then the second and third. Reilly was the last to board the fourth. He stood facing the passengers.

"Everyone okay?"

He got a mix of nods, thumbs up, and okays, though he could feel the apprehension in the air.

Volosin stepped into Reilly's bus and gave him a walkie talkie.

"Keep chatter to a minimum. My rule is no one keys a mic unless it's important." He showed Reilly the unit. "Earpiece in your ear, press to talk."

"Got it."

"Okay. See you at the airport." Volosin checked his watch and radioed to his team, "*60 sekund. Odna Khvylyna.*" Then he left the last bus to board the first.

"We'll be leaving in a minute," Reilly told his passengers. No one spoke. No one coughed. Reilly had seen this in troops going into battle. A natural reaction. Even the most fearful had to brace themselves.

Reilly heard Volosin radio the drivers. "*Hotovyy.*" Ready. The engine in bus one revved. Then bus two with the same "*Hotovyy.*" Volosin called bus three, the one in front of Reilly. No reply. He called again. "Kolisnyk!"

Bus three driver, Kolisnyk, finally keyed his microphone. "*Zahubyvsya klyuch.*" He recognized the last word from its Cyrillic cousin. *Klyuch.* Key. He didn't know the first word, but in context it didn't sound positive.

"What's the matter, Volosin?" Reilly asked.

* * *

An hour out, the Jordanian charter was ordered to a holding pattern.

"Zhytomyr control, this is Charter 1066, we have limited fuel. We were not cleared to land at Kyiv Oblast or Zhuliany. We are on a United Nations mission of mercy. We must land and pick up our passengers, currently en route."

It was more information than Reginald Thompson's pilot wanted to give. He counted on mission of mercy and his lack of fuel to get him on ground. One was true. One was not.

"Roger, understood," the base replied. What is your bingo fuel?"

The pilot of the mercenary Airbus lied. He had more than enough to land, take off and get to their destination in England. But not so if they were in a long holding pattern off the southern coast of Ukraine. Russian fighters might take interest. Maybe they'd ask questions. Maybe they wouldn't and just fire their air-to-air missiles.

"Standby Charter 1066," the Zhytomyr ground controller responded. "Prepare to reroute." He gave a heading.

The problem at the airfield was the impending helicopter arrival of the Ukrainian president who was on a mission of self-preservation.

"Roger, Zhytomyr control."

The charter began to circle as instructed over the Black Sea. The pilot was pissed. He decided to give it 30 minutes. No more. Thirty minutes maximum. Then he would return to Jordan. A fucked mission.

* * *

"*Ebat!*" Volosin yelled.

Reilly understood little Ukrainian, but given the context, it sounded like a familiar Russian expletive. *Blyad! Fuck!*

"Volosin, what's wrong? We're ready to roll."

Now Reilly heard shouting back and forth on the open mics. He motioned for his driver, who had started his bus, to open the door. He got out. Flanders followed.

"Stay in the bus" he ordered.

"Where you go, I go."

Reilly had no desire to argue with his shadow.

"Suit yourself."

He ran to bus three, directly in front, which was filled with confusion and more shouting. Volosin's men, equipped with flashlights, were searching for something. The *klyuch*. Volosin was inside doing the same. The driver was checking under his seat.

Volosin screamed at his man, which made the passengers more nervous than they already were. Reilly tapped Volosin on the shoulder and signaled with his thumb to come talk to him—outside.

"Asshole!" The Ukrainian paced, shaking his head. "He was supposed to stay with the bus. But he goes out for a smoke and loses the fucking key! Imbecile."

Reilly demanded. "Can't you jump-start it?"

"Like in your movies? Not this."

"Then we'll split the sixty here in the other three buses. They can stand in the aisles and double up."

"And start a riot because now there'll be no room for any carry on?" Volosin replied. "No. Three buses leave. One comes back."

"That could take hours," Reilly responded. "And if things don't hold—" Reilly didn't need to complete the thought. They both had been measuring the elapsed time between bomb flashes and the sound of the blasts. Time tightened. They didn't have hours.

"I'll get another bus!" Reilly declared. "If I'm not back in fifteen minutes, load everyone up in the three buses, toss out whatever's necessary, steal cars if you have to, and leave."

Volosin smiled. "Where will you find another fucking bus?"

"Saw one on our way in. Possibly guarded."

"Then you're going to need this." Volosin reached behind his back, under his leather jacket, and produced a Soviet Marakov PPM 9x18 mm handgun.

Reilly took it, expertly released the twelve-round magazine, checked the capacity—fully loaded—and slammed it back into place.

"Jesus, Reilly," Flanders exclaimed.

Volosin snickered. "Standard training for a hotel executive?"

"Fifteen minutes!" Reilly snapped. He checked his watch.

"Got it."

Reilly started down Prorizna.

"Wait!" Flanders shouted. "Like I said, where you go, I go."

"Then keep up!" Reilly replied.

* * *

Twenty-five minutes before turning back. The Airbus pilot wished he'd only given it fifteen, not thirty. According to Zhytomyr he was to continue to circle and await further instructions. Radar showed air traffic avoiding Ukrainian airspace and fewer planes taking off. Twenty-five minutes more was all he'd allow himself. Money be damned.

* * *

President Dmytro Brutka was tightly buckled into his seat on his Mil Mi-8 Russian-built twin-turbine helicopter. He traveled with two suitcases full of Euros, equally secure. Fifty million. Just part of the bounty he had squirreled away. The copter, normally his presidential airborne command post, flew at maximum speed, 260 km/h. Fast, but as far as Brutka was concerned, not fast enough.

"ETA?" he demanded over the intercom.

"Twenty minutes, Mr. President."

"Twenty!" Brutka complained.

"Yes, sir. Air traffic."

"I don't care about any other traffic."

"Enemy forces, sir."

This quieted the president. Brutka checked his watch and worried more about his money than the country he was abandoning. His Minister of Defense had his orders. Defend the country from what Nicolai Gorshkov was selling inside Ukraine as pro-Russian nationalism.

A minute, two minutes later, Brutka was all the more impatient.

"Faster!" he yelled over the comm.

"We are at top speed, sir. Seventeen minutes."

* * *

"Zhytomyr Tower, this is United Nations 1066 requesting status."

"Charter 1066, remain in a holding pattern at 28,500 and await further instructions." He was at the far end of his circuitous route. Fifty minutes from the airport on a straight shot.

"Charter 1066 requesting new flight plan." He radioed the coordinates that would at least get him closer.

"Negative Charter 1066. Hold. Will advise."

* * *

Reilly turned down Pushkinka Street. Looking south, nothing but cars. He ran.

"This way," he yelled to Flanders. She kept pace with Reilly.

At the next intersection he turned right onto Bohdan Khmelnitsky Street. Ahead, a building he remembered.

"There!" Reilly said.

"There, where?"

Five minutes into the fifteen, they came up to an historic blue and white mansion converted into The National Museum of Natural History. Across the street, were three museum vans and a school bus in a fenced-in parking lot. Reilly and Flanders crossed over.

"Locked," Flanders said.

A thick steel cable chain was wrapped around the fence gate, secured with an over-the-counter keyed Master Lock. Impossible to break apart—but not impossible to shoot apart.

"Back! Behind me," Reilly ordered. He aimed the Marakov from an obtuse angle three feet from the lock, held his breath, let it out slowly, and fired a single shot. The first missed. He adjusted his aim and squeezed the trigger again. The lock shattered.

"Now let's hope there's a key somewhere."

They ran to the bus, checked under the front bumper, the foot panel at the door, and behind the front license plate. "Got it," Flanders announced. She found it hanging on the driver's outside mirror.

"Thank you," Reilly said. He opened the door, sat in the driver's seat, and examined the console.

"Tell me you know how to drive a stick," the reporter asked.

Reilly inserted the key, started the engine, released the brake, and put the bus into gear. It stalled immediately.

"You do know how to drive it, right?" she reiterated.

He started it again, got a feel for the gas and clutch and inched forward, first scraping one of the vans, before he had real control.

"Yes."

Ten minutes down. Five before the caravan was to leave.

As he rolled forward an army LuAZ, the Ukrainian version of an American jeep, pulled into the lot and blocked Reilly's exit. The doors flew open and two uniformed soldiers exited with weapons drawn.

"Prypnennya!"

Though he didn't speak the language, it was clear the soldiers were ordering him to freeze.

* * *

Amateur Facebook Live videos streamed around the world. Ukrainians were on Facetime with relatives in Europe and the U.S., and CNN and BBC bureaus sent out footage from the apartments atop the 533-foot tall

Klovski Descent 7A—the city's tallest building. Viewers from across the globe watched, including millions in Moscow and Stockholm. Meanwhile, U.S. audiences also learned that Russian T-62 tanks were pressing forward from the border and Ukraine's president was unaccounted for.

Inside the Kremlin, Nicolai Gorshkov beamed. He was following through on Vladimir Putin's incursion into Crimea: finally taking Ukraine back. In addition to the tanks and paratroopers and ground forces, he had S-400 Triumph surface-to-air missiles to guard against incoming aircraft. The guiding belief was to hold and protect the capital, because once Kiev fell, all of Ukraine would fall.

Gorshkov already had intelligence that Dmytro Brutka was on the run. His command had coordinates indicating where he was currently heading: Zhytomyr Airport, west of Kiev.

"Sir?"

His command requested an order to attack.

* * *

The soldiers' headlights blazed straight at them. Reilly thought this would not to end well. *Two Americans breaking into a private lot, stealing a bus, and armed in the middle of an invasion? They're scared. We're out of our league.* He pressed the talk button on his radio.

"Volosin come in." The radio squawked.

"You're running short on time, Reilly."

"Got a bus. Up and running, but we're staring at two assault rifles. Ukrainian Army regulars. Any words of wisdom?"

"Yes, stay in the bus. Repeat everything I say. Loudly, friendly. Then tell me what they say."

"Okay."

He had stopped the bus some twenty-five feet in front of the soldiers—close enough they couldn't miss if they fired. Reilly kept his hands visibly on the steering wheel. Volosin slowly dictated a response.

"Say it. Slowly. No sign of a threat in your voice. I'll give it to you in pieces. Just repeat it."

Reilly shouted what Volosin told him as best he could, not knowing what he was actually communicating. After the fifth of five short sentences, the two Ukrainian infantrymen argued.

"What's happening, Reilly?"

"They're thinking."

"Your Ukrainian is piss-poor, but they're trying to figure you out."

"With their weapons still on us."

"Time to see if money changes their minds. How much do you have?"

"Two envelopes. No Ukraine hryvnas—five thousand euros."

Volosin dictated another message for Reilly to repeat.

"Okay. Put two—no, three thousand in one envelope. And is that reporter with you still alive?" he asked sarcastically.

"Yes."

"Then tell her to do something useful. Take the fucking money and walk with it raised high. Nothing threatening. You go with her, but keep my gun tucked in your belt in the back. If all goes well, they'll be thinking about the money more than killing you. If they make any threatening move, don't hesitate, shoot them."

* * *

Every minute Butka looked at this watch he got more worried. His pilot dropped to under 91 meters, barely 300 feet above the ground. That's what saved his life: the Russian pursuit jets lost him. But so did Zhytomyr radar.

* * *

"Charter 1066, Zhytomyr clears you to approach."

Instructions came through for a new west-to-east flight plan which was going to cost more fuel. But at least he could continue. A minute later, when Zhytomyr re-established contact with Butka's government helicopter, the charter was put in a holding pattern again.

Ten minutes, the pilot said to himself. *Ten more minutes.*

* * *

Flanders stepped out. She had both hands raised. In her right hand, a business size envelope from Reilly. The money. Reilly received one more instruction over the radio from Volosin.

"Got it," Reilly replied. He followed Flanders.

The reporter stood three feet from the door, allowing room for Reilly to stand beside her, but he held back a step and to her right side. He had his hands in the air as well. They waited.

"Tell me you've done this kind of thing before," Flanders whispered.

"I have."

"And you've lived to tell the story."

"I'm here."

She looked at him briefly, then back into the jeep lights.

"And we'll be talking about this tomorrow?"

"If we stick with the plan." The jeep's lights blinked once.

"That would be our signal," Reilly said.

"How do you know?"

"I know." They walked forward. "Smile," he said under his breath, "and stay close. The more they look at the pretty girl, the less they think about me."

They were getting too close to talk aloud. Especially in a language the soldiers didn't understand. They could see the two Ukrainian soldiers now rising behind the open doors. Young, maybe nineteen or twenty. Three thousand Euros could make a difference in their lives. Most of all, they could leave the parking lot richer than when they arrived. Reilly counted on that.

Be smart, he thought. *Take the money, call it a day.*

Reilly stopped short of the jeep by ten feet. Volosin had told him to say these words: "*Boh stvoryv nas yak vil'nykh stvorin'.* Say them warmly," the Ukrainian underscored, "with a nod and a smile. They will either lower their weapons, return the greeting, take your money and leave, or you will have to quickly kill them."

Reilly offered the soldiers a friendly nod and rattled off, "*Boh stvoryv nas yak vil'nkykh stvorin'."* Flanders quickly glanced at him, not under-standing, but catching the need to smile. He repeated the phrase and Flanders did her best to mimic him.

Ten seconds. Five more. Then a monotone "*Tak,*" from the soldier on the driver's side.

"*Tak,*" repeated the other.

"*Tak,*" Reilly replied. *Yes.*

The two soldiers relaxed their aim. Savannah Flanders brought her hands down and forward, offering the envelope. The second soldier slipped his rifle strap over his shoulder and approached the attractive woman. She nervously handed him the money, now also adding, "*Tak.*"

Reilly lowered his hands, but this time with a slow parade salute. He had given them more than they expected. Respect and money. The Ukrainians returned to their vehicle, backed away, and waved them forward.

"Wait," Reilly said. "Just nod. No quick movements."

Flanders didn't need to be told twice. Once the LuAZ was away, Flanders asked, "What was it that you said?"

"A quotation Volosin gave me from a Ukrainian cleric who died awhile back. Apparently, his memory meant more than a Spetsnaz major's name."

"But what does it mean?"

"I don't know, he just said memorize it and try it. We'll have to ask."

"First thing when we hook up with Volosin," the reporter replied.

"Second. First, we get our asses onboard and out of Kiev. Fast."

64

Brutka's helicopter touched down. The president barreled out with his suitcases, ducking under the still rotating blades. But he didn't know which way to go. An officer appeared out of the darkness.

"This way, Mr. President," he said. He offered to take the bags. The president held onto both tightly.

Two minutes later he was onboard a Gulfstream charter, *on loan*—actually requisitioned from an oil executive seeking new business in Ukraine. A government pilot instructed Brutka to fasten his safety belt and prepare for immediate takeoff. It wouldn't be soon enough.

* * *

"Charter 1066, you are now cleared to approach," Zhytomyr Tower advised. The mercenary pilot was instructed to drop to 25,000 feet and come in on a new heading. The money seemed real again, but the landing would be fast and the takeoff even faster.

* * *

The buses rolled slowly and cautiously through the inner city with escaping traffic, past armored vehicles heading in. They stayed true to Volosin's plan, taking a meandering route. The interior lights remained off making it relatively impossible for other vehicles or posted sentries to peer inside. They moved as a loose group. Never speeding, allowing other vehicles to move around them. Always in radio contact, on course, until—

"We've been waved to stop," Volosin announced from the lead bus. "Stay cool," he said in English. "Don't come out unless I say."

Reilly detected a few more colorful Ukrainian words when Volosin gave the instructions to his team in his native language. The caravan slowed and finally rolled to a stop on the T0611 heading north, just before the M06 onramp to Zhytomyr. The radio was silent. Reilly assumed Volosin would bound out in some official manner, flash an old ID, bark orders or outright lies about the buses and the passengers. Undoubtedly, he would count on the guards being nervous, uncertain what their real duty was, and not able to easily communicate with command, which was likely confused.

Sixty seconds into whatever was happening, Volosin radioed.

"Reilly, we're going to make it very easy for these young men. You pay the toll, then they let us through."

"How much?" Reilly now asked.

"Five hundred per bus. Two thousand."

* * *

The president boarded his jet and put safety belts around the two suitcases. He was surprised to see a woman and child already onboard.

"Who are they?" Brutka demanded of the pilot, a Ukrainian air force colonel he didn't recognize.

"My wife and child. You're giving us all an all-expense paid vacation."

He now stood over the president, appearing more in command than Brutka.

"I've got the keys to the plane and," he looked at the suitcases, "you've got means to pay for your flight."

"This is the government's money," Dmytro Brutka replied coldly.

"Of course, it is," the pilot bellowed. "Of course, and you're keeping it safe."

"I'll have you court martialed," Brutka screamed.

The pilot's wife turned in her seat and smiled. A cold smile that showed no sympathy for the country's president who had slipped away from his own security, stealing money, and unwilling to fight the Russians.

"And what will you do to *me*, Mr. President?" she said producing a gun.

Brutka lowered his shoulders. Defeated.

"You are a coward and a thief. Abandoning your troops and your country."

"How much do you want?" Brutka said.

"We'll see how the flight goes," she replied.

Brutka had the sinking feeling it wasn't going to go well at all.

* * *

A payoff. A bribe. A toll. As far as Reilly was concerned, they could call it anything they wanted. Divide it anyway they saw fit. However, the danger of handing over money to men with guns is that they might think you had more. Two things could happen at that point: a temporary standoff leading to more cash, or an escalation leading to some of players being permanently eliminated. Reilly had gotten through one negotiation already. *Now?*

There were four soldiers. One in particular who did the talking and the deciding. He seemed to show some respect for Volosin, but he looked at Reilly suspiciously. This was clearly different. Not the case where a simple homily was going to get them out.

Volosin waved Reilly forward. He knew the drill. A disarming smile, which only sometimes served to actually disarm. The conversation was in Ukrainian. Volosin showed patience, experience, and control. What Reilly heard sounded calm, no raised voices, no animus. Then, *"Hi,"* from Volosin. Not a greeting. They'd gotten past that. *Hi* in Ukrainian meant *no*. Volosin's *no* was tough, definitive. No meant no.

One soldier's hand gripped the barrel of his rifle. He began to raise it. The one who spoke for the group put his hand out across his comrade's body. The soldier brought his weapon down.

Reilly noted it was a good decision because he'd seen the driver of bus two getting out the back door and circling around to cover Volosin. He would be able to dispatch all four soldiers before they fired a shot.

"Okay," the lead soldier said. This time he used English for Reilly's benefit. Volosin waved his left hand for Reilly to step forward. He never took his eyes off the men. Reilly handed the young soldier the money.

"We're good?" Reilly said. The soldier didn't understand.

"*My dobre?*" Volosin repeated.

"*My dobre.*"

Volosin backed away. Dan Reilly did the same. The last to leave was the unseen driver. Two minutes later, the soldiers removed their armored vehicle and waved the buses ahead.

"More expensive than the New York Thruway toll," Savannah Flanders quipped when Reilly returned.

"Definitely," Reilly replied.

* * *

Reilly rejoined his bus hoping there'd be no other delays. At the same moment, a private jet was taking off from Zhytomyr and a Jordanian charter was thirty miles out on final approach.

An hour later on the runway, with Flanders beside him, Reilly counted yellow shirts. Everyone had made it. He personally shook the guests' hands as they climbed the portable stairs to the plane. But because of the pilot's insistence over weight, some handheld bags were left at the airport. Volosin said he would get them to London…for an additional fee. Reilly smiled.

"Of course." They settled up with the money brought in from Dubai.

"As agreed, my friend."

"*My dobre.* We're good."

"One question for you."

"Oh?" Volosin replied.

"How ex-Spetsnaz are you?"

Volosin laughed heartily.

Reilly had his answer. He was targeted from the beginning at the airport. Volosin was undercover, tasked with spying, and was now better off for it.

"I've got a couple of questions, too, Major," the *New York Times* reporter stated.

"Yes, Ms. Flanders."

"What was it that you had Reilly tell the two soldiers in Kiev? It made the difference."

"'*Boh stvoryv nas yak vil'nkykh stvorin*'. A simple quotation by a beloved Ukrainian, Cardinal Lyubomyr Husar, revered throughout the country. The quote translates as 'God created us as free creatures.' Meaning, everyone has the freedom to make the right decision. And considering the gun Reilly had, they made the right one."

"And one last question," the reporter asked. "What will you do now?"

"We're going to fight the Russians. We'll fight them until we drive them out, whether or not NATO and the United States stand by us, whether it takes a month or a year or ten years. Then we'll elect a new president. We're going to need one." He now spoke with some knowledge. "I've gotten word that our last president, how shall I say, took an unexpected fall tonight."

PART THREE

SHOCK WAVES

65

LONDON

TWO DAYS LATER

Secretary of State Elizabeth Matthews arrived in London to talk with her former employee. She met Reilly in one of the Kensington Royal conference rooms, the Montgomery, often referred to as The Monty. The room, like others in the hotel, was named for great British military tacticians. This one honored Field Marshal Bernard Montgomery, a decorated general who served with distinction in both World Wars.

The staff had put out coffee and pastries. Reilly poured coffee for both of them.

Matthews, dressed in a gray suit, black blouse and freshwater pearls, opened with a comment Dan Reilly couldn't quite categorize as a compliment or a criticism. But it certainly was the truth.

"Dan," she said almost affectionately, "you're a constantly moving target."

"Apparently with a bullseye on my back," he replied. "And I assume that's the reason for your unexpected visit."

"Smart as ever."

"You're late. The FBI gave it their best shot. And Agent Moore and I are becoming fast friends. Once he got past me being on his most wanted list, we've had a number of solid conversations on the Three Ts."

Terrorists. Targets. Timing. The Three Ts had also been Matthews' work for twenty-five years. From the time she was an Air Force fighter pilot to her four terms in Congress, her distinguished State Department career, to serving as the nation's Secretary of State—Crowe's Secretary of State. Matthews didn't know if she'd last long if Battaglio remained in office.

"You know there are people around D.C. who don't trust you, Dan."

"There are people all around the world who don't trust me. Is that why you're here?" She smiled. "Elizabeth, you've come a long way to talk. How about you make it easy for yourself. Straight out."

"Okay, straight out. It's not exactly about you; I don't know if Crowe will make it. If he doesn't, we've got Battaglio for the next two years. And to be perfectly honest, he's doesn't have enough experience behind the wheel. He's impulsive and prone to tirades, and can get irrational. I saw it in Congress. So far, he's kept it under control in the White House, but soon he'll slip. And this is no time for slips. I'm afraid he'll make the wrong decision and fuck up bigtime."

Reilly reacted in a way she expected. With a direct question.

"What are you really saying?"

"How about coming back in?"

"No, thanks."

"Battaglio is dangerous."

"He's no Crowe, but he could rise to the job."

She ignored the comment, instead trying, "I could use you."

He said nothing.

"At least think about it."

The last comment had the weight of an order.

66

TRACY, CA

THE SAME TIME

Pak Yoon-hoi checked into a motel along North Tracy Blvd. under a new name, Tom Pond. He had a driver's license and credit card to support his new identity, and a smile that might have earned him an upgrade in another property. But at the Motel 6 all the rooms were basically the same. He put his team of eight men in three rooms at the nearby Microtel Tracy.

Yoon-hoi avoided hotels and motels near airports and at city centers. The cheaper ones were often off the country's Interstate highway system and further away from FBI and Homeland Security scrutiny. Tracy was just 56 minutes from the Oakland Bay Bridge in normal traffic—rush hour would take longer. Yoon-hoi's team would be leaving at 0350, ahead of the commuters but in time for the 0600 crunch.

They had their weapons. They had their explosives. Yoon-hoi was confident that they'd succeed, escape to San Francisco, board waiting fishing boats, and quickly disappear in eight different directions. They'd run the maneuver nearly a hundred times on a military base in Russia and twenty-five times, all at dawn, on the Kerch Strait Bridge, also known as the Crimean Bridge, an 18.1 km span built by the Russian Federation between the Taman Peninsula and the Russian-annexed

Kerch Peninsula of Crimea. It was the longest bridge in Russia or Europe, and served as a perfect model for the North Korean squad. American satellites overflew the Crimean Bridge most mornings. Of course, Russia followed the orbits. But the bridge's anchor rooms were covered in canvas, which raised eyebrows in Langley, but never rose to the level of actual concern for CIA analysts.

The night before the mission, Yoon-hoi toasted his comrades' courage with beer in the traditional manner, holding the bottle with two hands, pouring it into their glasses all the while looking away so when they drank, he didn't see them consuming the alcohol. A long-held tradition.

"*Goenbae!*" Pak Yoon-hoi declared.

"*Goenbae!*" the men replied.

The toast literally meant 'empty glass,' a Korean equivalent to the English 'bottoms up.' They drank and laughed until Yoon-hoi called an end to the revelry. His killers looked like they belonged in the North Bay; tan slacks, blue shirts, and loose-fitting jackets. Jackets because it was chilly at the early hour even in California, and loose-fitting to hide pistols and knives. Over their jackets they slipped on orange vests similar enough to standard Caltrans wear to pass as the real thing.

Outside the motel, in the dark, they removed magnetic white horizontal stripes on their rented and repainted Dodge pickup trucks, revealing orange Caltrans stripes and the state transportation agency logos. They screwed on fake license plates and fastened caution light panels above each cab. To anyone's eye, they were legitimate state vehicles. The last thing they did was load the four vehicles with supplies they had stored in their rooms, the most important being C4 for blasting open the steel doors leading to the bridge cables.

They had practiced the task in Russia until they were fluid and fast. Their best time from exiting the truck to blowing the door was forty-two seconds. That was without obstacles, human or otherwise, thrown into the mix. With obstacles—reinforced doors or guards—it would take longer. Yoon-hoi counted on his men's adrenaline pumping, but he didn't discount the unexpected. CCTV cameras also had to be dealt with swiftly. But at this hour, before the morning shift change, overnight eyes would be straining to stay open.

Getting through the steel doors was only the first step. It was step two that would take real time. That's where two of the faux Caltrans trucks with programmable electronic signs would come into play; they'd light up with alternating warnings: Stop and Accident Ahead. This would block all traffic, quickly giving the teams in the second trucks time to fire up and use gas cutters to sever the cables.

Yoon-hoi sent his crew off with a wave. He would not hear from them again until a designated time two days later. But their accomplishments would be heard around the world. They would be reported in Russia and celebrated back home in Pyongyang, where he longed to return and be honored as a hero. But that would not be after this attack; he still had one more assignment to complete.

* * *

LONDON
Savannah Flanders filed the article on the Kiev evacuation she'd written on the plane. 2,251 words including her byline; descriptive without revealing Dan Reilly by name, and detailed without giving away the identities of the Ukrainians. Promises made, promises kept.

Her *Times* editor agreed to the deal she struck and said the story would break first on the paper's web edition before hitting print. CNN, FOX, MSNBC, NPR, AXIOS, and AP would immediately pick it up. She'd be quoted for the next news cycle. Not a bad day for her career.

* * *

"You're nothing if not persistent, Ms. Flanders," Reilly said when he took her call.

"Really, I think we can graduate to first names."

"Okay, Savannah."

"My story's going to hit in an hour. Everyone's protected," she said, "as agreed."

"Thank you."

"Have time for a drink?" she proposed.

"Can't. Heading out again."

"The NATO Summit?" Flanders noted.

He said nothing.

She continued, "I hear Stockholm's nice this time of year."

"Savannah, there are far more important stories than me," he replied. "Go after them."

"No chance. I'll see you there."

* * *

THE OAKLAND BAY BRIDGE

Tolls on the Bay Bridge are only collected from westbound traffic. There were two choices: cash or the automatic lanes, which required the state's FasTrak transponder on the car dashboard. The four fake Caltrans trucks didn't have transponders, but it didn't matter to the lead driver, at least for the next half-hour. He steered into a FasTrak lane. What he didn't know was that vehicles without transponders were still seen, in technical terms, by the bridge's toll sensors. In a fraction of a second, multiple cameras snapped pictures of the trucks' license plates and their drivers and passengers. It was a computer-mechanized program designed to ultimately send evidence to the registered vehicle owner that they owed the state money, and would face penalties if they didn't pay promptly. The process usually took more than a month. In this case, the cameras would provide additional evidence of a crime in the making.

The trucks continued slowly across the bridge in the right lane. The last truck illuminated the digital left arrow sign for traffic to move past. Nothing out of the ordinary—just as they trained: calm, methodical. Timing was key. So was surviving. No active radio transmissions in this phase, only concentration on the job at hand and all the variables that could get in their way. The terrorists drove to their objectives: two targets fifty yards apart at the midpoint over the bay. They were on schedule.

Terrorists. Targets. Timing.

The two lead trucks each slowed to a stop. The following trucks triggered their pre-programmed electronic arrows for traffic to merge left into one lane. It took thirty seconds to create the necessary gridlock, precisely as planned. Next, the teams exited their trucks with the tools they had smuggled into the country. Cars began to honk, but the terrorists ignored them.

While one man held up traffic, another patrolled back and forth between the vehicles. Two others from each team simultaneously put out work cones and flags, and began to jackhammer multiple holes in the cement. They would accomplish that in just under four minutes, to the annoyance of hundreds of cars backed up. They were still on schedule.

Using only hand signals, they returned to the trucks for the C4 and the timers. Once the detonation was set for three minutes, they'd leave the cones around the worksite, get back into their vehicles and head to solid ground. The gap in the traffic flow in front of their trucks would guarantee their safety—at least, it had in all of their run-throughs.

Through the process, few took notice of the ostensible Caltrans workers who had guns slung over their shoulders. They were formidable weapons: CMMG MK47s, nicknamed The Mutant, with 30-round magazines. Reliable enough to dispatch any annoying commuters who might approach. None did.

Now for hooking up and starting the timers.

"Junbidoen?" radioed the team leader over the car horns.

"*Junbidoen*," confirmed his counterpart behind him.

The terrorist in front checked his watch. All was good. They were only twenty seconds off their pre-established timetable. Satisfied, he held up five fingers and began a loud countdown. At one he yelled another

"Junbidoen!" *Ready!* Ready to trigger the timer, to get back into their fake Caltrans vans, and to drive off as patriotic heroes. Not ready for the booming, ear-rattling pressure that preceded the blast of wind as a pair of MH-60M helicopters from 160th SOAR, the Army's Special Operations Aviation Unit, rose from below the bridge to the deck.

Of all the things the saboteurs were trained for, this was not one of them. Not the Black Hawk Helicopters that came out of nowhere. Not the nine FBI HRT (Hostage Rescue Team) operators rappelling from each bird. Not the warning shots from the door gunners.

The terrorists were prepared to fight, but the birds that had been idling below, adjacent to the bridges on Treasure Island, completely surprised them. So, the armed men fired their Mutants on the attackers because surrendering was not an option. Surrendering would bring shame to their families. Shame would bring death to loved ones.

The onboard FBI marksmen opened up with their M-240H machine guns to cover the teams rappelling onto the bridge. Two terrorists were cut down instantly; the rest found cover behind their trucks. Once the FBI HRT operators were on the bridge deck, the helicopters pulled back to avoid taking direct fire. The battle was now between the remaining six terrorists and eighteen FBI agents.

One of the terrorists made a decision—a suicidal decision. He ran to the nearest timer to re-set the C4. But before he could enable the device, an agent cut him down from behind. The timer's countdown never moved past the new five second mark.

Within two minutes the terrorists were all dead. It was time for mop up.

Another two Black Hawks dropped additional teams, including trained EMTs out of the Washington Field Office's OpMed Program. Six FBI Tactical Mobility Teams converged from the San Francisco side in armored LENCO BearCats and Humvees. Behind them, four EOD (Explosive Ordnance Disposal) trucks and their teams would examine, defuse and remove the explosives.

The agents closed the bridges for four hours, checking each vehicle in the immediate area before turning them around. Provisions had to be made for bathrooms and other emergencies, including a pregnant woman who was rushed to a hospital to deliver twins.

They tagged eight bodies. None of the combatants carried identification, so it would be up to the FBI labs to try to identify the dead. But there was a hint to their origin: it had been captured by FBI microphones and cameras wired days earlier throughout the bridge cable housing, and reviewed by Vincent Moore in the lead helicopter.

Junbidoen. They had been ready.

LONDON

Flanders watched the breaking news bulletin on CNN: the FBI had thwarted a terrorist attack on the Bay Bridge between San Francisco and Oakland, California. Traffic was at a standstill. Talking heads could only speculate beyond the limited first reports. From live news helicopter cameras she saw what looked like bodies under a tarp. It eclipsed her story, but she somehow thought there had to be a Reilly connection. She called his cell.

"Reilly, it's Savannah. Watching the news?"

"Yes, we got lucky," he replied.

"We?" She noted that Reilly's voice was confident, the way it had been in Ukraine.

"They. The FBI," he quickly added.

"What do you know?" He didn't respond. "Damn you, Reilly. Give me something! At least off the record!"

She only heard the sound of Reilly's TV in the background.

"Who are you!" she demanded.

"A guy who thought he could help. It's what I do."

"Oh, you're much more than that. You want to know what I think?"

Reilly didn't really want to hear.

"I'll tell you. And maybe it'll be part of my article. You're Cecrops."

"What?"

"Cecrops from Greek mythology. Cecrops was the first king of

Athens who reigned for fifty years. A cultural hero. Legend has it that Cecrops brought the alphabet to the Greeks. Quite the guy. Like you."

He ventured, "Is there a moral to this story?"

"Yes, relatively speaking. Relative to you. Cecrops had two halves to his being. From the waist up he looked human. The man who taught the Greeks to read and write. The man who introduced the concept of marriage, political representation, and ceremonial burial. Good things. The Acropolis was also known as Cecropia in his honor."

"Glad you've got your ancient history down," Reilly said offhandedly. "I've got more pressing things to deal with."

"Precisely. But wait, this is where it gets really interesting. From the waist down, Cecrops was a serpent, coiled and dangerous. Two parts of the same figure. The top, enlightened and informed. The bottom, a snake; always observing, calculating, ready to strike."

She paused for reaction. Reilly didn't offer any, so she made her point.

"You're like Cecrops, Dan Reilly; smart and cultivated. A man of the world. But there's that other part. The part that knows how to act in the moment. On the 14th Street Bridge. Along the backstreets of Kiev. And if I dig further, I'm sure I'll discover more of what you do and who you are."

"You're reaching."

"Then talk to me, Reilly. Really talk to me. I am going to get my story. It would be far better if you participate."

"I'm sorry," he said. "I can't help you further."

Before hanging up, Flanders made one final declaration. "I'm not dropping this. I'll see you in Stockholm."

67

WASHINGTON, D.C.

THE WHITE HOUSE

They watched what America was watching—the foiled terrorist attack at the Oakland Bay Bridge, the eight bodies, and one recorded word, now translated.

"*Junbidoen*," FBI Director Reese McCafferty said.

"June-what?" Battaglio asked.

"A word recorded moments before their intended detonation. *Junbidoen*, Mr. President. Korean. It means *Ready*. It's clear even through ambient noise. Our translators have no doubt that was the word."

"Meaning?" Battaglio wondered.

"Ready to start the clock. Meaning the terrorists are speaking Korean and therefore probably are Korean, likely North Korean."

CIA Director Gerald Watts took the point further.

"It supports the video of Asians walking away from the 14th Bridge. Our analysts also ID'd them as likely Korean."

"And eyewitness descriptions from the Virginia motel where we recovered battery packaging," added Watts.

"Battery packaging?" Ryan Battaglio demanded. He didn't understand.

"Sir," McCafferty explained, "from batteries used to power remote detonation devices or the electronics onboard. Hard evidence found by a smart motel housekeeper. And then there is the Denny's waitress murder outside of Las Vegas."

"Excuse me, but would somebody give the president a concise report with everything in it?" Battaglio complained.

The FBI and CIA directors shot each other looks before glancing over to the National Security Director.

"Actually, sir, it was in a paper prepared for you yesterday," Simon said, hiding his immediate frustration.

"Well, from now on, do more than hand me something. Tell me what it is, its relevance and importance. And show me photographs. I want to see pictures of what you're talking about!"

"Yes, sir," Kimball said, noting both Battaglio's short temper and short attention span.

"And?" Battaglio continued.

"Mr. President?"

"What the hell went on at Denny's?"

"After finishing the late shift, a waitress was murdered in her home." FBI Director McCafferty stated. "Sir, we believe she took too much interest in a conversation. Perhaps she overheard details on another attack, making her enough of a threat to one of the individuals that he eliminated her. Brutally sir, while she was in bed."

"A Korean?" Battaglio asked.

"Possibly."

"Great. I've heard *likely, perhaps, maybe,* and *possibly*. Is that how America does investigations these days? By speculation?"

"In the pursuit of facts, Mr. President, yes."

All of this was in the report the president didn't read, but McCafferty felt it was useless to make a point of that. Instead he continued.

"The cook at the restaurant never saw the patron, but he had two orders. One from a regular, the other a semi-regular. The semi-regular didn't show up that often, but the regular was known and we currently have him under surveillance. Mr. President, he is the prime suspect in a plot we've uncovered. We're already surveilling his place of employment."

"Which is?" the acting president asked.

"A pumping station," McCafferty said. "A pumping station connected with Hoover Dam."

68

ONE HOUR LATER

Dan Reilly took the British Airways flight from Heathrow to Stockholm, which lasted two-and-a-half hours. It was a smooth trip from takeoff to 33,000 feet, spacious in First Class. A finely cooked medium-rare steak and perfectly paired pinot noir appeared at the appointed time; luxury in the air. Momentarily, it distracted him from the uncertainty on the ground.

It was vastly different for career Air Force pilot Cpt. Chad Barquist in the tight cabin of his U-2S reconnaissance jet at 70,000 feet. The cockpit was his second home, the one his wife Janis didn't know much about. Few people did. He claimed, quite truthfully, that in addition to being a jet pilot, he was a military photographer. All true. It's just that the photos he shot were from fourteen miles above the earth and usually over foreign countries trying to hide things.

His in-flight movements were restricted by his Navy Mark IV high-pressure suit, required for the extreme altitudes and the mission. Barquist was hooked up to a relief tube for urination. When on-call, he stuck to a high-protein, high-fiber diet. He told Janis it was for his sensitive stomach. It wasn't. It was to minimize his need to go.

Today's takeoff from Howard AFB in the Panama Canal Zone quickly put Barquist over the Chinese ships heading toward Venezuela.

He was one of two men in the air: one trying to relax, the other working. Dan Reilly was mulling what he already knew, what he had seen and reported to the CIA while detained in Venezuela. Cpt. Chad Barquist was flying almost three times as high as Reilly in a U.S. spy plane, to photograph more evidence.

Reilly jotted down and prioritized his immediate concerns:

Accommodating the Russian delegation in Stockholm.

Confirming the requirements for elevating the hotel to RED threat level status.

Staying in contact with Heath, and now Secretary of State Matthews.

Keeping Savannah Flanders at bay.

Barquist's concerns were far different. He was focused on getting clear photographs of the three ships; mission coordinates were programmed into his onboard computer. He would make two passes over each vessel at the current maximum altitude, then drop down to 40,000 feet for a second set of passes.

Two men in the air—thousands of miles apart, but unknowingly connected.

STOCKHOLM
THE KENSINGTON NORDISKA HÔTEL

Reilly forgot his concern about Marnie the moment he felt her breath on his neck at check-in and the words she whispered in his ear, "Get two keys."

He smiled but didn't turn around. At his request, the clerk gave him a suite on the second floor. When he finished checking in, Babbitt was gone. He looked around. She was waiting at the elevator bank already, her hands folded, alternatingly looking impatient and very excited.

They produced their identification at the lift and showed their keys.

Once in the room, Marnie kissed Reilly and began unbuckling him.

"Seems like months," she murmured.

"Years," he countered, as he unclasped her bra.

It had been what, a week? An ill-timed trip to Venezuela. The Ukraine evacuation. Terrorists at the door, a reporter on my heels. A very busy week.

* * *

Later that evening, Reilly walked the grounds of the Nordiska Hôtel. Security guards were at the entrance and the elevators. Stockholm police were posted outside. Plainclothes Russian security officers were visible everywhere. They looked to be the toughest: tall blocks of muscle standing at check-in, feet away from the elevator banks, peering out windows and roaming common areas. Each group had discrete wireless communication channels. But Reilly was certain that someone—or multiple someones—in the hotel, or in nearby black vans, were listening remotely. Russian, American, British intelligence. Possibly Iranian. Undoubtedly they all knew about one another.

The Kensington Royal Nordiska Hôtel sat on the Stockholm waterfront near the Old Town and the Royal Palace. Dan Reilly had overseen the purchase and renovation of the classic brick property, which stretched halfway across a city block. KR brought the hotel, built in 1872, back to its historic glory. Millions went into recreating the lobby's gold leaf walls, Persian carpets, statuary, and a Michelin 3-star restaurant with one of the best Swedish smörgåsbords in all Stockholm. Tapestries throughout the hotel depicted Sten Sture the Elder, a Swedish separatist who took the city from Kalmar Union loyalists in 1471 and became the ruler of Sweden until he died thirty years later at 63. Elsewhere hung a painting of St. George and the dragon dating back to the 1480s, historical works illustrating the old walled city, and photographs chronicling the 1917 Stockholm Peace Conference, which sought to end the First World War.

During the renovation, Reilly had successfully lobbied EJ Shaw to bring the Nordiska up to international safety standards in order to make it a diplomatic destination; this meant secure entrances and exits not known to the general public, motion-detecting surveillance cameras in every hallway and elevator, and bulletproof windowpanes in the suites likely to be used by visiting dignitaries. For the NATO summit the Russian Federation had booked 32 of them, the biggest and best for Nicolai Gorshkov. The majority of the Russian group had already arrived. That meant senior officials in expensive Italian suits, generals in uniforms weighed down with metals and decorations, and undercover FSB agents—some passing as tourists, others as Russian thugs.

Reilly surveyed the lobby again; right now, anyone could be an operative. Many probably were. With a little time before his next survey with hotel staff, he left the hotel for some air.

A block away, walking along the Södra Blasieholmshamnen Riverwalk, Reilly was aware of a tail. Subtle, but not so subtle he wouldn't notice—two men followed him roughly a hundred feet back. Another, diagonally across the street, twenty feet behind. They all looked Eastern European.

Reilly stopped, as a tourist might. He took out his phone and shot typical touristy pictures of the yachts moored in the harbor, followed by five smiling selfies with his phone high and wide. High and wide enough to include his trackers: photos to send to Langley. Before moving on he took a dozen more sightseeing pictures of activity along the wharf.

A block further, Reilly snapped another set of pictures. The tails were still with him. He paused to scroll through the photos he'd already taken, which were decent shots thanks to the fact that the sun set so late. He dubbed the lone man on the opposite side of the street Moe, for a lock of hair falling over his forehead. The second with frizzy short hair was Larry, and the third, a bald guy, Curly—The Three Stooges.

Reilly emailed the photos to Bob Heath with a short, cryptic note. *Any idea who my ugly friends are?*

When he returned to the hotel, Moe was sitting in the hotel lobby with a cup of coffee. Larry was positioned next to the concierge. Curly wasn't in plain sight, but that didn't mean he wasn't there. They looked different, but cut from the same Russian cloth. Reilly actually expected better, but he wasn't about to complain. He wondered whether Gorshkov had sent these three stooges to rattle him. *Psych ops? Mind games, or part of a greater strategy?* He decided he needed Alan Cannon's help.

He was about to join his walkthrough when Reilly spotted a familiar face sitting at a corner seat at the lobby bar. A striking woman. Now wearing blue instead of red but looking every bit as seductive.

Reilly crossed over to talk with her.

"Ms.—" he struggled for her last name.

She looked up and tilted her head.

"Ah, Mr. Reilly. Nice to see you again. And it's Pudovkin. Better yet, Maria."

Her perfume filled the air. *Rosemary,* he believed. *Fresh and inviting, like her smile.* But if legend served him right, a scent associated with fairies and weddings, but also witches and burials.

"I'm flattered you remember me," she said.

"Hard not to. You made a strong first impression."

"Well then, care to join me?" Pudovkin replied. "I hope my second is even better."

Reilly smiled, not showing his true belief—that she was a spider laying a spider's web—for him.

"I'm sorry, Ms. Pudovkin. Perhaps another time. Unfortunately, I've got a meeting coming up."

Reilly glanced in the mirror. Moe moved in closer to them, within eye contact of Pudovkin.

"I'm not used to taking no for an answer." She signaled the bartender then pointed to her glass and Reilly. "Just a few minutes to get better acquainted."

Her accent made her sound all the more seductive.

"Just a few, but it comes with some questions," he replied.

"Professional or personal?"

"Definitely not personal. I'm involved."

She pouted a little girl pout, then said, "Well good for you, Mr. Reilly. But in your travels you must meet with so many interesting people. Don't you ever…"

Reilly interrupted. "You're here on business?"

She fixed her eyes on him and cheerfully said, "Ah, a boundary. I'm sorry, she must be very special."

"Yes, she is," he replied.

"Well, then professional it is. I'm a Moscow tourism attaché. Work takes me everywhere. Right now, Stockholm. The NATO summit gives me opportunity to make connections, create business opportunities, and develop new relationships. Like with you."

Another smile. Another comment that tended toward the personal. Reilly said nothing.

His drink came. She raised her glass and offered a toast. "To surprise encounters. You never know where life will lead you."

He clinked her glass and said without much inflection, "To surprise encounters." Reilly took a sip. "I imagine you're very good at sales. Your superiors," a word he intentionally chose over *bosses*, "must be very pleased. You know how to work a room and," he laughed, "develop new relationships."

"Not unlike your work, Mr. Reilly."

He never gave Pudovkin permission to use his first name.

"Yes. I work hard for my company. As we discussed in London, I'm President of our international division. It's why I hotel-hop so much."

"Then it seems we're both in the same business," she replied.

"Apparently. And you're busy at it right now."

Now Pudovkin laughed. "Very astute, Mr. Reilly." With that, she took a slow sip, traced her tongue across her top lip, leaned forward, and looked into Reilly's eyes.

"We must do this again."

She went in for a kiss. A light kiss. She eased back, smiled and kissed him again. This one lingered.

"One for each of our meetings," she said playfully. "But I've always felt they come in threes."

Reilly had no comeback as she left the bar. Pudovkin hid a broad smile from him, but it was clearly seen by Moe. A few more encounters, she thought, and she might successfully ensnare and compromise Reilly, turning him into a useful asset. But that wasn't the plan. *What a shame,* she thought.

* * *

An hour later, Reilly was on another walk and a call with Heath.

"Got your photos," Heath said. "We're on it."

"Thanks. I'll have another friend for you, but I have to pull it off the computer. In the meantime, a name."

"Names are good. Quicker. Are your friends with you now?"

Reilly looked about. First over his shoulder across the street, then behind him. He saw the bald one, Curly.

"Just one. Non-threatening." He privately thought, *I hope,* realizing he still needed to call Alan Cannon.

"Who's your other friend?" Heath asked.

"A woman. A femme fatale. Looks that could kill."

"The worst kind."

He spelled out Pudovkin's name, described her, and estimated her age. Heath read it back and typed it into a database that instantly searched a thousand sources. State, federal, and international. CIA, NSA, FBI, Interpol, and more. Not the usual library sources, although Heath's computer automatically ran Google, Facebook, Instagram, and other social media sources simultaneously.

"While I have you," Reilly continued, "any updates you can share?"

"Yes and no."

"I'll take the *yes.*"

"Not now. Hope you understand."

Reilly did. Heath would brief him, but only in a SCIF in the American embassy. That meant he had something relevant, but sensitive.

"Can't head there right now. I've got Curly on me."

"Curly?"

"One of my Three Stooges."

"With the curly hair?"

"Come on, Curly's the bald one. Larry has the curly hair."

"Right."

At that moment, Heath had results from his first-level search for Maria Pudovkin.

"Okay, buddy. Your girlfriend is either a cheerleader in Glendale, California, which I doubt; a sixty-eight-year-old mother of four in Indianapolis, which I also sincerely doubt based on your description; or about 1,451 girls and women outside the parameters. I think she gave you—"

"A fake name," Reilly interrupted. "No kidding."

They both understood the meaning of what remained unsaid.

"Get me the photo," Heath instructed.

"Will do. Anything else pressing?"

"Just my hemorrhoids," the CIA Officer replied.

"Too much information."

"You asked. But—" Now Heath stopped short.

"What?" Reilly asked, sensing trouble.

"Something. Just coming in."

"What?" Reilly repeated.

At that moment, another call rang through on Reilly's phone. A number showed up screen that he immediately recognized.

"Getting another call, Bob. A *New York Times* reporter."

"You're not going to want to take it. Not until I tell you what's happened."

69

STOCKHOLM

"The story broke online. It's blowing up the Internet," Heath quickly explained.

"What story?"

"A partially redacted copy of a sensitive government report that—"

"Shit," Reilly said under his breath. "Am I identified?"

"Hold on." He scanned the article written by a *Washington Post* reporter, Peter Loge. "Don't see it. But that doesn't mean—"

Reilly understood why Savannah Flanders was on him again. She was putting things together. And if she could, others might as well. He imagined how conspiracy theorists would run with it and launch attacks on the radio and feed Deep State voices in the political echo chamber.

Reilly stopped walking. So did Curly. He felt like waving hello but didn't.

"We have to get this quashed," Reilly said.

"That's a domestic call. The Bureau. The White House. They can try, but you know reporters, they'll protect their sources."

"Unless the *Post* is being used." Reilly collected his thoughts. "Bob, if you had the actual document the paper received, can your folks or Watts' people track it to any specific copy machines at State, the National Security Council, or DHS?"

"Copy machines do have subtle signatures. Chances are it's a copy of a copy. That makes it more difficult."

"But not impossible."

"Not impossible," Heath affirmed. Reilly's mind raced.

"You said some sections were redacted."

"According to the online story, yes. Solid black ink through sections."

"Then can we find out which office in which department has a copy that matches the redactions?"

"It would need approval."

"Actually, Elizabeth Matthews could make that call since the work originated in State. Best if that request comes from you, Bob. Still have a good relationship with her?"

"Sure," Heath replied.

"Good. Let her know we talked. She can do it any way she sees fit. Even in a dark parking lot, Watergate-style."

Reilly sighed. Things were going from bad to worse. He did a 180 to return to the hotel. Curly was caught off-guard by the sudden move. Reilly shouted, "It's okay, we're going back now!"

"Who are you talking to?" Heath asked.

"Curly. I figured I can save him a few steps."

* * *

Reilly's phone rang minutes after he hung up with Heath. Savannah Flanders again. If he didn't pick up, she'd just keep calling. Besides, he might get more information without giving up much of his own.

"Reilly."

"Flanders," she said. "We need to talk."

"About?"

"Come on, Reilly, don't screw with me."

"We're back to last names? Okay, I'm in Stockholm. Got a lot to do. What's up?"

"Why don't I believe you? Whatever," she replied. "The *Post* just broke a story and I have a feeling deep down that it should have been mine."

"Why's that, Flanders?"

"Because it has your name all over it."

"My name?" Reilly choked. Heath had thought he was in the clear.

"That's quite a reaction from someone playing stupid. You worked at State, the report covered the first three targets, the bridges in Pittsburgh, and there's a whole lot more a Mr. Dan Reilly, former United States State Department analyst, would have predicted."

Reilly walked past the hotel. Now Moe picked up his trail.

"Well, can I get a comment from you?" Flanders asked. Cars honked. "Did you say something?"

"Just listening and making my way through traffic," Reilly replied.

"Just tell me, did you write the report? Reilly, is this your work?" She heard Reilly breathe into the phone. Nothing more than that. "Dan?" she continued.

"I'm here."

"Look, assuming it is you, you probably have a better idea what's next. That's what I really want to get at: what should we be worried about now?"

"For your story or for you?"

"Set the rules."

"Not for publication. Not yet."

"Agreed."

"We're focused on the attacks back home. But I think it's a deception for a much grander play."

70

WASHINGTON, D.C.

WASHINGTON POST EDITORIAL OFFICES

THE NEXT AFTERNOON

Peter Loge had expected the visit from the FBI. Upon their arrival he notified the paper's lead Constitutional attorney, Jim Harris. Ten minutes later, Agents Moore and Kaplan were led to the *Post's* glass-enclosed conference room. Loge and Harris were already seated. They introduced themselves from across the table. No handshakes; Moore and Kaplan produced business cards. Harris passed his to the agents.

Moore studied the lawyer's card and opened with, "You understand why we're here."

Harris, mid-60s and lanky, showed no fear. He replied, "And you must equally recognize our position." The conversation was already punctuated by Harris speaking and Loge remaining tight-lipped.

"We can't comment, and we definitely can't divulge anything regarding our sources."

Moore folded his hands and leaned in. But instead of speaking to the attorney, he looked at the reporter.

"Mr. Loge, we're not the enemy. I'm not the enemy. But that doesn't mean we don't have enemies." Loge held his gaze, as he had been instructed by legal. "I've read the report that you've been given. I believe you recognize why keeping it secret was vital."

Getting no response, Moore pressed ahead.

"That was the intention of the State Department. I've met the analyst who authored it, that was his intention as well. The report laid out vulnerabilities and the means to attack them. It was researched, written, and used to help strengthen our defenses, to harden targets against attack. But the report was clearly leaked, stolen, or sold, we don't know by whom or to whom." Still a frozen look from Loge. "And now you have a copy, likely from whatever source has been using it to hit us. And they want you to run it to imply we knew these targets were vulnerable and we did nothing to protect them." Moore tapped the paper. "Mr. Loge, you're being co-opted."

"The public has a right to know," the reporter suddenly declared.

"In time, maybe. This is not that time. It's in the interest of national security for you to put the report aside and to let us investigate whether the leak is part of a larger conspiracy against the United States."

The lawyer was about to speak; Loge tapped him on the arm, a signal to wait. "Go on."

"With all due respect, you're being used to embarrass American intelligence. And since that is where you find yourself, unwittingly, I'd like to propose a way *we* can also use you."

Harris abruptly stood. "I think we've spent enough time on this, Agent Moore. No sources," he said.

"It would make things so much easier if you would, but we know your answer. We know you'd accept a jail term, Mr. Loge, and the *Post* would still put out more stories. It's also apparent that if you stop, the same study will show up in other hands. Maybe at the *New York Times* or *Los Angeles Times*."

Vincent Moore hesitated. There was an unspoken *and* that he left dangling.

"What do you want?" Loge asked.

"Rather than an answer coming from the Bureau directly, I'd like to bring in another voice."

"Who?"

"One moment." Moore dialed his cell and turned it on speaker. It rang three times. A man answered. "Moore, FBI. She's expecting my call."

"Please wait, Agent Moore." Ten seconds later, a woman was on the phone.

"This is Secretary of State Matthews."

Loge swallowed hard.

"Mr. Loge, are you on the line?"

Harris intervened. "He's here. I'm a lawyer for the *Washington Post*." He introduced himself.

"Thank you, gentlemen. I appreciate your time and I will cut to the chase. Of course, we want the name of your source for the report. But I'm certain you're not prepared to give that up."

"Correct, Secretary Matthews," Harris declared. "It's not even on the table."

"So, instead, here's an alternative: we'd like the actual report."

"Absolutely not!" Loge shouted.

"I'm not finished. Make a duplicate for yourself but give us the one you originally received."

Loge was confused. "Our copy?"

"Yes."

"Why?"

"Forensic footprints, Mr. Harris. It may contain clues to where it came from—a specific office at the State Department, or possibly the identity of who may have leaked it, most likely to a foreign power. We figure out those answers, we could have a way through this mess."

She paused to choose her next words carefully. "Keep *a* copy, but in the interest of national security, we ask you to write around the actual targets, allowing us the opportunity to prevent additional attacks." She referenced the assault on the Bay Bridge. "There are plenty of other stats to pull from. Just don't name targets."

"That's all?" Harris was surprised, but not willing to give in on behalf of the *Post*.

"But, there's one more thing. We don't know if you have the name of the report's author. However, for his safety, it's absolutely imperative that you do not reveal his identity."

Harris leaned back. Loge leaned forward.

"A trade before agreeing," the reporter proposed.

"Mr. Loge, lives are in the balance."

"I recognize that, but…"

Harris grabbed his arm and started mouthing *no, no, no.* Loge continued.

"…here's my deal. If we comply, then when you're ready to charge the government leak, I get to break the story."

Moore relaxed in his seat and looked at the other agent who had not said a word. They waited for Matthews to answer.

"Depends."

"Depends?" Loge responded.

"Depends on who it is."

71

STOCKHOLM

THE NEXT DAY

The Stockholm committee chose neutral ground for the meetings: *Riddarhuset,* the House of Nobility. That meant American, Russian, and NATO security forces had hundreds of tasks to coordinate with Swedish officials before the delegates would be allowed on the grounds. And with conflicting safety priorities, checkpoints and event-specific identification to coordinate, it was no quick task.

It was decided that Sweden's president would hold a welcome reception in the building's Lord-marshals' room. During the 18th Century, the room was originally a meeting place for the Secret Committee of the Swedish Riksdag, the parliament. Following the reception, participants would be ushered into the Great Hall of the House of Nobility, first used by the aristocracy for parliamentary meetings, and now where the Assembly of Nobles gather every third year.

Swedish army snipers would take up posts on the roof in a tight perimeter around *Riddarhuset,* and another wider circle on the property, while drones would feed real-time video to American Secret Service agents, Russia's SPB, and NATO officers. English was chosen as the common language for all open-channel dialogue. Advance teams moved in shortly after NATO agreed to meet with Gorshkov. Acting President

Ryan Battaglio was the latecomer to the list of invitees.

Now three days out, as the deadlines grew tighter the problems became greater. SPB and NATO were at odds on everything from where President Gorshkov and NATO commanders would sit to food preparation. When the Secret Service entered the picture, it got worse. NATO commanders had to move down the conference table and the agenda was expanded.

STOCKHOLM
THE KENSINGTON ROYAL NORDISKA HÔTEL

Reilly followed his own rule in the hotel restaurant. He asked for a table where he could face out. The predator position. That's precisely where Marnie Babbitt found him. She wore a short red print skirt, a white silk blouse, gold hoop earrings, and a gold and freshwater pearl necklace. Her long black hair was up, for now.

Reilly stood and embraced her. She pressed her lips against his, slipped her tongue inside, withdrew, smiled, and whispered. "There's always more where that came from." She took the seat opposite him and soon decided on the *Rebuli Superiore*, an Italian prosecco. When it arrived, Babbitt proposed a toast. "Six months today."

"Oh my God, you're right. Six months to the day since we met in Tehran."

Reilly looked back on the chance encounter when they were both in Iran to meet government officials. He was there to discuss hotel construction. She was flown in by Barclays to talk about financing ventures.

"See what happens when you open your eyes to possibilities," Babbitt said. "To us."

"To us," Reilly replied.

They toasted to one another and clinked glasses, as they always did. She kicked off her heels, caressed his leg with her toes, and worked her way up. But she wasn't getting the reaction she wanted.

"You're worried."

"Lots on my mind."

"More than the usual?"

"All things considered, yes."

"The conference," Babbitt suggested.

"Not so much the conference. Things back in the States."

Babbitt leaned in. "You keep so much inside when we're together. Come on, let go. You can tell me anything. You have to talk if we're going to grow our relationship."

Reilly nodded. He was holding back. Maybe it was time.

At that moment, Reilly noticed Maria Pudovkin entering the restaurant. A waitress led her to a table near Reilly's. Before sitting she spotted Reilly and crossed over.

"Well, hello, Mr. Reilly. Look at this. Our third meeting."

Reilly smiled politely. He looked at Marnie as she turned to the voice. She flinched.

Pudovkin caught the look.

"I'm sorry. I shouldn't have interrupted."

"No worry. Marnie, this *is*," he paused as if to remember. But he had memorized her name. "Maria Pudovkin, she's with..."

She filled in the answer, "Russian Federation tourism. We met briefly in London and at the bar the other night."

She offered her hand to Marnie who was slow to respond.

"Oh, no worries, Ms.—"

"Babbitt," Marnie said bruskly.

"Ms. Babbitt," the Russian continued. "He's quite devoted to you."

Reilly thought he saw the Russian take Marnie's hand and hold it just a little too long. *Affectionately. This spider was always laying a trap. Even for Marnie.*

* * *

Reilly led Marnie into his room. Once the door was closed, she flicked off her heels, stood on her toes and kissed him deeply. He eased away.

"Something's really getting to you," she noted.

"Just thinking."

"About what."

"That woman in the restaurant."

Marnie stepped back and said, "Oh?" It was the kind of *Oh?* you don't want to hear from a lover.

"Not that way."

"It seemed too coincidental when she came over to us—"

Babbitt corrected him. "To you. She hardly saw me until you did the introduction."

"Okay, coincidental to me."

"Do you ever just allow yourself to relax?" Marnie said coaxingly.

"With you, yes."

"Then—"

She kissed Reilly again. He had the same tentative reaction.

"There you go again. Still focusing on that woman?"

"She's Russian government, Marnie. There's more than what meets the eye."

"There's a lot to look at," she joked.

"Come on. I don't mean that."

"Then what do you mean?"

"I'm sure she's a Russian agent. Possibly FSB."

"Why would you suspect that?"

"The chance meetings."

"Hey, we met by chance. What does that make me?"

Reilly smiled broadly, "Totally different circumstances."

Marnie smiled. "And don't you forget it, Mister Reilly."

Reilly sighed. "Right."

"Forget her. Kiss me."

She moved in again; her lips ready, her eyes closing. He wasn't there. She opened her eyes.

"What now?"

"The way she squeezed your hand."

Marnie buried her head in his shoulder. "I wasn't aware of anything."

"I was. If she is an agent, she may use you to get to me. Or she could compromise you and your business."

Marnie nibbled on his ear and slipped her hand down below his belt. "Daniel J. Reilly, you really need to focus on more pressing things."

He sighed. It was even a deeper sigh than when her toes reached him under the table.

"See," she said.

"Just promise me you'll be careful."

Babbitt drew in a long breath and smiled. "I promise." Then she got right back to the situation in hand.

* * *

They made love. They spooned. They slept. Reilly awoke at 3:00 a.m., grabbed his phone and went to the bathroom. He checked for texts; the first one up was from Bob Heath.

"Phone Home."

Home was Langley. The fact that he wanted Reilly to call meant it was important. He dialed and whispered.

"Reilly."

Given the time difference Heath was still at work, but he would have taken the call at any hour.

"Got something interesting," the CIA operative said.

"Wait." Reilly put a towel on the floor to block the crack under the door and turned the shower on.

"We have a 70 percent positive match on your mystery woman," the CIA operative said.

"And…"

"Seventy percent isn't 100 percent. But speaking generally, and working from what you sent, we've come up with a six-year-old fuzzy photograph of a woman with colonel stripes standing in the third row of a Moscow parade stand. Two rows behind Number One. Seventy percent because she's in the shadows and wearing a uniform hat. Except—"

"Except what?"

"I can't get into specifics," Heath said. "But working with the State Department's Diplomatic Security Service, it's the only match we have, which is fairly unusual. A highly ranked woman officer in the Russian army is someone they'd ordinarily bring out. Market. Publicize. But they haven't. That suggests she either fell out of favor, was reassigned, or she's extra special."

"And you think…?"

"I don't know enough. Besides, we're starting at 70 percent. Anything beyond that is speculation."

"Okay, Bob, speculate."

"Remember, Number One," Heath said, referring to Gorshkov, "was master spy. During the Cold War he was able to turn and recruit more Westerners than probably anyone. But even he couldn't entrap subjects the way a woman could. I'm sure you've heard of the unique school where they were they trained."

"Red Sparrow?"

"In the day, yes. More recently, under the SVR, it became The Institute. Different name. Same purpose. Recruits are trained in befriending, seducing, and compromising foreign political figures, reporters, and business executives. Seducing being one of the most important tools in their portfolio. We know this through experience and confirmed by a former KGB general, Oleg Kalugin."

Reilly had heard the name but couldn't place it.

Heath continued. "For years, Kalugin was a top dog in Russian spy operations until he exiled to the U.S. in the mid-90s. We learned a great deal about Russian operations from him. Don't laugh, but Kalugin famously boasted, 'In the West, you ask your men to stand up for your country. In Russia, we ask our young women to lay down.'"

Reilly nodded. In his mind Pudovkin fit the profile perfectly.

"Such a woman operative, especially adept at running other Russian agents around the world trained to snare new assets, would surely earn Gorshkov's respect and rise in responsibility."

"And she's one of them," Reilly observed.

"Worse. She could very well be one of the best they have."

"Seventy-percent certainty, Bob?"

"What's in a percentage?"

"It's important. She's gotten close to me, and…."

Reilly had another troubling notion. Two, in fact. First, what if the Russian woman was trying to get through him to Marnie? The second was more disturbing.

"Bob, can you do me a favor?"

"Sure."

"It's an awful one."

"It's an awful business."

Dan Reilly told him what he wanted.

72

STOCKHOLM

TWO DAYS LATER

Nicolai Gorshkov traveled through Stockholm's streets in an armored caravan coordinated by the Swedish Military Intelligence and Security Service, approved by Gorshkov's Presidential Security Service (SBP), and with consultation by Kensington Royal security head Alan Cannon. The Russian entourage comprised six armed Russian all-purpose, multi-terrain 4x4 GAZ *Tigr* infantry mobility vehicles—two in the lead, two in the back—and one on each side of Gorshkov's armor-plated *Aurus* limousine. The name *Aurus* is a linguistic blend of the Latin word for gold (Aurum) and the first syllable of Russian (Rus).

Reilly watched the arrival through the underground service entrance with Cannon, the hotel general manager and ten members of the security team. No one was present without permission. Everyone had a job to do: that's what made the arrival appear seamless.

Gorshkov waited for an SBP officer to open his limo door. He was the second to get out. The first was a man who looked like a bodyguard, but Reilly pegged him as much more: an FSB officer. He'd be joining the Russian contingent in the hotel. Gorshkov straightened and smoothed his black suit. He nodded to the first man and to the Russian soldiers who took up positions in the garage with their Kalashnikov

AK-12 assault rifles at the ready. They surrounded the Russian president for the twenty-four steps to the elevator bank. The elevator was open and waiting. It was keyed to skip all floors but the fourth, where Gorshkov would reside.

"So far, so good," Cannon remarked.

"That sounds so temporary," the general manager said. "Like it's only the beginning."

"It is, and it's never the same with these people," Reilly added. "Come on, our turn."

The KR team went to a second elevator bank.

"Make sure everyone's always three steps ahead of their needs and completely alert, 24/7," Cannon instructed. "These people are impatient and hard to please."

"Try impossible," Reilly said, "which is all the more reason to anticipate."

He thought again about the Russians constantly on his tail. The trio of Moe, Larry, and Curly. Then the notion, *who's anticipating whom?*

STOCKHOLM
AMERICAN EMBASSY
THE SAME DAY

Ryan Battaglio read through the talking points prepared by the State Department, and a CIA analysis of NATO's position. He focused on committing the relevant facts to memory. He had instructed Chief of Staff Lou Simon that he was not to be interrupted, but National Security Advisor Pierce Kimball had urgent information.

"Just in from Watts, sir. U2 flyover confirmation of the North Korean shipments to Venezuela."

Kimball held a folder containing multiple pages. The cover was marked Top Secret.

"Summarize it for me, Pierce."

"I'd prefer you read it. One specific paragraph, then we can discuss it."

Battaglio took the folder and read the first few lines of the top sheet:

On the basis of the report of the Southern Pacific Watch Committee, the following advisory is issued regarding five (5) container ships that departed from the port of Wŏnsan, Democratic People's Republic of Korea. USSPACECOM has tracked the cargo vessels even after the ships turned off location tracking devices, a procedure North Korea often employs when it transports coal to China.

He was instantly bored by the intel-speak. Kimball prompted him to the bottom sentence:

Intelligence concludes the shipment includes forty (40) ICBMs capable of reaching major cities in the United States. They must be considered weapons of mass destruction and their transportation an overt act of war.

Battaglio exclaimed, "They can't!" He handed the summary to Simon.

"They are," Kimball said.

"Don't they know what we'll do?"

"I suspect they're counting on you doing nothing, sir."

"Well, they're damned wrong!" Battaglio shouted. "And they'll find out the hard way. Now give it to me in plain English."

Kimball did, reciting details from the Appendix: precise dimensions of the containers; computer overlays of the Hwasong missiles within them; and most importantly, photographs of North Korean military personnel including Major Kim Noh, identified by the CIA as a member of the famed Pyongyang Missile Quartet, the nation's leading nuclear scientists.

"Cuba again," Simon declared.

Battaglio missed the reference. He looked to Kimball for clarification.

"Read Bobby Kennedy's book *Thirteen Days* about the Cuban Missile Crisis," he said solemnly, but knew Battaglio wouldn't.

73

Savannah Flanders started her article at least ten times but she still had more questions about Dan Reilly than answers. Reilly was a man who seemed to have an uncanny ability to insert himself into trouble.

"Christ!" she blurted out of frustration. She tossed the pencil she'd been twirling at a corkboard in the London bureau cubicle. It stuck like an arrow piercing a target.

I'm not getting anywhere here when the story's out there. When he's out there, she thought. Flanders sharply stood, collected her laptop, purse, and the always-ready carry on suitcase. Before boarding a Norwegian Air flight from Gatwick to Stockholm she called Blowen in New York.

"Good timing," her colleague said. "Check your email. I'm about to send you a pdf. Not a lot, but some."

She listened.

"More on Reilly's military record and the woman he's seeing."

"What woman?"

"A VP at Barclays in London. Travels constantly. Not much on her yet, but I'm working on it. Her name's Marnie Babbitt." He spelled it.

"Sounds haughty."

"Hey, she's British."

HENDERSON, NV
THE SAME TIME

The FBI posted undercover officers at the Denny's on a rotating schedule. They came in trucks and rented cars, on motorcycles and as walk-ins. They looked tired, busy, self-absorbed, in a rush, and carefree. Men and women. They made ordinary calls on their phones, sent innocuous texts to unlisted numbers, looked up trivial things on Google. They ordered food and they ate. They paid in cash and with their personal credit cards. They were observed from the building across the street and listened to by wireless. And they watched and waited. Day after day, night after night.

So far, the only positive thing to come out of the FBI SSG, the Special Surveillance Group, was the extra revenue for the restaurant and generous tips for the waitresses. Vincent Moore was back and hating the oppressive Nevada heat. The lack of results from the stakeout only made it worse, but he couldn't pull his team out. Reilly had identified the water system as a target and the death of the Denny's waitress appeared to confirm that suspicion. So they'd stay, watch and wait.

At 2 a.m. on the seventh night a man entered, took a seat in the corner, and ordered a Grand Slam. Nothing unusual until the chef peered out through the opening after the new waitress came in with the order. It was the right time. He looked to the corner, swallowed hard, and nodded to a young woman flirting with a date across their table as they held hands. The woman caught the sign and surreptitiously tapped her associate three times with her index finger. The man slid his right hand back and under the table, touching the number zero on the cell phone that rested on his lap.

Across the street, Moore's lead agent was sleeping and missed the tonal alert. Moore didn't. He shook his man and tapped one of the four monitors covering the restaurant.

"There. The guy in the corner." They could only see the man's back.

"Him?" the sleepy agent asked.

"We got the signal. The cook ID'd him."

Moore watched the monitors closely. He saw the subject eat three pancakes, three eggs, and three sausages. His Grand Slam. But he didn't move. Neither did the romantic couple nor the pair of two-man teams at opposite corners on Warm Springs Road. The FBI agent had laid out his standing order for the way everything would go down. He reiterated it each night: "Identify one or both of the terrorists at their meeting place. Then a game of cat and mouse. And in this scenario, the FBI is the cat."

"What if we're sure we have him?" the woman agent asked hours earlier.

"Stick with the plan," Moore said. "Observe, identify, follow. Do not engage without my approval. We'll take him down when I give the order. Not before."

Vincent Moore knew the man was a threat. The worst kind; he was well-placed, an inside man. Moore recognized him: the subject was the supervisor from the pumping station, Richard Harper.

74

STOCKHOLM

THE HOUSE OF NOBILITY

THE NEXT DAY

Twenty stone-cold faces sat staring at one another across the conference table—adversaries wearing their game faces. Gorshkov had his people, strictly for show, and Battaglio had his, though he wasn't inclined to listen to them. The NATO delegation was further down Battaglio's side of the table. Stacks of yellow pads remained in the middle for jotting notes or making deals. Files were stacked within reach of each camp, some opened and others not.

Sitting with Ryan Battaglio were his translator; National Security Advisor Pierce Kimball; Chairman of the Joint Chiefs General Robert Levine; Chief of Staff Lou Simon; and Secretary of State Elizabeth Matthews. Matthews had chosen a conservative blue suit and white blouse for today's meeting; below her left shoulder she wore a small silver brooch in the shape of a bald eagle. Those who knew her, including Kimball and Simon, understood what it meant: honor, respect, and dignity. But Battaglio neither noticed nor got the meaning. Depending upon how the meeting went, Matthews might flip the pin upward or downward to express her assessment—it was a non-verbal cue she had borrowed from former Secretary of State Madeleine Albright. With the exception of the four-star general in his service dress uniform, the other Americans wore dark suits and red ties. NATO's three-man contingent wore their neatly pressed uniforms.

Gorshkov was in a classic black pinstripe suit, identical to another fifty in his closet. They were all handmade, with hand-stitched vertical gold thread piping of his name running through the fabric. His white shirt had a cutaway spread collar, and a dark blue Italian tie matched his imported Salvatore Ferragamo shoes.

"Mr. President..." Gorshkov addressed Battaglio in English.

Battaglio liked the sound of that. *Respectful.*

"Please extend our sincerest wishes to your nation and to the family of President Crowe. Your country is suffering, and you have our heartfelt wishes."

It was impossible for Gorshkov to sound completely sincere through his accent and delivery, but that worked to his benefit. He showed no real empathy, which Secretary Matthews noted, but Battaglio didn't.

"Thank you, Mr. President," the acting president said. "We all pray for President Crowe's swift recovery." To Matthews, Battaglio's words fell as flat as Gorshkov's.

Gorshkov gave a cursory nod, the kind that meant nothing.

"We have much to discuss, President Gorshkov," Battaglio continued. "Your incursion into Ukraine, your troops on the Latvian border. Neither bodes well and may lead to terrible calamity."

Gorshkov cocked his head, as if he could no longer understand English. Gamesmanship. He looked to his left and his aide quickly translated. Gorshkov replied in Russian.

"Mr. President, the good people of the Russian Federation seek a secure life now, as they did following the Great Patriotic War. All we want is security for our homeland, and freedom for Russian nationals living outside our borders without their rights and privileges. You would not consider such a situation if it were reversed, and Canadian and Mexican alliances threatened you and Americans by birthright living in those countries."

Battaglio heard the English translation and swiftly replied, "There are no similarities, Mr. President. We are not at our neighbors' doors with troops."

"Well then, you live a safe life, while we do not."

National Security Advisor Pierce Kimball, to Matthews' immediate right, felt the new president was quickly being outclassed and out maneuvered. *It was going to be a long session*, he thought. *No, sessions.*

STOCKHOLM

Savannah Flanders arrived, stiff from sitting in the cramped last row of the Norwegian Air flight. The Kensington Royal was impossible to book, but she secured a room at the Hotel Skeppsholmen, a small boutique property nearby. She took a long, hot shower and instead of resting, she set to tracking down Reilly again and gathering whatever she could for her story.

While toweling she called Reilly's cell. He didn't answer, which was not much of a surprise; the conference had already begun and he might have things to do. Next, she texted him; it was probably easier for Reilly to discreetly respond that way.

Flanders thought about napping but dismissed the idea. Instead she dressed, signed onto the hotel Wi-Fi, and checked her email. The usual: her editor, her mother, Facebook friends celebrating birthdays, airline mileage updates, and *NYT* and CNN news alerts. And one other email: it was from Mike Blowen. A note and a file. The file contained a photograph of Marnie Babbitt from a Barclays newsletter.

Flanders wondered whether she'd be willing to talk. Likely not, but it would be worth asking.

If sleep wasn't an immediate option, coffee was. First in her room, then downstairs at the Panorama Restaurant.

Twenty minutes later, Reilly returned her text with: Busy now. It was likely one of the auto-replies he'd programmed. Flanders decided to go to Reilly's hotel and wait. *Why not?* she thought. It was where the Russian delegation was staying. She might pick something up. Besides, waiting for Reilly was becoming her full-time job.

* * *

Reilly's outside work was again impinging on his full-time job.

"What's up?" Reilly asked when Vincent Moore called in from the US.

"We've got a bead on a guy in Nevada." It took a moment for Reilly to focus on the context. When he did, he was careful what he said next.

"Oh?"

"Oh yes. And you were right."

'Right' could mean a number of things: right about the dam, right about the water supply. Right about Lake Meade. Right about Las Vegas.

"About—?"

"Yes," Moore said cryptically. "And we're taking our time for obvious reasons." To Reilly, that meant the subject was under surveillance.

"Don't wait too long," Reilly said.

THE HOUSE OF NOBILITY

TWENTY MINUTES LATER

Three hours in, the two sides had hardly gone beyond trading political slogans. Gorshkov, channeling Lenin:

"History has presented my country with an immediate task. The fulfillment of this task, protecting our people, is our right, our duty."

Battaglio, summoning Reagan:

"Mr. President, our responsibility is to the present and the future, between North America and Europe. A Europe including the Russian Federation. Surely we can both recognize that this is the foundation on which the cause of freedom so crucially depends."

Gorshkov employing Castro:

"Not without recognizing that NATO's military alliance is an instrument of repression; perhaps not from your perspective, but certainly from ours."

Battaglio channeling George W. Bush:

"The unity between NATO and the United States of America, and our commitment to freedom, carried us to victory in the Cold War.

Take heed that this remains the mission that history has set for NATO, and the United States is committed to that mission, Mr. President."

The two sides postured; a typical opening round. Gorshkov finally called a break. Each group went to opposite anterooms with ample coffee, tea sandwiches, fresh fruit and pastries. Battaglio promptly pulled Pierce Kimball to the far corner.

"So far this has been a waste of time."

"It's how it starts, not how it ends," Kimball explained. "It's a big game board, Mr. President. Big egos, big stakes. And it takes time to move the pieces around correctly. Stay in it, we'll get to the issues." Kimball wondered if the new president was up to the job. He felt Battaglio could use a Cold War primer.

"You have to remember, sir, Gorshkov thinks and acts like a spy. KGB and FSB—no one ever leaves that behind. Once a spy, always a spy."

"And?"

"Gorshkov has been in it for the long game since he served as Chief Intelligence Officer in Dresden in the last years of Soviet rule. In late '89, with the end in sight, the Kremlin ordered Gorshkov to burn all the files he and his predecessors had accumulated: names of contacts, assets who had been turned, and those who could be blackmailed in the service of the Soviet Union. Gorshkov adamantly complained. He was overruled. The final command from Moscow, 'Close it all down. Burn everything. Return home.'"

"Yes, yes, yes, I know all this!" Battaglio hated being lectured.

"But you need to realize who you're dealing with—a ruthless, manipulative dictator who rose out of the ashes of the Soviet Union determined to seek revenge on all those who abandoned him and rebuild Russia into a full super power.

"Mr. President," Kimball said, "with the U.S. so preoccupied, Gorshkov believes he's free to tear through Eastern Europe. Georgia and Crimea were the first and second steps under Vladimir Putin. Gorshkov intends to take the rest back."

Battaglio dismissed the assessment with a wave of his hand. "I can make a deal that he's going to have to take. It'll calm things down."

The National Security Officer was aghast, effectively shot down. Secretary Matthews, who had overheard the conversation, was speechless.

"Don't worry. He'll listen," Battaglio concluded. He took a few cookies from a platter and walked across the hall to meet with the NATO officials. It was a meeting that ended with grim faces.

75

HENDERSON, NEVADA

Vincent Moore's team remained in stealth mode, invisible to Richard Harper but not to the man assigned to watch him for Pak Yoon-Hoi—an Uber driver named Jimmy Boyd, who wasn't interested in picking up fares.

"You asked me to let you know if you had a problem," Boyd reported. "Well, it looks like you have a problem."

Boyd was a local hire: well-paid but uninformed. A Las Vegas hustler, or in the words of Yoon-Hoi's Russian teachers, a disposable pawn.

"People in vans are following Harper from a distance. They went to his apartment and now they're heading to the plant." Pak Yoon-Hoi listened. "Good, right? You wanted to know."

"Very good, Mr. Boyd."

"You want me to stay with them?"

"No, that won't be necessary. Go back to work but don't talk to anyone. I'll make sure you're taken care of." Boyd smiled, pleased with himself and unaware that he only had another day to live.

STOCKHOLM

THE HOUSE OF NOBILITY

The meeting reconvened.

"Mr. Gorshkov, there's something you don't understand," Battaglio declared as soon as they were seated again. The Russian didn't like his tone and replied in kind.

"What is that, Mr. Battaglio?"

"You're not dealing with President Crowe. Though by now, I believe he would have come to the same conclusion as I have."

"Which is?"

"You're making the mistake of listening to America's polls and political commentators who are ignoring what's happening in the rest of the world."

The Russian president glared.

"I don't," Battaglio stated firmly. "And during our break I made a call."

Gorshkov raised an eyebrow before the translator started.

"Mr. President, I'll dispense with any mystery because your own people will soon alert you: I ordered operations at Ramstein Air Base in Germany to full tactical ready in support of NATO troops in Ukraine and Latvia. That means…"

Gorshkov listened, but he already knew what it meant. Ramstein was home to the United States Air Forces in Europe and Africa as well as AIRCOM, NATO's Allied Air Command. Altogether at least 54,000 servicemen and women were now on alert and poised to fight the Russian Federation.

Nicolai Gorshkov sat erect and expressionless. He remained focused on Battaglio as he finished speaking.

Threat received, Battaglio thought. He waited for a response.

* * *

Savannah Flanders's press credentials earned her entrance into the Kensington Royal Nordiska Hôtel even with its elevated security. But when she texted Reilly, she got the same auto-response and couldn't be sure if he'd even seen her message. She was determined to hang around until she could gather some useful information, whether it was directly related to Reilly or not, so she settled into the lobby restaurant and ordered a much-needed coffee. Flanders positioned herself facing the lobby, and observed the various government functionaries milling around while she drank her Americano. Suddenly she spotted Marnie Babbitt stepping off an elevator, clad in a bright summer dress and flats. Babbitt moved with a sense of self-assurance, exuding power and success; no wonder Reilly liked her.

Flanders promised herself she wouldn't talk to Babbitt without first speaking with Reilly. But that didn't mean she couldn't tag along and see where Babbitt was headed.

* * *

Battaglio hadn't anticipated Nikolai Gorshkov's response: he clapped. He clapped for ten seconds.

"Mr. President," he said, "no one should ever underestimate you. You have a full grasp of the situation. You have allies to answer to. It's a perfectly rational response to a situation you view as dangerous. But I ask you to view it from the Russian people's position, from the perspective of our history."

He paused for the translation, then continued, indignant.

"The Germans in the Great War. The Germans in the Great Patriotic War, Mr. President. Russia attacked both times. In each war, we braced against the enemy at the cost of millions of men, women, and children. Today, the same unsettling political waves are sweeping across Europe. Fascists, right-wing extremists. The EU is splintering. Brexit-light and Brexit-heavy is seeping into political discourse everywhere, including your own nation. You have to admit, it's part of the fabric of America now. This makes the world unsettled in a way Russia knows all too well. We are bracing for history to repeat itself."

Battaglio wasn't convinced. "Yes, but times have changed, President Gorshkov. Military regimes are not at your doorstep now."

"Not today. Maybe not tomorrow. But tell that to those men, women, and children in 1914 and 1939. Ah, but we can't. History only allows us to go forward and hopefully act appropriately on what we've learned," Gorshkov continued. "And so, I was elected to do just that. So, stand down, President Battaglio—we can remain trade partners. Russia's relationship with America doesn't need to change, but we can agree to focus on our own problems and peoples. And the countries I welcome into the new Russian Federation will benefit from our protection—which, considering the state of NATO, I imagine looks better every day."

Battaglio was accustomed to standoffs in Congress, but this had an order of magnitude beyond those partisan stalemates. He widened his eyes at Pierce Kimball, as if to say, 'What now?'

Gorshkov saw it. He had the American president exactly where he wanted him.

76

STOCKHOLM

Marnie Babbitt casually strolled through the aisles of Stockholm's most famous department store, Åhléns City. She was focused on finding a sexy black bra and matching negligee. For Dan Reilly to see, to get aroused by, to remove. There were other high-end shops, but Åhléns on Klarabergsgatan was an experience all its own and a perfect place to meet. The store took up an entire block. It offered a range of price points and endless choices. Everything for everyone. And considering Stockholm was a true international destination, on any given day, dozens of languages could be heard.

Babbitt found what she thought would entice. A sheer bra with delicate shoulder straps and satin ribbons drawing attention to her curves. It had a perfect name. *Passionata.* She walked toward the dressing rooms to make sure it delivered precisely as advertised. That's when she heard a woman's voice from behind.

"*Ideal'nyy vybor.*"

Russian.

The woman continued.

"*On budet lyubit' tebya v etom…I vne.*"

Babbitt turned.

"Ah, but I should be using my English more."

Babbitt smiled. "That's alright. I have had some Russian. And yes, it is an ideal choice. He'll love it on and off."

"So nice to see you again, Ms. Babbitt."

"And you, Ms. Pudovkin."

"Nothing like lingerie to whet a man's appetite and wet your own."

The conversation was overheard by another woman a few racks away looking through clothes. Savannah Flanders.

* * *

Gorshkov was performing, reveling in the drama he'd plotted. He considered slamming his hand on the table. But no, not yet. Save that for the right moment to scare the inexperienced American president. *The acting president.*

"Mr. President, you have made a huge mistake. It is you who has set the clock ticking to war. I will tell you what will happen and in precisely what order should you continue test Russian resolve: your American planes are about to take off. Do not be mistaken, our defenses are poised to respond. The conflict will quickly escalate; your NORAD computers have Russian installations targeted. And at the moment the first American missile crosses Russian airspace, we will respond, Mr. Acting President." The last slight was delivered with particular venom.

"History will blame you. While you come ready to lead us to nuclear winter, I come with a desire to make a summer of peace."

Battaglio allowed himself a subtle laugh.

"You can move beyond your rehearsed Cold War speeches. You're very good at it, but I suggest we start getting to the substance of our meeting." Hearing the translation, the Russian president shook his head, a dismissive gesture. More theater. Satisfied that he had taken up enough time, he pressed on.

"Mr. President, here we are deliberating in one of the most beautiful cities of the Old World. 'A city between bridges.' Isn't that how they refer to it?" The American president was not familiar with the description.

"A city between bridges. Bridging islands. Bridging

cultures—Scandinavian and Russian. It's interesting that the Swedish Vikings, the Varangians, sailed across the Baltic in the 10th Century founding states in Russia, Belarus, and Ukraine. They pillaged the Jewish *shtetls*, killed the men, raped the women. Tragic on one level. But on another, they actually saved the bloodlines in those communities, introducing new DNA, reversing the ravages of generations of intermarriage.

"Yes, 'a city between bridges.' And perhaps here," Gorshkov stopped as if to think, but he had planned for the moment, "let us find another bridge to build."

* * *

Savannah Flanders watched the encounter, first from some twenty feet away, then even closer holding an armload of clothing. She caught much of their conversation in English but noted that some had been sprinkled with fluent Russian.

"I'm sorry, but this is inappropriate," Marnie said.

"You're so right. Forgive me," Pudovkin offered.

"Of course."

"And you. It is Marnie, right?"

"Yes, Marnie," Babbitt replied. "Marie?"

"Maria."

The woman passing as Pudovkin touched Babbitt's hair lightly. Marnie didn't recoil.

"Beautiful silky hair."

"Thank you."

Pudovkin lingered. The way she did when she touched Marnie's hand.

Marnie breathed deeply and closed her eyes for a moment. She looked around. From her vantage point, no one took particular notice.

Pudovkin laughed. "I'm sorry. You remind me of someone."

"That happens."

The Russian withdrew her hand and looked around.

"Well, try it on. I'm sure he'll be pleased. And if you need another opinion, I'm here."

"I think I'll be fine," Babbitt replied.

"I'd go so far as to say you're better than fine." Then the Russian woman leaned in and whispered into Babbitt's ear. Babbitt smiled and nodded.

* * *

"Help me understand whether any agreement we come to will be supported by your Congress? Considering the temporary position you hold, are you actually viewed as your nation's leader?" Gorshkov asked.

"Make no mistake, I am America's chief executive. In case you're looking for a title to use, president works just fine."

"My apologies, Mr. President. I intended no disrespect, but I have to understand if you speak for the American people." The question, once translated, cut to the quick. Battaglio fought to keep his frustration out of his voice. He knew that was what Gorshkov wanted.

"I'm here. That's all you need to know."

"Of course, of course," Gorshkov replied. "Then we shall proceed, but I cannot hide the feeling that you have an agenda not yet revealed." Battaglio kept his eye contact on Gorshkov, looking neither left to his team nor right toward the NATO command, and pushed ahead.

"Mr. President, three Chinese container cargo ships are on their way to Venezuela. That's three more in addition to those already docked."

Gorshkov quickly replied with a wave of his hand, "China is a long-standing trading partner with Venezuela. What is your point?"

"The ships contain missiles, Mr. President. Intercontinental ballistic missiles that will be joining others already deployed. By our count, forty; soon pointing to forty-two American cities and major population centers."

"A bold claim," Gorshkov declared.

"Oh, it's more than a claim."

"Well, if you have proof, you should present it to the United Nations and Chinese diplomats, not me. Those are the proper channels."

Battaglio nodded to Secretary of State Elizabeth Matthews, who removed a file from her briefcase and handed it to Battaglio. The acting U.S. president slid it across the table to Gorshkov, the tension in the room becoming palpable as the folder slowly moved from the American side of the table to the Russian. Battaglio watched closely as Gorshkov examined the photographs and notations; when he finished a cursory review, he passed them to a general whose name Battaglio couldn't remember.

Gorshkov leaned in and asked Matthews sharply, "How do I know these are not doctored?"

"Send your spy satellites over," she replied with a sly smile. "The coordinates are on the photographs. They're less than six hours old, completely relevant to today's business. There are other missile sites we believe are already online and we view them as a great threat to our borders. I am prepared to establish a military blockade of all Venezuelan ports: any vessels that don't stop, agree to boarding, or turn around will be fired upon with extreme prejudice.

"You remember the last time the United States of America was faced with a threat of equal proportion? It nearly brought us to war. Kennedy and Khrushchev—the world watched, Mr. Gorshkov. The world will be watching again today. So now mark my words, we *will* fire on those ships. And we will take out each of the missile sites."

"I fail to see what this has to do with the Russian Federation?"

"I hope nothing, Mr. President. And everything related to our negotiations. We believe the Chinese ships are transports hired by North Korea." The translator changed North Korea's name to the Democratic People's Republic of Korea.

"I still fail to understand the direct relevance," Gorshkov professed.

"You are allied with both nations. But I will get to that. For now, it's absolutely imperative for you to recognize that the United States is prepared to, and will within the next six hours, establish a no pass blockade in international waters, to be maintained by the Fourth Fleet. Those ships will be poised to intercept the transports, as will Los Angeles class submarines below the surface, and Navy jets from on high."

Gorshkov turned his attention from Matthews to Battaglio. "Mr. President, assuming this is all true, your issue is with the government of China, presupposing your accusation about the Democratic People's Republic of Korea."

Battaglio slammed his fist on the table when he heard the translation.

"It is 100-percent true, and I believe you are equally 100-percent aware."

Gorshkov attempted to answer after the translation, but Battaglio pushed on.

"Should I consider the Russian Federation complicit in this action, President Gorshkov?"

Gorshkov's eyes narrowed to furious slits. He fixed on Battaglio and suddenly spoke in precise English.

"Are you coming to a point?"

"Yes I am."

* * *

Savannah Flanders was an investigative reporter. What she observed made her nervous. And now she couldn't *unsee* what she'd seen: how the two women seemed to practice using each other's names. The whispers and the touches. It appeared to be a rendezvous more than just a casual meeting. An English business executive and a Russian woman.

Flanders returned the clothes–her props–to the rack. She continued to look like an undecided shopper working her way out of the lingerie department. *Now for the nearest exit,* she thought. She had to reach Reilly. As she rode down the escalator, she texted him again:

Need to talk Urgent

This time, a fast reply from Reilly:

RU here?
She replied with a Y for yes and texted:

Meet you at your hotel in 15 min

Will u b there?

Reilly responded with his own:

Y

She ended the text stream repeating one word, this time in all caps:

URGENT

* * *

"Turn those ships around, Mr. President," Battaglio commanded, trying to give it a Reagan ring.

"That's a demand to the wrong nation," the Russian president replied. He held up a finger and conferred quietly with his aides. Battaglio shot a glance to his translator, who nodded in the negative. He couldn't hear the conversation.

"Of course, we both have our channels to Beijing—diplomatic, trade, cultural. I caution you, any statement from the United States of the type you describe would have the sting of an ultimatum."

"Fully intended."

The Secretary General of NATO blanched. Carlos Phillipe reached over and whispered in Battaglio's ear. "We're here to discuss *Russia and NATO*." Battaglio ignored Phillipe's plea.

Gorshkov countered, "A dangerous posture, Mr. President."

"A most dangerous situation, Mr. President," Battaglio replied. "The transports are Chinese. The missiles, we believe, are North Korean. Together they are complicit and threatening us."

Gorshkov replied under his breath, "*Delat' iz mikhi slana.*"

Battaglio's translator blanched.

"What?"

"It's an expression we have. Don't make an elephant out of a fly," the translator offered.

Battaglio clenched his fist.

"Well, we have an expression in America, too, Mister Gorshkov. It's simply that there's an elephant in the room. It means there's a problem you don't want to recognize! But now is the time to do so."

Battaglio continued after the translation went unanswered. "We've retraced the cargo ships' route via satellite: China to Wŏnsan Harbor, North Korea, via the Sea of Japan. The containers were loaded under cover of night; large enough to contain Hwasong-15 missiles."

Gorshkov understood, but he still waited for his translator to do his work.

"The Venezuelan armed forces have been working with North Korean advisors to bring the missiles online. We know of one." Battaglio stated the name. "Kim Noh, a leading nuclear scientist. And if there's one, there are more. And so, to be abundantly clear, when I present to the American people evidence of North Korea's deployment of ICBMs in the Western Hemisphere, it will be viewed as a supreme threat. America will demand I consider it an act of war."

Gorshkov took a conciliatory tone. "Tell me more of this elephant in the room."

"The elephant is not to be ignored. We must find a solution, Mr. President. Are you willing?"

Gorshkov took a long drink of water from a bottle his own staff had provided. He was always mindful of possible poisons. Battaglio now smiled for the first time in hours; he felt he had Gorshkov where he wanted him.

"Given our understanding of the facts, I am prepared to offer a proposal," Battaglio stated.

NATO Secretary General Phillipe whispered again in his ear. "Mr. President, we should take a recess to discuss this. May I remind you the purpose of our meeting is to—."

"No!" Battaglio replied far too loudly. "There are multiple considerations to our sessions which not only include Europe, but the safety of the American people. That is my foremost concern."

The NATO Secretary looked to the other members of his negotiating team, Chairman of the European Military Committee General Jules Rother, and General Alias B. Turnbull, Supreme Allied Commander Transformation, SACT; each was appalled by the new president's demeanor. Jules Rother, the Frenchman, spoke.

"Mr. President, we insist on a recess before proceeding." Rother stood. The other NATO delegates did the same. Gorshkov leaned back in his chair.

"Perhaps this would be a good time for a break. I propose we continue this evening. At 1900."

Not waiting for the translation to be completed, the Russian president also stood. With two of the three negotiating parties leaving, the meeting was over for now.

* * *

Flanders walked briskly out of Åhléns City and turned left on Klarabergsgatan. It was busy with pedestrians, fast-moving cars and city buses. She stopped at the crosswalk and waited for the light to change. The sun was beginning to drop, but in Stockholm, it would be another six hours before something approximating night would descend on the city.

She looked left and right. She felt a slight breeze. There were horns, birds, and the sounds of footsteps as people lined up behind her. There was conversation in multiple languages and the distinctive scent of perfume. She recognized it from somewhere, somewhere recent. She heard people talking on their cells. More pedestrians got ready to cross but not yet, not while a red Hop on/Hop off bus bore down at roughly 50 mph. As a New Yorker accustomed to crazy traffic, Flanders automatically planted her feet on the edge of the curb and braced herself. That was a mistake. Instead of anchoring her, it made her unprepared against—

The crowd. But not the crowd—one person who came from behind and pushed her with such force that Savannah Flanders lost her footing and was thrust directly into the path of the oncoming tourist bus.

There were screams, but not from Flanders.

77

The hour came and went. Reilly texted Flanders. Once, twice, then a third time. No response. He called. No answer. *That's not like her*, he thought. Ten minutes later he tried again. Nothing. He reread her earlier texts. The single letter Y for yes. Urgent twice. Meet in 15.

Reilly phoned Alan Cannon.

"Got something for you."

"What is it?"

"My radar's up. Maybe for no reason, but—"

"Sometimes we don't need a reason," Cannon said. "We just have to listen to instinct. What is it?"

"I'm trying to get in touch with a *New York Times* reporter." Reilly spelled her name and gave Cannon a brief description. "She showed up in Kiev wanting an interview about what happened on 14th Street Bridge after the explosion. I've been trying to talk her out of it but she's very persistent." He didn't get into any details about where her research had led. "Now she's in Stockholm and texted a few minutes ago that it was urgent to talk. But I can't reach her. Like I said, my radar's up."

"On it. Let me see what I can do." Cannon replied.

* * *

Marnie Babbitt knocked on Reilly's hotel room door. She carried her shopping bag from Åhléns.

"Who is it?"

Reilly was expecting Babbitt, but half-hoped it was Flanders to ease his mind.

"The woman of your dreams. Now open up!"

Reilly unlocked the door. He smiled and was ready to kiss her, but Babbitt strolled right past.

"Wait, wait!"

"You wait. I want to tell you something." Babbitt kicked off her heels and put the bag down.

"Drink?"

"Sure," she replied.

Reilly poured from an open bottle of Albert Schoech Alsace. The Sylvaner, Chasselas, Riesling, and Muscat blend was light and sweet, like their conversation.

She took a glass. They clinked in a toast to one another as they always did and she sat on the bed.

"You were right," Marnie said.

"About?"

"The Russian woman. She followed me. More than that. I think she came on to me."

Reilly closed his eyes and swallowed hard.

"What's wrong?" she asked.

"Actually, nothing," Reilly replied. He looked relieved.

"Really? I just told you that woman came on to me. That's nothing?"

"No, it's something. Look, Marnie, she's dangerous. She wants to get close to you, maybe to get close to me."

"No way."

"Seriously."

"What do you mean?"

Reilly said, "It's what she does. She's a...."

"A what?"

He paused. He needed the right word. A safe word for her that didn't say everything. "A predator."

Babbitt laughed. "I got that much."

"The way a…" he paused again. "The way a corporate spy tries to ensnare and entrap."

Marnie lightened up.

"Whoa. She was just making a pass. I shouldn't have said anything. Besides, I've had training."

Reilly said, "Just be careful."

"Always am." She snapped her fingers. "Oh, which reminds me, I forgot to take my pill."

Marnie retreated to the bathroom with her wine glass. There, she changed into her new purchases—the lace bra and a matching silk negligee she'd bought. *Passionata* and *Awakenings*.

"By the way," Marnie called from the bathroom. "Why all the worry?"

"I think I'm just working too hard."

She poked her head out. "I've been trying to tell you that. You need to start listening to me."

"I will."

Reilly laid down on the bed and kicked off his shoes and removed his socks. A minute later Marnie re-emerged. She walked quietly over to him. He watched. She ran her left hand over her nipples and her right hand under the appropriately named silk *Awakenings*. He sat up. She covered the remaining six feet and took his hand and put it under hers.

Reilly sighed. "Did you find her attractive?" Reilly asked jokingly.

"What is it with you men and Russian women? *Kak Ukus zmei.*"

Despite his knowledge of Russian, he didn't get the meaning.

"Like a snake bite. An Aesop Fable. *The Peasant and the Snake.* It means, '*What a bad name snakes have gotten from you men.*'"

A thought flashed in Reilly's mind. Vipers. All the more dangerous because they could open their mouths wider than most to deliver their venom. And Maria Pudovkin was a viper, filled with poison.

Marnie made the thought go away with what she did next.

78

Alan Cannon first called Flanders' *New York Times* office and spoke with Michael Blowen. The reporter explained he hadn't heard anything from Flanders since she'd checked into her Stockholm hotel and said she was going to head out to Reilly's to see him. Cannon thanked Blowen and went to the Kensington hotel security office to review CCTV lobby footage. He produced his VP of Security identification when questioned by a young guard and explained what he needed. Cannon was quickly set up with a screen and instructions on how to scroll through, freeze, and blow up footage. Before screening, however, he Googled a photo of Flanders from her job at the *Times*, printed it, and with the image placed beside the monitor, began watching footage from 1500 hrs., or 3:00 p.m. on. He screened in real time; when the time stamp hit 15:47:06, he stopped the playback. A woman who resembled Flanders entered the frame, wearing a navy blue and white-striped long-sleeve blouse with a light blue sweater, slim khaki slacks, and peep-toe wedges. The angle wasn't good enough to make a clear determination, so he hit play again and picked her up on six different cameras. A different camera angle from behind the front desk provided the best view. He froze the image; the time stamp was 15:48:52. Cannon grabbed a freeze-frame, pasted it to a new window, and compared it with his Google image.

"Bingo."

He returned to the moving images. The woman sat on a couch

beside a small round table for drinks. She rested her purse beside her, taking out a folded piece of paper. She opened and scanned it, then placed it face down on the table.

Cannon wondered what it was. *A memo? A schedule?*

At 15:51:03 a waitress came by and took an order. A cappuccino or some other specialty coffee arrived at 15:56:20. She paid in cash. Cannon could clearly see the denomination. A one-hundred Swedish Krona bill and six tens atop it. Roughly eighteen bucks American. She let her coffee cool until 15:58:10 then took her first sip. At 16:12:23 she sat up, alert. Something or someone caught her eye. Cannon glanced across the screen to the direction Flanders was looking. The elevators. He froze the frame again.

Marnie Babbitt. Cannon her—Reilly's girlfriend. It seemed logical that Flanders might want to talk to Babbitt if she was doing a story on Reilly.

As the video continued, Flanders raised her paper again and seemed to be comparing it with the woman she was looking at. A beat later, at 16:12:37, she quickly folded the paper and stood.

Cannon whispered to himself. "Okay, time for a little chat."

But she didn't. At 16:13:15 Flanders started following Babbitt out of the hotel. Jesus, *she's tailing her. Why?* Cannon wondered. The hotel video wouldn't do him any more good—he'd have to pick up the pair on city cameras.

* * *

Cannon headed to meet an old friend at *Polismyndigheten,* Stockholm's Swedish Police Authority, located at Kungsholmsgatan 43—Detective Inspector Erik Eklund. Eklund greeted Cannon warmly, but stated he was busy with an investigation and couldn't spend time helping. Instead, he assigned a precinct sergeant to set up the street CCTV camera playback. It took a few minutes for Cannon to navigate smoothly and figure out how to have one camera position lead him to another. After a few false starts, he got it. He saw Flanders exit the Kensington, cross the street, turn right and walk along the river. He watched her casually trail Babbitt some fifty feet behind. Never close. Never too far away. Past boats, around bicyclers, street venders, and musicians. Around a corner, through a park, and down another avenue until Babbitt arrived at a huge department store. Åhléns City.

From the camera mounted high on a pole across the street he watched Babbitt enter, followed 30 seconds later by Flanders.

Now what? he thought. Shopping could go on for hours. And there were multiple ways in and out of the store. Then he remembered Reilly had told him the approximate time of the last texts. He fast forwarded to just five minutes prior and called up the cameras that covered the exits.

* * *

True to the officer's prediction, he finally spotted Flanders leaving thirty-two minutes after Marnie Babbitt entered the store. He saw her move quickly along the sidewalk to a corner in order to cross the busy street. Cannon watched closely. She moved to the head of the queue, took her cell out and appeared to be texting. More people came up behind her. Fast moving traffic passed by. The video had no audio, but Cannon heard the sounds in his head. People talking as they pressed forward. Cars honking. A red Hop-On Hop-Off bus speeding up to make the light before it changed. Then another person working her way up to the front of the crowd. A woman wearing a blue hat that obscured her face, but not her intentions to Cannon's trained eye. Someone who was calculating time and distance, speed and energy.

Without realizing, he screamed out as if to warn Savannah Flanders. Of course, she couldn't hear him. He saw the woman appear to bump the reporter. Actually, it was more than a bump. A push. A deliberate, two-handed shove that sent Savannah Flanders to her death.

79

Alan Cannon showed the video to the police sergeant assigned to him. He phoned Detective Inspector Erik Eklund, who was on his way back from taking statements where an unidentified woman had fallen in front of a bus. Eklund intended to check the CCTV cameras himself and was surprised that Alan Cannon was reviewing the same scene.

"She didn't slip or fall," Cannon explained when Eklund sat next to him. "She was pushed. Watch." He turned to the computer playback that he'd frozen and slowly moved forward through the footage.

The scene turned hectic; people shocked. Hands in the air. Cries. The bus stopped some 30 meters down the street. They went back and forth trying to see the moment clearly. Cannon was convinced it was intentional. Eklund wasn't so sure.

"Alright, then where's her purse?"

The detective hadn't found it at the scene, but Cannon had his own supposition. It was taken in the confusion by the woman in the blue hat." He scanned the images frame-by-frame. Right after the collision and feet from the impact, the purse was clearly on the ground. For the next 45 frames, a second-and-a-half, another bus drove by obscuring the mounted CCTV camera. After it passed, everything was the same except for one detail. The purse was gone. So was the woman with the blue hat.

* * *

Cannon decided to tell Reilly in person, not over the phone. He cabbed back to the hotel and spotted Reilly talking to three security officers in the lobby. Cannon waited a few steps away. Reilly finished and crossed to his associate.

"Hey buddy. Plugging last holes here based on the Russians' needs. How'd it go for you?"

"Let's walk," Cannon said.

Reilly asked why. Alan Cannon wore the kind of expression that said, *Not here. Not until we get out.*

They walked outside in tandem, past the house security, the Stockholm police, and the army officers posted around the hotel.

"Okay, talk to me, Alan."

A block away Cannon stopped. He faced Reilly and told him directly. "Flanders is dead."

Reilly's shoulders slumped. He felt his legs weaken. Cannon explained what he'd seen and the police's investigation. He described the moment and his belief that Flanders had been intentionally pushed.

"I don't understand." But he suddenly flashed on Marnie's Åhléns shopping bag.

"She followed her in," Cannon said, "and was spotted by another woman. A woman with a hat. Then this happened outside. On the street."

Cannon showed Reilly printouts of still frames from the outside surveillance cameras. The images were sharp. He saw how the woman, somewhat blocked by other pedestrians, pushed Babbitt in front of a bus.

The two men did not move. Reilly straightened and stared into nothingness as thoughts began to flood him. *Flanders's dogged pursuit of facts. My not picking up the phone at a critical moment. My complicity.* Then, pure guilt.

And then there was Marnie Babbitt. Beautiful, sensual, hypnotic Marnie Babbitt. *Marnie Babbitt who always seemed to show up. In Tehran, in England, Brussels, and now Stockholm. Marnie Babbitt who was interested in him, but equally interested in his work, his contacts, what he knew. Marnie Babbitt who seemed more than comfortable meeting Nicolai Gorshkov in Russia on their second chance encounter. Marnie Babbitt whose Russian was a little too good. Marnie Babbitt who he'd just ...*

"Pieces," Reilly whispered. "Parts that form the whole."

"The whole what?" Cannon asked.

"The whole truth."

80

Marnie Babbitt left Reilly's room and walked with a spirited step toward the elevator. She was feeling good and wanted some fresh air. She heard a greeting. "Well, hello again Ms. Babbitt, you look absolutely radiant."

Marnie Babbitt turned to a recognizable voice. A voice that always seemed to come from behind. This time down the hallway. The last time, in the department store dressing room.

"Ms." Marnie hesitated. "Pudovkin."

"Maria's good."

"I'll remember. Maria."

"That's good, Marnie. *Praktika delayet ideal'nym.*" Practice makes perfect.

Babbitt nodded. She looked past the Russian woman, then to her back. No one else was in the hall. "Are you on this floor, too?"

"No. I got off early. But a pleasure bumping into you again."

Babbitt knew it was no accident. The Russian had been waiting. She took a deep breath, shuddered, and walked forward. Pudovkin gestured to the overhead camera at the end of the hallway. Marnie stopped short.

"Well nice seeing you again," Pudovkin said politely.

"Nice seeing you, too."

Pudovkin brushed passed Marnie and slipped her a plastic card. A room key in a sleeve with a number written in black.

Marnie Babbitt palmed it like a pro. Like a pro who had rehearsed the move a hundred times.

* * *

Reilly returned to the hotel, shaken. He went directly to the security office wanting to do his own viewing. "Show me the Russian hallway cameras," Reilly sharply ordered the hotel security chief. "Fifth floor."

"Of course, Mr. Reilly," the uniformed officer replied. "From when?"

"An hour ago." His cell rang almost immediately. Marnie. *Take it or ignore it?* He answered.

"Hi," he said. He was chilly. She noticed.

"What's the matter?"

"Just busy. Why?"

"Dinner soon. Out of the hotel?"

Reilly didn't answer immediately.

"Dan?"

"Yes, sorry. Preoccupied."

"Dinner?" she asked again.

"When?" was all he could manage.

"An hour. I'll be in the room waiting. I'm all yours."

Reilly wasn't so sure anymore.

* * *

Babbitt had called Reilly from the hallway near the elevator. She hung up the phone and pressed the up button on the lift. It arrived. She took it up two flights. The door opened to a pair of Russian guards who were at the ready when she emerged. Babbitt showed them the room key. One of the guards keyed his wireless and whispered. He got an immediate reply in his ear and motioned for Babbitt to proceed down the hallway to her right. Some fifty steps further, Marnie found room 545. She used the electronic key card to gain entry without knocking. Two steps in, she closed the door.

"Welcome," the Russian said.

Marnie Babbitt nodded, dutifully stood at attention and saluted Russian Colonel Martina Kushkin.

"Sit," the colonel ordered. "You look nervous."

Marnie remained standing. "I just talked with him. He didn't sound right," Marnie said, facing Pudovkin/Kushkin.

"Then it's time to clean things up," she said coldly.

"I can still bring him in," Babbitt's eyes remained locked on Kushkin's. "I've spent so much time and he's—"

"You've run out of time. The warning I whispered to you in the department store was necessary. She followed you. She saw us together. I discovered from her purse that the woman was a reporter. She would have figured things out. I took care of that."

Babbitt stiffened to hide her shiver. "Colonel, I believe I can fix this."

"I'm counting on you to do so. By now he must know. He's smart. You were sloppy. If he doesn't suspect you already, he will."

"He loves me."

Kushkin laughed. "You're a good fuck, but I'm not so sure you're that good an agent."

Now Babbitt realized her own life was in the balance. She nodded compliance. "I'll make it up to you, Colonel."

"Yes, you will. And this is how," Martina Kushkin explained to her sleeper spy.

* * *

Reilly scanned through the lobby cam video. He spotted Marnie returning to the lobby with her Åhléns City bag. The bra and negligee. She went to the elevator bank, pressed the button, and entered. Reilly switched to the third-floor cameras and picked up Babbitt going to his room. If the security guard made the connection, he didn't say anything.

"Back to the lobby. Scan at double speed."

"What are you looking for?"

"Another woman. A woman wearing a blue hat. Wide brim."

Forty minutes in, he saw his subject. She kept her face intentionally obscured from the camera. But Reilly definitely recognized her from the CCTV footage at the scene.

"Follow her off the elevator," Reilly instructed.

They picked her up as she stepped off on the fifth floor. One of the Russian floors. For a moment he saw her face. Maria Pudovkin.

Reilly stopped to think. "Back to the third floor," he said. He gave the security officer the time when he left his room. "Okay, now scrub ahead. For the next few minutes they scanned. Nothing but the empty hallway, then they saw Reilly's exit. "Alright, fast forward again." At triple speed it didn't take long.

"Stop!" Reilly pointed. "Back up and play it slowly. Half speed."

Reilly watched once, twice and a third time. There appeared to be a polite encounter in the hallway between two women. *Marnie and—*

"Okay, even slower. I'll tell you when to freeze."

On a single frame, Reilly tapped the officer's shoulder. "There! Can you pan down and blow that up for me?"

The security officer obliged.

"Bigger." Reilly pointed to Marnie's hands. "That's it."

Blown up, he saw her adeptly palm a small, flat, rectangular object from the second woman—the Russian.

"Damn. A room key," the guard said.

Damn didn't begin to cover it for Reilly.

* * *

Kushkin had Babbitt repeat the instructions she'd been given. "Good, and he still trusts you?"

"We just made love. Of course he does."

"Well, he won't have to for much longer. It will be easy and painless. Do your job and he simply won't wake up."

"Yes, Colonel."

Kushkin smiled approvingly, like a teacher to a bright student or a parent to an obedient child. Then she stepped forward, kissed Babbitt on the lips. Her hands eased down and traced Marnie's breasts. "And

Svetlana," she whispered, employing Marnie's real name, "you'll return to London, and after you grieve we'll find you another subject. In a few months we'll find time together. I haven't been to St. Lucia. Have you?"

"No," Babbitt sighed.

Kushkin smiled again. "Now one more thing. To make sure all goes right." She inserted a miniature radio transmitter in Babbitt's handbag. Babbitt watched.

"Just so I can hear everything."

"Yes, Colonel."

81

"You look concerned," Acting President Battaglio noted in a secure conference room at the American Embassy.

National Security Advisor Pierce Kimball was worried. So were the other members of the West's negotiating team, including a new face that had been flown in.

"Mr. President, this is Dr. Veronica Severi. She's the CIA's top psychologist. She's served at the agency for more than thirty years, advising President Crowe and four prior administrations on the character and psychology of world leaders. Director Watts recommended she stay close to the negotiations to provide insight. We feel her critical assessment would be important for you to hear."

Battaglio fixed an icy stare on the shrink and then transferred it to the National Security Advisor. "Are you questioning my ability, Dr. Kimball?"

"Mr. President," Elizabeth Matthews interrupted, "the State Department has also benefited greatly from Dr. Severi's consultation."

Dr. Severi tipped her head, indicating she would take it from here. "If I may, Mr. President, with no disrespect..."

Battaglio shrugged. "You have five minutes, doctor. Make it count."

Severi was an expert analyst, particularly when it came to evaluating the psychological profile of foreign dictators, sociopaths, psychopaths, and plutocrats. She had already determined Battaglio required intellectual reinforcement. She would go slowly and measure her tone.

The doctor removed her tortoise-shelled glasses, folded the temples, and hooked them on the neckline of her off-white blouse. It was a friendly move making her appear less academic, more approachable. In reality, Dr. Severi could be stone cold, clinical, and absolutely direct. She had turned what had been a practice few understood at the CIA into a vital resource for America's security. But today, she would tread lightly.

"Mr. President," she began reassuringly, "my job is to help you. I analyze foreign leaders so we can better understand what they will do when pushed too far, when cornered by rivals, when their time is running out. The scenarios are endless. We have to think it all out ahead of time in order to set strategies, prepare counter moves, consider military action, and hopefully negotiate out of crises successfully. To put it another way, I try to figure out what makes them tick. And to the business at hand, it's important to understand that President Gorshkov is a complicated subject, worthy of understanding."

"Okay, enlighten me."

"Of course. Gorshkov relies on three elements of power he learned and mastered first as a KGB officer, then as an FSB agent. Coercion, incentives, and persuasion. Consider the position the U.S. and NATO are in right now. Coercion. He has forced us to deal with the geopolitical hand he has dealt. Ukraine and Latvia. You're at his back door and he believes he is in the position to dictate terms."

"Excuse me. No one has dictated terms but me."

Severi did not argue the point, but she saw his eyes dart. A sign of discomfort. Based on her own comprehensive and classified psyche workup on him when he became Alexander Crowe's choice for a running mate, she concluded Ryan Battaglio over compensated for any inadequacies with bravado and bullying, quick answers and a short temper. Delving into his personal and political history, she found this to be true. Moreover, in light of his inexperience on the global stage and facing an enormous personality in the Russian leader, he was clearly the lesser of the two, yet he couldn't admit it.

"Mr. President, Nicolai Gorshkov is a master gambler who has stacked the deck. In another sense, he's running the table." She stopped short of adding, *on you.*

Battaglio was stung by what was left unsaid.

"He's completely adept at the game. Remember, his background. He has lived in a dark space for the past four decades. Unquestioned and unbeaten. Almost a third of Russia's top officials, and more than half of his closest advisors are former intelligence officers. They succumb to his will or face death. He eats, sleeps, and breathes diversion, deception, and deceit."

"And you think he is getting the better of me?" Battaglio sharply asked.

"To answer that, I'll move onto Gorshkov's third element of power. Persuasion. He is relying on you being convinced that you are driving the deal. When in fact, he has his plan. His deal."

Battaglio turned to Kimball. "I've heard enough." To Severi he added, "Thank you for your time, doctor. I hope you have a pleasant trip back."

"Sir, you offered her five minutes. Give her that time," Matthews appealed.

Battaglio rolled his eyes and waved his hand.

"Thank you, Mr. President," Severi politely replied. "If you'll allow me a bit more analysis on the Russian president."

"Whatever."

"Gorshkov is counting on America's turn toward ideological *illiberalism* and the fragility of our democracy today as a self-regulating, self-correcting constitutional system. He has watched and waited. Planned and schemed. Now he's acting. Again. And he's counting on the obvious."

"Which is?"

"Inaction, sir, based on political realities. Only 30 percent of American millennials consider living in a democracy crucial to their lives. That's compared to 75 percent of people born prior to World War II.

To put it another way, our traditional liberal values supported tolerance of others, individual rights, and civic and international engagement. On the other hand, *illiberalism* supports populism, protectionism, and nativism."

Battaglio sat quietly, running the clock out.

"All the more reason Gorshkov wants you to think you get the win while he gets precisely what he wants."

"A trade."

"In part, but much more. He sees what's occurred in Europe: the Brexit mess. Italy, where more than half the population voted for anti-European parties. Hungary and Poland, two nations moving toward openly illiberal governments. The rise of extreme right factions in France and Germany. Authoritarian regimes ascending throughout the world. And leaders who view their own power over citizens' rights and liberty, who openly criticize the judiciary, create and threaten enemies within, rule by decree, and rail against what they deem as unfair media coverage. We're not immune either, as you know. And he is likely to view the world's disunity and our own internal chaos as reason to believe we will do nothing as he continues to annex country after country."

"Dr. Severi, are you implying I'm not up to facing him one-on-one?"

Severi ignored the defensive attack. "No, Mr. President, I am painting the sharpest picture of your adversary so you can make informed decisions. Right now, pump the brakes. In other words, slow the process down. He will get frustrated, but you will make him think twice, possibly increasing his respect for you as a skillful opponent. And in taking your time, listen to your esteemed advisors, they have the experience to…"

That was more than enough for Battaglio. He thrust his hand up for her to stop.

"Spoken like a true shrink, doctor. I see what you're doing. Own the decisions and the consequences of those decisions."

"A president's responsibility."

"That's all, Dr. Severi." He suddenly stood. "We're done here."

Dr. Severi rose.

"Have a nice flight home," Battaglio said dismissively.

The CIA psychiatrist left. The Acting President turned to Pierce Kimball and asked, "Thirty years?"

"Yes, sir."

"Fire the bitch."

82

KENSINGTON ROYAL NORDISKA HÔTEL

Reilly paused the playback on a telling security camera frame—Marnie Babbitt entering the Russian woman's room. He stared at the image. Evidence of so many things. Deceit, betrayal, manipulation, and perhaps worse.

The door closed. He scanned forward. It remained closed for fifty minutes. Until Marnie Babbitt left, went to the elevator, pressed the down button, and then, as he saw on the third floor hall camera, returned to his room.

He ran through a mental checklist.

He would confront her.

He wouldn't.

He'd call and wait for Alan Cannon.

He wouldn't.

He'd get hotel security to accompany him.

He wouldn't.

He'd notify Stockholm police to arrest the Russian woman.

Dan Reilly decided he'd give Babbitt the chance to explain. Maybe he was wrong. Maybe she was developing a deal in Russia. Maybe her intentions were innocent. *Maybe, maybe, maybe,* he thought. Then personal warning bells sounded. Like the ones he heard going into combat in Afghanistan. The ones that guided him at State. The bells that led him to establish the hotel security priority system.

He needed two things. A diversion and a tool of the trade. Reilly stopped at the hotel florist. He bought a bouquet of pale purple roses. Next, he went to the Kensington Royal security office.

* * *

Nicolai Gorshkov relaxed in his hotel suite. He held a vodka in his left hand and a French Gauloise in his right. Though he didn't smoke often, he preferred Gauloises over any Russian brand. None of his aides told him smoking was not allowed in the hotel. Gorshkov spent his life doing things that weren't allowed.

While he drank and puffed, a general updated him on the status of his troops.

"Good," he said. "Make sure they're well fed and rested. No further advancement. The Americans are on edge. I want this acting president to act with his own interests in mind and not see mine."

He took a final sip of his drink and doused his cigarette in what remained. He motioned for an aide to get his jacket and prepare to leave for the next, and possibly final session of the *mirnyye peregovory.* The peace talks. He laughed at the notion. *Peace.*

* * *

Reilly considered knocking. *But who knocks on his own door?* He used his key, held the flowers to the side and entered. Marnie was on the balcony looking out. "Hi," he said warmly.

She spun around. "Hi there," she said. She had a wine glass in her hand. Another was on a small table waiting for him. "Looks like we each have something for the other."

He held out the flowers as he joined her. She smiled. "They're beautiful. Thank you. Now come, relax," Marnie implored. "We have nowhere to go until dinner and lots we can do."

She picked up the second glass and exchanged the flowers for the wine. Babbitt took in the scent and Reilly swirled his wine. He brought the glass to his lips but stopped when she looked away.

"What is it?" he asked before tasting.

"A French red." She reached for the bottle. "A Bordeaux blend."

"Are we celebrating?"

"Always," she said, dropping her eye contact.

"To our tomorrows?" Reilly replied. He didn't drink. Instead he studied Marnie.

"Of course, darling. Drink up."

He lowered his glass and placed it on the bureau.

"What?" Marnie asked.

"We always toast. From the first time we met in Tehran. And every time after. But no toast now. Why not?"

"I'm sorry. Yes, to…"

"Tomorrows," he repeated.

"Of course."

Marnie tried her best to force a smile. But her voice betrayed her. She quickly picked up his glass, handed it to Reilly and said, "Yes to all our tomorrows."

They clinked. She took a sip. He did not.

"Anything wrong?" she asked.

"I've had a hard day," he said, wondering how she'd react.

"I'm sorry. Then forget the wine for now. Let's just relax."

She crossed to the bed and patted the mattress. Reilly shook his head and walked to the French doors leading to a balcony off his suite.

"Did you hear the news?"

"No. What?"

"A reporter was involved in a terrible traffic accident."

"Oh?" she asked.

"Actually, not an accident."

He waited for a reaction. It came slowly. *Slowly,* he thought, with the time it took consider how to respond.

"Not far from here. Outside a department store." He looked at the shopping bag from Åhléns City. "That store, Marnie."

"Oh my God," she exclaimed. "That's horrible."

"A *New York Times* reporter. A good one tracking me down for a story. Good enough to find things out. Good enough to get her in trouble. Good enough," he paused, "to be considered a threat to someone."

Marnie approached him on the balcony. He turned to her.

"She was pushed in front of a bus, Marnie. She's dead."

Marnie looked up. She began to speak, but no words formed.

"Yes, I imagine it's hard to talk about," he said. "She followed you from the hotel to the store, Marnie. What she saw got her killed."

* * *

At the same time the Russian president stepped into his blast proof limo in the KR underground garage, the American acting president was leaving the Embassy in his. Battaglio was ready to close a deal, but without unanimity from his advisors. No one had successfully convinced him of the Russian president's long game. Not his National Security Advisor, nor his Secretary of State. Not the CIA psychologist. Not NATO command.

* * *

Reilly slipped back away from the balcony, leaving his last declaration to settle in. Inside the suite he retrieved his wine. He raised the glass.

"Come now Marnie. Our toast. Would you say to my health?"

She stood silently. Neither yes nor no.

"I'll take that as a *no.*"

He tilted the glass over the flowers and poured while keeping his focus on Marnie. She followed his every move. Now to her purse on the desk.

"Coincidences, Marnie. I've been trying to piece together seemingly unrelated coincidences. Like the many times you just appeared in my life. You knew so much about me from the start. Just being a smart businesswoman?"

She looked at him stone cold silent.

"Or," Reilly continued, "a foreign operative."

Her eyes darted again to the desk. Reilly caught the look and took three steps toward it.

"What I don't know is whether Pudovkin turned you or you're the real deal, a Russian-born spy. One sends you to prison for treason. The other could earn you protection in the U.S. if you agree to cooperate. I'm sure you'd prefer the latter. For that matter, so would I."

She said nothing.

Reilly shook his head wondering how he could have been so wrong about her. He reached her purse. "Was it my business that you wanted to compromise? No, probably not big enough."

Babbitt fixed her eyes on her purse.

"*Bol'she?*" Reilly asked in perfectly delivered Russian. "*Politicheskiye kontakty?*"

She stiffened.

"*Net. Dazhe bol'she. Pravitel'stvo.*" *Bigger than politics. Government.* "My Russian can't possibly be up to yours."

"It's passable," she finally said.

"Thank you."

He dumped the contents of the purse onto the desk and ran his fingers through the items. Wallet, lipstick, keys, phone and loose change. He moved them to one side. He saw a small vial. He picked it up, unscrewed the top and sniffed.

"I can explain."

"I bet you can. But will it be the truth?"

"They forced me, I…"

"Odorless. I suppose tasteless, too."

She lowered her eyes.

"Was any of it real, Marnie?"

Marnie Babbitt barely spoke above a whisper. "My family."

"What about your family?"

"He'll kill them." She looked up. "*She'll* kill them."

Marnie breathed deeply and started to take a step toward him.

"No," he shouted. "Stop." He was not about to test her fighting skills. She could very well kill him any number of ways. Stay there until I figure things out."

"You figured out enough," she said. "How?"

"You forgot a basic I once told you," Reilly said. "There are no secrets in hotels." He paused. "*If* you know where to look."

Reilly slid his finger across the desk to another object from her purse. It was flat, larger than a nickel, smaller than a quarter. He'd seen them before. He'd worked with them. Lithium-powered UHF spy bugs. The ones he'd handled in the State Department were good to about 1,000 feet. He knew what was likely to happen next.

* * *

Gorshkov's five-vehicle motorcade queued underground in the hotel service driveway. Two cars led the president's Aurus. Two more followed, Gorshkov's security forces within. They were held up as five Stockholm motorcycle cops took positions at the head of the escort. Two more lined up on either side Gorshkov's limousine and four others waited to take up the rear. Overhead, circling at 800 meters and 60 meters apart, two police helicopters. Another 500 meters north, a fully armed Swedish UH-60M Black Hawk. Two others were hovering along the route. All prepared to track and protect Nicolai Gorshkov.

* * *

Reilly tossed the bug at Marnie. It landed at her feet. Instead of picking it up, she smashed it with her heel.

"They're probably on the way," she said. "She'll have sent them by now."

"Who is she, Marnie? Who are you?"

"She can't let you go."

"Who is she?" he demanded.

Babbitt shook her head. Reilly cocked his ear to the distinctive sound of a slide being pulled back on a pistol in the hallway. He turned and, from under his sports coat, wedged into his belt, he withdrew the Glock that he had taken from the hotel security office.

* * *

The police accompanying the motorcade and the helicopters above were all moving as one. They got the go signal and began rolling up the ramp, and out the service entrance of the Kensington Royal Nordiska Hôtel.

* * *

Reilly instinctively stepped to the side of the doorframe and raised a finger to his lips, signaling Marnie to remain quiet. He stood two feet back from where the door would open, allowing him to see the assailant before he'd be seen. It would be one or more of the Russians who had been following him.

Marnie stepped backwards toward the balcony. Reilly steadied his gun with both hands. He expected the Russian copped a passkey off a housekeeper. He might knock first, or just unlock the door and enter.

Reilly would only have one chance. He took in a deep breath, focused his thoughts and waited.

No knock. Seconds ticked by. Then he heard the click of the electronic entry. The big bald Russian led with his 9mm Marakov. He inched forward. Marnie was straight ahead. He saw her and looked for a signal. Her eyes shifted slightly to the right and forward again. He whipped the pistol around the entrance and fired twice.

* * *

The Stockholm police motorcycles made a right onto the one-way street along the north side of the hotel. The Russians followed. With everyone at street level now, the police paused for radio clearance from above. Once received, they made another right in front of the Kensington Royal Nordiska. Officers posted on the street held traffic as the motorcade turned the corner. Gorshkov leaned low into his seat, made sure his windows were rolled up, and his safety belt was secure. He put his hands on the leather seat, as if to brace himself. Across from him, a Russian general scanned the sidewalks.

"Ready, sir?" he asked.

Gorshkov nodded. He'd been ready for months. So was his driver.

* * *

The Russian Reilly dubbed Curly followed his shots with a turn of his whole body. The American was not there. But a gun was now at the back of his head.

"*Bros' I zhivi.*" Reilly demanded. *Drop it and live.*

The bald agent complied. But in the same instant, ducked, swiveled, and planted a roundhouse kick to Reilly's stomach.

Reilly's gun arm went high, but he remained on his feet, because there was nowhere to go. He was already pressed against the wall. The Russian came on hard. He grabbed Reilly's outstretched arm, pinned it to the wall and delivered a knee to his gut. Reilly absorbed the full force. It nearly knocked his breath out. The next punch was intended for his chin, but Reilly parried right. The Russian's fist smashed into the wall. He lost his hold on Reilly's gun arm. Reilly brought the pistol down hard on the Russian's head.

He stumbled back and retrieved his gun. Reilly didn't wait. He fired. The big Russian dropped, never to rise again.

Reilly looked at Marnie. She had given the Russian a cue at the door. The wrong cue.

"Why?" he asked.

* * *

To witnesses, it was either the speed of the vehicle or the reliability of the M202A1 Flash, an American 66mm, four-tubed incendiary shoulder-fired rocket launcher, that apparently saved Gorshkov's vehicle from being hit.

Actually it was neither. It was pure timing and training. The attack went precisely as planned.

The payload—TPA, a thickened pyrophoric agent—exploded on contact with the three-foot high cement bollards anchored outside the hotel. It's what spared the lives of thirty-four guests in the lobby. That, and the blast-resistance upgrades. The design included a combination of modular pre-cast cement, steel threaded windows with aluminum glazing. Most of it held, preventing the 1600°C white-hot compound from exploding inside. It did take out the two Russian vehicles following Gorshkov and everyone within, as well as the Stockholm police cruiser behind them, four hotel employees, and three passersby. Searing heat also shot straight up the front of the building in one massive wave.

* * *

First the flash. Then the deafening sound of the explosion. The heat. The sudden and violent change in air pressure. The vacuum it created. The wind and the force it brought.

"Marnie!" Reilly shouted. She was looking directly at him when the inferno overwhelmed the balcony. For an instant he thought he saw sadness and regret, then there was nothing.

83

Gorshkov's assemblage sped up. The aerial surveillance quickly spotted the assailant. Russian guards appeared to come out of virtually nowhere, shouting orders over their radios. Kill orders. They succeeded in under thirty seconds. Almost as if it were planned.

* * *

The fire alarm blared. The piercing, high-pitched, modulating wail brought Reilly to full consciousness; to his feet, to his job.

The ceiling sprinklers engaged and immediately soaked Reilly. That was good. It meant that the hotel's defensive systems were working. He stepped over the dead Russian and ran into the hallway. Since it was early evening, he figured most people were out exploring the city. Another good thing: fewer people running down the stairways. He passed the elevator bank and cut into the nearest corner stairwell, not one deeper inside. A middle-aged French couple, clearly disoriented, staggered out of their room.

"*Aidez-nous!*" the man pleaded. *Help us.* Reilly noted burns on his head and hands. He cradled his wife who was in shock. The 14th Street Bridge all over again.

"*Suivez-moi. Attention!*" They followed him as instructed to the stairwell. There, they met others. Reilly held the French couple back until room opened up.

"Stay calm," Reilly shouted to everyone. "Don't push!"

Four floors. Given the traffic, at least fifteen seconds per floor. *One minute.* And, for the first time, he replayed what had happened. *Bomb blast. Fireball. But not just a bomb. Ordnance, then the explosion.* He'd heard the combination before, outside of Kabul. *Shoulder-fired.* Considering the immediacy of the two sounds, the shot was from within fifty yards of the hotel.

Now he heard gunfire. *Another shooter?*

Three more floors. "Keep moving," he implored. Two floors. "Look for security officers. They'll direct you to a safe way out," he commanded.

One floor. Then they were down. The door to the northwest corner of the hotel was open and Kensington Royal security was there.

* * *

The Secret Service vehicle in front of Ryan Battaglio's armored limo got an emergency call.

"Vacate. Vacate. Vacate." It was an order to proceed directly to the airport—fastest route, fastest speed. The agent riding shotgun requested confirmation.

"Confirm, base."

"Repeat. Vacate. Vacate. Vacate."

The same order was received in Battaglio's Beast. The acting president, who had never rehearsed for any crisis maneuvers, was thrown hard into his seat with the sudden acceleration.

"What the hell's happening?"

"Sir, we have a situation," the Secret Service agent explained in the fewest words possible. He pulled Battaglio down below the bullet-hardened windows. A moment later, the agent learned more details. "Sir, bombing at the Russian delegation's hotel. We're heading to the airport. Wheels up in thirty."

"Gorshkov?" Battaglio asked.

It took more back and forth with base operations to find out.

"Unharmed. The attack missed his motorcade."

"Is he leaving?"

"Stand by, sir." The Secret Service agent requested an update. It took a minute for an answer.

"He's on his way to the destination. No change of plans."

"Then we'll do the same."

"But sir—"

"You heard me!"

Acting President Battaglio peered out the right-side window. A motorcycle hugged close. Another was on his left. *One more meeting,* he thought. *That's all it will take. Then out.*

* * *

Reilly took a minute to survey the lobby. Through the smoke he counted probably two dozen people ambulatory, but in pain. Another nine down and eerily still. Dead or unconscious. Tables overturned and shattered glass everywhere. Billowing smoke, but the fires were out. His security team, communicating to one another on walkie-talkies, attending to victims.

"Keep everyone calm," he told the officer nearest to him. "Check the upper floors for fires." He barked another five orders that came naturally from his training, but realized the staff was following procedures perfectly with no regard to their own safety.

Since ambulances and paramedics would soon be on site, Reilly focused on his other immediate concern: the Russians.

Reilly saw FSB officers quickly moving out. Some had suitcases. Two men and one woman approached the side exit where the flow headed. He couldn't immediately identify the woman. He recognized the men—the Russian thugs he dubbed Moe and Larry. And...*the woman.*

They saw one another at the same time. Reilly mouthed her name. "Pudovkin!"

She tapped Larry on the back and pointed. The agent separated. Moe stayed with her.

"Stop!" Reilly shouted. She ignored him. But now Larry was on an intercept course.

Reilly stepped backwards onto crushed glass. He kept his eyes on the agent who removed something from under his leather jacket—a Marakov; the same weapon Curly had used.

Reilly continued to back pedal. He yelled, "Pudovkin! She's dead! Babbitt's dead!"

The Russian colonel froze short of the exit.

"Your girlfriend is dead!"

Pudovkin straightened. The declaration stung. She stared hard at Reilly. He read hatred. Deadly hatred. But her expression slowly changed to a cold, heartless, emotionless smile, as if it didn't really matter.

Her Russian muscle closed in. Reilly reached to the gun tucked in his belt, but rejected the idea. *Too dangerous in the lobby.* Instead, he shouted, "Everyone, keep moving. Out! Out now." He moved toward the rear exit, losing himself in the crowd and repeating, "*Spring! Lauf! Allez! Go!* Out now!"

Larry searched for his target. He was nowhere in view so he also pushed through the panic to the exit. People who didn't move quickly enough got the butt of his Marakov. A woman went down. Then an old man.

A young security officer saw the hits and the gun.

"*Txepe!*" There!

It drew the attention of another security officer who took up the chase. But it was short lived. Moe had his partner's back. The guard went down with a swift thrust of his *Vityaz*, a narrow, long-blade Spetsnaz knife.

84

Reilly ran to the service ramp. At the top he had a simple decision to make. Left or right. *Which way would the Russian go?*

He pictured her at the bar. She'd held her cocktail in her left hand. *Dominant left.* But was it her decision which way to go or Moe's? *Hers,* Reilly reasoned.

He ran. He ran without a plan.

What would he do if he caught her? She'd have diplomatic immunity. And he realized he had no legal authority over her. Reilly stopped three blocks beyond the hotel. He leaned over, caught his breath and thought about what had just happened. Everything became clear except one final point. Marnie was a plant. A sleeper spy. She'd entrapped him with the hope of turning him. Failing that she was willing to poison him, and yet by not proposing a toast, did she intentionally send a clue for him not to drink the wine?

A car honked. It snapped him back to the moment. Reilly took off again focused on catching up with the Russian. Now he focused on Pudovkin's immediate moves. *Would she try to commandeer a vehicle at gunpoint? No. Better to be lost in the crowd. The subway!*

Even though Reilly usually traveled in a company car, cab, or Uber when he worked, he made it his business to memorize a city's key subway stops relative to where he stayed. An old habit from college days when he first toured Europe on twenty dollars a day. *So which subway station?*

In his mind, the one with the most options. *T-Centralen.*

The T stood for *tunnelbana,* Swedish for the underground. The station formed the apex of Stockholm's metro system where all the lines met including the regional trains. From T-Centralen the Russian had options. Fourteen directions, fourteen ways to escape through more than ninety other stations. That, of course, was assuming Reilly was correct and she was headed toward T-Centralen. But then again, if the situation were reversed, that's where he'd go.

A five-minute fast walk, Reilly thought. *A two-minute run.*

* * *

Gorshkov's motorcade shot through traffic at nearly highway speeds.

Acting President Ryan Battaglio's procession converged at the same rate, which was good because the Secret Service wanted him in and out fast. Battaglio figured he could present his proposal authoritatively, presidentially. Gorshkov would discuss it with his aides. They'd agree, work through the timetable, sign a preliminary document, shake hands and the world would be safer. To Battaglio and his tentative presidency, the solution would offer a concession to Gorshkov while still being a win for the U.S.

* * *

Pudovkin had a running head start. Reilly raced to catch her. Four blocks from T-Centralen, along Klarabergsgatan, he saw Moe peer out from a storefront. A Pizza Hut. Moe was on his cell phone, undoubtedly talking with Larry. He calculated the woman would be another block away, still three from the subway station.

He thought quickly. Rerouting around the block to cut her off would take too long and if he stayed on this side of the street he'd be spotted. The only possibility was to cut across and use cars and trucks for cover. He started, but then he faced a new problem. The center strip was cordoned off by four-foot-high fences. He swore.

At that moment, a motorcyclist sat on his parked Triumph

Scrambler. He started the engine and prepared to put on his helmet. Reilly acted. He pushed the driver off without apologizing. The cycle listed, but before falling away from him, he grabbed it, hopped on, and raced off to the man's screams.

Larry saw it down the block. Still on the phone, he alerted his partner.

Reilly didn't see the man behind him, he had his eye on Moe who now ran out into the road. The Russian raised his gun. Reilly began to swerve making it too hard for Moe to get off a clean shot. He sped up, figuring he had less than ten seconds to catch up to an oncoming city bus that, if he judged right, could provide cover from the gunman. It was a good idea except the bus driver was slowing for a red light ahead.

This gave the Russian an unexpected opportunity to cross to the center strip behind the bus and get off a shortened round.

Reilly braked. Too fast. He began to wobble. He shifted down and dragged his left foot on the ground to steady the motorcycle. The friction on his leather soles and the immediate resulting heat made him lift his foot and brake more, which cost him precious seconds to catch up with Pudovkin.

Three other things happened in quick succession. The light turned red in four directions, allowing pedestrians to cross. The bus gave him cover past Moe. The gun slipped out of his belt when he leaned forward to speed up.

Two more blocks driving against traffic. No police around and he knew why. All forces not assigned to cover Gorshkov and Battaglio were undoubtedly rushing to the hotel, fearing there might be another attack.

He wished he had called for help from Alan Cannon. But Cannon was likely wrapped up getting staff and guests to safety at the property. He was on the own.

He passed Moe. Another block, some 100 yards ahead, he spotted the Russian spy. She was on her cell.

They had eye contact. Distant, hate-filled. Reilly shifted, accelerated and saw her race into the metro entrance. Pudovkin still had twenty seconds on him. Twenty seconds and fourteen choices leading to a hundred potential subway stops.

He came to a quick stop. Reilly dumped the Triumph outside the station and ran into what was as much an art installation as a metro stop. Staggering, breathtaking, dynamic. He entered a huge, bustling transportation hub with hundreds of citizens walking to the lines they knew and pockets of tourists with phone apps open, trying to navigate the system.

The main terminal was bright with a golden hue. Voices echoed off the marble floors and the massive curved ceiling. He stopped twenty feet in to get his bearings and scan for the Russian. As he turned 360, he caught a commotion. A young boy was on the ground crying. His mother was helping him up. The woman was shouting and pointing to an escalator.

Reilly ran past the woman and child into another slowdown—people queued to take the escalator down to the platforms. Reilly slid down the metal barrier between up and down.

At the bottom he emerged in what appeared to be a surrealistic cavern; bigger than life and from an alternate reality. Faded denim-colored walls curved up to soaring snow white ceilings adorned with paintings of leaves suggesting giant fossils. It was as awesome as he remembered when he first came to Stockholm years earlier. That day he took his time to appreciate the architecture and the art. Not today. He ran down to the center platform where he could go in either direction. A train was just departing south. The T19. If Pudovkin had boarded, he'd missed her. Now he felt the rush of air as another green line subway approached. One of the westbound trains. The subway rolled to a stop. There she was at the far end, waiting for the door to open to the first car. He ducked behind a group of tourists. She stepped in. Reilly did the same five cars back.

Reilly read the stops on a route grid. He was on T17, which shared many of the stations of the other two subways on the green line. *Where? Where are you going?* Too many choices. Then one station jumped out.

Thorildsplan! Of course, he thought. *It stops at Embassy Row. Pudovkin is heading to the Russian Federation embassy. Escape and diplomatic sanctuary.*

Six stops. He walked toward the front subway car, timing his confrontation. *Not on the train or at the platform. Above ground. Outside Thorildsplan.*

At each stop he stood near the open door ready to bolt if she moved. She didn't get off at *Hötorget.* Not at *Rädmansgatan, Odenplan,* or *St. Ericksplan.* The subway rolled into *Fridhemsplan,* one stop before *Thorildsplan.* Now he was one car away. Pudovkin didn't get out. He let out a long, deep breath. The subway moved ahead.

The long train began to brake an eighth of a mile from *Thorildsplan.* Reilly held onto a metal pole near the door.

Slower. Slower. The train emerged from a tunnel into the daylight and stopped. The doors opened. He waited. A couple pushed past him. Reilly strained to see who was exiting the first car without being seen himself. An old man with a cane. Three students. A businesswoman with an attaché case and a Gucci bag. A blind woman with a seeing-eye dog. Then Maria Pudovkin.

85

"Mr. President. It seems that your life was spared by a matter of inches. Are you certain you're willing to continue today?" Ryan Battaglio asked before sitting.

"I am, but considering the dangers, we must come to an agreement quickly. My security forces will not allow me to return to the hotel, which itself is not even habitable. I understand there were many deaths in the assassination attempt against me," Gorshkov said, showing a modicum of compassion. "Sixty minutes, Mr. President. Whatever you have to present, I'll give you one hour. My plane will be ready whether or not you are."

Battaglio nodded. He was prepared to present his proposal despite the opposition in his camp. To get, he had to give. He figured getting was more important. He could take that to the press. He could take it to voters if Crowe didn't recover. Americans didn't care about Eastern Europe anyway. But they did care about the threats to the homeland.

The opposing sides took their seats and traded polite comments. Battaglio cleared his throat.

"Mr. Gorshkov, the solution to everything comes down to one word."

The Russian president cocked his head, understanding the English and not waiting for the translation. Battaglio felt he had set up his position perfectly.

"Venezuela."

* * *

Reilly held back. Just enough to make sure that his prey wasn't going to return to the subway. Pudovkin quickly looked up and down the platform. Clear. She pressed on. Reilly stepped off into another world. A life-size video game. The artistic inspiration for *Thorildsplan* station was Pac-Man complete with representations of the Ghosts, Pac-Man's enemies, Inky, Blinky, Pinky and Clyde; all against a blue tile background that ran the length of the station. Another day, under other circumstances, Reilly would have laughed. Not today. Not now.

The Russian walked through a connecting Pac-Man route. Past arrows and hearts. Down a flight of stairs, heading toward a huge red cherry outlined in black. She stopped midway and looked over her shoulder.

Reilly ducked behind four Chinese tourists. He waited a few seconds that seemed like minutes. He straightened. She was walking again.

* * *

"Venezuela?" Gorshkov asked.

"Mr. Gorshkov, the time to intervene is now. Talk to Beijing, then we will have something to discuss."

"China?" The Russian president straightened up. "What can you possibly be thinking?

"China can defuse the crisis and bring the Supreme Leader of the Democratic People's Republic of Korea to his senses."

NATO General Rother scribbled a note to Turnbull, who passed it along to Secretary General Phillipe. It simply said, "What's he doing?"

Battaglio continued, "Get China to solve this mess if you can't yourself. Don't let this turn into another Cuban crisis."

At first, Gorshkov silently considered the request, then he whispered to his generals to his right and left. They whispered back. Gorshkov sat and thought, cleared his throat, and leaned toward Battaglio across the table. "And for this gesture?"

Secretary of State Elizabeth Matthews, blindsided like the NATO allies by Battaglio, left her seat and with her back turned to the Russians, whispered to the president. "He won't do anything out of the goodness of his heart. He'll drop another shoe."

"Of course he will, Elizabeth. It's called negotiating."

"Not if this is all his doing," Matthews said. "We're scrutinizing intelligence to confirm whether Russia also has operatives in Venezuela working with the North Koreans. Remember Dr. Severi's caution. Gorshkov can run the table on you and…"

"Thank you, Madame Secretary," Battaglio replied dismissively. "You may sit down."

Gorshkov waited for the exchange to end. He cleared his throat, again demanding everyone's attention. He looked serious, but inside he was beaming at how well the inexperienced acting president had fallen into his trap.

"President Battaglio, you speak of Cuba. It is worth considering that after the United States' failed incursion into Cuba, what you Americans call the Bay of Pigs, Premier Castro sought protection from the U.S.S.R." Gorshkov intentionally meant his reply to sound like a lecture. "Through that union, came the Soviet Union's obligation to defend all its interests. If Moscow wasn't willing to defend Cuba, what faith would the Soviet Union's other allies have in the Kremlin? So yes, Nikita Khrushchev shipped missiles to Cuba. To defend the country allied with Russia."

"And Russia backed down."

"Negotiated, Mr. President; negotiated for the removal of missiles in Turkey that threatened our people and our major cities."

"Which would have been removed eventually," Battaglio said, relying on the primer he'd gotten.

"Which were removed sooner than eventually. And so, here we are with a similar situation. Perhaps the Venezuela government fears for its survival. But, my friend, you strike the right tone now. I am willing to make the calls for the sake of peace—to Beijing, to Pyongyang, to Caracas. But we also seek peace in Europe. Security on Russia's eastern borders."

Phillipe shuddered. As he'd feared, Battaglio was about to use NATO as a pawn.

"And this brings me back to Latvia and Ukraine," Nicolai Gorshkov stated. "Think of it as our Venezuela, Mr. President."

* * *

Reilly held back as the Russian woman took the stairs, then proceeded cautiously. He reached for his gun. It wasn't there.

Shit!

At street level Reilly looked left. Nothing. To the right, no more than twenty feet ahead, Pudovkin, standing, watching, and waiting.

"Mr. Reilly, you're certainly persistent," she said loud enough for him to hear.

He walked toward her. Ten feet away he asked, "Who are you?"

She smiled confidently and looked around.

"The woman you met in England. The woman you met here."

He stopped five feet from her.

"FSB? SVR? GRU?" Reilly asked, listing three Russian spy agencies.

"What's in a name?" she responded.

"You're in Stockholm. Gorshkov is in Stockholm. The GRU doesn't report directly to the president, but the SVR does. But your president was KGB, then FSB. He values FSB training over all others. I'd say that makes you an FSB Chief. But then again, you could be with the foreign ministry intelligence, which puts you in the GRU as a uniformed officer working directly under Gorshkov?"

Reilly decided for himself. "Yes. Under him," he said suggestively. "A lieutenant? A colonel? And surely, Pudovkin isn't your name."

"And hotels aren't your only interest, Mr. Reilly. You could very well be a spy yourself. But that's only conjecture based on Babbitt's reports." She paused. "Did you love her?"

Reilly glared.

"She said you did. And she was very lovable. I trained her well."

"Don't you even want to know how she died?"

"You killed her?"

"No. The explosion. I suspect from a shoulder-fired missile. Yours?"

She said nothing. Enough of an admission.

"A deception for something bigger going on."

"Oh how you do sound so much like a spy, Mr. Reilly. But it is what it is," she said defiantly. "So now, we must say goodbye. You, the jilted lover who can't stop me. Me? A Russian tourism attaché being stalked by an American."

"But your problems don't disappear," Reilly said.

"I have no problems."

"No? You fucked up. Your agent is dead. We're out here under," he turned counting the buildings and posts, "ten, maybe more surveillance cameras. And eyewitnesses."

"We're simply having a conversation. Two people just off a subway."

"But your men will make a report. Your work outside of Russia will be over. How long will Gorshkov want to keep a burned agent around?"

She laughed, but without her usual bravado. "Are you trying to turn me?"

"Like Marnie intended with me?"

She stopped laughing.

"Here's reality," Reilly continued. "You career is over. And with it, I dare say, your life."

"You don't scare me, Mr. Reilly."

"I think I have. Come with me and you'll have a future. Keep walking and you will be dead in a month. You're good. But you're not that good."

* * *

"You've heard my offer. What do you want?" Battaglio asked Gorshkov.

Secretary General Phillipe feared the worst. The American president was willing to trade away Ukraine and Latvia or both to prevent a conflict with Venezuela and North Korea.

The reply confirmed his worry.

"Sovereign elections in Latvia and Ukraine," Gorshkov stated.

"The countries are not mine to give," Battaglio postured.

"And the missiles in Venezuela are not mine to negotiate. But sometimes we must do what is most expedient. Free elections would be a way through the current disagreement."

"I object," General Phillipe said. "You said it yourself, Mr. President." He addressed Battaglio sternly. "The countries are not yours to give."

"Do you not have faith in the electoral process, Mr. Secretary General?"

"Not with Russian hackers manipulating campaigns and the results."

"Let's hear what President Gorshkov has to say," the acting president replied.

"Thank you, Mr. President. Of course, this is all very sudden and without much advance consideration." A lie. "But here is what the Russian Federation seeks."

"For having North Korea remove its missiles immediately," Battaglio reinforced.

"That is what you require."

Gorshkov stood and paced as he often did when dictating terms to anyone lesser than him.

"One: Within twenty-four hours, Russian Federation troops currently deployed in Ukraine will withdraw to the Russian side of the border. Two: Russian military exercises previously scheduled on Russian Federation territory east of Latvia will be postponed. Three: The government of Latvia will grant free and open elections within sixty days."

"*Non!*" Phillipe blurted in French. He turned his back to Gorshkov in protest.

"Please continue," Battaglio urged. "We've come to find solutions."

"Four, our Russian brothers and sisters in Latvia must be given full voting privileges, to participate in the determination of their future governance."

General Phillipe slammed his fist on the desk.

"No!"

Gorshkov looked to Battaglio, who in turn shot Phillipe a visible rebuke, adding, "Let's hear President Gorshkov out."

"Thank you again. Ukraine shall also have open elections, also sixty days."

Battaglio was willing to agree, but to calm down the NATO team he proposed, "A ten-minute break, Mr. President. And during that time, I believe you have a phone call to make."

Battaglio failed to notice that Elizabeth Matthews had turned the head of her bald eagle pin downward.

* * *

"This is your plan, Mr. Reilly?" Colonel Kushkin declared. "Wooing me into a safe house, promising me asylum? I expected more from you. At least a threat from a broken hearted lover."

"Her death is on you, not me."

Reilly looked beyond the spy. The two Russian thugs, Moe and Larry, approached. Reilly widened his view and panned the street. Two more Russian teams, some thirty feet away, now stood alert at forty-five-degree angles.

"Time's running out," he boldly told the Russian. "Your muscle has arrived. And they're not coming for me. They want you. They have their orders. They'll quietly walk you away. You might even have another meeting with Gorshkov. And then… ." He saw the Russian tense.

"You're trying to confuse me."

"You're smarter than that. I gave you a very easy offer to accept," Reilly said. "For a few more seconds it's entirely your decision. But from what I hear, Gorshkov has personally been willing to permanently solve certain personnel problems right in his office. Is that true?"

She said nothing. Reilly nodded in the direction of the agents. She also saw them moving in.

"They're coming for you."

* * *

In a room down the hall, free of Russian ears, Battaglio dismissed the Belgian general's concerns, promising safeguards against hacking and supervised voting.

"Impossible within sixty days," the NATO Secretary General contended. "Absolutely impossible."

"Then ninety days."

"One hundred twenty."

Battaglio nodded. *Wiggle room*, he thought. *Counter offer four months, settle for three.* He reasoned Ukraine would be the bigger diplomatic problem, but Battaglio could threaten loss of U.S. support if Ukraine failed to comply. In his mind, another win.

Ten minutes into the debate there was a knock at the door. An American Secret Service agent's knock.

"What is it?" President Battaglio bellowed.

The agent opened the door. "They're ready, sir." The thirty-two-year-old Secret Service agent from the Presidential Protective Division—the agents who served closest to the president—conveyed the word from an officious Russian counterpart.

"We'll be out in three minutes."

"But we're not through," Phillipe argued.

Battaglio declared, "I am ready to close a deal. Our nation's security demands it."

"Please reconsider," Elizabeth Matthews cautioned. "This rush to judgment, Gorshkov's sixty-minute demand, is all is highly manipulative and suspect, intended to force your hand."

"Jesus, Elizabeth! The man was attacked today. His security wants him safe. We'd do the same thing."

"It reads like a page out of Machiavelli," she countered. "He could have planned the attack himself. A near miss, timed perfectly. Don't be taken in."

"Bullshit!" Battaglio shook his head. "This conversation is over. We're going."

Battaglio stood and strode quickly to the conference room door. The NATO team entered first, followed by Pierce Kimball. Elizabeth Matthews was next in line, but Battaglio held her up, allowing the U.S. translators to pass.

"Actually, Elizabeth, Pierce and I will handle this. Go back to the embassy."

"Sir?" she responded sharply.

"We'll be fine."

"With all due respect, it won't look fine," Matthews replied.

"I'll make appropriate excuses. See you in Washington, Madam Secretary. You're excused."

* * *

Pudovkin's two men now flanked her. Moe asked. *"Yest' problema, polkovnik?"*

She shook her head *no.*

"Well, one thing's cleared up," Reilly said. "They're addressing your army rank, *Polkovnik*–Colonel.

"Poydem s nami," Moe declared.

"I believe that's an order." Reilly instantly translated. *"Come with us."* He addressed Moe. "What happens if she doesn't want to go?"

Moe signaled to Larry. They closed in on Pudovkin, hooked her arms and squeezed hard.

She didn't wince. She also didn't move.

"Your colonel is thinking," Reilly declared.

Larry reached inside his leather jacket and slid his pistol halfway out; enough to be seen.

"Really? Here?" Reilly said.

Moe leaned into Pudovkin's ear. Reilly overheard and understood. *"Net otveta ot Peterova."*

"Ah," Reilly said in English, "You won't get a response from Petrov. I called him Curly."

They looked confused.

"You won't be hearing from him."

Moe studied Reilly.

"Ever."

Now Moe tugged Pudovkin like he was in charge. *"Seychas!"* She attempted to pull free. Larry drew his Marakov. Moe repeated his order. *"Seychas!"* Now!

"It's too late," she said to Reilly.

"It's not," he replied.

Moe laughed. "It is," he said in perfect English.

* * *

Gorshkov spoke sharply.

"Here's what will happen. The Chinese cargo ships will reverse direction. The missiles will be dismantled and loaded onto ships of another registry to be verified by the United States. There will be no further missile deployments in Venezuela. The United States will not establish a blockade. The United States will not take any punitive action against the government of Venezuela in the form of further sanctions, or against the Democratic People's Republic of Korea, or for that matter, the People's Republic of China."

Battaglio smiled. He was getting what he wanted. Now to the cost. "As for the stand-down in Europe," he began.

Gorshkov rose again. He smiled—the kind of smile that comes from someone who holds the high cards in a poker game and doesn't have to bluff anymore. All the money was on the table. It was time to call.

"As offered, the Russian Federation will remove its observers from Ukraine."

Battaglio looked pleased. Gorshkov continued.

"However, the United States and NATO agree to allow elections as I proposed."

"Actually, we have a different time frame," the acting president interrupted. He stated the terms, and as expected, they settled on three months, which was precisely Gorshkov's plan, though he didn't indicate that.

"Agreed, ninety days. And one more point," Gorshkov added.

"Oh?" Battaglio replied.

Gorshkov walked to the window and looked out onto the grounds of Noble House. He smiled, but out of view of everyone. He knew Swedish Special Forces were on the roof along with American and Russian snipers. There was no danger here, just as there had been no real danger for him outside the hotel. The maneuver had been rehearsed more than a hundred times. Much like the recent terrorist attacks on the U.S. targets.

"Yes," he said swiveling around. "My position is firm. The elections will be open to all Russian nationals living in Latvia, and those Latvian nationals residing in the Russian Federation."

National Security Advisor Pierce Kimball reacted before Battaglio. "That could drastically alter the government of Latvia."

"Brussels cannot agree," the NATO Secretary General roared.

Battaglio looked to his left and right, to each of the dissenting voices.

"The United States and NATO will monitor the elections. We'll take precautions."

"Mr. President, Mr. Secretary General," Gorshkov said, "Is it too much to ask that all Latvians have a voice in self-determination? Two-hundred thousand Russian-language nationals have not been heard from in Latvian elections. Trust in the democratic process."

"And if we cannot gain a consensus from NATO?" Kimball dared. "Then the Russian Federation troops posted at the border shall find another way to open the polls."

Battaglio inhaled deeply, and to the dismay of his allies said, "If you put fair elections on paper, I'll sign."

* * *

Colonel Martina Kushkin, aka Maria Pudovkin, struggled against Moe's grip. Reilly moved a half-step forward, but Larry raised his gun.

"Colonel? As of now, you're a woman without a country. You can choose America."

Moe removed a silencer from his jacket pocket and quickly screwed it on his Marakov. Larry did the same.

"Really, an international incident right here? Cameras everywhere," Reilly warned. "You'll be just as burned as your colonel. An embarrassment. According to everything I've read, Gorshkov doesn't tolerate embarrassments. So again, Colonel. Shall we go?"

She took a half-step forward. Moe and Larry held her. But her momentum gave her pivot room, enough to raise her right elbow and drive it into Moe's gut. As he doubled over, with her hand free she drove her knuckles into his Adam's apple. He grabbed his throat and dropped.

Next, she swept around hard with a high right kick that should have connected with Larry's stomach. But the agent anticipated the move. He side-stepped. Her kick went wide, but hit his gun hand, dislodging the Marakov.

Reilly moved toward the gun, but Kushkin dove for it first and won the scramble. With the Marakov in hand, she returned to a standing position, aimed the gun at Larry, then at Reilly, and back to the Russian agent.

One of the Russian soldiers from the embassy was instantly on his radio. At the same time, a young woman eyewitness dialed 1-1-2, the Stockholm emergency number.

Reilly caught the woman's attention and waved her away, but not before another Russian soldier confiscated her cell phone.

Reilly turned to Pudovkin. "What's your real name, Colonel?"

"Martina. Martina Kushkin."

"Well, Martina Kushkin, I strongly suggest we go."

Seconds ticked as she continued to hold the gun on her fellow Russian.

"We've got less than a minute before your men get permission to shoot and maybe two minutes before the local police show up. Either way—"

Kushkin finally nodded. She took a step toward Reilly, but Moe was up and behind her now.

"Nyet, Polkovnik!" He repeated the order in English. "No, Colonel!"

Kushkin felt his Marakov in the small of her back. She smiled. A fateful smile.

"Seems the decision has been made for me." Nonetheless, she dared another step.

Moe's silenced Marakov ended it. He wrapped his arm around Kushkin to prevent her from falling forward. Larry rose to steady her. The other Russians closed in and blocked any real view from the area's surveillance cameras. Even the eyewitnesses wouldn't be able to agree on what occurred.

"We're finished here," Moe said. "Your work is done. So is ours."

Reilly stood drained. He silently watched as they maneuvered Kushkin's limp body to the nearby embassy. They did their best to make it look like she was drunk. Not an unusual sight given Stockholm's widespread sidewalk drinking.

86

NEVADA

FOUR DAYS LATER

Vincent Moore, wearing all black, led the briefing in a freestanding rented warehouse on Whitney Mesa Drive in Henderson. His team of eight, five men and three women, were suited up in jackets with bold FBI letters on the back, which covered their Kevlar vests. For now, they had on baseball caps. In a few minutes, they'd replace them with helmets.

"Questions?" Moore asked.

Nicky Jewel, an FBI special agent out of DC, raised her hand.

"Resistance?"

"Assume the subject is armed."

"Desperate?"

"Let's take him down before he gets that far."

"Affirmative," she said.

"Affirmative," the others in the team replied.

Moore continued, "We go in hard and fast. Announce, no delay, in. I want the subject on his stomach and cuffed in under thirty seconds. We roll at 0300."

"And then a quick extraction to Guantanamo?" Agent Jewel asked.

"Above our pay grade, Nicky. We're just cowboys at a rodeo."

Moore now replayed the events that brought him to this moment.

About his initial presumed guilt for Dan Reilly. About the realization that Reilly was also after the truth. About the targets and attacks. About bringing the terrorists down, *No,* he thought as he prepared to move in. *It was far more than a rodeo. It was a non-stop wild ride.*

* * *

The team quietly exited two black vans a half block from Richard Harper's rented single-family wooden house on Spotted Eagle Drive. Heat sensors from a surveillance run determined that he slept in the second master bedroom, located in the back of the house, away from the street. From the blueprints filed with the city by contractors, the front door would be the quickest way in. Then up fourteen steps, seven before a landing, seven more on a slight turn to the left. Three seconds to get in, seven seconds on the stairs. Ten to disable or disarm Harper. Ten to lay him out and cuff him. Moore's thirty.

Moore staged the assault. One at the front door lock with a battering ram. Three immediately in, with teams simultaneously hitting the back door. Moore was with the agents at the front of the house.

Radios linked them and on a count of ten from Vincent Moore—

Shock and awe. That's how they intended to storm the house. But they didn't expect the front and back doors to be wired with explosives. A fatal mistake. The blasts instantly killed the first four agents in front and three in the back. Vincent Moore among them. Only Nicky Jewel was able to struggle away before the entire house went up in flames.

* * *

Two time zones away at a Dallas airport Hilton, Pak Yoon-hoi, checked in as Billy Park, closed the app on his phone. The app was connected to a video camera attached to a tree on Harper's front lawn. There was another in the back. Whenever anyone crossed a laser beam to the door, it sent a cellular signal to Yoon-hoi. Most of the time it was a coyote or a stray dog. But the sight of FBI agents targeting Harper was something else. And so he quickly dialed another number, which took nine seconds to be bridged through a cellular tower less than a quarter mile away, to a master hub in Dallas, which sent the signal across state lines to Las Vegas, bounced to a local tower in Henderson, to a hidden phone on Spotted Eagle Drive, which triggered explosive devices at the front and back, and on the second floor where Harper slept.

* * *

FBI Director Reese McCafferty led a sweep of the Southern Nevada Water Authority's Intake Station No. 2. Cameras followed. They found eleven devices wired to C4, each tied to individual cell phones. Each planted along the supply chain that could have drained Las Vegas dry for weeks or longer. Each waiting for Harper's activation calls which now would never come.

The phones gave the FBI something to work with, something to trace. They also learned that Richard Harper was a pseudonym. Someone who had passed as Richard Harper from Bellingham, Washington for two years; had worked his way up at the plant, credentialed and promoted. A sleeper spy. The only clue to his identity came from his autopsy: poor dental work. It had all the signs of having been done in Russia.

87

Reilly was called in to debrief with Bob Heath at the CIA. He also gave EJ Shaw at Kensington Royal headquarters an abridged version of the events in Stockholm. It made Reilly uncomfortable not to be able to explain everything, but he couldn't. Not yet. Issues of national security.

He had three other appointments on his calendar—memorial services. The first in Washington, D.C. for FBI Agent Moore. Then Newtown, Pennsylvania for Savannah Flanders. Finally, Cambridge, England where he stood alone in the back of the church and heard speeches from Barclay colleagues who praised Marnie Babbitt as a loyal employee. They didn't know otherwise. Reilly slipped out after the last *Amen* without talking to anyone.

The next day, Reilly landed at Dulles. It was a particularly hot afternoon. Traffic was still being routed to the district across the Potomac through Arlington, onto the Theodore Roosevelt, the Key and the 11th Street Bridges. Repairs would continue on the 14th Street Bridge through the end of the year. This is where it had all begun for him less than three weeks earlier. A lot had changed for Reilly in that time. A lot had changed in the world.

He arrived late for his appointment at the Harry S. Truman Building, the headquarters of the State Department at 2201 C Street, NW, but no apologies were necessary. Everyone was late these days in D.C. and other cities hit by the terrorists.

"Daniel, thank you for coming," Secretary of State Elizabeth Matthews said. She rose from her austere oak desk, which once belonged to President Eisenhower's Secretary of State, John Foster Dulles. "You've been through a lot. I'm sorry."

Reilly expressed his appreciation and accepted her invitation to take the leather chair facing her; a signal that this was going to be a formal discussion.

"Coffee?" She gestured to a silver pot on a mahogany shelf to her right.

"Rather we just get to business, Elizabeth. What's on your mind?"

"Daniel, you were instrumental in confirming the North Korea connection in Venezuela. For that, and so much more, thank you. I wish I could make that public. I can't."

"Of course."

"We're not out of it yet. We have a great deal to sort out." She paused and lowered her voice. "I'll get right to the point. I called you in for a reason."

"Elizabeth, I'm retired from government work. Remember?"

"Right," she said with a hint of irony. "Retired."

Reilly didn't respond.

"I'll be blunt. Battaglio gave away the store in Stockholm. He caved. In Russian terms, he was a classic useful idiot. It was masterful on Gorshkov's part—I believe everything from the domestic attacks right to President Crowe's—" she hesitated, "—assassination attempt. Even the missiles in Venezuela: they wanted us to see them. You just happened to be the first."

"You shouldn't be telling me this, Elizabeth."

She ignored him. "A deception and Battaglio played right into him."

Reilly was uncomfortable. He sought to change the topic.

"Will Crowe make it?"

"According to his doctors, yes," she replied, leaving more unsaid than said. Reilly restated his question.

"Will he return to the White House?"

"We don't know."

If she had more, Reilly believed she'd tell him. He switched to another open topic.

"Have you found out who's responsible for leaking my State Department report?"

"Yes."

"A name?"

"Strictly off the record?"

"Who?"

"I mean never," she added. "Ever. No cocktail conversation. No memoirs."

"Who, Elizabeth?"

"No name. Not impossible to discover, but don't."

"Go on," Reilly said neither agreeing nor disagreeing.

"The FBI targeted everyone who might have had access to the report and identified a significant person of interest, let's call her Subject One, based on sudden out-of-town trips beginning last Christmas and the numerous times during that same period she had checked out of work extremely late and alone. Enough red flags to set up a sting. A week ago, the subject was seen leaving the Chairman's office with confidential files, planted by the bureau. They were labeled top secret. They were totally manufactured. The FBI exercised a warrant and found a hidden safe in her Bethesda home and walked away with photographs of a very intense extramarital relationship she'd been having. And as you predicted, we ultimately nailed her through her office copy machine. The copy signature matched the *Post's* copy. The leak, shall we say, has been plugged, and word circulating among her coworkers is that she's on personal leave."

"Does Battaglio know?"

"Knows, but doesn't grasp the significance. Said we do the same thing all time and therefore we shouldn't be surprised. He wrote it off as normal meddling. But it was much more than that."

"Caught in a classic honey pot operation. Sexpionage."

"You could call it that."

"What about the agent? Have you identified him?"

"Not a *him*. A *her*. A *her*, Daniel. In fact, in a direct way, the FBI was able to make the connection thanks to you."

"Kushkin," Reilly said resolutely.

"Correct. Colonel Martina Kushkin. AKA Maria Pudovkin, Nikki Romanovich, Rhonda Nealy. Just a few of her aliases. On this mission, she was Sally Ann Chalmers, a Miami divorcee. Attractive, fun, and sexy. She set her sights on her mark. It took time and opportunity. Nothing rushed. First, a friendly encounter during a family ski trip to Vail. Innocent conversations on the slopes, a seemingly chance meeting over a latte, and since they hit it off, flirtations, and an invitation for dinner in Washington if Chalmers ever made it there. Which of course, she did. We've got CCTV footage of them together at hotels, streets, stores."

Though the locations were different, Reilly thought, it was precisely how Marnie Babbitt had zeroed in on him. *Probably for corporate secrets.* First in Tehran, then in Moscow, and on and on. He was grateful he never provided her with any confidential information or even talked about his State Department report. Nonetheless, she likely suspected he had more going on and had advised Kushkin.

"Subject One confessed to everything. It was all new and exciting for our bored middle-aged Capitol Hill lawyer, a textbook seduction. Pure Cold War tactics still very much in the Russian spycraft handbook. And once seduced, Kushkin had a highly placed asset. Compromised by letters, texts, photos and videos. You get the picture."

"I do," Reilly replied.

"We suspect she's not the only one recruited by Kushkin. We've got our work cut out for ourselves. She handed over intelligence and strategy. Your file, Dan. And now she has deaths on her conscience," Matthews said somberly. "She'll be thinking about that in protective custody for the rest of her life. 18 U.S Code section 2381 is quite specific."

Reilly was familiar with the penalty for treason.

"Of course, we'll bury her with some other charge. Give her a new life and a pretty ankle bracelet she'll never take off. She's already said goodbye to her family."

Reilly nodded.

"Speaking of pictures, I have some you will be interested in seeing," Matthews said.

She handed Reilly a file containing a series of long-lens photographs. His eyes immediately went to the most identifying elements.

"What do you see?"

"Surveillance of a—" he paused and evaluated the clues. "—Russian port?"

"So far, so good."

"And what looks like a Korean ferry docking."

"That would be North Korean. Keep going."

Reilly examined more photos. The ship mooring. The gang plank being lowered, and then tighter shots of—

"Just one person disembarking?" he asked. "Only one?"

"One," Matthews affirmed. "Which makes him a person of interest"

Reilly noted the date on the photo. "It's a few years old."

"Yes, taken by one of ours overlooking a dock in Vladivostok."

"Who's the guy?"

At that moment Reilly's cell rang.

"Sorry." He pulled his phone from his suit jacket pocket and looked at the incoming number. Edward Jefferson Shaw calling from Chicago. He hadn't checked in with his boss all day.

"Need to take that?"

Reilly shook his head and, conflicted, sent his boss to voicemail.

"I'll get back to it. Go on."

"At this moment, we're convinced he's the point man on the domestic attacks and the operative behind the remote bombing that killed Moore and his team. His description matches eyewitness accounts at various locales near the targets. Hotels included, Daniel. The FBI is on it."

"Any leads?"

"None so far, but he's not as invisible as he once was. That's all I can share with you now."

"*Now?* That seems tentative. What do you really want from me, Elizabeth?" Reilly asked directly.

88

Dan Reilly settled onto a weathered park bench in Edward J. Kelly Park just east of the State Department at 21ˢᵗ and Virginia Avenue. He needed to rest and process what he'd heard. Most of all, Reilly had read anxiety in Elizabeth Matthews's voice as she explained how ill-prepared Battaglio was for the job. Actually, in retrospect, the greater clue was in her eyes. It was more than anxiety. She showed true worry for the country. Now alone, he contemplated all the variables. From his perspective, none of them had immediate positive outcomes.

Reilly tried to relax. He took in his surroundings. To his right, a tourist asking a stranger for directions; approaching, a woman pushing a stroller; and in the distance, a couple racing to catch a bus. All normal.

Reilly took out his iPhone and was about to hit the programmed speed dial button and finally call his boss back, but a familiar large bronze sculpture pulled his eye. It shimmered particularly brightly in the late afternoon sun. He knew the piece; a replica of a classic Greek work, *Discobolous of Myron*, or as it was called in the park, The Discus Thrower. It depicted a young athlete, perhaps an Olympian, in the act of throwing.

The figure's body was curled, his concentration fixed. His muscles swelled with immense energy. His mind was focused on a single purpose: to unwind and hurl the discus with great fury. Except he wouldn't. The motion had been frozen by the artist's hand sometime between 460 and 450 B.C. when the original work was sculpted.

Now Reilly's thoughts shifted to the identity of the Greek who had posed for sculpture. He looked the part; muscular, fit, and focused. But was he actually an athlete or just a brawny model standing in for one? Then Dan Reilly tensed. He considered his own identity—an international hotel executive who brought experience, professionalism and honor to his job. Yet, at the same time, was he being sculpted by America's intelligence community to serve their purpose, much like *Discobolous of Myron,* The Discus Thrower?

Reilly shivered even though the temperature pushed past 90. He forced himself to dismiss the notion as he put the call through to Edward Jefferson Shaw's office. Reilly had a pleasant, but short conversation with the Kensington Royal president's secretary. A minute later she put him through.

"Are you packed?" Shaw barked. His manner was friendly, but without a hello. Hello was always implied, but often never offered when Shaw wanted to get right to the point.

"Always," Reilly replied.

"Good. Back to England before the end of the month. Then Beijing and Nairobi, or whatever order you want to circle the globe. Oil ministry meetings coming up. You should do a swing around. Make sure everything is okay.

"Oh, before you fly off," Shaw said almost as an afterthought, "You and I need to have a serious conversation on Twenty-one." Twenty-one was Shaw's floor at the Chicago headquarters. "Off the phone. Just you and me."

Reilly had been anticipating this, too. He'd been involved in too much intrigue too publicly to hide from his boss any longer. He owed Shaw an explanation. Just how much detail did he want to give? How much did Shaw want to hear? Reilly ended the call with the promise to himself to have that conversation.

He looked at the sculpture again, this time considering the Discus Thrower more as himself. *Was he also a model simply striking a pose? Or was he the real thing capable of competing at the highest level?* These were the questions, once answered, that would determine Dan Reilly's future.

89

THREE DAYS LATER

The call went out from the White House press secretary at 7 a.m., enough time to assemble the press at 8901 Rockville Pike. President Alexander Crowe would address the nation from Walter Reed National Military Medical Center in Bethesda, Maryland at noon. Five hours to prepare. The Secret Service took control of the perimeter; by 10 a.m. helicopters circled overhead and drones flew even higher. Rooftop snipers covered angles in all directions.

Rumors over whether Crowe had died circulated for weeks despite White House denials, actual Instagram photographs, Twitter postings, and YouTube video. Such was the world where conspiracy theories replaced facts and the nation faced an ever-worsening case of truth decay.

Mainstream media commentators had picked up on the old saw, "A lie can travel halfway around the world while the truth is still putting its boots on." The phrase has been alternately attributed to Mark Twain and satirist Jonathan Swift. But the truth was, no one really knew any more about the origin of the expression than what Crowe would decide today, including Acting President Ryan Battaglio.

While Battaglio publicly prayed for Crowe's return, privately he had already begun maneuvering to reshape the administration. His handling of Ukraine and Latvia demonstrated the extent to which he was eager to set a new course for American foreign policy even through Crowe's recovery. The fact that Crowe had remained in a coma through the Stockholm negotiations worked to his favor: he didn't have to consult with the president. And considering most Americans polled proved they didn't truly understand the issues that faced NATO, it strengthened his resolve to withdraw from many historic commitments so long as Crowe stepped down…or died. Either way, he hoped it would happen soon.

At precisely noon, President Alexander Crowe was wheeled to the front lobby from the elevator. From there Crowe told the Secret Service and his doctors he would walk across the lobby with his wife on his arm to steady him. They had practiced already. Once in front of the cameras, Crowe would anchor his hands on a bulletproof White House podium, acknowledge everyone with an appreciative nod, and when comfortable wave to the cameras: a front-page photo opportunity, an image that could appear in a box behind TV anchors.

Cued by the Marine Band playing "Hail to the Chief," President Crowe stepped forward, confidently approaching the podium. Once in place, he kissed his wife Sasha and stood as straight as he could while acknowledging the thunderous applause and cheers. White House staffers, aides and reporters all focused on a president some thirty pounds lighter than when they'd last seen him. His wife had his favorite blue suit tailored from 44 to a 37. She dressed him in a new white shirt with a 15½-inch collar, a full two inches smaller than before the assassination attempt. Buttoned and with a proper blue tie, it hid Crowe's loose neck skin.

After a minute he gestured for everyone to quiet down. It took another minute of applause and three attempts before he could begin. "Well, I'll make it easier for you all. Am I a sight for sore eyes?"

The crowd of nearly one hundred roared their approval. Crowe went on to thank his doctors and his family. His wife smiled. She'd stood by his side through his four Congressional runs, eight years in the Senate, his one term as Vice President, and nearly three years as President of the United States. But just prior to heading downstairs, she had whispered in his ear, "You look so handsome. Now go get 'em. Then, let's go home."

And so President Alexander Crowe announced his retirement. Gasps rippled through the throng of well-wishers. The Secret Service agents stood expressionless. However, inwardly, the senior member of the detail silently worried over how well his successor would fare as president. There were already ripples of discontent in the White House.

Secretary of State Elizabeth Matthews watched from her office. The announcement was not a complete surprise. In a phone conversation, Crowe had indicated he would likely step down even though she strongly advised against it. He had told Ryan Battaglio the same thing. But it was truly his wife's wishes minutes before speaking that cemented Crowe's decision.

Battaglio watched the announcement from the Oval Office. When the news became final, Battaglio shouted a resounding, "Yes!" heard down the hall. Then he began drawing up a list of names: those to keep, those to cut, and who he could truly count on as political allies. *No drastic changes immediately*, he reasoned. The news channels, columnists, and commentators would be all over him. *Patience. Measured steps.* But in time, he knew the changes to make. High on the to-go list was Matthews. Further down, Pierce Kimball.

* * *

Crowe's resignation speech at Walter Reed and Battaglio's White House swearing-in led the news for only five hours. Then another story grabbed the headlines: Russia was on the move.

"Jesus!" Battaglio shouted to the people he'd called into the Oval Office. "We had a deal."

He'd summoned Matthews, Defense Secretary General Ellis Chase, National Security Advisor Pierce Kimball, and CIA Director Gerald Watts. They stood facing him while Battaglio held court from behind his desk.

"What the hell is that fucker doing?" he demanded. Matthews took the lead.

"Exactly what he intended from the start. Mr. President, you trusted Gorshkov. He can't be trusted." Implied was *I told you so.*

Battaglio stammered, "What do we have? In detail!"

Already knowing that Battaglio was not a detailed person, General Ellis replied in simple terms. "In the last three hours, Russian troops seized Kiev. They now completely hold the city." He had Pentagon assessments including satellite imagery in a file on his lap. He handed it to the new president. It was marked TOP SECRET with a time stamp.

"This is up to date, sir." Battaglio didn't open it.

"For God's sake, just tell me!" He threw the folder to the corner of the desk. Ellis cleared his throat, took out the photographs and explained what they showed, slowly. Troop deployments, artillery and tank units rolling into the city, and how quickly the Russians were able to take the airport.

"He claims it's not an offensive move," Ellis continued. "He wants to guarantee honest elections. After all," he read from a translation of a Gorshkov statement, "Ukraine is notoriously corrupt, evidenced most recently by the failed escape attempt of President Dmytro Brutka, and by other prior administrations that answered to the whims of the United States. The new government cannot be expected to be any different. Therefore, I have ordered Russian Federation forces to safeguard the integrity of the elections on behalf of the good people of Ukraine."

"Bullshit!" Battaglio screamed, a continuation of his meltdown. A meltdown within his first few hours as president.

Though she didn't say it, Matthews was convinced that Gorshkov had waited to see whether Crowe would remain in office or resign. Once he stepped down, the die was cast. He ordered his troops to swiftly invade Ukraine and hold Kiev. He had counted on Battaglio doing nothing, and he'd been right.

Battaglio stood and paced. At first he used his desk as a barrier to keep distance from the others. Speaking to the air rather than anyone in the room he said, "Okay, so we spin this as a positive. Which it ultimately is." He paused when no one reacted. "Take a seat and come up with a marketable approach. I'll wrap it into a tweet. That'll buy me some time."

General Ellis had nothing. Likewise, CIA Director Watts. Elizabeth Matthews remained silent. Finally, Battaglio voiced his own suggestion. "We'll broker a goddamned ceasefire. Gorshkov will move his troops back across his side of the border, in return for us allowing him to advance the date of the vote. Something for something."

Matthews winced. "Gorshkov has Kiev. He won't budge."

"Elizabeth, just shut up! I asked for an approach and none of you came up with one. So, I'm going to go with the ceasefire." He turned to his National Security Advisor. "Pierce, go to Moscow and broker it."

"Yes, sir," Kimball replied knowing he'd never get such a meeting.

Matthews had a pad on her lap on which she had taken some notes. Now she wrote a number in the lower right hand corner: 25. She circled it and lightly tapped it with her pen as if she was thinking. The move caught the attention of the only other Cabinet member in the room, her couch partner, Chase Ellis. He glanced down, then up. They exchanged eye contact. He slowly closed his eyes. A response, neither good nor bad, but perhaps an acknowledgment that might lead to a conversation outside the Oval Office, outside the White House…a conversation that could eventually include other Cabinet secretaries.

With her pen pointing to the number, Matthews held her focus on Ellis until he opened his eyes. He found her gaze, looked to the page again, then up, and blinked purposefully once. A sign: he recognized the significance.

Twenty-five: the number of an Amendment to the United States Constitution. And within it, the fourth stipulation, or as ratified in 1967 and identified by the Latin Numeral IV, the section most relevant to what Matthews viewed as a real and present internal danger.

Since there was no current vice president to add weight to the issue, there were really two relevant numbers: Fifteen and eight. Fifteen, the number of Senate confirmed Cabinet members. Eight, the majority of fifteen; the number of Cabinet votes required to remove a sitting president from office.

Matthews had to be strategic. She hoped General Chase's nonverbal reaction meant she had two of the eight. If so, six to go. The fate of Eastern Europe depended on it.

EPILOGUE

That night, Dan Reilly strolled along Georgetown's tree-lined cobblestone streets, where America's founding fathers and future presidents had once lived; where they designed the layout for the capital city over beer at taverns, where they struggled over the character of what would become the United States. Where they took sides on freedom and slavery.

Georgetown's history is full of patriots and scoundrels, diplomats and spies, deals brokered and alliances broken. If the walls could, they'd talk of presidential trysts, a last toast before duels, assassination plots, and tactics to keep the republic standing. Unbeknownst to him, Elizabeth Matthews was having one of those conversations just a few blocks away.

Dan Reilly loved meandering through the city, discovering unique architectural details that had weathered over the years and hearing stories from locals who uncovered centuries-old papers when rehabbing their brownstones. He'd just finished a leisurely dinner with Bob Heath at the Mansion on O Street, an eclectic hotel and restaurant favored by artists, actors, and hip Washington residents. They'd talked openly about friends and family, and quietly about Stockholm. Reilly hadn't shared his conversation with the Secretary of State and Heath didn't bring up the CIA's concerns about President Ryan Battaglio. Both topics would be left for more secure quarters.

When they finished their last glass of Japanese whiskey, Reilly passed up Heath's offer to drive him to his Dumbarton Street apartment. He had beds in Washington and Chicago, and wherever else in the world work took him—which was everywhere.

"Are you sure?"

"Absolutely," Reilly said. "I need to walk off dinner."

They parted, and Reilly headed home a little more than a mile away, usually a fifteen- or twenty-minute walk. Tonight it would be more like twenty-five. He casually observed the Georgetown students out on pub crawls, Congressional staffers making their way to their apartments, and delivery services in cars and on scooters rushing late meals through the narrow streets. There was a certain pace to the city at this hour, not as fast as the morning. And the sounds that carried were different, too: footsteps landing heavier than earlier in the day, tired goodbyes rather than energetic hellos. And dogs on their nighttime walks, barking at shadows across the street: Georgetown at 11:15.

Reilly was relaxed as he strolled, mostly thanks to the cocktails, wine, and after-dinner drinks. He smiled to passersby. He whistled an old TV show theme he couldn't quite place. He nodded to couples holding hands and gave lovers ample room. All was quiet in this part of town.

Reilly had one more block to go. He crossed the last intersection. About halfway down the street, a man stepped out from a shadow under a tree and glanced left and right, as if looking to see if anyone else was around other than the two of them. The sidewalks were otherwise empty.

Reilly now tensed but continued to walk forward. At sixty feet, the man began sauntering slowly toward him. Reilly fixed on him for a moment. He looked to be in his mid-fifties, but it was really hard to tell at this distance and in limited light. Eighty feet, Reilly changed his thinking. He was younger and walking purposefully. *Maybe forty to forty-five.* He wore a black suit with a dark shirt.

The footsteps grew louder as he came closer. But they were not the sluggish nighttime steps he had heard from others. Reilly saw he was carrying a stick—no, an umbrella; a large black umbrella. The handle was in his right hand. He angled toward the right side of the sidewalk.

At no time did he tap the ground with the tip as people tend to do.

The thoughts took Reilly to fifty feet. One streetlight towered between them. Reilly now reconsidered the man. He was definitely younger. Early thirties with an athlete's body. Or a soldier's. The man glanced from side to side again and peered further down the street, seeming to grip the umbrella more tightly as he raised it inches above the ground, as if to almost point it.

Another thought hit Dan Reilly: *there's no rain in the forecast today or tomorrow. So, who carries an umbrella when it's not going to rain? No one,* Reilly concluded. *No one except—*

In an instant he called up an event from his intelligence studies in the Army: London, September, 1978. Bulgarian dissident Georgi Markov, then a BBC broadcaster and award-winning author, was waiting for a commuter bus on Waterloo Bridge when a man approached him with a raised umbrella. As the stranger passed him, Markov felt a sudden prick in his thigh. The man said, "Sorry." He wasn't. He had fired a ricin pellet from his umbrella and left the scene in a taxi. Markov ignored the immediate stinging pain. He shouldn't have. Within three days he was dead.

Reilly calculated the distance between the two of them. Forty feet. Sixteen steps or less. Little time for options. Maybe no time.

Fight or flight. Fight options were bad. Flight offered two: in the direction he'd come or dodging across Dumbarton? A foot chase was a bad choice against a younger and likely faster man. As he evaluated his second option, Reilly saw headlights illuminating parked cars ahead. A vehicle was coming up the street from behind him—a diversion? He quickly looked over his right shoulder and made a calculation. With a feint to the left he might throw his adversary's balance off. Then, he would dart into the street and if he timed it right, the oncoming car would block the man. He just might get enough of a lead to reach safety; it was his best—and only—choice.

At the exact moment Reilly started to break, the car rolled to a stop. The driver, a woman, called to the man through her open window.

"Hey, sorry I'm late. Thanks for grabbing my umbrella."

"No problem," the man in black replied. He crossed the sidewalk only a few feet ahead of Reilly, stepped into the road and got into the passenger seat.

Reilly watched them kiss and drive off. Taking a deep breath, he wondered whether recent circumstances were making him see threats where there were none. He exhaled. *No.* This was the life he now lived. He had to become more aware of his surroundings, the people he met, and others who suddenly stepped out of the shadows.

So it wasn't tonight. Not along his quaint Georgetown block at the hands of an innocent man returning an umbrella. But Dan Reilly resolved he would have to sharpen his senses to recognize danger and how to defend against it. He also needed to figure out how he could better function in the dual worlds he inhabited—business and intelligence.

Dan Reilly had important decisions to make. He scanned the street and listened for footsteps. It was quiet. He continued home, no longer whistling.

ACKNOWLEDGMENTS

RED Deception is a thriller about the global hotel industry in a challenging and dangerous world. Gary and I used many fictional characters and incidents which occurred in the forty years I worked with Marriott and the twenty-two years I was President and Managing Director of the International Lodging Marriott. During that time I founded and led the Marriott International crisis committee.

I am grateful to the individuals listed below who made our successes possible, who influenced, mentored, guided me, and played key roles in making this novel possible. Several of them might find themselves in this creative work.

Linda Bartlett, Yvonne Bean, Katie Bianchi, Harry Bosschaart, Stan Bruns, Nuala Cashman, Paul Cerula, Weili Cheng, Don Cleary, Mark Conklin, JoAnn Corday, Henry Davies, Victoria Dolan, Roger Dow, Brenda Durham, Ron Eastman, Joel Eisemann, June Farrell, Franz Ferschke, Jim Fisher, Fern Fitzgerald, Paul Foskey, Geoff Garside, Robert Gaymer-Jones, Jurgen Giesbert, Will Grimsley, Marc Gulliver, Tracy Halphide, Debbie Harrison, Ron Harrison, Pat Henderson, Jeff Holdaway, Andrew Houghton, Ed Hubennette, Gary Hurst, Beth Irons, Andrea Jones, Pam Jones, Simon Jongert, Nihad Kattan, Kevin Kearney, Chuck Kelley, Karl Kilburg, Kevin Kimball, Tuni Kyi, Buck Laird, Henry Lee, Mike Mackie, Kathleen Matthews, Alastair McPhail, Scott Melby, Raj Menon, Anton Najjar, JP Nel, Scott Neumayer, John Northen, Jim O'Hern, Alan Orlob, Manuel Oview, Jim Pilarski, Belinda Pote, Barbara Powell, Reiner Sachau, Mark Satterfield, Bill Shaw, Brenda Shelton, Craig Smith, Brad Snyder, Arne Sorenson, Alex Stadlin, Jim Stamas, Peter Steger, Pat Stocker, Susan Thronson, Chip

Stuckmeyer, Myron Walker, Bob Watts, Hank Weigle, Steve Weisz, Carl Wilson, and Glenn Wilson.

I want to thank my Orange County friends for supporting me through publishing *Red Hotel* and the completion of *Red Deception*. These friends include Haris Ali M.D., David Brouwer M.D., Jeffrey Bruss M.D., Jay Burress, Lynn Clark, Michelle McCue, Paulette Lombardi-Fries, Christina Palmer, Micky Rucireta, Sharon Sola, Chip Stuckmeyer, Tingting Tan M.D. and the staff at City of Hope, Nicky Tang, Christy Teague, Dominique Williams.

Through memberships with various boards, I have received inspiration and engaging conversations. My thanks goes out to The Orange County Visitors Association Board Members, Caroline Beteta, and team at Visit California, Doug Muldoon and the FBINAA, MIND Research, Boston University Boards, Cal State San Marcos Foundation Board, and Althea Foundation Board. It is a pleasure being involved with all of you.

Several people encouraged me to take a leap from my business book, *You Can't Lead with Your Feet on the Desk*, to writing a novel. These people include my coauthor, Gary Grossman, Bruce Feirstein, June Farrell, Pam Jones, Pam Policano, Andy Policano, and my wife, Michela Fuller. Thank you all very much. I must admit, it's been a lot of fun working with Gary Grossman.

And finally, there are simply no words to describe my enduring thanks to J.W. Marriott.

ED FULLER

Thank you to Ed Fuller for our most wonderful creative collaboration. You are a true friend and an inspiration. Your experiences give life to our character Dan Reilly and your friendship fills me up.

Special thanks, once again, to screenwriter, author, producer and columnist Bruce Feirstein for putting us together. Additional thanks to our agent Carol Mann, the Carol Mann Agency; our marketing and publicity guru Meryl Moss at Meryl Moss Media; Roger Cooper for his ongoing belief in me and for launching my thriller writing career; and our publisher, Eric Kampmann, President of Beaufort Books and Megan Trank, Managing Editor. Thank you one and all.

There's our extraordinary business and creative team. Now for the engine behind the effort.

Thanks to Sandi Goldfarb for her editorial assistance throughout the creative process; Bruce Coons, lifelong friend and technical advisor for all my thriller writing; intelligence and Beltway experts—author and Lasell University Professor Paul DeBole, Homeland Security Special Agent Edward Bradstreet, and Professor Peter Loge, School of Media and Public Affairs.

Additional thanks to ThrillerFest Executive Director and author Kimberley Howe; all my friends and colleagues at the International Thriller Writers Association; and ITW authors Jon Land, W.G. Griffiths, Raymond Benson, Steve Berry, Daniel Palmer, and R.G. Belsky. Also, Tanya Zlateva, Dean, Boston University Metropolitan College; attorneys Tom Hunter, Ken Browning; Chuck Barquist, Jim Harris; my Hudson High School classmates (we're a tight group!), Linda Mussman and Claudia Bruce at Time and Space Limited, and of course, friends Stan and Debbie Deutsch, Jeffrey Davis, Vin DiBona, Jeff Greenhawt, Robb Weller, Nat Segaloff, Fred Putman, Michael O'Rourke, and Ryan Fey of the Grill Dads.

And finally with true loving thanks, my wife, Helene Seifer; and family Jake Grossman, Sasha Grossman and Alex Crowe, Zach Grossman and Tory Sparkman. You keep me going. You inspire me. And you all make me proud.

GARY GROSSMAN

ABOUT THE AUTHORS

ED FULLER is CEO of Laguna Strategic Advisors, a global consortium providing business consulting services worldwide. He has served on both business and charitable boards during his forty-year career with Marriott International where he served as Chief Marketing Officer, followed by 22 years as President and Managing Director of Marriott International. Under his management the international division grew from 16 to 550 hotels in 73 countries with 80,000 associates and sales of 8 billion dollars.

Upon retirement, Ed repurposed his career in several arenas. He has served on five university boards and has been an adjunct professor for both MBA and undergraduate students. For more than four years he was a blogger for Forbes and other tourism and lodging industry media. As an author, Ed published *You Can't Lead With Your Feet On The Desk* in English, Japanese, and Chinese, which has been distributed throughout the world. In 2019, he and co-author Gary Grossman released their high-energy thriller *Red Hotel*, *Red Deception* in 2021, followed by *Red Chaos* in The *Red Hotel* Series. Ed served as an Army captain in both Germany and Vietnam, receiving the Bronze Star and the Army Commendation medals. He and his wife Michela reside in Orange County, California.

GARY GROSSMAN's first novel, *Executive Actions*, propelled him into the world of geopolitical thrillers. *Executive Treason, Executive Command*, and *Executive Force* further tapped Grossman's experience as a journalist, newspaper columnist, documentary television producer, reporter, and media historian. In addition to the bestselling *Executive* series, Grossman wrote the international award-winning *Old Earth*, a geological thriller that spans all of time. With *Red Hotel* and *Red Deception*, his collaborations with Ed Fuller, Grossman entered a new realm of globe-hopping thriller writing.

Grossman has contributed to the *New York Times* and the *Boston Globe*, and was a columnist for the *Boston Herald American*. He covered presidential campaigns for WBZ-TV in Boston. A multiple Emmy Award winner, Grossman has produced more than 10,000 television series and specials for networks including NBC, CNN, ABC, CBS, Fox, History Channel, Discovery, and National Geographic Channel. He served as chair of the Government Affairs Committee for the Caucus for Producers, Writers and Directors, and is a member of the International Thriller Writers Association and Military Writers Society of America. He is a trustee at Emerson College and serves on the Boston University Metropolitan College Advisory Board. Grossman has taught at Emerson College, Boston University, USC, and currently teaches at Loyola Marymount University.

FOR MORE INFORMATION AND TO CONTACT THE AUTHORS
WWW.REDHOTEL.COM